Amanda Prowse

A Mother's Story

First published in the UK in 2015 by Head of Zeus Ltd.
This paperback edition first published in the UK in 2015
by Head of Zeus Ltd.

9 7 5 3 1 2 4 6 8

A catalogue record for this book is available from the British Library.

ISBN (PB) 9781781856604
ISBN (E) 9781781856574

Head of Zeus Ltd
Clerkenwell House
45–47 Clerkenwell Green

'I wouldn't have felt so alone, so frightened knowing I was in a club of many thousands, rather than a club of one. The scariest thing has always been how it crept up on me, throwing its dark cloak over my head so I couldn't see what was happening.'

Prologue

There was a small camera winking at the duo as they waited to be let in. A woman half stood, raising her hand in recognition of Dr Boyd. She pressed a buzzer out of view and the door whirred open, admitting them to a large square hallway. The woman sat at a pale wood reception desk that curved round in an arc, with a large row of pigeonholes on the wall behind it. The decor was simple: mainly white walls, with brightly coloured accessories on the desk – red files, green pen pots – and a large yellow clock on the wall that ticked loudly. The place had the false gaiety of a children's hospital.

Without being told the drill, Dr Boyd signed a book for them both and waited. A heavyset woman of indeterminate age appeared, her demeanour telling anyone who cared to notice that this was not where she wanted to be. She ignored them and bustled past with an armful of files.

A smiley nurse then appeared. She searched Jessica's overnight bag and patted down her clothing. Jessica was quiet and polite; her earlier misgivings disappeared. She felt a sense of relief that she was going to find some peace in here. It wasn't as scary as she had anticipated, so far. The nurse seemed kind and business-like. 'We'll get you settled in your room, Jessica, okay?'

She nodded. Dr Boyd went into an anteroom off the reception area and she didn't see him again. She was taken deeper into the bowels of the building. Beyond the hospital-like reception, the facility looked a bit like a cheap hotel, the only difference being that instead of carpet tiles, the floor was grey linoleum. Chocolate-box-style pictures were screwed to the walls, depicting meadows abundant with flowers and the sun peeking over rolling hills. The nurse linked arms with Jessica as though she were elderly or infirm. This made Jessica smile. Despite being neither, she had to admit it was a great comfort to have this woman to lean on as they made their way to her room.

'Is Matthew coming here later?' she asked, realising that she hadn't said goodbye properly.

'No. Not tonight.' The nurse patted Jessica's arm.

'Tomorrow then?'

The nurse didn't answer. Jessica wondered if she had heard.

'Will he come and see me tomorrow?' she repeated, this time a little louder.

The nurse blinked quickly, but remained quiet. Jessica swallowed, wondering if she had said the wrong thing. She couldn't remember where Matthew was or why he wasn't with her, but judging from the nurse's silence, she felt it best not to mention him.

The woman's rubber-soled shoes squeaked as they made their way along the glossy linoleum. Jessica stopped and gasped as a deafening wail of distress hit her ears. She gripped the nurse's hand.

'It's okay, Jessica. It's just someone calling out. There's

nothing to be afraid of.' The nurse smiled and squeezed her hand, which helped a little.

The nurse pulled at a swipe card that was anchored to a spring-loaded cord and held it against a small black panel by a wide door; the door swung open outwards. Jessica found herself in another section of corridor. The strip-lighting overhead was too bright and the artificial glare made her eyes squint in defence. Jessica noticed the glass-fronted cabinet set high in the wall, full of phials and syringes; she tried not to think of when they might be needed and what they might contain.

They stopped abruptly. The woman again pulled on her card and swiped the panel by the side of another door. Jessica noted the little window near the top of the door. She wandered into the small room and cast her eye over the melamine-topped chest of drawers and the single bed in the corner. The window had bars over it and pale grey vertical blinds that reminded her of an office block. She sat on the bed and ran her hands over the blue blanket that was the kind she had only ever seen in hospitals; it was tucked neatly under the mattress and sandwiched between white sheets that were folded over at the top to form a thick white border. Here too, the floor was squeaky and dust-free. She liked how clean everything was, uncluttered. It made it easier to think.

Another woman came bustling into the room. She was less smiley than the first one and was holding a clipboard. She sat on the orange plastic chair, which creaked under her weight, and put the clipboard on her lap. 'I need to ask you some questions.' Her mouth was set in a sneer, as if she was irritated or in a hurry.

Jessica nodded.

'You know where you are, do you?' She spat the words.

Jessica nodded again.

'Go easy,' the smiley nurse whispered to her colleague.

'Go easy? You do *know* what she's done?' she fired back.

Jessica felt her body shake.

'Have you in the last twenty-four hours had any suicidal thoughts?' The woman stared at her in a way that made her feel very uncomfortable.

Jessica shook her head and looked down into her lap.

'Feel free to speak up, Jessica. We are here to help you.' Nice nurse spoke softly, kindly, in spite of the disapproving twist of her colleague's mouth.

Jessica had a sudden flashback to her wedding day. She remembered standing and trying to make Jake, and Matthew's other mates, be quiet so Matthew could speak. *'We all knew Jess wouldn't be able to resist getting involved during the speeches, right? Apparently the trick for me is going to be how to get her to shut up, not just today but throughout our married life. Roger has very kindly given me these for use in extreme emergencies!'* She pictured the ear defenders her dad had supposedly given him.

But now it was as if she had stopped owning her own life. A decision had been taken without her consent, arrangements made without her involvement; people had started talking about her in hallways and into phones with palms cupped over the mouthpiece. From that moment, she had no longer been responsible for herself. At first she'd felt quite relieved and a little petrified. As time went on, she'd felt less relieved and more petrified. Because if she wasn't responsible for herself, then how could she control what happened to her? And the answer to that was that she couldn't.

Her tears came quickly and without warning. She stayed silent, as her hot distress tumbled down her face and clogged her nose and mouth.

'Where have I gone, what has happened to me?'

One

It was a beautiful May day. Orange-tipped butterflies danced in the clear blue sky, kissing the sunny yellow flowers on which they rested. The apple trees were in full bloom, abundant with pink and white blossoms, some of which had fallen to form a floral carpet across which the guests tramped.

The crisp, clear sound of a fork hitting the side of a glass echoed around the marquee. Conversation levels dropped to a burble and those who had migrated to other tables, crouching on the coir matting to chat to their friends, made their way back to their own. Clusters of girls rushed back from the loo arm in arm, holding sparkly clutch bags and with perfume freshly spritzed. Three pretty waitresses navigated their way through the maze of tables, distributing chilled flutes of fizz in readiness for the toasts. Jessica felt a current of joy travel through her. Her day was perfect.

It was the kind of wedding she had seen in magazines, the kind of event that featured in movies – a million miles from what she had envisaged for a girl like her. Jessica, whose mum and dad thought pasta was an exotic food, who had grown up in a world of coupons, saving stamps and thrift, whose school uniform came from the second-hand shop and who had received a book token for every birthday as far back as she could remember. She was at the most exquisite wedding she had ever attended and she was the bride! It was, as her mum had reminded her earlier in the day, like a blimming fairy tale.

Matthew's childhood had been very different. Jessica was marrying a man whose parents nipped to France in the way hers nipped to the supermarket. They were the sort who knew which wine to drink with fish, and at the supper table they made jokes about the cabinet of the day and shared amusing snippets they had picked up from Radio Four. It was a world away from her home life. When she'd been introduced to his family for the first time, she'd felt awe and fear in equal measures. One year on, both had subsided, a little.

Polly hurried round the back of the top table and placed her head on her best friend's shoulder. Her large green fascinator sent feathery fronds up the bride's nose, which Jessica snorted away. She could smell the boozy fumes that wafted from her friend's mouth. This was not unusual for Polly: since their teens, both girls had lived by the mantra 'it's wine o'clock somewhere!'

'There is something you need to know, Jess,' Polly said in a solemn whisper.

'What's that?' Jessica was intrigued.

'We probably should have discussed it before now, but the fact is, now that you are a married woman, your husband might want to do *S-E-X* with you.' The s-word was mouthed, not spoken.

'Really?' Jessica placed her hand over her mouth and widened her eyes.

'Yes.' Polly nodded. 'It's what married people do. My parents have done it twice, as I have a sister, and I don't think your parents have done it for a while.' Both girls glanced at Mr and Mrs Maxwell, sitting further along the table in their finery, and giggled.

'Stop laughing, Jess. This is very importatant, impor… tatant. Importatatnt.' Polly tried but failed to get the word right, making Jessica giggle again. 'Whatever! Doesn't matter.' Polly waved her hand in front of her face. 'The rule is: just lie back and think of England. Don't say a word, don't move and it should be over before you've managed to sing the second verse of "Jerusalem". In your head, of course – not out loud, that's a no-no. Got it?' Polly straightened up and kissed her friend on the cheek.

'I think so…' Jessica bit her lip. 'Is the second verse the "Bring me my bow of burning gold" one?'

'Yep. You might want to practatise.' Polly winked.

'Because it's importatant?' Jessica asked.

'Zactly!' Polly fired imaginary pistols at her mate as she backed away from the table.

Jessica laughed at her dear, sloshed friend, who had in fact, as a young teenager, been a mere two park benches away from her when she'd had her first sexual experience after a rather flirtatious game of rounders with the choir of St Stephen's. Things would have got a lot more steamy had it not been for the intervention of Reverend Paul, who had shown up at a crucial moment, shushing them from the park like an agitated giant crow, just in time to save their souls and their reputations.

Polly teetered across the dance floor in perilously high

heels. Jessica watched as she sucked in her stomach and jutted out her ample chest as she walked past Matthew's boss, Magnus, who she had a crush on. The fact that he was older than her father, married and rather arrogant didn't seem to deter her. Jessica loved Polly like a sister. Only last night they had sat in their pyjamas in Matthew's parents' spare bedroom and written a list of all their sexual conquests, each fondly remembering the lamest of victims that the other had conveniently chosen to forget. Rather embarrassingly, they realised that there were at least two shared names on their lists; this had sparked a fit of uncontrollable laughter, which even the smallest of things was prone to do. Polly, who jumped from job to job and was currently temping as a PA, made Jessica laugh like no one else could. So much so that sometimes Jessica barely made it to the bathroom in time, much to her shame.

Jessica patted her tiara, making sure the delicate headpiece and her perfectly curled chocolate-coloured locks were just so. Swallowing her nerves, she touched the pad of her middle finger to her bottom lip, which was still slightly sticky with gloss, meaning her mouth would shine during the close-ups that would inevitably be snapped during the speeches.

Looking at her mum, Coral, who sat a few seats away on the top table, Jessica tensed her cheeks and pulled a wide mouth, indicating both excitement and nerves. Coral winked at her daughter and took a deep breath. She too was trying her best to hide her anxiety. Jessica felt a wave of love for her mum, who she knew had been anticipating this day with trepidation, fretting over her outfit, her hair and what the rest of her family might do or say to embarrass them. It was a minefield. Jessica had tried to reassure her that if Uncle Mick *did* decide after a couple of glasses to do his fart trick, it wouldn't be the end of the world. Both she and her dad had been sent into a tailspin wanting to contribute financially and yet not wanting to set a budget that might thwart Margaret's grand ambitions for her only son. Jessica had watched them trying to navigate the unfamiliar world of canapés, wedding favours and linen samples and knew it took all of her mum's strength not to suggest that she could make the buttonholes, write the place cards and knock up a platter or two of sausage rolls to save a few quid.

Jessica had, during the process of planning the wedding, learnt how to communicate with her mother-in-law. Quite unlike her own mum, Margaret didn't want to be bothered with detail; she simply wanted her decisions approved so that she could rush them into action with gusto. She raced everywhere, as though time was always in short supply, and she always, always looked neat. She was fastidious about her appearance, her little waist often emphasised by a huge tan leather belt that wouldn't have looked amiss on Lennox Lewis. Coral was the exact opposite, pausing often, sometimes lumbering and frequently distracted. She worried about whether a bow would sit right and whether Aunty Joan could manage to last all day with her dodgy hip, but the bigger questions left her in a state of flux, nervously chewing her nails.

Jessica looked out at the expectant faces of the beautifully turned-out guests who were all beaming in her direction as they sat in the elegant ivory marquee on her in-laws' lawn. She felt like a princess and couldn't help smiling as she thought back to that fateful rainy day a year ago, sitting in Sainsbury's car park.

The rain was pounding on the car roof, sounding like small pebbles hitting metal. She'd watched as Matthew sprinted across the grey tarmac in his sneakers and tried the car door handle. Finding it locked, he knocked on the glass of the passenger window.

'The door's locked, Jess! Open up!'

She shook her head, which he may or may not have seen as she slunk down further into the driver's seat, her bony shoulders hunched and the sleeves of her sweatshirt pulled over her hands.

He knocked harder. 'Jess! I'm getting soaked, it's tipping down! Open the bloody door!' This time he bent down, joined his fingers in a salute against his forehead, then rested them on the glass as though it were sunny and not pissing down with rain. 'Jess! What are you doing? I'm getting drenched and so is the shopping.' As if proof were needed, he held up a soggy French stick that looked rather sorrowful and was bent in two.

Jessica folded her arms across her chest, which heaved in an effort to contain her tears. 'I'm not opening it. So go away!'

'What? For God's sake, Jess, look at me!' With his one free hand, Matthew pulled his sodden jersey away from his chest and watched as the waterlogged wool remained mis-shapen. 'Open the sodding door. This isn't funny.'

'Do I look like I'm laughing, Matthew?' she shouted as she leant across the passenger seat, her voice catching in her throat.

Matthew dropped the bag of groceries onto the ground and laid the soggy French stick on top of it. Then he skirted around the front of the car, squeezing through the space between 'Ross', his Fiat Panda, and the car in front. Bending down until his face was level with hers, he pushed the wet hair back from his forehead and tapped on her window. Jessica turned to face him and couldn't help the twitch of laughter on her lips as she watched the rain running off the end of his nose in a steady stream. He looked even sexier than usual, if that was possible.

'Go away, Matt!'

'What do you mean, "*go away*"? I nip into Sainsbury's to pick up some supper and by the time I get back I've been barred from the car? From *my* car!' he shouted and laughed, more than used to his girlfriend's slightly erratic behaviour. She was what Jake had described upon first meeting her as 'a bit of a handful'.

'I came in to find you, Matt, and I bloody saw you,' she barked.

'Saw me what?' Matthew raised his hands as he stuck out his bottom lip and tried to blow the rain away.

'Talking to Jenny! I saw you both in the *champagne* aisle.' She emphasised the word champagne, as though this gave the observation added salaciousness. How could she explain that she still felt nervous and inadequate around these posh girls whose confidence danced out of their well-spoken mouths, and that every swish of their blonde ponytails left her feeling insecure? This was especially so with Jenny, the sweet, leggy American, whose easy manner and fabulous teeth set her apart. Jessica doubted her childhood had been one of sitting on the step of the pub, sharing a packet of Hula Hoops while her dad played skittles in the back.

'That's because I was buying a bottle of champagne! And it was only Jenny, I've known her forever,' Matthew offered, shaking his head in confusion.

'Well I know that, clever clogs. As I said, I saw you! And it's not *what* you purchased that bothered me. It was Jenny throwing her arms around your neck, kissing your face. *And* she had her leg resting up on your thigh, what's that all about? And then I saw you look left and right to check I wasn't watching – well, I was – and then you put your finger on your lips as if to shush her. I'm not stupid, Matt. I know something is going on. Or are you going to tell me I imagined the whole thing?' Jessica felt her mouth crumple in the beginning of tears. This little development was no good at all. She really liked him, more than liked him, she loved him! She dug her fingernails into her palms as a distraction.

Matthew stared at her open-mouthed as if figuring out what to say next. There was a sudden thunderclap overhead. Jessica jumped. She hated thunder. Matthew ran back round to the passenger side of the car. He pulled the bottle of champagne from the bag and held it up to the window.

'You didn't imagine the whole thing. But I bought this for *you*, you idiot.' He smiled.

Jessica felt her stomach bunch, still unused to these extravagant gestures.

'Why don't you give it to Jenny!' She tried to halt the smile that threatened – he had bought her champagne!

'Jenny? No! You've got the wrong end of the stick.'

Matthew shook his head and placed the bottle on the ground. 'If you're not going to let me in, then just open this window a little so you can hear me properly. Please. I hate having to shout, and people are watching,' he yelled.

'I don't care who's watching!' she shouted back, which was a lie. She cared a lot. She rolled Ross's passenger window down by two inches.

Matthew bent down and spoke through the gap. 'Thank you for opening the window.' He smiled. 'I bought champagne because we are celebrating; you and I. Jenny threw her arms around my neck because she *knows* we are celebrating. And the reason she knows is because she has spoken to Jake, who couldn't keep a bloody secret if his life depended on it.'

'What are we celebrating?' Jessica looked across at her rain-soaked, bedraggled boyfriend as he clung to the window, his fingers gripping the rim of the glass in a monkey-like pose, his body pressed against the side of his car in the driving rain. She watched as he arched his body backwards and reached into his wet jeans pocket. Using two fingers, he pulled out a small square red box.

Jessica flung her hand over her mouth as her tears finally found their release. *Oh my God! This is it!*

Matthew suddenly dipped down until all that was visible were his head and shoulders. He shook his head to rid his eyes of the rain. Jessica wound down the window fully, caring little that Ross's upholstery was getting a good soaking. Matthew pushed his forearms into the car and, leaning through the open window, carefully opened the little red box that rested in the centre of his palm. In it nestled his grandmother's Art Deco engagement ring. The square emerald was flanked by two baguette-shaped diamonds and the whole beautiful composition sat on a worn platinum band. It was stunning. It was the ring she had admired when last at his parents' house. Now she knew why it had been sitting there on the mantelpiece, not waiting to be cleaned, as his mother had burst out, but waiting to be collected, by Matthew, in preparation for this moment. Although being locked out of the car on a rainy Tuesday in the car park had probably not figured in his plans.

'Jessica Rose Maxwell...' Matthew paused to compose himself. He gave a small cough and started again, seemingly unaffected by the rain that continued to plaster his hair to his face and his clothes to his body. 'Jessica Rose Maxwell, I love you. Even though you drive me crazy and are undoubtedly the most bonkers person I know. You are also the funniest and the most beautiful. I can't stand the idea of not spending every night with you or not seeing your face on the pillow next to mine when I wake up. I want you to have my babies. And I can't imagine any other future than one with you. I love you.' He pushed the box further into the centre of the car until his arm was fully outstretched. 'Will you marry me?'

Jessica opened Ross's door and tried to jump out, but was anchored by the seatbelt that had tightened across her chest. She laughed as she waited a second and then pushed the button for release. Slipping from the car, she ran through the downpour, edging around the bonnet and into Matthew's arms.

'This is just what I have always dreamt of, being proposed to in Sainsbury's car park!' She kissed him hard on the mouth. 'I love you too!'

'Is that a yes, then, Ms Maxwell?'

'Yes! It's a yes! Of course it's a yes!' Jessica jumped up and down in the rain until she too was soaking wet. She threw her arms wide. 'I'm getting married!' she shouted at the elderly man in an oversized high-visibility jacket and peaked cap who was collecting stray trollies in the car park.

'Congratulations!' he shouted back through the haze of droplets, and waved.

Jessica leapt into Matthew's arms; luckily he was used to this and caught her with ease.

'I'm sorry about your French stick.' She kissed him again.

'Jess, if that's the worst thing we have to contend with in our married life, then I'd say we are going to be just fine.'

Matthew lifted her higher above his waist and held her firmly, with her bottom resting in his hands, as she wrapped her legs around his torso.

'I love you, Matthew.'

'I love you too.' He smiled.

Jessica placed the flat of her palm against his cheek, her expression deadly serious. 'No, you don't understand. I love you more than I knew I could ever love anyone. I love you more than I will ever love another person in the whole wide world and I always, always will. The thought of you not loving me…' She drew breath as if she'd been struck.

'Jess, my Jess. There is nothing you can do, nothing that would make me stop loving you.'

She buried her head in his shoulder. They would wake tomorrow knowing that they were going to be husband and wife, forever.

One year on, Jessica studied the plain platinum wedding band that now sat next to her engagement ring, on the third finger of her left hand. She splayed her fingers, admiring the new addition.

Matthew's father once again tapped the fork against the glass. 'Ladies and gentlemen, could I please ask you to be seated for the speeches.' Jessica caught the way Margaret flashed her husband a look, as if to say, 'Remember, short and sweet, this isn't your floor show.' As was his habit, he jutted his chin, shot his cuffs and ignored her.

Matthew's university chums threw back the shots they had lined up on the starched white linen tablecloth, knowing that time was of the essence. Who wanted to listen to speeches sober? Led, as ever, by Jake, they had long since shed their suit jackets and morning coats; their ties were slackened or absent, their sleeves unevenly rolled.

At twenty-three, Matthew was the first of the gang to marry and this catapulted him into the adult world. They saw it as their duty to both celebrate and mourn the fact that one them had been snared. Their girlfriends exchanged glances; the group of pretty plus-ones had little in common other than that their respective partners had all done very well at A-level, had read law at Nottingham University and were now sitting at the Pissheads and Reprobates table in this fancy tent in the Buckinghamshire countryside.

One of the Pissheads had won an enviable internship, the Chief Reprobate was studying for his Bar exams and at least two of the others were earning mega-bucks in the City, but when the group reassembled, they threw off their career labels and behaved like the twenty-three-year-olds they were. Getting plastered, making crude jokes and trying to get laid became the order of the day.

Matthew's colleagues – or those in the Shark Pool, as the sign on their table tagged them – gripped their glasses of Pinot Grigio Grand Cru and Châteauneuf-du-Pape, carefully chosen to accompany the fish and venison. Their signet rings made pleasing clinks against the sides of the glasses. The practising lawyers eyed the young bucks on the neighbouring table with a mixture of disapproval and envy.

Anthony Deane stood at the top table and pulled his cream silk waistcoat down a fraction, trying to hide the bulge of good living that crept over his waistband with alarming speed year on year. He coughed and lifted his chin. 'It's wonderful to be able to host you all here today in celebration of the marriage of our son Matthew to the delightful Jessica. I would now like to hand the floor over to Jessica's father, Roger.'

Jessica didn't think of him as her father, he was Dad, her dad. A loud 'woohoo!' came from the back of the marquee. Anthony raised his glass. 'Well thank you, that man. One woohoo already and we are not even close to the finale – this bodes very well.' There was a ripple of laughter. Anthony sat and folded his hands across his stomach as all eyes turned to Roger Maxwell.

Jessica watched her dad stand. He smoothed his tie against his chest, removed his glasses from the case that usually sat on the arm of his favourite chair, and placed them on his nose. He pulled the folded sheets of A4 paper from his pocket. In no particular hurry, he coughed to clear his throat. His words when they came were delivered clearly and sincerely. Jessica had to stop herself rushing over and holding him close. She felt a swell of affection and gratitude towards this man during his first ever public speech. She knew how nervous he was and loved that he didn't try to refine his Essex accent, proud of his roots and what he had achieved for his family with nothing more than hard graft and an eye for an opportunity.

Roger looked up at the assembled guests. 'I don't think I can go any further without mentioning quite how beautiful my daughter looks today.' This prompted a round of applause, in response to which, Jessica placed her head in her hands and tried to hide. Matthew pulled her hands from her face and encouraged her to stand. She felt the scarlet stain of pleased embarrassment creep up her neck as she put her hands on her impossibly small waist and gave a half turn to show off her dress to its full advantage. The tiny crystals sewn into the delicate cream lace of her fitted bodice sparkled in the candlelight. She gave an awkward bow before resuming her place next to her husband and gripping his hand on the tabletop. Her action elicited numerous wolf whistles and cheers and to try and quieten her racing pulse, Jessica laid her manicured hand against her chest.

Roger paused to let the ruckus die down; he was handling the speech like a pro. 'I remember the quiet Saturday night we were watching the telly when Jessica came home and told her mum and me that she had met a man at a barbecue who had been so sloshed that he called her Joanna all night. I didn't think much of it, but three months later young Matthew was knocking at my door informing me of his decision to propose to Jessica! I asked if he meant Joanna

– I think that broke the ice a little.'

More laughter rippled across the room.

Matthew nodded; it had.

'The word whirlwind was invented for these two. My first question to Matt was, quite naturally, are you *mad*, son?'

'Oh, Roger!' wailed Jessica's mother, Coral. Then she laughed with her hand covering her mouth.

'My second question was, of course, who do you support?'

'Queens Park bloody Rangers!' came the shout from the Pissheads and Reprobates.

'Yes,' Roger answered, pointing at the rowdy table, 'and as a lifelong Hammers fan, let me tell you, those clearly weren't the words I wanted to hear. But it could have been so much worse. He might have been a Millwall fan or, worse still, been one of those blokes who only likes rugby!'

The room erupted into laughter. Anthony's passion for rugby was well known. Jessica beamed at her dad. He was doing great.

'I think this topic will only rear its ugly head if we are ever blessed with a grandson, when I will be charging up that maternity ward with a claret and blue strip. No arguments there, boy.'

'Ooooh! Harsh!' Matthew's friends heckled from afar.

Roger reached for his glass. 'But all joking aside, there is no finer bloke to whom we could entrust the care of our child. We are so proud of our beautiful girl, our clever girl, and an artist no less. We love all that she is and all that she will be. It feels like only moments ago that she was holding my fingers and taking her first steps along the path in our garden.' He paused and swallowed the lump in his throat.

'From the very first moment I held you in my arms, Jessica Rose, I loved you and I will love you until my last breath. I know that Danny is looking down on you today and probably laughing at his old man done up like a kipper!' He plucked at his tie. 'Your mum and I wish you both every bit of happiness in the world. And if we can give you one bit of advice, it's this: nobody's life is perfect. Be patient on the dark days, because they pass.' The room was silent. 'No matter how dark it gets, sit it out. Even if you think you are alone, when the light comes back, if you are lucky, you'll look to your right and realise that the person you love was sat by your side, holding your hand, though you might not have seen them.' He stole a glance at his wife and smiled. Then he raised his glass. 'To Jess and Matt.' He took a sip and everyone followed his lead.

Matthew raised his wife's knuckles knitted against his own and kissed them. He would give her the ocean in a box if he could; nothing would ever be too much for this girl who he loved more than life itself. Jessica smiled at him, fixing him with a knowing look.

Coral cried. This was to be expected at the mention of Danny on a day like this. Jessica's girlfriends whooped and hollered on cue; in fact everyone on the Tarts and Slackers table was giving as good as they were getting in terms of banter. They were all, however, similarly affected by the words of Jessica's dad, which made their tears flow. They had all known Danny, remembered Jessica's quiet older brother who had now bizarrely become her younger brother, frozen aged fourteen. Polly in particular sobbed noisily into her linen napkin, smearing it with lipstick and mascara in the process. Their collective outpouring was partly in response to Mr Maxwell's loving sentiments and partly because none of them could imagine how life might be now that Jessica, who in their school-leavers' yearbook was described as 'Little Miss Chatterbox, the girl who even talks in her sleep!', was a married woman. It felt like the end of an era and was a timely reminder that they too would be jumping off the ship that sailed on the sea of singledom sooner rather than later.

Matthew tried several times to begin his speech, but with the persistent chanting of 'Deano!', his student footballing nickname, it was almost impossible. Eventually Jessica stood and with arms outstretched and palms facing down, patted at the air, signalling for Jake and the boys to be quiet.

'You're so bossy, Jess!' Jake yelled. 'Poor Matt!'

'I am *not* bossy, I'm assertive.' She smiled at her husband's best friend.

'Thank you, my assertive darling.' Matthew kissed her forehead and she nodded gratefully in response.

'We all knew Jess wouldn't be able to resist getting involved during the speeches, right? Apparently the trick for me is going to be how to get her to shut up, not just today but throughout our married life. For the days when that proves impossible, Roger has very kindly given me these for use in extreme emergencies.'

Matthew bent down to reach below the table, then straightened up to reveal a pair of orange ear defenders in his hand. Everybody laughed and clapped, her parents included. Jessica thumped her groom on the bottom as he continued. 'Wow! In all seriousness, how to follow that?'

He looked at Roger. 'And I must say, a good summing-up from my father-in-law. Ever thought of leaving the sales game and taking up law, Roger? We could do with your sort in the courtroom!'

'Hear! Hear!' his colleagues concurred.

Jessica was happy beyond words that her dad and husband were friends. It would mean that all the Christmases, birthdays and holidays at the seaside that she pictured in her head, where they and her parents laughed as they played cards or ate fish and chips on a pebble beach, would come to fruition. Her stomach knotted in anticipation.

'I am quite possibly the happiest man on the planet today…' Matthew began.

Jessica smiled up at her husband on this, the happiest day of her life.

18th January, 2012

Dear Diary

I think that's how I'm supposed to start. The doctor's instructions weren't that specific. So here goes. What to say? It's hard to know what to put. It's not like anything much happens.

There was a treat this afternoon. I use the term loosely as participation was compulsory. It's strange, isn't it, that even supposedly nice things, when done under instruction inside these magnolia-painted brick walls, have the joy sucked from them.

It was a visit from a beautician called Kimberley. She wore long, thick, false eyelashes and her blinks were slow and languid, as though weighed down by the feathery fronds. It made me want to rub my own eyes. She arrived carrying a plastic box that I'm sure was designed for tools. I remember my dad owning one that was similar, full of paint-spattered brushes, screwdrivers and, bizarrely, odd buttons that he must have found around the house.

Kimberley was accompanied by a young, silent apprentice who blushed with awkwardness as she massaged oil into our cuticles and painted pastel-shaded glitter onto our nails. I wanted to smile at her and tell her not to worry, we aren't contagious, but I don't smile any more.

I sat on a stool that was bolted to the floor; God forbid someone might actually give in to their simmering rage and lob it at something or someone. As instructed, I sat with my hands stretched out on the tabletop, flexing downwards from the wrists and resting on a rolled-up white towel as Kimberley sawed back and forth with the emery board. I glanced to the left and right at the girls who sat either side of me. I was transfixed by the sight of our hands. Hands that could not be prettified or cleaned simply by washing them and applying a coat of nail polish. Hands stained with blood and violence. One pair choked the life from an ageing aunt for money; others cut the throat of a lover. Then I started to think about what my own hands had done. I studied my fingers and I remembered.

I cried then, as I often do. Kimberley's assistant glanced at me nervously from the corner of her eye, distracted from her task. I saw the lump in her throat as she swallowed her fears. I could guess at her thoughts: what comes after tears? Will she fly into a rage? Hurt me? She for one would be glad that those stools were immoveable. I wished I could summon a smile to tell her not to worry, that I would not fly into a rage or hurt her.

I looked at my thin wrists and hands with disgust. The act they have performed taints everything they come into contact with. The food they touch turns to ashes in my mouth, flowers lose their natural scent, taking on the smell of the bathroom on that day, and any skin they happen upon shrinks from my touch as if burnt.

All of this and more I deserve because I did the worst thing a woman could do.

The very worst.

Did I do it on purpose? Yes, yes I did.

Am I a bad person or do I deserve the kindly words and knowing smiles that sometimes float my way across the games room or exercise yard?

Truthfully? I don't know the answer to that question.

Two

It was less than twenty-four hours after the wedding speeches that a naked Jessica flung open the doors on to the balcony of Matt's parents' Majorcan villa. The wood and wrought-iron shutters were thrown wide to reveal the bright blue Mediterranean morning and the gauzy curtain panels arched in the early breeze. Beyond their window and the ornate scrolled iron balcony they could see nothing but the green tops of the Tramuntana Mountains. Even at this early hour, the sun was giving off warmth and there was the distant ring of bells from the Church of San Juan Bautista in the village. Jessica looked back at Matthew, resting her chin on her shoulder.

'This is so perfect! I think it's the nicest place I have ever been and I can't believe we're here!' She tucked her hair behind her ears and turned to her husband, who lay in the crumpled bed with the edge of a white sheet wrapped around his toned legs. 'And I can't believe your parents just leave the key in a tin behind the bush! I'm surprised you haven't got squatters.'

'I think that's unlikely. Everyone knows everyone – anything suspicious and Mum and Dad's phone would be ringing off the hook.'

'We should go for a walk, stop somewhere pretty for coffee and fresh bread and then come back for more sex!' She ran at the bed and landed with a thud against the antique, brocade-covered headboard.

'For God's sake, Jessica, you can't want more sex! You're going to kill me!' Matthew pulled the pillow over his head.

'I can't help it, I find you irresistible. You should be glad I do. Lots of women don't like sex.'

'Is that right?'

'Yep. I read it in my magazine.' She smacked his bottom. 'Think yourself lucky you didn't marry one of those,' she said as she chose a chocolate Hobnob from the biscuit selection in her handbag and shoved half of it into her mouth.

'Firstly, this morning I wish I had married one of those; I could do with the rest. Secondly, you are covering this bed in crumbs!' He groaned.

'Matthew, we are on our honeymoon. You can't moan about me wanting lots of sex or eating biscuits in bed. You can only be miserable after we've been married forever and I repeat myself and you have to wee every five minutes and you have one of those bloated fat tums that old men have, tucked under a belt with your jumper pulled over it.' She popped the other half in her mouth.

Matthew propped himself up on his elbow. 'I could never moan at you. You're amazing. I think I'm the luckiest man alive. Don't you ever change.' He ran his thumb over the inside of her arm.

'I won't. Apart from getting wrinkly.' She grimaced.

'I shall love each of your wrinkles.' He leant forward and kissed her knee.

'And I shall love your little fat tum and skinny legs!'

'I object! I haven't got skinny legs!'

'No, but I've seen your dad in shorts and I bet you *will* have. You are going to turn into him, I can see it.' Jessica reached for another biscuit.

'Blimey, and you still married me?' He laughed, pulling her on top of him until they lay skin to skin, letting the warm Majorcan breeze flow over them.

Jessica wriggled down the bed until her head rested on her husband's chest. 'I didn't know another person could make me this happy.'

'Me neither.' He smiled.

Jessica pressed her body against his.

'Oh God! This is going to mean sex again, isn't it?' Matthew closed his eyes and sank his head back into the pillows.

'I'm afraid so,' she confirmed. 'Just lie back and sing "Jerusalem" and with any luck it should all be done and dusted before you've got through the second verse.'

With her basket on her arm, Jessica picked her way down the steep path and on to the shingle beach. She looked up at her husband, who, more confident of the route, had strolled ahead, carrying the towels and a thick blanket to lie on. She hesitated, pausing to shield her eyes against the sun and to stare at her man as he placed the rug on the ground and spread the towels on top. She knew this was the most perfect time in the most perfect place. Her face ached from smiling, but she couldn't stop. She was filled with happiness and excitement.

Looking over at Matthew, her heart skipped and joy bubbled up into her throat. He was in his shorts and flip-flops, going from corner to corner, crouching down, making the makeshift sunbed the neatest and comfiest it could be. Jessica pushed her sunglasses further up her nose and gazed at him. He looked beautiful; the sun lit him from behind as he stood in a golden haze. It was a moment of realisation that her whole happiness lay in this man's hands. It felt like a fragile thing that might, if wrongly handled, take flight. The thought, the idea of him turning off the love that poured from him was enough to make her feel sick. His love was like an addiction, a drug. He was so much more than her. Smarter, posher, better looking. Just better. And she realised in that moment that she was vulnerable and that the happiness she had found could be taken from her with nothing more than a change of heart. This thought terrified her. She remembered taking Matthew to the pub to meet Polly for the first time and hurrying to the loo so she could get her feedback. Polly had leant on the sink and said, 'Bloody hell, Jess! He's Manchester United!' She knew what this meant: out of her league and it wasn't only about looks. It was so much more than that.

'Here we go, madam.' Matthew bowed. 'Your bed for the day awaits!'

Jessica giggled, depositing her basket by the blanket, their lunch of freshly baked bread, slices of Serrano ham and a small punnet of olives safely wrapped inside. She kicked off her sandals, abandoned her sunhat and strolled to the shoreline, letting the lapping waves foam over her toes.

'Ooh, that water's quite chilly!' She stepped backwards.

'Rubbish!' he scoffed. 'You just have to be brave.'

'I'd rather be warm than brave,' she said over her shoulder.

'Is that right?' he asked as he removed his sunglasses and threw them down near the basket.

Jessica screamed in anticipation as he covered the space between them at speed, his head bent low, like a bull on the charge. Before she had time to protest, he had grabbed her around the waist and was hurtling into the water, taking her with him. The salt water was kicked up in an arc, soaking them both before he lost his footing and sank down into the sea, dragging his squealing bride with him. They immediately bobbed to the surface, Matthew laughing and Jessica spluttering with the shock. She raised her fist to thump him but he caught it, pulling her close, lifting her like a baby until she rested in his grip with one head on his shoulder and her legs dangling over his arm. He swirled her around in the water as the waves gently broke over them, leaving a salt residue on their skin and their hair plastered to their faces.

'See, it's not cold, not once you are in.' He smiled.

She nodded. He was right.

'Don't ever leave me, Matt.'

'I'll never leave you.' He kissed her nose. 'Lie back. I'll hold you.'

Matthew moved his hands to the small of her back as Jessica slid down and lay flat on the water with her arms outstretched and her head back in the sea. She lay very still as the small waves lapped over her ears. With nothing more than Matthew's gentle support keeping her up, Jessica looked up towards the mountaintops.

'I feel like I'm flying,' she breathed as he moved her gently across the surface.

'Fly high, golden girl. I've got you.'

Jessica arched her back slightly, pushing back further into the water and enjoying the feeling of weightlessness. She was overcome with a sense of peace. She wished they could stay like that forever.

14th March, 2012

Some days I feel as though I am inside a small box. Everywhere seems airless and claustrophobic, particularly when it's sunny and bright outside. If I could scratch away my skin to get out, I would. There is no quiet space I can hide and no place I can be by myself to think for any length of time.

The dining room smells of bad breath, old food and boiled vegetables. It reminds me of a school canteen and although I am sure I will get used to the smell, I haven't yet. Today, I was given a helping of corned beef with a couple of limp salad leaves that had stuck to the warm plate. I stared at it and the woman in the hairnet who had given it to me said, 'What's the matter, Rapunzel, did you want something different off the menu?' If only I could, but she was just being mean.

People have regular seats on the benches fixed on either side of the long, thin dining tables – some groups huddle together, whispering, others laugh and chat. I sat alone at an empty table as usual, but a woman lowered herself onto the bench opposite me, following my every move. She was desperately thin and drummed the tabletop with stained yellow fingers; her long nails made an unattractive click. She was wearing a misshapen grey T-shirt with the word 'Nagasaki' in peeling raised print on the front. Her arms were stick-like and hung from the gaping armholes like spaghetti. 'Got any baccy?' She grinned at me and I could see little black stumps instead of teeth as she flicked her lanky fringe from her face. I just shook my head and did my best to ignore her. It's not as if this kind of thing hasn't happened before. It's just that sometimes I can keep a hard shell fixed around my heart, and sometimes I can't. Today I couldn't and I felt scared. Sick and scared.

When I was growing up, it didn't matter how rubbish my day was or how overwhelmed by life I felt, I always thought my mum and dad could fix everything, because they did! Stepping inside the front door of our little house in Hillcrest Road, Romford was like being wrapped in a warm safety blanket. I don't remember being aware of the seasons; in our house it was always warm and cosy. My dad would peel me a clementine, removing all the white pith that I hated and singing 'Oh my darling...' and no matter when or where I fell asleep, he would put a blanket over my toes and draw the curtains.

But on the day I followed the policeman up the path and into the hallway, the day I lay on my bed and listened to my mum screaming and swearing as my dad held her down, the day my heart beat so fast I thought I might die too, I realised that my mum and dad had failed. There was no safety blanket. They couldn't keep us safe and I knew this because they had let Danny die. And I lost my faith in them.

I have considered the possibility that they were being punished. Maybe they had done something wrong and so Danny got taken from them. Like there is this unseen force totting up the good and bad and making everything balance. That's how the world works sometimes; it is cruel, hard and difficult to live in.

Three

It was dusk in London and despite being September, when winter pawed impatiently at the break of dawn and blew its cool breath over the sunniest of afternoons, there was still the lingering promise of a warmer day tomorrow.

Matthew felt a swell of pride every time he placed the key in the willow-green front door of their red-brick Edwardian terrace on Merton Avenue off the Chiswick High Road. Having a key to his very own front door – their first house – felt like a huge deal. It was more than enough to counteract the gut-churning worry that preoccupied him at three in the morning when he got up to pee and thought about the size of the mortgage that they had taken out and the hefty deposit they had been gifted by his parents.

Anthony had made his fortune buying then renovating houses and building new ones, lots of them. He was adamant that homeownership was the only way to safeguard his son's future. With that in mind, not long after their engagement, the equivalent of Matthew's yearly salary had been transferred into his account without comment. His parents had of course insisted it was a gift, but Matthew felt it was in some way a test. Would he pay it back? Could he?

Jessica had fallen in love with the property the moment they had arrived, before the estate agent had even opened the front door. She ran her fingers over the pale pink dog rose that clung to the trellis at the side of the front door and hung in a heavy bower over the lintel. It gave off a heady scent as they entered the house.

'Just think of all the people who have walked through this door since it was built.' She turned to Matthew, beaming. 'I can see women standing here waving their men off to war and I bet they had a street party for the Queen's coronation!'

Matthew nodded, knowing that she was right there and then picturing herself walking through this door in all seasons, planning how she would greet Polly and her parents from the other side of the etched glass panels.

Jessica had then leapt and squealed her way around the house, shouting, 'I love it! I absolutely love it. Look at the space! And it's so light, I can work here. Oh, Matt, look at this place!' So much for appearing cool and indifferent in front of the estate agent, the better to try and negotiate a favourable price. Matthew smiled as he remembered that day.

It was also the day they had met their next-door neighbour. The woman had loitered around the mini wheelie-bin behind her gate, wearing a green cardi, brown tweed skirt and what looked like men's shoes. Her movements were slow. She seemed to be taking a very long time to deposit the half-full carrier bag, clearly hoping for a glimpse of the young couple, if not an introduction. Jessica waved at her as they left, full of excitement at the prospect of the house becoming theirs.

'I have lived here all my life. This was my mother's house.' This was her opener, delivered with narrowed eyes and without even the hint of a smile.

'Well, lucky you. It's such a lovely street!' Jessica beamed, trying to win her over.

'Used to be.' The woman tutted, jerking her head towards the opposite side of the road, which left Jessica and Matthew wondering who had moved in and put an end to the good times. The woman was tiny, in her seventies, not quite five foot and of slight build. She had a blunt grey bob and wide fringe that from a distance looked like a helmet. Her lips were almost non-existent and her eyes tiny behind her John-Lennon-style frames.

'I am Mrs Pleasant,' she said before scuttling back inside.

Matthew and Jessica had fallen around laughing when they'd got back to their flat.

'At least we know we won't be living next door to a crack den and I shouldn't imagine there will be many sex noises coming through the walls,' Jessica said.

'At least not from her side!' Matthew quipped.

'She creeped me out.' Jessica shuddered. 'The way she announced "I am Mrs Pleasant"; that was just weird.'

'I tell you what's weird – her name, when she is one of the least pleasant people I've met!'

'I know, right! It only works if her first name is Not-Very!' And the two fell onto the sofa, laughing some more.

Matthew now hovered at the door of the sitting room, watching his wife, who sat curled into the window seat.

One leg was tucked underneath her bottom, the other stretched in an elegant arc with her oversized sketchpad resting on it. Her thick hair was in a messy ponytail on top of her head and her leggings had gone baggy around the knees from sitting in her favourite pose all day. It was on days like this that he thought her most beautiful: no make-up, no fancy clothes and lit from within, consumed by the task in hand. Her face was contorted with concentration; a little crease had appeared at the top of her nose and her tongue poked from the side of her mouth. She had been taken on by a freelance agency and this was her first commission. Jessica had excitedly read the brief aloud. 'A children's book!' she'd squealed. '"We are looking for woodland creatures both male and female that should be appealing and non-threatening and will incorporate elements of nature in both their physique and costume." How brilliant is that!'

Jessica looked up and stared at her husband, his tie askew, the stresses of the commute etched beneath his eyes. 'How was your day, Mr Important Lawyer?'

'I'm not an important lawyer yet, Jess. If I were, I wouldn't spend most of my day shuffling paper and searching for things at the request of my dickhead colleagues further up the ladder. Today was really, really boring. And long. As soon as anyone mentions the word "background" in relation to a client, I know that means me with my head in a file two inches from a screen for the next day or so.'

'Oh, poor Matt.' She sighed.

'Did I mention it was boring?' he asked as he dropped his briefcase to the floor, threw his keys onto the console table and slumped against the door frame. ‘Do you know how much I envy you, being able to work in your pyjamas, sip tea when you feel like it and lounge in the window seat with the radio on? You live the life of a lottery winner, not a care in the bloody world!’ He smiled at her.

Jessica nodded. ‘You are right, but in exchange for my fabulous career choice as a freelance illustrator, I earn barely enough to keep me in baked beans, maybe half a tin at the most, and if I didn’t have a clever, well-paid man to support me, I’d be destitute.’ She shrugged.

‘There are women all over the country squirming inside their “All Men Are Bastards” T-shirts at that very statement.’

‘It’s true though.’ Jessica placed her pencil in her mouth and flipped the pages of her pad. She felt a surge of self-doubt. She loved drawing, it was one of the few things she knew she was good at – really good at – but if she couldn’t make any money from it, what was the point?

‘I doubt you’d be destitute for long,’ Matthew added. ‘Not looking like that.’

‘Look what I did today.’ Jessica ignored him and turned the pad to face her husband, revealing the intricate pencil drawing of a creature, part girl, part pixie, with pointy little ears that poked from beneath the lustrous layers of her curled hair. Her eyes were vast and sat inside a heart-shaped face. Her tiny mouth was pouting and on her head sat a crown of wild flowers. ‘She’s a woodland sprite and she tries to save the world from the evil wizard’s spell.’

‘Wow, she’s beautiful!’ Matthew was, as ever, quite taken aback by his wife’s talent. It was alien to him how such detail could be achieved with nothing more than shading and pencil strokes. 'She reminds me of you.'

'It's the pointy ears, right?' Jessica tucked her hair behind hers.

'Yep. And the sexy pout.'

Jessica sighed. 'What do you want first, supper or sex?' she asked matter-of-factly as she stood and placed the pad on the floor, laying her pencils on top.

Matthew pulled his tie from his collar and flung it on the sofa. 'That depends. What's for supper?'

'I was thinking pasta with a handful of prawns, bit of chilli, splash of cream, chunk of garlic bread, nice warm glass of red...' she parroted from the cookery show she'd caught on TV at lunchtime. As she spoke, she pulled her hair from its band and let it fall over her shoulders.

'Oh, supper sounds good!' Matthew teased as he walked over to his wife and took her in his arms. 'But I guess a quick round of sex wouldn't do any harm, in fact it might be the least boring part of my day.'

'Good, that's settled then. Here or upstairs?' Jessica shrugged him off with a dry expression and removed her socks, flinging them in the air.

'I think upstairs.' Matthew kicked off his shoes and undid his shirt buttons. 'In fact, I'll chase you – think of me as that evil wizard!' He let out a roar as he dived towards her with his palms raised and fingers bent to imitate claws.

Jessica screamed as she hot-footed it up the stairs and hurled herself onto their bed. She hated being chased. Matthew grabbed her and nuzzled her neck until she shrieked with laughter and her face split with happiness.

*

With her head resting on her husband's chest, she let her breathing slow, matching the rhythm of his heartbeat. She purred at the feel of Matthew's hand stroking her hair, which lay in a gossamer sheet against his skin.

Jessica glanced at the bedside clock. It was nearly ten o'clock. 'I rather think we've missed the supper boat. It's a bit late for pasta and plonk.' She giggled.

'I'll get up in a minute and return with toast, honey and tea. How does that sound?' He kissed the top of her head.

'It sounds brilliant.' Jessica propped herself up on her elbow and stared at her man, who looked decidedly ruffled, his hair stuck up at odd angles.

'I'm really happy.' She smiled.

'Well if I'd known the offer of toast and honey was what it took, I would have offered you some a long time ago.'

Her face was suddenly serious. 'I mean it, Matt. I knew I loved you and wanted to be with you, but I had no idea what being married would be like and I feel…' She plucked at the plain white Egyptian cotton bed linen, trying to find the right words.

'You feel what?' he encouraged.

'I feel very safe and secure.'

'That's good. That's my job, to make you feel that way.'

'I feel relieved that I know where my life is going and that I don't ever have to get tarted up for a date again. Apart from dates with you of course!'

'Of course.'

'I sometimes wish I could crawl inside you and stay there

forever, just curled up into a little ball, inside your tummy. I think it's the closest to you that I could possibly get and I'd like that.'

'I have to say, I rather like having you outside of my tummy. It would be very difficult to shag you and I don't see how you could cook supper.' He laughed. 'Not that you do cook supper much. And when you do, you're hardly Nigella!'

'I'm trying to be serious, Matt. I didn't know how different it would feel being Mrs Matthew Deane, but it's very different, in a good way. I feel safe.'

'You are safe,' he whispered. 'I would never let anything happen to you.' He ran his thumb along the inside of her arm, following the purple vein as it meandered under her white skin.

'I know we are young, and it might sound stupid, but I used to worry about getting old. I couldn't imagine what it would be like. But now I don't worry any more. I know that if I'm with you then everything is okay. Even if that means being old and wrinkly and smelling of wee.'

'I shall still find you sexy when you are old and wrinkly and smell of wee.'

Jessica laughed and kissed her husband full on the mouth, feeling a rush of love for the man and his body. She rolled on top of him and kissed him again. The toast would just have to wait.

29th August, 2012

The long, long days of summer are nearly over. I can't see the trees or smell the flowers on the breeze, except for forty minutes each day, not nearly long enough for me. I stand and gulp in great lungfuls of wonderfully fresh air that hasn't been filtered through the air-conditioning system.

It's not my favourite time of year – that would have to be autumn. Even though it was an autumn day all those years ago. The air smelt like Bonfire Night, earthy and damp, a scent I have always loved. It was five o'clock. Cars had their lights on even though it wasn't quite dark; it had been raining and everything was a little hazy, dazzling. I zipped my coat up to my neck as I was a bit chilly. Up until that point, there was nothing to mark the day in my mind; it was just a regular school day. But I can still remember the littlest details. I remember sitting on the bus wondering if I could get my homework done while I watched *Malcolm in the Middle* or whether Mum would make me go upstairs to my room.

I sat alone halfway up the bus on the left-hand side, pushing my foot against the floor to keep steady as the driver swung the vehicle around the corners. I heard the hiss of his brakes and stood up just before the bus pulled over, ready to retrieve my rucksack from the wire rack overhead. It was heavy. I was watching it fall, making sure my hands were positioned just so to stop it crashing down on top of me. My arms were raised high when the doors scraped open, then I heard the noise. A prolonged screeching followed by a high-pitched squeal of rubber on tarmac, then smoke and a smell that was like a mixture of fish, chemicals and something burning. Someone was screaming. I remember that too.

Then I was in the back of the police car. The light swirled a purple-blue beacon across the houses, though they turned the siren off. When it pulled into the quiet road where we lived, just the presence of a police car there was enough to get the curtains twitching. The driver and his colleague put their helmets on and walked up the path to our front door. I wondered if they had forgotten about me and was about to knock on the window when one of them turned and gave a tight-lipped smile. I knew then that they had left me there on purpose.

My mum opened the door and stood wiping her wet hands on a tea towel. Who'd have thought that small orange and red striped thing would shine so distinctly in my memory.

I wound down the window and breathed in the cold night air. They didn't know I was listening. I picked at a loose thread on the hem of my skirt, watching the seam unravel as I pulled it.

The policeman said, 'There's been an accident,' and I heard my mum say, 'Not Danny?' and then she gasped. I can hear it perfectly even now, over a decade later. Something stopped me from rushing out of the car, stopped me running into her arms and burying my face in her chest, letting her hold me tight.

I watched her face as the words filtered back to me. 'Your son was in a hurry to get off the school bus, he ran out from behind... It was getting dark... Car braked... but... Oldchurch Hospital.'

I have replayed those two words so often, over and over inside my head, trying to figure out why they caused me so much pain. 'Not Danny? Not Danny?' she said, bringing her hand to her chest with the tea towel scrunched inside her palm. And then the sharp intake of breath.

And back then I was so sure she was right. Danny was golden. I was like the consolation prize, bronze at best. Later on, Matthew would often call me his golden girl. That was before I ended up in here, of course. I don't know what he would call me now, if he were here to call me anything at all.

Four

Jessica paid the cab fare, shoving the scrunched-up tenner at the driver in her haste to get inside as quickly as possible. 'Thank you!' she shouted, waving over her shoulder as she skipped across the pavement and fumbled in her bag for her front door keys.

'Evening, Mrs P!' Jessica regretted the overfamiliar greeting the second it left her lips. 'Got anything planned for Halloween? You can have these if you like!' Jessica held out the white plastic vampire teeth that she and Polly had been wearing all afternoon.

Her neighbour ignored the offering in Jessica's outstretched palm. 'It's *Mrs Pleasant*,' she uttered before disappearing inside with a disapproving shake of her head.

'Waaaaaaagh! Matt! I'm so sorry. Oh my God, I've had a complete mare!' Jessica hollered as she let herself into the house, dropping her handbag behind the front door as she raced along the hallway's stripped-wood floor. She came to an abrupt halt in the light, airy kitchen that occupied the glass-roofed extension at the back of their home.

Matthew was sitting at the breakfast bar in his dinner jacket, white shirt and black bow tie, his newly polished shoes resting on the bar of the stool and his glasses on the end of his nose. He was scanning his iPad, reading the day's papers while sipping on a gin and tonic infused with plenty of lime. He looked up and sighed.

'Well hello, Mr Bond. I believe you have been exthpecting me?' Jessica lisped through her ill-fitting vampire teeth. 'No! No! No! Please don't be in a huff. I'm sorry, my love. I know you hate being late.' Jessica pulled out her teeth and held up both her palms as if she were directing traffic.

'I'm not in a huff,' Matthew countered a little coolly, lightly tapping his fingers on the counter top.

'You are a little bit, I can tell. Because that was funny and you didn't laugh, not even slightly. Plus you have the beginnings of your huff face. But I promise I'll get ready at super-speed and let's see if we can't turn that frown upside down!' She grinned.

Despite his irritation, Matthew smiled at his effervescent wife as she babbled.

'It's not even my fault I'm late! I'm so sorry, baby,' Jessica continued as she pulled her cowboy boots from her feet and flung them into a heap in the middle of the floor. 'I was out with Polly and Jayne in a pub down by the river and I *told* them I had to get back for your very important lawyery-night thing and Polly even set an alarm so I could head off in plenty of time and it was only while we were sharing a massive Eton mess, which was delish actually, just the right mix of cream and strawberries. Anyway...' She swallowed. 'Jayne asked what I was planning on wearing tonight and I remembered I'd sent my dress to the cleaners and hadn't collected it. So I left, didn't even pay my share, which no doubt Polly will slate me for, even though she never gave me the money for Max and Drew's civil partnership gift, do you remember? The ugliest teapot in the world that we got from Greenwich Market? Well, we were supposed to go halves with Polly. Anyway...' Jessica rolled her hand in the air. 'I hailed a cab, but when I got to Mayflower's on the Goldhawk Road, guess what?' Jessica finally drew breath as she slipped out of her jeans and flung them, inside out, over the back of a dining chair, before shrugging her arms from her jersey and tossing it over her head.

'They were closed?' Matthew offered as he powered down his iPad and decided instead to watch his wife strip in the kitchen.

'They were! Bastards. And I just accidentally called our neighbour "Mrs P" and I don't think she was that chuffed. Ooh, I need a drink. Do you think I have time for a quick one?'

The hands of the kitchen clock were quickly making their way towards 7 p.m., which was precisely the time they needed to leave in order to make the banquet at the Guildhall that started at 7.45. Jessica looked at the clock guiltily and pulled out a three-quarters-full bottle of Pimm's and a chilled litre of lemonade from the fridge.

'Be a love, Matt, and pour me a big one while I go and find shoes.' She smiled as she plonked the bottles on the work surface and scooted along the kitchen floor in her bra and pants before coming to rest in front of the huge scrubbed-pine linen-press in their hallway, which was brimming with numerous pairs of shoes and boots, most of which, if Matthew were to be honest, looked remarkably similar.

'Oh, come to Mumma, you little beauties!' Jessica bent over and dug deep into the closet, withdrawing with a pair of beautiful silver Louboutin shoes in her hand. She leant on the kitchen worktop and kicked up her left foot. 'Matt, I am being as quick as I can. Just look at this red sole; tell me it isn't the most fabulous thing you have ever seen! God, if someone had told me when I was eighteen that in five years' time I'd be a married woman who got to wear Louboutins to a posh work do, I'd have told them pigs were flapping past the window!' Jessica flicked her long, dark hair back over her shoulder and grinned excitedly.

Matthew poured his wife's drink and swallowed. He had known her for the best part of two years, they had been married for five months and the sight of her in her white lacy underwear and killer heels had the same effect it always did. He knew he would never, could never, grow tired of this vision of his perfect, excitable, sexy, unreliable, disorganised, tardy wife.

'They are indeed things of beauty. Now get this drink down your neck while I call a cab. We can't be late. Again.' Matthew reached for his phone while Jessica necked her Pimm's and scoffed the little strawberry he had placed in the bottom of the glass.

'Tell you what, I'll go same again.' She pointed at her empty glass. 'And I promise to be ready by the time the cab gets here. Deal?' She beamed.

'Do I have any choice?' Matthew smirked as he reached for her glass and collected one for himself from the floating shelf above the sink.

Jessica opened her make-up bag and patted dark smudges of powder around her green, almond-shaped eyes before swiping her lips with a wand that dripped with hot-pink gloss. Bending over, away from her husband, she turned her head upside down and tousled her roots with her fingers before flicking her head up the right way and slowly righting herself. She turned to Matthew, who was back on his stool, took the glass from him and downed her second large Pimm's in less than five minutes.

Matthew knocked back his drink and looked at the clock, the hands of which were now motoring. 'We really have to get going, Jess. We're on Magnus's table and you know what he's like.'

'Absolutely. Nasty boss. He was a topic of discussion today at lunch. Polly says she would like to sort him out, give him something to smile about. I told her it was unlikely to happen, but you know Polly, she's a trier! Have you had a bad day, baby?'

'Not a bad day, exactly, but a busy one and I find being late stressful. But this you know.' As Matt sipped at his drink and looked at his beautiful wife, now bent over the open drawer, rummaging for a pair of stockings to go with her shoes, he found that being late was suddenly the last thing on his mind.

Jessica felt his gaze and turned around, a slow smile lighting up her face. 'Well, I suppose there is one thing we could do to relieve your stress,' she said coyly, coming to nestle in the space between his legs as she toyed with his bow tie. She leant in to kiss his neck.

'Jess, you minx! We *have* to go out!' Matthew wiped his brow and fought the flames of longing that reared up inside him, trying to focus on the fact that he was expected to be somewhere and it was work related. 'This is very different from blowing Jake off last minute for the pub quiz or lying to my parents that we have colds and can't make brunch. This is my job!'

'I know that.' She nodded. 'I can't help it that I find you completely irresistible. And we could be very quick!' Jessica laughed, loving how this man made her feel like the sexiest woman alive. He gave her confidence that she had never experienced and she loved it.

Matthew shook his head and placed his hands on his wife's waist. 'I love you, Mrs Deane. I love you so much.' He kissed the base of her throat.

'Good job, isn't it?' She lowered her head and looked up at him through lowered lashes.

'It bloody is.' He smiled.

Jessica kissed him on the mouth, reaching up and enjoying their Pimm's-infused connection.

'I guess ten minutes late isn't going to make any difference, is it?' Matthew sighed as Jessica whipped the tie from around his neck and placed it around her own. She then undid the top buttons of his shirt.

'It'll be fine and we can have the best ten minutes ever, ever, ever!' She laughed as she slipped her hand inside the white cotton frontage and stroked the skin of his chest.

'I'm never going to get promoted!' Matthew yelled. 'How

can I admit that I am *never* going to get promoted and the reason for that is I can't leave the house on time because my wife is too sexy. It doesn't make any sense!' He shook his head and ran his palm over her back, lingering on her bra strap, enjoying the promise of what lay ahead.

'You don't have to worry about promotion. I am very cheap to feed and my only indulgence is flashy shoes.' She threw her head back and laughed.

'We still have the mortgage to pay,' he reminded her.

'I don't care about mortgages. I'd live in a tent with you!' she shouted.

'God, you must be pissed! I know you love this house.' Matthew laughed.

'I do, but not as much as I love you.'

Matthew reached for the remote control and pointed it towards the docking station. Calvin Harris's 'Feel So Close' blared from the speakers.

'Woohoo! I love this song! It reminds me of when we met. Come on!' Jessica swooped over and pulled Matthew towards her. 'Come and dance with Joanna!'

She ran in her heels back to the dock and turned the volume up even louder until the beat hammered against their ribs and the bass made the glasses on the shelf jump. With her hands above her head, Jessica spun and danced to the song, stopping only to swig from her glass and pass it back to her lover. Matthew, as ever, was quickly hypnotised by his gorgeous wife, dancing in her heels and underwear in their kitchen. The Pimm's disappeared and the song changed beat. The fast dance rhythm was replaced by Adele's soft and haunting 'Someone Like You'. Jessica walked slowly over to her man and slipped into his arms as she clasped her hands behind his neck. Matthew held her as they swayed in the middle of the kitchen, fuelled by the Pimm's. They danced slowly, then progressed to kissing and eventually to falling onto the floor, where Jessica shed her Louboutins and Matthew his inhibitions before making love to his irresistible wife.

Matthew slicked back his hair and shot his cuffs as he sidled into the chair next to his boss. He nodded hello to his assembled colleagues, who appeared to have polished off their first course and were awaiting the next. Jessica kissed Magnus's wife on both cheeks.

'So sorry we are late, Magnus, traffic was absolutely horrendous, some kind of problem on the A4. It was completely snarled up.' He avoided eye contact and concentrated on spreading the napkin on his lap.

'Oh, you should have called me.' Magnus paused. 'We could have picked you up. We came in from Heathrow, practically drove past your house. Whistled in with ease.'

Matthew reached for the water jug and tried to think of something to say.

'Maybe there are two A4s, eh, Matthew?' Magnus winked at his young protégé and thankfully chose not to mention the lipstick that sat on his collar and matched a smear on his neck.

7th December, 2012

I was given this little red book a while ago and had quite forgotten about it until I unpacked my bag here on that first, lonely day inside this horrible place. This is a good use for it. It's nearly the end of my first year in here. I remember when I'd just arrived and the doctor said, 'It would be a good idea, don't you think, to write everything down, everything good and everything bad. How does that sound, Jessica? Think you can manage it?' trying to get me to commit, coaxing like I was a child. I shrugged my agreement. I never wanted this to be a chore, like writing an essay or filling out a form. I decided at the beginning to ramble and see where it takes me, knowing I can always rip the pages out if I don't like what I've put. Anyway, I've only written a measly four entries this year – probably not enough to convince anyone that I am 'coming to terms with it' as they insist on calling the guilt and fear that gnaws away every day. I was pleased to find this book among all my possessions, though I don't know who packed it for me. Its crimson cover is a lovely splash of colour in this world of grey and beige. And it has beautiful creamy hand-pressed pages. So perfect I can hardly bear to write on them.

I've never written a journal before, not properly. I tried once, not long after Danny died. I sat on my bed with the duvet over my legs, leaning on the wall with a pillow stuffed in the small of my back and a little book perched on my knees. I thought I had something important to say, but I didn't. Instead, after much consideration, I decided to write about what I'd had for lunch, who I fancied at school and which song I loved. But then one day I came home early from school to find my mum reading it in the kitchen. I couldn't believe she had stolen my private diary, but some instinct made me duck behind the door instead of shouting. She didn't see me, but I saw her face crumple with tears as she put the book down on the table. I could imagine her anger: 'How could you write about stupid things like lunch, music and boys when we have lost Danny! Lost him forever!' She didn't say those words, but I heard them anyway. I was convinced they were there under the surface at all times.

After that, I made a few brief entries, things I thought she would want to read: *I see the stars and think of my brother. I hate it when Danny's bedroom door is left open and I see his bed, knowing he will never sleep under his duvet again.* These were both true, but so far from what I wanted to write that my diary soon felt like a work of fiction, snippets of someone else's life. And so I stopped writing it altogether. I left the book on my bedside cabinet, hoping that maybe Mum would see it and realise that I did care about Danny, and that I was a good daughter and a good sister. That part was true: I did care about my brother. But I still knew my diary was meaningless and fake, and that ruined it for me.

This diary will be different. No one will ever see it or read it. I shall destroy it when I have said all that I want to. It isn't for the benefit of anyone else. This is for me and me alone. I can say what I want, how I want. I shall prove it right now. I shall write three things that I have never, ever told another living soul. Okay, here goes.

Firstly, the car keys didn't miraculously disappear when we were camping in Devon; I threw them into the river. After I'd done it, I sat on the grass and watched as Mum and Dad argued, then Mum cried and Danny, who hated any kind of conflict, went all withdrawn. I was six. We waited hours for a man to come and change the locks. He charged 'an arm and a leg!' The reason I threw away the keys was because I figured if we couldn't drive the car home, we could stay on holiday forever. Mum wouldn't have to go back to her shitty job as a dinner lady and every day Dad could nap in the afternoon and drink beer in the evening before we all fell into our beds laughing. But we didn't stay on holiday forever. Instead, we drove home in frosty silence and Dad kept shaking his head as he had spent the next month's petrol money on getting the car sorted. I still feel bad about that. Particularly because I spoilt one of Danny's last holidays. I spoilt it for him and I spoilt the memory for everyone else.

Secondly, I cheated in my Biology GCSE. I copied a diagram from Neil Whittaker's paper. He was sat to the side of me and by copying him I went up a whole grade. A whole grade! I accepted the hug from the teacher on results day and her words of congratulation stuck like sticks in my craw, I couldn't swallow.

And thirdly...

And thirdly.

I don't know how to write this, but here goes. Thirdly, if I think about the terrible thing that I did and if someone offered me the chance to rewind time, would I stop and do something differently, change the outcome? And the answer to that is no, I don't think I would or could and that frightens me more than I can say.

Five

With fingers quickly numbing in the cold, Jessica twisted the wreath on the door and adjusted the tartan ribbon so it sat just so against the willow-green front door. She gave a little jump, beyond excited. Their first Christmas in their new home and she wanted everything to be perfect.

'Looks like someone died.' Mrs Pleasant's voice drifted from the other side of the low hedge.

In the half-light, Jessica looked over at the woman's sour expression. She wasn't going to let anyone or anything take the shine off her planned evening. 'Not yet, they haven't, but the night is young!' She shut the door and skipped up the hallway, pleased by her confidence and audacity.

Kneeling on the kitchen floor, she prodded the side of salmon that had been generously slathered in herbs and lemon, just as the recipe had prescribed. 'Look at you, my leaping beauty! Admittedly, your leaping days are over, if you ever had any – more likely you bashed your head on the wall every time you tried to turn around in some cramped fish farm and were only allowed to visit your family once a week, looking at them through a green net. Blimey, it's not much of a life, is it? But on the plus side, you will bring my guests and me a lot of joy and you are still quite beautiful!' She shoved it back inside its tinfoil tomb, popped the tray back in the oven and closed the door. She was getting the hang of this cooking lark, but couldn't resist opening the oven door every few minutes to check on progress.

This was the night of their much anticipated Not-Christmas Dinner. As their best friends were understandably committed to attending family celebrations over the festive season, they thought it would be a good idea to have this pre-Christmas get-together. Jessica had eschewed turkey, figuring that by the time December the twenty-fifth arrived, they would all be sick of the sight of it. She had spent the whole day preparing and yet had still managed to run out of time, forced to rush at the end to catch up.

The work surfaces were wiped down. The peeled veg and spuds were roasting, a posh tiramisu was defrosting on the drainer and the dishwasher was half stacked. She loved the excited flutter in the pit of her stomach at the thought of what the evening might hold, feeling like a proper grown-up with her lovely house and her wonderful husband. There was something great about the prospect of having friends for dinner, not least the opportunity to show Matt how accomplished she was. The kitchen might have only been cleaned in the last half hour and the sofa needed a plump, but the food was on the way to being ready, lamps were on, beer was chilling and the one large glass of plonk that she was entitled to while cooking was beginning to do its job.

Matthew sauntered into the kitchen and looked from left to right, wondering if Jake or Polly had arrived early. 'Oh! I thought I heard you talking to someone!'

'I was.'

'Who?' Matthew scanned the room a second time.

'The salmon.' Jessica smiled.

'The salmon we are having for supper?'

'Uh huh.' She nodded.

'Did it have anything interesting to reveal?' Matthew raised his eyebrow at his wife.

'Not really.' Jessica sighed. 'I think it might be a bit shy.'

'That'll be it.' Matthew grabbed her bottom and cupped her denim rump in his hand. 'That and the fact that you have imprisoned it in a hot oven.'

'Don't say that! You make me feel guilty!'

'Actually, Jess, not sure how to break it to you, but it was already dead.'

'So *that's* why he didn't answer me!' She threw the tea towel on the sideboard and slapped her forehead.

'You know the worrying thing about living with you is how normal your crazy has become to me.' Matthew cracked open a pistachio and threw it into his mouth.

'What do you mean?' Jessica asked from the sink as she filled the ice-cube tray and popped it into the freezer. She remembered how impressed she'd been when Matt's mother had offered ice when they visited.

'I dunno, I guess it's the small things that have become normal. Like not mentioning in front of any appliance that we might be considering getting a new one, for fear of upsetting them.'

Jessica scooted across the floor and placed her finger on her husband's lips as she closed in and whispered in his ear, 'You weren't going to mention the toaster situation, were you?'

Matthew shook his head.

'Good.' She exhaled. 'Because if I was Tiny the toaster and I found out you were thinking of replacing me with Bertha big toaster, I might just think about packing up altogether, or catching fire in protest!'

'Our toaster is called *Tiny*?' Matthew whispered.

'Yes. Because she is small and can only take two slices.' Jessica curled her lip and scrunched her nose as though he were stupid. 'Anyway, naming our things isn't crazy, it's normal. You need to give me a better example.'

Matthew rubbed at the one-day stubble on his chin and tried to think of an answer. 'Okay, well you still make me check under the bed and in the wardrobe every night for monsters and vampires.'

'It's not vampires, it's werewolves,' she corrected him. 'Vampires wouldn't really bother me, not after watching the *Twilight* series. I can see they have some endearing qualities.'

'Fine, but that's not really the point, Jess.'

'What is, then?' she asked, looking into the face of her husband.

'Well, none of them exist!' He chuckled. 'Talk about having to state the bloody obvious.'

Jessica stared at her husband wide-eyed. She paused before saying, 'The thing is, Matthew, I think they do and I'm scared of them, but you are categorically certain that they do not exist and yet it's *you* who looks for them every night in the cupboard and under the bed, so doesn't that make you madder than me?'

'I'd never thought of it like that.'

'So why do you look for them? Why don't you just tell me there is no such thing?'

Matthew put his hands on her waist and pulled her towards him. 'Because, Jessica Rose, I would go to the ends of the earth to make you happy. I would do anything to bring you a moment of joy and a worry-free sleep.'

Jessica laid her head against his chest. 'I don't think anyone else in the whole wide world has ever loved anyone the way I love you and you love me.'

'I think you are right,' Matthew concurred. 'I love you completely.'

'Even though I talk to the supper?' she asked.

'Because you talk to the supper.' He kissed the back of her neck. 'The place looks great, by the way.'

She felt her heart swell at the compliment.

The doorbell rang.

Jessica wriggled free and ran down the hallway. Polly and Jake stood side by side, having shared a cab from Clapham, where they lived three streets apart. Both clutched bottles of wine.

'Polly! Happy Not-Christmas!' Jessica shouted her happiness as though it had been months not days since she had last seen her best friend.

'And to you, honey. Now let us in. It's bloody freezing out here!' Polly shivered.

Jessica stood aside and swept her arm towards the kitchen. 'Matthew was just telling me how mad I am.'

'Well you are, but he knew that before you got married, so he can't renege now,' Polly replied, gazing at Matthew through narrowed eyes as she hugged her mate.

'I wasn't thinking of reneging, Polly.' Matthew sometimes found it hard to tolerate the outspoken Polly.

'If it is all going tits up, mate, then my flatmate is moving out end of the month so you can come and bunk with me. We can reinstate Thursday-night curry and karaoke, back of the net! Boys'd love it, just like old times!' Jake stood behind the hugging girls, nodding sagely at his friend.

'What is it with you two? My wife and I are deeply in love and happily married and we will remain so!' He tutted.

'Well said, my gorgeous man.' Jessica turned and jumped onto her husband's back, hitching a piggyback all the way to the kitchen.

'Blimey, Jess!' Polly cast her eye around the place. 'Cooking supper and a tidy house – you're turning into your mum!'

'I like making the place look nice.' Jessica pouted.

'You can come and give mine a whizz over if you feel like it,' Jake suggested.

'That's very kind of you, Jake, but I think I'll pass.'

The skeletal remains of the salmon sat on a large oval plate in the centre of the table. No one mentioned the rather blackened outside or the fact that it had been glued to the base of the dish. The buttered spuds had been polished off and all that remained of supper were a few sprigs of long-stemmed broccoli and the licks of tiramisu stuck to the side of the glass bowl that the spoon hadn't managed to reach.

‘I’d like to propose a toast,’ Matthew announced. ‘To my wonderful wife, thank you for cooking that incredible supper.’

‘Hear! Hear!’ Jake bashed the table.

‘And may the coming year bring us lots of wonderful things!’ Matthew lifted his glass and sipped.

‘Oh God, this isn’t a clue that we are awaiting the pitter-patter of tiny Louboutins is it?’ Polly shouted.

‘No.’ Jessica waved her hand as she sipped her wine. ‘Definitely not. We’re still getting used to being married.’

‘And having too much fun,’ Matthew added.

‘Yes,’ Jessica agreed. ‘We have a five-year plan. I shall get pregnant when I am twenty-eight. Matt will have been promoted and I will be earning proper, good money for my illustrations and then we shall have two beautiful babies to make our lives complete. A boy and a girl.’

‘Blimey, sounds like you have it all planned out,’ Jake scoffed.

‘We do.’ Jessica nodded.

‘God, I love my wife!’ Matthew beamed. Polly mimed retching. ‘I apprcciate her every day, especially when I look at my neighbour, to whom I’d also like to propose a toast.’ He raised his glass. ‘To Mrs Pleasant, next door!’

‘May she learn how to smile!’ Jessica added.

‘Yes, Mrs Pleasant! Learn to smile!’ Jake shouted very loudly at the kitchen wall.

‘Shhhh!’ The three looked at him and Polly placed her cupped hand over his mouth. All were laughing and cringing, hoping she hadn’t heard.

Jessica coughed. ‘And a toast to me! I handed in my first

illustrations today. They are awaiting approval, but the point is, I finished them!'

'Yay!' they all chorused. 'Congratulations!'

The four, now well lubricated by the four bottles of wine they'd drunk during dinner, slumped in their chairs and hacked at a lump of Dolcelatte that they popped onto salty crackers and washed down with glugs of ruby red port.

'I've eaten too much,' Polly wailed as she reached for the cheese knife and cut a fresh lump.

The other three laughed.

'Then why are you reaching for more cheese?' Jake crossed his eyes at Matthew to show he still thought Polly was an idiot as per his first snap decision on her character and despite many meetings since.

'Because I figure, as I've already broken my diet, I may as well *really* break it – you know, in for a penny and... however that partic... particleear phrase finishes. Plus I'm thinking of getting lipo and I want my money's worth.'

'You don't need lipo, Poll, you are beautiful.' Jessica smiled at her friend. She knew that, despite her bravado, Polly harboured insecurities about her appearance and her future.

'Oh my God! Talking of beautiful...' Polly slapped her forehead. 'I nearly forgot! The most amazing piece of gossip. You know my cousin, Callum?'

'Geologist, tall, bit superior, red hair?' Jessica asked.

'The very one. Well, he has just told the family that he is no longer going to be Callum and as of now is living as a girl called Collette! My aunt and uncle are under sedation. Can you believe it?'

'No! I can't!' Jessica squealed.

'Has he got boobies and things?' Matthew was curious.

Polly shrugged. 'Apparently!'

'Good on him, that's not easy,' Jessica said. 'It's a very brave thing.'

'It's a very weird thing,' Jake replied. 'Urgh, makes my flesh creep!'

'When did you become so enlightened, Jake?' Matthew asked his clueless friend.

Jake flicked the Vs in response.

'Anyway...' Polly once again steered the conversation. 'Going back to my weight, it's easy for you to give advice, Jess. You have nothing but plain sailing ahead.'

'What d'you mean? Why's it easy for me?'

'Well, you've already landed Mr Perfect – not perfect for me, but perfect for you,' she clarified as she pointed her finger and narrowed her eyes at Matthew.

'The feeling is entirely mutual!' Matthew raised his glass at his wife's best friend.

Polly continued. 'You have the lovely house, the gooey marriage and in five years, apparently, there'll be the pitter-patter of tiny trolls on your stairs...'

Jessica smiled. Polly was, unlike her, not fond of babies. Or, more specifically, not fond of the prospect of looking after them.

'But some of us are still in the race, trying to make it to the finish line.' Polly sighed and crunched on another cheese-laden cracker.

'We're not gooey. Are we?' Jessica looked at their guests.

'No, you're just sickeningly happy. And seeing someone

that happy with their lot in life can be seriously irritating!' Polly delivered this with a straight face and was rewarded with a high five from Jake.

'We really must do this again soon: please come over to our house, eat our food, drink our wine and insult us. How are you fixed for next week?' Matthew shouted.

'Don't be grumpy.' Polly wagged her finger at Matthew. 'And don't worry, you know we'll be here again next week.'

'Well thank goodness for that!' Matthew gave a sarcastic clap.

Jessica stood and pointed towards the sitting room. 'I think it's charades time!'

The other three got up noisily from the table, wobbling as the effects of the booze travelled to their unsteady feet. They shoved the chairs under the messy table and elbowed each other out of the way: no one wanted the end seat on the sofa and the last one in was the first to start, that was the rule. Jessica laughed as her husband and friends fought for space, running into the sitting room and jumping onto the sofa, hugging cushions to their chests and squawking with laughter. They might be a gooey couple with a lovely grown-up house, but they still knew how to have fun.

4th February, 2013

They finally took down the bare tree today. It was long overdue. The sight of the spindly arms and dried needles was quite sad, the last thing we need to look at is more decay. My first Christmas in here was horrible. I felt like I was carrying a boulder in my stomach that grew heavier and heavier until I could barely move. I ached to be home – home, wherever that was. The thin strips of tinsel in the recreation room, the plastic baubles hung from light fittings and the paper plates of biscuits with fingerprints smudged into the melting chocolate had the opposite effect to what was intended. They just highlighted the fact that we were trapped; the forced cheeriness jarred with the depressing, clinical environment. Mostly I try and pretend I am somewhere else, anywhere, fooling myself into calmly passing another day. But with the Christmas decorations everywhere I found it harder to pretend. They reminded me of what I was missing. What I had lost.

Our first Christmas after Danny died was even worse. None of us wanted to celebrate, but no one had the confidence to say so. I guess we thought we might spoil it for everyone else. I was only ten, but I wanted the day to be over the moment I opened my eyes. My mum went through the motions, trying to smile. My nan cooked our lunch. My dad made a joke about overcooked sprouts and we all laughed awkwardly. We were still at that new stage of grief where laughter is immediately followed by all-consuming guilt. The food was like cardboard on my tongue.

Our tree was sparsely decorated, as though someone had lost interest halfway through the job. Even the fairy lights flickered on and off, as though they couldn't be bothered to make the effort either. We didn't put the telly on and there was no music. If I had to give the day a colour, it would be grey. Everything was muted and sad and no one knew what to say. I was embarrassed in my own home, with my family.

Opening presents was excruciating. I was watched by three pairs of sunken eyes and everyone must have been thinking back to the previous year, wishing we'd all paid more attention, captured more detail, unaware it was to be his last.

I went upstairs after lunch and lay on my bed. I could hear my mum crying in her room. My dad stayed at the kitchen table and I imagined him trying to make small talk with my nan, bless him. I opened the little drawer in my bedside cabinet and I saw the 3-D bookmark Danny had given me the year before. It was a crappy present that I hadn't really liked, but as I lifted it towards my face and tilted it back and forth to make the teddy bear smile and wave, I realised it was the last present he would ever buy me and how much I loved it. His hands had touched it and those hands were now cold. I placed it on my chest and sank down under the duvet. Closing my eyes, I decided to pretend that he was downstairs with Dad and Nan, doing his crappy magic tricks like he used to. I smiled, remembering the corner of the ace that used to poke out of his sleeve. He was really crap at magic.

Six

'Jess? Jessica?'

She heard Matthew call out and the familiar clatter as he threw his keys into the bowl on the console table in the hallway and stamped the rain and dirt from his shoes.

'Where are you, wife of mine?' He was home early. It was only four o'clock. She hadn't expected him until later. She pictured him performing his little rituals, placing his briefcase on the table in the empty kitchen, walking around as he loosened his tie. He was probably glad to be home if their conversation before lunch had been anything to go by. He had apparently been enduring a very dull day.

'Hey, honey, I'm home!' For this kitsch statement he employed his best Midwestern accent.

Jessica smiled from her hiding place and chose not to respond, not yet. She heard the faint sound of water running and the tell-tale flick as Matthew filled the kettle and flipped the switch before grabbing a mug, the clunk of it hitting the work surface reaching her ears upstairs. Jessica pictured him running his eye over the empty oven and pristine hob that had taken her a good hour to scrub. Matthew knew how much she hated cleaning, so he would be touched by the time she had taken over it.

Jessica had recently been preoccupied with drawing flowers, repeatedly trying to capture the delicate, almost transparent nature of the poppy and to perfect the shading of variegated ivy. She wanted to do the very best job she could for the publisher who had commissioned her, knowing this was how to get repeat work. Her obsession had been worth it; she had heard today that her work had been very well received. She'd done some work and cleaned the house, but she hadn't planned anything for supper. She smiled to herself, imagining Matthew's father's reaction if he were to arrive home to find that dinner hadn't even been thought about. Anthony Deane was used to walking into a kitchen where sauces simmered, cakes rose, freshly baked bread cooled and meat roasted, all in preparation for the daily feast. Today of all days, this was the last thing on her mind. She was somewhat distracted.

Jessica heard the slam of the metal bin lid as Matthew lobbed a teabag into it and made his way along the hallway. She heard the sitting room door creak as he poked his head inside. 'Jess? Je-ss?' he shouted, louder this time.

'Up here. I'm in the bathroom!' Her voice echoed around the sparkling, white-tiled walls.

She heard the familiar groan of the bottom three Victorian stairs as he climbed towards her.

'What *are* you doing?' he enquired.

'I'm in the loo!' she called.

'Well I know that.' Matthew laughed. 'That's why I'm talking to you through the door. The question is, what are you doing in there?' He tapped an irritating irregular rhythm on the frame.

'What kind of question is that? What do you think I'm doing in here?' She rolled her eyes.

'You know what I mean – you've been a very long time.'

'Well hey, Mr Lawyer, your interrogation skills need to be a little sharper and more specific. And what do you mean "a very long time"? How long am I allowed, exactly?'

'Jessica, stop mucking about and please tell me why are you locked in the loo when any business you might need to conduct in the loo is usually taken care of after a few minutes and even then rarely with the door locked. And by my reckoning...' Matthew pulled the sleeve on his shirt and glanced at his watch. 'You have been in there for at least ten minutes.'

Jessica was silent. How to start? She wanted to be alone. She was nervous.

Matthew made a fist and used his knuckles to tap on the door.

'You are banished,' was her response. 'Leave me alone.'

'You can't banish me! Not from the bathroom – it's not your kingdom. You are not queen of the loo!' he hollered from the landing.

'I think you'll find I am, actually,' she replied casually as she rested her back against the side of the bath and read the instructions. 'Go away and come back in four minutes!'

'Four minutes? Jesus Christ,' he muttered. She heard him cross the landing into their bedroom, where the television sprang to life with the sound of canned laughter and the bed springs squeaked under his weight.

Her fingers now shook as she fumbled with the foil

wrapper and grimaced at the indignity of having to pee on a spatula. Jessica did her best to pee adequately, finding it harder to wee on demand than she had anticipated. She placed the test on the side of the sink and washed her hands, thoroughly, hardly daring to glance at the little stick and not wanting to jinx the result by looking too soon. She was flooded with excitement and nerves. This might just be the very moment that their lives changed forever.

The result appeared almost instantly. There was one dark blue line and a second that was slightly fainter. Clutching the little plastic wand to her chest, she closed her eyes as her stomach leapt with excitement. *Oh my God! We did it! We actually did it! Oh my God!*

Suddenly floored by uncertainty, Jessica retrieved the crumpled instructions from the bin, unable to believe the result. Had she got it wrong? Was this a positive reading? She needed to be certain. What did two blue lines mean? She squinted at the results paragraph and stared in the mirror, beaming at her reflection. 'I'm going to be a mummy! Oh my God!' she whispered, feeling a wonderful combination of happiness, pleasure and something else... She felt satisfied, content that she knew where her life was heading. Holding the test in her hand, she ran her index finger over the little window, a glimpse into her future. She couldn't wait for it all to happen.

'Okay, Jess.' Matthew's voice drew her; she had quite forgotten that he was waiting for her. 'I'm going to give you two more minutes and then I'm going to kick the door in.'

She laughed. 'I don't think you know how to kick a door in, Matt.'

'I do, actually. I might not have grown up on the mean streets of Romford like you, but I know a thing or two about forced entry.' He sounded indignant, as though her comment was in some way a slight against his masculinity.

Jessica ran her palm over her still flat stomach and pictured the teeny tiny seed of a baby on the other side of her tum. 'I shall always take care of you, baby. I love you already.'

'I love you too, my mummy!' The little voice was clear and golden. It rang out and made her heart sing. Jessica beamed.

'Right, that's it. I'm going to barge the door in now!' Matthew shouted.

Jessica cracked open the door a fraction of an inch and put her face to the gap. Matthew was equally close on the other side; their noses practically touched.

'Hi,' she whispered.

'Hey, Jess. How are you?' Matthew enquired, softly.

'I'm good.'

'How was your day?' he asked, raising the mug of tea in his hand and sipping at it.

'Fine.' She smiled.

'Well I'm jolly glad to hear that. Are you coming out of there?' he asked with his head tilted to one side.

She shook her head. 'Not just yet.'

'Right.' He smiled. 'In that case, can I ask why you are hiding in the bathroom? Have you got your hot Spanish lover in there? Did I come home early and catch you unawares; are you planning on sneaking him past me while I get changed out of my suit? Is that it?'

'No.' Jessica smiled. 'Juan always leaves before three o'clock, just to be on the safe side.'

'Very wise.' Matthew nodded. 'Can I come in?'

Again she shook her head.

'Well, this is all very mysterious. Can you at least tell me what you are *doing* in there?' he asked, calmly.

Jessica took a deep breath. 'I'm doing an experiment.'

'Oh right.' Matthew pretended to be placated, folding one arm across his chest and drinking his tea, which had almost cooled to the right temperature. 'What kind of experiment? Is this like the time you bought that science kit and we made a volcano in the sink?'

'No, this is more like a "how do Matt and Jess cope when an unexpected meteor comes along and explodes the world as they know it" kind of thing.'

'Okay, well that sounds a little more taxing and expensive. Have you broken something? Should I be worried?'

'Depends,' Jessica whispered again, feeling coy and unexpectedly tearful. She watched as Matthew leant in even closer.

'Jess, can you please come out of the bloody bathroom!' He raised his voice a fraction. The joke, whatever it was, was wearing a little thin.

'I can't. I'm shy.' She nodded. This was close to the truth.

Matthew threw his head back and laughed loudly. 'Oh, Jess, that's priceless. Some of the things we do on a very regular basis are illegal in several countries and you won't let me in because you are *shy*?'

'This is different…' She couldn't explain why. Maybe, secretly, she had wanted the knowledge to be all hers, just for a short while. 'I have been peeing on a stick,' she said.

'Why are you peeing on a stick? I don't get it!' He shook his head.

Jessica reached behind her, gathered the pregnancy test from the sink and poked the end of it through the gap in the door. She watched Matthew's expression change as he instantly recognised the enormity of her experiment. He placed his mug of tea on the chest of drawers and grabbed at the plastic strip. He stared at the little window as Jessica finally crept from the bathroom and stood in front of him on the landing, holding her cardigan close around her body with one arm, and with her thumbnail firmly between her teeth.

Matthew looked from her to the pregnancy test and back again, staring into her eyes. 'Is this two lines good or two lines bad?' he asked.

She smiled at his Orwellian humour, even at this pivotal moment. 'That depends…' She bit her thumb, anxious; this was about five years ahead of schedule and not even close to what they had planned.

'On what?' he countered.

'On whether you want to be a dad, Matthew.'

It was a loaded question. Was he ready for fatherhood? The top of Matthew's nose creased as he responded. 'I do, Jessica. I want to be a dad as long as you are the mum and I want to take care of you, for always. That's always been the case, nothing's changed.'

Her response was considered and slow. 'Then it's two lines good, Matt, because this means that I am having our baby.'

Her husband stepped forward and held her with a new tenderness in his touch. 'My darling!' She was already a precious thing, carrying their offspring, which he would protect and shield.

Jess felt as if she'd been elevated to a higher status. No longer was she simply sweet and slightly bonkers Jess who drank cocktails and danced in her pants – she was going to be a mother. *A mother.*

'Oh, baby! This is wonderful! Wonderful!' Matthew held her tight.

'Are you sure? We were supposed to wait. It's not what we planned,' she prompted, biting her bottom lip, remembering their discussion and agreement that five years on would be a good time to start thinking about a family.

'Nothing is ever, ever what we planned. I figured that out a while ago. With you, Jess, there is absolutely no point in having a plan. It's best to just go with the flow.'

'But we're only twenty-three, how will we know what to do?' She blinked away the tears that gathered.

'Lots of people do it a lot younger and manage just fine.'

'I guess...'

He placed his hand under her chin and tilted her face upwards until she had no choice but to meet his gaze. 'You and I can do anything, anything as long as we are together. That's what we've always said, isn't it?'

Jessica nodded.

'And this is one of those things. Together we will be the best bloody parents in the world! It's going to be brilliant!'

She reached up and kissed her man.

'Do you feel okay?' he asked, holding her at arm's length.

'Yes, of course! Bit sick, but I think that's normal. And I've got a funny taste in my mouth like I'm licking a copper coin! But I'm fine. I'm not ill, just pregnant. There is no way I am going to be one of those women who go all earth mother and start chanting and building a yurt in the back garden.'

'That's a relief, we haven't got room for a yurt *and* my gas barbecue.' He smiled. 'Oh Christ, I'm going to be a dad!' Matthew punched the air. 'Back of the net!'

'You are not to tell a soul. No one! Seriously.' Her expression was suddenly solemn.

'Why, isn't it mine? Damn it! Don't tell me old Juan got there first.' He stole a kiss from her.

'I'm serious, Matthew. It's best not to tell people until more time has passed. I think a few months or something, just to make sure.'

'Make sure what?' He scratched his stubble.

'Oh I don't know! It's just not the done thing.'

She watched as Matthew drew a cross with his finger over his heart. 'Okay, scout's honour.'

'Oh my God, Matt, this is huge! Can you believe it?' Jessica bit her bottom lip and felt her tears pool. 'This is one of those moments that when we are old and grey we will talk about and remember, the day we made a baby! Our actual baby! Not that we made it today, but you know what I mean.'

'When did we make it? I thought you had that cap thing.' He squirmed, still not good at discussing anything to do with the female body.

Jessica patted her tummy. 'This baby is two parts you and me and one part Pimm's. It was our kitchen party night, on Halloween. I was too sloshed to care.'

'Oh God! Does it matter that we were sloshed? Do sperm get drunk?'

Jessica laughed. 'I have no idea! I think I'm nearly three months.'

'Wow, so when will it be born?'

'July sometime, not sure exactly.' She smiled.

'That's perfect. Right before the football season. I won't have to miss any games.'

'You can take the baby with you!'

'Can I?' Matthew looked a little nervous. 'Are you allowed to take little babies into football stadiums?'

'How should I know?' She shrugged. 'This is going to be one steep learning curve for both of us.' She felt a warm rush of excitement flow through her body as she jumped up and down. 'You're going to be a dad!' Her tears finally found their way to the surface and fell down her cheeks.

'And you are going to be a mum, a fantastic mum.'

'Fucking hell,' she said, 'I'm going to be a mummy!'

'Yep.' Matthew wrapped his arms around her. 'We'll stop having sex and you'll start baking and knitting and tutting at all the bad language on TV. You'll carry sucking sweets in your handbag.'

'Is that what happens?' She laughed through her tears.

'Yes, next time you go to the doctor's, you'll get fitted with a mummy microchip and all the knowledge in the universe will whoosh into your brain. You will then know how to kiss a knee better, how to remove stains from clothes and the recipe for Yorkshire puddings off by heart. You'll keep spare buttons in a jar and you will always have a fresh packet of tissues and something to read just in case.'

'Wow! I'm looking forward to all of that. And if you don't mind me saying, you seem to know an awful lot about it.'

'Well, I should. I've had a mum ever since I was born.'

'Come on, we need to celebrate!' Jessica grabbed her husband's hand and led him into their bedroom.

Abandoning his now cool mug of tea, Matthew kicked off his shoes as they fell onto the bed. Jessica grabbed the remote control and switched off the television before drawing the curtains and clicking on her lamp. She slipped out of her jeans to get comfy and turned to see Matthew place his phone on the bedside table and open his arms to receive her.

Lying with her head on her husband's chest, she wrapped her arms around him. 'I'm so excited, Matt. Scared but really excited. I love you.'

'I love you too, my clever girl. Don't be scared. We can do this.'

Jessica looked at the spatula that she had propped by her bedside lamp with its two little lines that seemed to be getting darker as time passed. 'Do you know, I do feel very clever!'

'That's because you are. This is by far the cleverest thing that you have ever done.'

'No, it's the cleverest thing *we* have ever done!' she corrected him, before kissing him passionately on the mouth as his hands stroked her back.

Matthew's phone beeped. He pulled his arm free and swiped the screen, then laid it flat on their duvet.

'Who's that?' she asked, craning her neck to look up at him.

'No one.' He stared at her, unblinking, which she knew meant he was up to no good. It was the expression he pulled whenever he'd been caught out.

'Oh my God! What have you done?'

'Nothing.' He stared at her.

'Who have you told?' She reached up as Matthew grabbed the phone and held it out of her reach.

'No one! Get off!' He giggled as she climbed up him as though he were a fallen tree, placing her bare foot on the back of his calf to gain leverage. He placed his free hand over his groin, wary of her flailing limbs. Jessica pushed upwards on the bed with her hand on the top of her husband's head until she was able to grab the phone. Then she collapsed back down onto the mattress. Matthew, rendered weak through giggling, grabbed her legs and pulled her onto him, where she stayed, still clinging to the phone. She ran her finger over his phone screen and read the text that had just arrived.

Jessica twisted her mouth sideways and with one arm across her chest held the phone in the outstretched hand of the other, this time reading aloud from a distance. 'Oh, Matt, how lovely. It's from Jake. He says, "Fucking hell, mate! Good to know you aren't firing blanks – this requires MAJOR celebrations. What exactly will my role as godfather entail?" You told *Jake*! Jake? Of all people? I told you not to tell a soul and you chose him! I'd rather you'd taken an advert out in the local paper,' Jessica wailed. She dropped the phone onto the bed as she covered her eyes.

Matthew lay on his side and propped his head up on his raised arm. 'I know what you said, but I couldn't help it!

I'm too excited. But don't worry, I told him not to tell anyone.'

'You told him not to tell anyone? Oh, well, that's okay!' She winced. 'You do know we are talking about Jake?'

Matthew nodded.

'Do I need to remind you that he hung a sheet with his tally score of shags out of his window at university?'

Matthew giggled at the memory. Jessica wasn't done.

'Jake who posted the *positive* result of his STI test on his own Facebook page as though it was a badge of honour?'

Matthew laughed even harder, clutching his chest and wheezing slightly. 'Stop!' he begged.

'Jake who told my mother at our wedding that we had sex on our first date in the back of your car!'

'He wasn't lying – we did!'

'That's not the point. He told my *parents*! On *my wedding day*!' she squealed.

'Don't be mad at me. I had to tell someone. I'm excited. I'm going to be a dad!' Matthew looked at her sheepishly.

'Urgh, I get it, but of all the people you could have told, you told him…' Jessica placed her face in her hands.

Matthew pulled them away and held them inside his own. 'I love you, Mrs Deane. I love you so much.' He kissed her cheek.

'I love you too, but I just wanted a little time. The pregnancy test is still wet with pee and already you and Jake are planning the bloody christening!'

'I can't help it – I'm excited!'

'So you said.' She smiled, finding it hard to stay mad at her husband, whose life was about to change as much as hers.

Jessica wriggled down the bed and lay against her husband. 'I'm excited too. We are officially the cleverest people in the whole universe!' She kissed him passionately and felt the swell of his body against hers. 'And now we don't need to worry about contraception!' Jessica shrugged off her cardigan, peeled her T-shirt from her body and unhooked her bra.

'My day just keeps getting better and better!' Matthew rubbed his hands together as he whipped off his suit trousers and dropped them in a heap on the floor.

'And perhaps you're right, maybe Jake *won't* say a word. I mean, this is not like regular gossip. He'll understand it's important, right?'

Matthew nodded. 'Absolutely.'

'Maybe I've got to trust that he is actually growing up.' Jessica smiled as her phone pinged on the bedside table. She reached across her husband and swiped the screen, sitting upright. 'I take it all back, it's from Polly.' Her phone pinged again. 'I don't believe it! She is basically screaming at me in text form and congratulating me, asking how come Jake knew before her? Oh and she's sent me a link for pregnancy incontinence pads and cracked nipple cream. Nice. Your friend is a big-mouthed dickhead!' Jessica shuffled from the bed and reached for her bra.

'What are you doing? Come back. No, no, no!' He held up his hand as though this might prevent her from getting dressed.

'Sorry, Matt, but it'll just have to wait.' She smiled as she fastened her bra strap under her boobs and twisted it until it was the right way round.

Matthew sat up. 'So hang on, are you telling me that just because I told Jake and he told Polly, *I* don't get to have sex?' He ruffled his hair.

'Yep. That's about the size of it.'

'Oh, Jess! Come back, please. Just for ten minutes, five even!' He wiggled his eyebrows.

'Ah, I'd love to, Matt, but sadly, because of your friend Jake and his unfeasibly large gob, I have to jump in Edith' – their Audi was blessed with the number plate ED13 and so 'Edith' it was – 'and take our unborn child to sodding Romford to inform my parents of the impending arrival. Because, in case you had forgotten, Polly and I have been friends since nursery and our mums are friends and neighbours. And if they hear via the grapevine, my arse will be grass!'

'I'll come with you.' He sat upright.

'No.' She took a deep breath. 'No, I'm fine. I am half joking, but seriously they would be so hurt to hear it second- or thirdhand. I'll literally just nip there and straight back. If you come, it'll turn into a proper celebration and I can't face that, not on a week night. Not that any celebrations from now on can include alcohol for me. I've stopped drinking.'

'Since when?' Matthew laughed.

'Since I weed on that stick about twenty minutes ago. I haven't had a drink since.'

'And how are you feeling?' He laughed. 'Missing it?'

Jessica exhaled. 'I'm managing.'

'Couldn't you just phone your parents?' he suggested.

'I don't think so. Phoning is for "we are going on holiday" or "I've chosen the paint colour for the front door," not for "your child is pregnant and you are going to be a nan!"' She tutted. 'Anyway, you know how they are. I have to tell them everything.'

'Not everything,' he corrected. 'I mean, they still don't know that you and your hussy of a mate have matching tattoos, do they?'

'True, only because we agreed not to tell. It's not worth the grief.' She shook her head.

'That's so funny. You are an adult, married woman, with your own Nectar card and everything and you're still scared of the grown-ups disapproving!' he teased.

'It's not that I'm scared of them...' Jessica couldn't phrase her thoughts. 'It's just that... Shut up, Matthew!' She decided that shouting at him was easier.

'I see. Charming. I'm being punished, aren't I?' Matthew grinned.

Jessica stretched, reaching for her jersey and allowing her black lacy balcony bra to hover in front of him. 'Don't think of it as punishment, my love, think of it as good practice for all that sex we are not going to have when I'm a mummy! I'll be back later for good loving and maybe a curry.'

'Is that because you have a craving?' He winked.

'No, it's because any plans I did have for supper have been hijacked by Jake and his loose talk! You can order one for delivery when I'm en route. I'll text you when I leave.' She blew him a kiss and went in search of the car keys.

Jessica sat in the car and turned up the heat to clear the windows. She watched as the ghostly mist cleared from the windscreen, then she lowered her head onto the steering wheel. 'Oh my God. I can't believe this. I can't believe it. A mum – me?' The truth was, despite being a wife and living in her very own house, she still felt like a child herself in so many ways. Matthew was right. She *was* still scared of the grown-ups disapproving, especially her in-laws. She raised her head and looked at the long, dark road ahead, praying that she would be the kind of mother that his parents expected and hoping beyond hope that she could be the kind of mother that this baby would need, that she'd be able to give it a safe, happy environment in which it would thrive.

8th July, 2013

I remember going to Matthew's home for the first time soon after we met. It was one of the scariest things ever. Not only because I was desperate for them to like me, but he had grown up in the kind of house that my mum had always admired. She used to point them out if we went on a trip or they popped up on the television, usually in *Midsomer Murders*. She'd nudge me in the ribs and say, 'Ooh, look, Jess, a criss-crossed-window house. Lovely!' And it was lovely. I used to feel that people who lived in houses like that, houses far grander than ours, must know things about life that I didn't. I thought they would be smarter, classier and more aware. Funny that, isn't it, that I would assume all this simply because they had more bedrooms than us and a utility room.

The Deanes' house had a large, square kitchen with fancy blinds all pulled to the same height on the three windows, a big bulky stove from which Margaret would feed friends and family with her fabulous bakes, and a big noticeboard on which were pinned seed packets, interesting snippets from newspapers, the odd photo and notes written in block capitals as if to give the message added importance. At the rear was an acre of perfect rectangle with a magazine-quality striped lawn. His dad fed it with a special mix he pumped from a plastic bottle strapped to his back, a chore he evidently enjoyed because he always grinned as he harnessed up and made for the back door. There was also a front garden with a circular driveway and a couple of nudey women statues.

The 'best' room they used only on special occasions. A rather neglected space, in my opinion, it always smelt slightly fusty, like it needed a good airing. The pale walls were packed with pictures of Matthew at various stages of his life, from his naked baby shot, which I loved, to him standing proudly in his graduation gown. There was a large fireplace, where a stack of logs sat next to a wicker basket full of kindling. Folded tartan rugs were thrown over the arms of the neutral-coloured chairs and copies of *Homes and Gardens* were neatly stacked on the low coffee table.

I know Margaret thought she had impeccable taste, but I found everything a bit dated, a bit old-fashioned. All the rooms had ivory five-arm chandeliers with candle bulbs that reminded me of the lights you might find in a pub, although I never said that to her. His dad had a grand workshop at the end of the garden where he framed pictures and did 'bits and bobs' – I think that was code for 'hide from Margaret'. Matthew said he had a chair out there and a radio, which was permanently tuned to the cricket during the season. I always thought it strange that in that big old house, Anthony needed his fancy shed to escape to, whereas my mum and dad, who don't have enough space in their little house, are happy to be side by side like a couple of bobbins in a box, as my nan used to say.

I remember arriving with Matthew for a dinner party at his parents' one time and hearing Margaret shout at Matt's dad, 'Right, Anthony, chop, chop!', pointing at the bottles of wine like he was the waiter. I couldn't believe the tone she used. Anthony stood to attention and saluted her. 'Yes, sir! Understood! Right away, sir!' Then they argued, as if Matt and I weren't there. I didn't know where to look. 'Oh, don't start!' she screamed. Matt just smiled, used to it, but I found it unsettling. I felt like I was watching a play and couldn't help wondering what my mum would have made of it all. She and my dad rarely exchange so much as a harsh word and there were these people bawling and swearing in front of me. Half of me wanted to phone my mum and tell her that just because you lived in a detached house with criss-crossed windows, it didn't mean you knew how to treat each other; and the other half of me wanted to say nothing and preserve the dream for her. I gripped Matt's hand as the row took its course. And I knew I wanted different for us, better. I made a vow that we would never argue or fall out like that. At least that's what I thought.

Seven

It was dark by the time she pulled up in front of her mum and dad's house in Hillcrest Road. Jessica noticed that the longer she stayed away, the smaller and shabbier her childhood home seemed when she did return. There was however something comforting about the gnome in Mr Fraser's front garden and the neatly trimmed shrubs of Mrs Parrish's opposite, familiar sights from her childhood that welcomed her back.

Her mum answered the front door and placed her hand on her chest, worry etched on her forehead. Her immediate response to any unplanned visit was to assume it meant bad news.

'Hey, Mum!' Jessica smiled broadly and gathered her mum to her, trying to reassure her that all was well. She inhaled the familiar scent of soap, fried food and worry.

'Oh, Jess, I wasn't expecting you! Is everything okay? Have you eaten?' Coral burbled without taking breath. She pushed some stray locks of grey-flecked hair behind her ears and wiped her hands down the cook's pinny that Jess and Matthew had bought for her last birthday. Matthew had joked that there was no point buying Jessica one as domestic goddessery wasn't exactly her thing. He didn't know how hard she tried.

'Yes, yes, I'm fine. And don't worry about food, we are getting a takeaway later.' She watched her mum's shoulders sag with both relief and disappointment.

Jessica stood in the hallway and let her eyes rove over the threadbare patches of carpet in the middle of the stair treads and the sheet of wallpaper behind the telephone table that had begun to peel away. A flush of guilt spread from her toes to the roots of her hair. Living with Matthew in his world meant she forgot how carefully her parents had to budget. A new carpet for the stairs would mean a year of planning, saving and going without. They constantly juggled things to balance the pennies. Picturing her beautiful shoe collection and all the presents from her wonderful husband, Jessica wondered how much carpet all her new possessions would buy.

'Come in, come in! You don't need telling!' Coral ushered her along the hallway. 'You look tired and I wish you'd cut your hair!' These were two of her mum's staple comments. Jessica ignored both. 'Matt okay?'

'Yeah, he's great. Working hard, you know, knackered as usual.' Jessica shrugged, feeling the usual flicker of embarrassment at mentioning her husband's fatigue when he got to sit in a plush office every day and return every evening to their luxurious home.

She stepped into the cosy kitchen, where her dad was sitting at the table, cutting into a pork chop. She had also forgotten how early they ate.

'Hello, Jess! I thought I heard you.' Roger wiped his lips

with his fingers, swallowed his mouthful and placed his cutlery on the table as he stood to embrace his daughter. 'Well, this is a lovely surprise. Matt not with you?' He looked over her shoulder as though his son-in-law might be lurking there.

'No, he's just got in from work. I've left him at home.' She pictured her excited husband secretly texting his friend with their news and smiled.

'Cuppa?' Coral was already filling the kettle.

'Finish your supper, Mum!' Jessica pointed at the abandoned plate on the table and wished she had said tea, not supper.

Coral made a dismissive gesture with her hand. 'No, no. I wasn't enjoying it anyway, only eating it for the sake of it.'

Jessica nodded, noting how easily the white lies slipped from her mum's mouth; anything to smooth a situation, ease a conversation or avoid having to tell the truth.

'Everything okay, love? We don't usually see you midweek.' Roger smiled and Jessica filled in the gaps: we don't usually see you unless it's prearranged and always on a Sunday, when we come to you.

'Yeah, everything's good. Great.' She smiled, feeling suddenly self-conscious about her pregnancy and having to confirm to her dad that she had indeed had sex.

'Work going all right?' Coral asked as she slipped teabags into mugs.

Jessica nodded. Her mum didn't fully understand how you could have a job but not go to an office, shop or factory. How you could earn money without having a weekly wage slip with the usual deductions. She didn't understand a lot about her daughter's life. 'Yes, I've been doing some lovely illustrations of flowers. And they got the okay today.'

'Oooh, will it have your name in it?' Coral smiled, giving this her full attention.

'Yes, I think so.'

'We'll have to have a copy then, won't we, Roger? We can leave it on the coffee table and when we have company, I'll say, "Oh, that old thing? That's our Jess's book!"'

'I'll get you a couple of copies, Mum.'

'Let me know how much they are and I'll settle up with you.'

Jessica nodded.

'I was going to call you, Jess. I've got something for Matt.' Her dad pushed past her and raced up the stairs.

As he left the room, Coral closed in on her daughter, whispering conspiratorially into her face, 'He wants Matt to have them. He's thought about it a lot.'

She withdrew as her husband came back into the room and placed an old green shoebox on the table. He removed the lid and carefully parted the tissue to reveal two shiny gold-coloured plastic trophies. Both were faux-marble pillars sitting on wooden plinths. One had a footballer balancing on the top, mid kick. A small plaque on the base read: 'Under 15s Player of the Year, 2000'. The other was identical but read: 'Golden Boot – Top Scorer 2000'.

'Oh, Dad!' Jessica ran her fingers over the precious mementos.

'I reckon Danny would like Matt to have them, even if he is a QPR fan.' He gave a half smile.

'I don't know what to say.' Jessica spoke the truth, overwhelmed by the gesture. 'He'll treasure them, Dad, I know he will.'

Roger nodded, choked.

She wasn't sure it was now appropriate to give them her news, not when the room was so full of Danny. 'I'll just spend a penny.' She ducked into the little cloakroom under the stairs and sat on the loo, looking at the small corner shelves crammed with photos of her and her brother when they were little.

Her eyes were drawn to one in particular. It made her smile. She was about five and was sulking on a step in a tutu with her chin on her fists and her elbows on her knees, clearly miffed about something. There was another of her blowing out the candles on a cake that was twice the size of her. She was seven; she didn't remember anything about being seven. Holding the picture, she studied every detail, laughing at her hair, which had been curled and anchored with a large velvet headband, and at the flecks of spit that an eagle eye could see flying towards the buttercream frosting. It was hard to blow with no front teeth. Narrowing her eyes, she studied the image of the boys and girls that stood either side of her, classmates from her primary school; Polly's was the only name she could readily recall.

Jessica looked at her mum, who was holding up the homemade cake at an angle. In the photograph she was a young woman with her head bowed slightly, a young woman whose hair fell in soft layers; she looked happy, satisfied with her lot and with no idea about the heartache that lay ahead. Now, she was hollowed out, cracked and stooped with grief. In the picture she was wearing a royal blue T-shirt and had a set of pink bangles sitting loosely on her wrist. Jessica felt a wave of panic spread through her veins. She was going to be a mum, a mum that would have to bake cakes, hold birthday parties, write thank-you notes and click the light off after checking under the bed for monsters. Jessica swallowed the wave of responsibility that threatened to swamp her. *Please let me be good enough. Help me figure it all out.*

Jessica clutched the photo to her chest and headed back along the hallway. Her parents were sitting quietly, staring at the shoebox with what could have been regret.

'I need to get back to Matt, I told him I wouldn't be too long.' She held the photograph in her hands before laying it on the table.

'Oh, okay, love, but you haven't drunk your tea!' Coral was confused; worried she had offended her daughter in some way.

'I don't really fancy a cup, Mum.' She took a deep breath. 'Matthew will be so touched with his present, Dad, he really will. Thank you. I think Danny would have liked him, don't you? I imagine them chatting sometimes, but it's difficult because Danny is still a little boy in my head. He never gets any older, does he? I can't imagine him in his twenties, going for a pint with Matt, so if I picture him, he's still young and Matt chats to him like he's a child.' She swallowed, knowing she was babbling, her emotions getting the better of her. 'It's when you reach milestones that you miss him the most, isn't it? And today's a milestone because I'm pregnant.' Her mum gasped as her hand flew to her mouth. 'And Matthew is the father of course, not Juan, my imaginary Spanish lover. Oh and I have a tattoo of a cherub on my arse and so does Polly.' With that she burst into tears.

September 24th, 2013

I didn't realise it was my parents' usual visiting day. They come once a month and it comes around more and more quickly. Too quickly for my liking. That's a horrible thing to say, but it's true. I feel guilty when people are sympathetic, which they are surprisingly often. I don't deserve sympathy and I definitely don't want it. They tell me that it wasn't really my fault, that I was ill – but I can't accept that. It just adds another layer of guilt for me to try and hack through.

I walked along the corridor and into the little room known as 'the family room'. I hate that term. To me, a family room is somewhere you choose to be to sit together with those you love, a place where laughter bounces from the walls and precious photos line the windowsill. A room like our front room at Hillcrest Road used to be, with its smear of meat sauce just above the skirting board and the tiny crack by the fireplace where Mum dropped a heavy plate one Easter Sunday. A room full of stories. This room is nothing like that. It's austere, cold and beige. Metal-framed chairs scrape along the industrial-style flooring. The windows are opaque and the outside bars cast long shadows on the opposite walls.

I peered through the door and saw my mum and dad sitting side by side, their thighs touching where they had pushed the chairs close together. Their forearms rested on the laminate-topped table. My dad looked older – he always does – and my mum looked... my mum looked like a ghost, frail, pale and just like she did when she was first grieving for Danny. She is grieving again and this time it's because of me; the wave of guilt threatened to engulf me.

None of us found it easy to start the conversation. It didn't matter that I hadn't seen them for a month: most normal topics are out of bounds. They couldn't comment on how well I looked, because I don't, and I didn't need to ask how they were because it was obvious from their faces. References to the outside world are too painful for any of us to mention; none of us wants the reminder that I am trapped in here. The weather is a no-go: they don't want to talk about a burst of sunshine when I am reduced to forty crappy minutes of fresh air a day, which I always take, rain or shine. My dad has given up work and my mum spends her days on the sofa, full of sadness and regret. This last month has been different for them, but we're all ignoring that. I know they've just had two weeks of respite. I picture them sitting on a plane with twitchy fingers and stomachs knotted with guilt and anticipation as they travelled overseas. The temptation to bombard them with questions is almost overwhelming. But I don't, knowing that their responses would keep me awake and drain the small amount of sanity I have stored inside my head. I can't cope with anything they might tell me. Better to pretend. Better for us all. Instead, they smile stiffly and nod as I sit down. My mum avoids my gaze and my dad opens his mouth as if to speak, but closes it again as words literally fail him.

I tell them that they don't have to visit. I say it with as much conviction as I can muster. The truth is, I don't want them here, I don't want to associate them with this place, preferring to think of them in the kitchen in Hillcrest Road, pottering and chatting with the radio on. I don't want them to see me like this.

The hour passed slowly, each of us periodically glancing at the clock on the wall, frustrated by how slowly the second hand crept along. My mum reached into her pocket and pulled out an acorn. 'A present,' she whispered. I took it from her shaking hand and placed it in my pocket. I have it on my bedside table.

When the bell finally rang, Mum looked at me and asked, 'Do you pray, Jess?' I didn't know if she was saying I should or merely asking out of curiosity. I was thinking of how to respond when a guard came along and, taking me by the elbow, escorted me from the room. I looked back over my shoulder in time to see my dad take my mum's shaking form into his arms and pat her back as she cried into his jumper.

Eight

Jessica felt the light touch of her husband's kiss on her forehead as he crept from the room. She smiled. This pregnancy malarkey certainly had its advantages. Instead of nuzzling her awake for speedy sex and then almost insisting on having coffee together before he left for the office, he now left her in bed every morning, encouraging her to sleep for as long as she was able. She was performing the very important task of baby growing, so Matthew had taken over most of the running of the house, not wanting her to hurt herself. Although how she might be injured by a hoover or a duster was beyond her.

Last night before falling asleep he had read aloud from their baby book, again. 'Oh my God! Our baby has fingerprints! Actual fingerprints, can you believe it? And if it's a girl she has eggs in her ovaries. That is mind-blowing.' He shook his head.

Jessica smiled. She loved that Matt was so involved, so excited about their future and so protective of her. Sometimes he could go a bit too far, like when they had rowed furiously about whether she should take on another illustration commission or not. He had inadvertently mumbled through a mouth full of food that she should relax, *it wasn't as if she had a real job*… She had shouted at him, and he had shouted back. It was one of those rows that had been simmering for some time and brought out into the open something she had long suspected. Matthew had tried to backpedal, but only succeeded in making matters far worse. Stuttering, 'But my mother was happy not to have the worry of working, she was free to keep the house nice—'

'You think my job is to keep the house *nice*?' Jessica had squealed.

'No! Well, a bit. Yes!' Worryingly, he didn't know why this might cause offence.

'Jesus Christ, Matt, what is this, 1950? Why don't you tell me which way you think I should vote while you're at it!'

'Don't be like that,' he said. 'You know what I mean. Just imagine if your mum didn't have to work every day at a job that she doesn't love, she'd have a much more pleasant life.'

'My mum has an unpleasant life because she is a dinner lady and isn't wealthy enough to stay at home?' This she squealed louder and higher.

'That's not what I meant!' He pushed at his eye socket with his forefinger and thumb.

'Well, that's what it sounded like. And for your information, my job, my creativity is a very important part of me!'

Matthew laughed. 'Oh God! You sound like one of those arty-farty types who carry a book bag and collect vintage teacups.'

He soon stopped laughing when he saw her stricken expression. He apologised straight away, and they had a proper talk about it all. In the end, though, she had agreed it did make sense and she gave up her job nonetheless. She loved her work, but she loved the idea of making him happy even more. Okay, her days were a bit more boring, and she missed the rush of a commission, the sense of promise she derived from a freshly sharpened pencil and a blank sheet of paper. But it was a small price to pay for the enormous amount of sleep she was now allowed.

Jessica buried her face in the pillow and sprawled against the mattress. Despite her initial misgivings, she had to admit that she rather liked the mornings when she was all alone. She could sleep like a starfish and snore with her mouth open, knowing she could wake naturally. No employment meant no boss to answer to. It had always been her definition of success and luxury to wake without an alarm clock. She was renowned for her sleeping ability. Her sixth-form report had stated: 'If sleeping anywhere at a moment's notice, such as in church, at assembly or during the fourth form production of *The Caretaker*, were a valid subject or sport, Jessica would be heading for a straight A.' She had meant to photocopy this and put it up in their loo.

A loud hammering on the front door woke her suddenly. Lifting her head and pushing back the thick curtain of hair that obscured her view, she tried to focus on Matthew's bedside clock. It was eleven o'clock. Surely she hadn't slept until eleven? But she had.

Grabbing her tartan dressing gown, Jessica thrust her arms into the holes and opened the front door. At first she thought someone had knocked and run away, a favourite prank of the schoolboys on whose route to school she happened to live. She was about to shut the door again when a hand waving from the ground to her right alerted her; it was accompanied by a trickling sound.

'What in God's name are you doing?' Jessica looked on horrified as she spotted her friend squatting on the small paved area where the wheelie bins lived, beneath the front bay window.

Polly looked up and smiled. 'I'm having a wee.'

'Christ, Polly! Why are you weeing in the front garden? Can't you just use the loo like a normal human?'

Polly snorted her laughter. 'I was absolutely, completely desperate! I got off the train and ran. I don't know how I hung on, I really don't. I only just made it to here. I banged on the door but couldn't wait a second longer. I'm nearly done. Don't watch.' She shooed at her friend with her hand.

Jessica drew breath and was about to respond when she heard Mrs Pleasant's door bang shut.

'Ah, morning!' Jessica waved at her over the shrubs and miniature wall.

'Mor—' Mrs Pleasant didn't quite manage to get her words out: the girl on the ground with her jeans bunched down around her knees fixated her.

'Sorry about my friend,' Jessica mumbled. 'She has an illness and has to go when the need takes her and... I'm just glad she managed to get behind the hedge in time.' She nodded apologetically.

'We are both glad about that!' Polly snorted again.

Mrs Pleasant fastened her mackintosh and hitched her shopping bag over her shoulder before making her way down Merton Avenue without uttering a word.

Jessica smiled widely at a mum with a pushchair that passed by, trying to look as if she had been awake for an age.

Polly came bounding into the hallway. 'Jesus Christ, you lazy cow! Come on, get up, get dressed.'

'I am up, just not dressed. I hope you are going to wash your hands!' Jessica shouted.

'Of course! Don't you have work to do?' Polly asked, who was herself between roles, having just finished her latest temping assignment, and considering training as a florist.

Jessica shook her head. 'No. I've kind of given up my illustrations for the time being. Matt thinks it's better I just concentrate on the baby and the house, y'know...'

'Actually, I *don't* know. You mean he just said "stop working" and you said "okay then"?' Polly asked with incredulity.

'Kind of.' Jessica looked at the floor.

'There you go again with the *kind of*! But you love drawing! And you haven't had the baby yet.'

'I know. But he's right, it does make life easier.'

'Bloody hell, mate, he'll be taking over the hoovering next and making you sit with your feet up!' Polly tutted.

Jessica smiled. 'Perish the thought.'

'I need some lunch!' Polly snapped her fingers and pushed past her friend, heading for the kitchen and no doubt the fridge. Jessica's food had always for some reason been more attractive to Polly than anything she might find in her own kitchen a mere seven miles across town.

'Don't they have supermarkets or cafés in SW4? I'm pretty sure they do.' Jessica yawned and stretched, raising her arms. Her T-shirt lifted to reveal the tiniest hint of a baby bump.

'Don't be sarcastic, your unborn child hears everything.' Polly nodded sagely and tapped her ears. 'We need to catch up,' she said as she ferreted in the cupboard and then the fridge, taking her haul over to the table. 'I have a target identified and need advice and assistance if I am going to proceed.'

This was how they had always referred to any new love-interest. 'Poor bloke.' Jessica yawned again. 'Does he know his days are numbered?'

'Yes and no.' Polly shoved a cracker in her mouth, followed by a lump of cheese. 'Yes, he knows I exist, and no, he doesn't know he is my potential future husband.'

'Where did you meet him?' Jessica filled the kettle and smiled, now fully compos mentis after her deep sleep.

'Well, here's the thing. I got chatting to him at the farmers' market and apparently he runs a pregnancy yoga class in a hall just off High Street Ken and I, like the best mate in the whole wide world that I am…' She placed her hand at her breast. 'Am willing to take you along for the good of your pelvis and the blob.' She pointed at Jessica's tum.

'You want me to schlep up to High Street Kensington for a yoga class because you fancy the instructor?' Jessica bunched her thick hair into a ponytail and fastened it with a band she had been storing on her wrist.

'Two words, Jess!' Polly shouted as she held up two fingers, looking like a forceful but less portly Winston Churchill.

'Oh no, don't say them!' Jessica stuffed her fingers in her ears.

Polly grabbed her friend's hands and pulled them onto the tabletop. 'Yes! I am going to say them!'

'Please, NO!' Polly yelled.

'Too late, Jess. I am saying them now. Conor Barrington!'

'No! Please don't pull the Conor Barrington card – again!' Jessica slumped down at the dining table, cradling her head in her hands.

'Yes, Conor Barrington! A promise is a promise.' Polly sat opposite her friend and smiled as she piled crackers high with strong cheddar, smeared them with Matthew's favourite spicy tomato chutney and crammed them into her mouth.

'I was fourteen!' Jessica banged the table with her flattened palm.

'So? What's that got to do with anything? You said if I double-dated with you and Rich, the Charlie from Busted lookalike, you would, quote, "Whenever you need me to, at any point in the future until we are old and grey, help you land the man..."'

'... of your dreams.' Jessica finished the sentence that was indelibly engraved on her mind and had haunted her ever since. 'I know, but what I hadn't banked on, Polly, was that you would need help landing the man of your dreams every bloody year since!'

'It was the worst Sunday of my *life*! Do I need to remind you of Conor's cheese-and-onion breath? His octopus hands? His sweaty palms that hovered dangerously close to my right tit? His constant sniffing? His boring conversation? It was torture, it was worse than torture!'

Jessica shook her head. 'No, you don't need to remind me. You have told me many, many times before. Don't forget he also told the whole of junior choir that you let him go under jumper over bra.'

'I HAD forgotten that! Right, you definitely owe me.' Polly grinned.

'What's your yoga man called?' Jessica picked up a cracker and snapped it in half, crunching it loudly.

'His name?' Polly kept her eyes on her cheese.

'Yes, what's he called?'

Polly sighed. 'His name is Topaz.'

Jessica sprayed her laughter and cracker crumbs over her best friend. 'Topaz?' she shrieked. 'Oh my God! Are you making this up? I am so coming to a class; I *have* to meet a man called Topaz! Are you kidding me? I can just see you taking him home to Romford: "Mum, Dad, this is… Topaz." Your dad would wet himself, literally. Your mum would draw the curtains in case any of the neighbours saw him. Does he wear those really baggy pants that hang down to his knees and carry a healing crystal?' Jessica laughed again.

'Yes and yes. But when you see the bod that sits inside those baggy MC-Hammer-style strides, you won't be laughing.'

'I think I might be, actually.'

'Look on the bright side, you can get a discount on baby yoga for the blob.'

'Poll, you have to stop referring to my baby as the blob.'

'Do I? Why?'

'Because…' Jessica tried to explain her feelings without sounding too mumsy, knowing this would only invite ridicule from her best friend. 'Because it is far from a blob. I'm just over thirteen weeks and this blob has a strong beating heart, it can move its arms and legs and it has fingernails!' Jessica felt a flutter of happiness ripple through her body. She placed her hand on her tummy and beamed. 'It's incredible, isn't it? We've got our scan tomorrow! I can't wait!' she clapped.

Polly placed her cheese cracker on the table. 'Do you mind if we stop talking about it?'

Jessica placed her hand over the back of her friend's. 'Aww, sure. Does it make you feel broody?'

Polly shook her head. 'Actually, no. It makes me feel sick!'

'How can it make you feel sick? God, Polly!' Jessica shook her head.

Her friend shrugged her shoulders. 'Just does. I mean, don't you think it's a bit yucky, all that stuff going on inside your body? Growing another human! It's not natural.'

Jessica shook her head and lifted her foot to rest on the chair. 'No, I think it's amazing and wonderful and exciting! And actually, Poll, it is the most natural thing in the world. It's what we are designed for.'

'You, maybe. Think I'll pass. I like having tits that I don't have to tuck inside my shin pads and I definitely don't want the whole stretch-mark thing – these hips should have a preservation order on them. And don't even get me started on breastfeeding.' Polly mimed retching.

'I can't wait to feed my baby.' Jessica felt her nipples tighten at the prospect, looking forward to the closeness it would bring.

Polly stared at her friend. 'But don't you think boobs are a bit...'

'A bit what?'

'A bit sexy. There, I've said it.' She exhaled. 'If I think of my boobs, I think of them as sexy and I can't imagine offering them to a baby.' She visibly winced.

'You are the limit. Boobs can be sexy, of course, but their primary function is to feed our babies. You'll probably feel differently if you ever get pregnant.'

'*If* being the operative word. I might consider it if there comes a point when I have achieved all my career goals and need to snare a Greek billionaire shipping tycoon.'

'Assuming things don't work out with Yoga Boy.'

'Oh, he's just fun. I don't really think he's my forever-and-ever lover.'

'Careful what you put out into the universe, Polly. That might come back to haunt you!'

Polly scoffed. 'Oh purlease, you're not going to go all hippified on me, are you, and start knitting your own jumpers and chanting to whale music?'

'No, Poll, I'm leaving that to Topaz. God, I can't even say the name Topaz without laughing. If I'm being honest, mate...' Jessica studied her friend's acrylic nails, strawberry-blonde hair extensions and the limited-edition Boy Chanel flap-bag that had been plonked on the table. 'I can't really see you hooking up with a yoga master.'

'Why not?' Polly paused in her eating, looking a little hurt.

'Because...' Jessica considered how best to phrase it. 'Because you are shallow and materialistic and he probably isn't. But I love you regardless, obviously.'

'Obviously,' Polly agreed. 'And I know you are right. I am indeed both those things. But I've thought about it. I have a plan.'

'Oh, well, good.' Jessica was intrigued. 'What's your plan?'

'I'm going to lie.'

'That's foolproof. What could possibly go wrong?' Jessica laughed.

'You can laugh, but I have it all figured out. I shall simply agree with everything he says and learn a little of his philosophy along the way. I've even bought myself a stretchy leotard thing and a sign that says "Love, Light, Universe" which I've put up in my kitchen.'

'What does it mean?' Jessica asked.

'Fuck knows, but maybe Topaz can explain it to me.' Polly grinned.

'I think it's going to take a bit more than a sign in the kitchen of your flat and a stretchy leotard for him to believe you are a spiritual being. Is he a vegetarian too? Like Mikey?'

'Oh God, don't talk about him. I can't even hear that name without wanting to puke!' Polly shuddered.

'But can't you see, this is Mikey all over again. He's a Mikey upgrade; he's like Mikey but with MC Hammer pants! You told *him* you were a strict vegetarian.'

'I had to! He ran the raw vegan restaurant on the Kings Road. I ate bloody alfalfa sprouts and drank broccoli juice for three whole months!' Polly hacked at a large lump of cheese and shoved it on her tongue as if to erase the taste memory.

'And why exactly did you finish, again?' Jessica was aware she sounded like a prompting primary schoolteacher.

Polly sighed. 'Because he caught me...'

'Caught you *what*?' Jessica wouldn't be satisfied until she heard it all.

Polly tutted and rolled her eyes. 'He caught me in the airing cupboard at three in the morning eating a bacon sandwich! Don't know what he was more mad about: the freshly scorched slices of pig I was gobbling or the fact that I'd gone for white bread and non-organic ketchup.'

Jessica slapped the tabletop and laughed loudly. 'Precisely. And that, my friend, is why you will not be able to keep up the pretence with Sapphire or whatever his name is.'

'Topaz,' Polly corrected.

'Yep. Him.' Jessica smiled and ran her fingers over the ends of her dark brown hair. 'I tell you what. You might think it's a little yucky, what's going on in my body, but my hair is glorious – thicker than ever and so shiny!' She pulled the band from her hair and let it fall over the back of the chair.

'You've always had fabulous hair; it's one of the reasons I hate you. Does Coral still advise you to chop it all off every time you see her?'

'"Oh, Jess, a shorter hairdo would look so pretty!"' they chorused before collapsing on the table.

Jessica stood. 'Bacon sandwich?' She had a sudden craving.

'Yep, on white, with ketchup. As long as I don't have to eat it in the airing cupboard!' Polly smiled.

*

Two hours later, Jessica held her fingers under her nose as if stifling a sneeze. 'This room stinks,' she whispered to Polly, who was busy applying bronzer and combing her lash extensions. 'It smells like old gym kit.'

'No it doesn't,' Polly snapped. 'Just suck it up, Jess. This is important to me.' She fixed her with a stare.

'Suck it up? I'm pregnant, I've travelled all the way here on public bloody transport, put lycra leggings on and am now stood in a room that smells of cheese and sweat! You need to be more grateful!'

'I *am* grateful, but I am only just about coping with this situation, and with you reminding me about the lingering smell of feet, you're making me feel sick. I'm nervous enough as it is.' Polly rubbed her enviably flat stomach.

Jessica pulled a face at her friend and looked around the room at the ten ladies and two men, who seemed to be lithe and limber, ready for their session. They all held towels and water bottles. She wished she had similar props to occupy her.

Suddenly, an uber-posh voice boomed from the back of the hall. 'Good morning, ladies, gentlemen, friends and those we carry within.'

Jessica shot Polly a look that she deliberately ignored; this was no time for inappropriate giggling. But Jessica knew if he used the phrase 'those we carry within' once more, she just might lose it. She stared at the floor and tried to think of something sad.

The voice continued. 'Welcome to all newcomers. I am Topaz and I will be your yogic guide, helping you reach a state of enlightened bliss and ultimate relaxation for you and your babies. Now, grab a mat, find a space and make it your own...'

Jessica felt the lightest touch on the back of her head as Topaz, with arms extended at shoulder height, made his way through the room, brushing his fingertips against the backs of the heads or shoulders of all those he could reach. Jessica shuddered involuntarily but also felt a warm quiver of joy; it was quite a nice sensation.

Topaz pranced to the front of the room and stood with his arms outstretched, his head thrown back and his eyes closed. Polly dug Jessica in the ribs with her elbow. Jessica looked at her friend, who mouthed 'WOW!' And she had to admit, he was indeed wow!

Topaz, resplendent in rose-pink cotton Indian pants, was naked from the waist up, baring a tanned and muscular torso. This, along with his lithe figure and fey head-twitching – necessary to shake his shoulder-length streaky blond-and-brown hair from his eyes – put him firmly in the rock-star bracket where looks were concerned. His bright blue eyes scrutinised everyone in the room and the smile that played about his mouth gave the whole experience an illicit air. Jessica was willing to bet her last cent that this guy would be able to score every single hour of every single day, even with a name like Topaz.

Suddenly he faced the group and announced, as though addressing an audience, 'Mothers-to-be, you are the creators of the fantastic! The coveted vessels that nature has blessed with the gift of life!'

Jessica stared at Polly's shiny pink toenails; bent double

with her face a few inches from the floor, it was the only way to control her giggles. She bloody well hoped Poll would get a date out of this, because trying not to laugh and not to pee at the same time for two whole hours was going to be a serious challenge.

September 25th, 2013

I'm feeling angry today. 'So you didn't like your parents coming to visit you? Do you like them?' That's what the psychiatrist asked me during my one to one and I wanted to scream. It's not that I don't like them, of course I do! I love them, I love them very much, and I always have. But the thing is, I don't want them or anyone I love coming in here. It's shit with its boiled vegetable smell and its magnolia walls, and I just hate the thought of them being in here, even for an hour. I tried to explain this as the psychiatrist adjusted her glasses and sat with her pen poised ready to capture any clues that tripped off my tongue. The worry and guilt I feel about those I love spoils any joy I get from their visit. I know they then go away and analyse how bad I look, how quiet I am, how sad. Well, they are right. I am sad. Sadder than I ever knew was possible. And I'm ashamed. And having them see me in here makes me even sadder and more ashamed. It's a horrible cycle.

She actually asked me to describe my shame – as if it wasn't obvious. But I tried anyway. I've learnt that the more I cooperate and the sooner I give the answer she is looking for, the sooner the session is over and I get a gold star on my crappy file. I always thought depression is for other people. I remember my mum saying, 'Oh, poor Mrs So And So, she's a bit depressed.' And I would think, Oh, buck up, woman! I thought depressed was another word for miserable or, worse still, weak. Even when Mum lost Danny, she didn't succumb to depression. Terrible things happen to people all the time and they just seem to cope, they can see the silver lining. But me...? I can't explain it. What did I have to be depressed about? I had it all.

At the group session afterwards, one of the girls was talking about her fella, remembering how they had met and how he had wooed her with mix tapes and love letters. It was sweet and nice to see the softer side of one of the tougher women in my block. I didn't share – I never do; my old life has no place in here – but I allowed myself to drift into the memory of meeting Matthew at the barbecue, something I usually try and block out. It was a sunny day. Polly and I arrived late. We'd been in two minds about whether to go or not as it was at the house of a friend of a friend. I sometimes think about how different my life would have been if we had decided to stay in the pub. I'm glad we didn't.

It was the usual set-up. A pile of charred meat sat in a heap, raided every so often by the drunkest of the crew, who grabbed and gnawed while they chatted to their mates. One of the boys was wearing a string of bunting around his neck. A couple of kids ran around the garden and the host's wife fretted and sweated about whether there was enough beer. Matt was standing under a tree chatting to Jenny, laughing at something. I noticed him because he was laughing so naturally, head back and loudly. He looked happy and happiness was what I wanted. He turned his head and caught my stare and something incredible happened. He looked, then looked away, then immediately looked back at me as if unable to take his eyes off me. His smile got wider. My heart hammered in my chest and we stared at each other, without embarrassment. It was as if he was saying, 'I've been waiting for you.' And in my head I answered, 'Well, I'm here now.'

He walked towards me and slipped on the grass. I caught his arm, just before he took a tumble, and he said, 'I don't know your name,' as though he should.

Polly answered, 'She's Jessica and I'm her smarter friend, Polly.'

'Dance with me, Joanna!' he said as he grabbed my hand and I smiled. It didn't matter that he'd got my name wrong, or that no one else was dancing. He beamed at me and I knew I loved him, just like that. I was wearing a red-and-white-striped halter-neck top and he called me a golden girl. Like I said, back then I really did have it all.

Nine

Jessica rushed into the room and smiled at her man, folded into a rather small plastic chair in the corner of the waiting room. He was thumbing through an old edition of *Woman's Weekly* and looked very obviously relieved to see her.

'You're cutting it fine.' He tossed the magazine onto the pile and wiped his hands on his thighs as he looked at the large clock on the wall. It was five to three.

'Sorry. I fell asleep! And then I couldn't park. I really wanted to be here nice and early.'

'You're here now.' He smiled. 'I was trying to work out how I could stall things if you were late. I was struggling for ideas. I'm glad you're here with the star of the show.' He nodded at her tum.

'The star of the show is making me want to pee. It said on my little leaflet that you get a better result if you have a full bladder, so I've downed a couple of pints of water and now I'm desperate!' She crossed her legs.

'Don't worry, not too much longer and as soon as we are done you can wee until your heart's content.' He kissed her nose.

'Bliss.'

The square room was a little cramped and stuffy. Pregnant women of various shapes and sizes sat along the walls and each had brought along at least one companion. Toddlers and other children were corralled in the middle of the room, crammed into the inadequate play area, competing over the wooden table-puzzle, the Lego scattered across the floor like corn feed and the various grubby, dog-eared books. A couple of little boys were squabbling over a plastic fire engine. Their respective mothers nodded at each other across the chaos, both declining to get involved. A little girl whined loudly when another accidentally trod on her finger.

Jessica looked at the tired faces of the mothers, who mostly just sat and stared at their offspring. She wondered why they weren't intervening and decided there and then that if ever her child were in a situation like this, she would entertain them, feed them and make sure they weren't left crying in the middle of the play square.

'Jessica Deane?' the nurse called from the corridor.

She and Matthew rushed towards the door, treading carefully to avoid little hands, feet and Lego bricks.

'Sorry about the wait. In you come.' The smiling lady in her pale green tabard ushered them into a room that Jessica thought was actually more like a cupboard.

She kicked off her trainers and lay back on the raised couch, with a paper sheet underneath her and her jeans and pants rolled down to below her bikini line. Matthew sat in the chair between her and the wall, with barely enough room to bend his legs.

'Feel free to ask any questions,' the woman said.

'Thanks. I've been writing up my birth plan today.' Jessica beamed as though she was handing in homework.

'Oh, that's exciting. And it'll be D-Day before you know it.'

Jessica gulped at the prospect. 'I have decided to go for a very natural birth. I don't want drugs. I figure if I'm being drugged then so is my baby.'

'Well, that's true, but the medical team will have had a lot of practice. They only use things that are safe and it's very well controlled.'

Jessica glanced at Matthew. 'I'm sure, but I still want it to be as natural as possible. I'm going to use lavender oil to soothe my aches and pains, initially anyway.'

The woman nodded knowingly as she scanned the screen. 'Okay, here we go!' She smiled as though they were on a rollercoaster just about to launch. Jessica was happy that even though the technician did this numerous times a day, she still managed to be enthusiastic and make the event feel special.

A viscous blue gel that smelt like hand-sanitiser was squirted across Jessica's stomach and then the woman used her right hand to roll what looked like a fat-headed white plastic microphone over it. With her left hand she manipulated a mouse and clicked buttons on the keyboard that sat in front of the large computer screen.

'We don't want to know what we are having, do we, Jess?' Matthew prompted.

'No, it'll be part of our surprise.' Jessica kept her eyes fixed on the screen. She recognised very little apart from some grainy whitish-grey lines on a black background.

'Oh don't worry,' the woman said without removing her eyes from the image, 'it's a little too soon for me to tell anyway.' She smiled.

'I can't see much of anything, let alone a willy,' Jessica piped up.

'Let me go in closer.' The woman twisted a dial and zoomed in.

Jessica squinted at the screen until she could see what looked like a fluttering tube.

'That's your baby's heart.'

Jessica inhaled sharply. 'Oh! Oh wow! My baby's heart!'

'And here we can see a good outline.' She clicked the mouse and zoomed in again.

Jessica watched as the picture of their baby came into focus. 'Oh, Matt! Look! Look!'

She couldn't drag her eyes away from the outline that was quite clearly a baby in profile. It was easy to make out a large head with two little arms being held up to the face. There was a well-rounded tum and two legs bent in an L-shape.

'Oh my God, that's our baby! Look at it. That's our little baby! It's amazing. Just amazing.' Jessica stared at the image on the screen as her tears gathered. Before long she was sobbing, unable to stop. She found herself quite overwhelmed, gripped by an intense fear. Wriggling from the couch, she pulled up her jeans, shoved her feet into her trainers and ran from the room.

'Jess?' Matthew smiled his thanks at the technician as he raced after his wife. 'Jess!' he called along the corridor.

He found her leaning on the car with her arms folded across her stomach. 'What on earth...? What's going on?'

Jessica shrugged.

'Jess, talk to me!' He gripped her arm.

'Can we just get in the car?' She looked up at him with the beginning of tears.

They drove in silence until Matt felt confident enough to speak. 'What are you thinking?' he coaxed.

'Nothing.'

'You must be thinking something!' He laughed.

'Well, I am now. I'm thinking about your question!' She gave the slow beginnings of a smile.

Matthew placed his hand on her thigh.

It was a while before Jessica broke the silence again. 'With every step of this pregnancy, I'm understanding more and more what Mum went through when she lost Danny.' She looked out of the window as the world sped by. 'I can't imagine watching him go from a tiny little dot to a living, breathing thing, a teenager, and then for him to just be gone. It's such a waste.'

'It is. I've always thought your mum and dad must be so strong to have got through it.'

Jessica looked at her husband. 'I'm not sure they did get through it, not intact. It changed them, sent them mad, and when they emerged, came out the other side, they were very different people.'

'In what way?'

Jessica considered this. 'My dad was quieter, more thoughtful, like he always had something on his mind. Burdened, I suppose. And my mum,' she sighed picturing Coral before and after, 'she lost her sparkle.'

Matthew nodded. 'Of course.'

'You don't know how children are going to change your life, do you? I mean, you only think about the good, the positive, the happy, but supposing they bring you heartache, sadness, loss. It's a gamble, isn't it?'

'I suppose it is.' He squeezed her leg. 'But one worth taking, Jess.'

'Oh yes.' She laid her hand over his. 'One worth taking.'

Supper had been cleared away and the dishwasher was whirring in the kitchen. Matthew beat the arm of the sofa with his flattened palm. 'Stop! Stop, Jess!' he wheezed, red faced. 'I can't listen to any more!'

As Jessica lay with her head in her husband's lap, she tutted. 'It's not that funny, Matt. We shouldn't be mean. I'm probably making it sound worse than it really was. I mean, it was only a yoga class and you'd think they were wacky anyway, all that finding your centre and concentrating on the now. And besides…' She reached across the floor for the bottle, poured the remains of the red wine into his large balloon glass and raised her head to sip her iced water. 'He may have a bit of weirdness going on, but he is really good-looking.'

'He'd need to be really good-looking to balance things out.' Matt placed his index finger on his thumb and chanted, 'Ommmm.'

'Seriously, Matt, he seems very nice, despite the weirdness!'

'I blame his parents. We need to make sure we raise a good solid child; none of this hippified arty-farty stuff for our child. I mean, calling him Topaz, that was their first mistake.' He rolled his eyes.

Jessica laughed.

'I'm glad you're laughing, honey. I was worried about you earlier, running out of the scan like that and clamming up on me. I didn't know what to do and I hate feeling that useless. If I don't know what's wrong, then I can't fix it.'

'I'm sorry.'

'No need to apologise. I just want you to be happy and I didn't know what the problem was.'

Jessica turned to face her husband. 'I felt a bit overwhelmed, that's all.'

'Well that's understandable, this is a big deal.' He rubbed her arm.

'In fact, more than a bit overwhelmed. I was scared. I am scared,' she whispered before the next sob built in her throat.

'What are you scared of?' Matthew held her close and spoke into her scalp.

'I'm scared I won't know how to do it,' she mumbled through her tears.

'Won't know how to do what?'

Jessica shook herself free and wiped her mouth and eyes. 'Mummying!' She pushed her hair from her face. 'I don't know about making birthday cakes and inviting kids to parties and stuff! It was all right when *I* was a baby – my mum had my nan a couple of roads away to call on whenever she felt like it. Plus her friends who had babies were close by too – like Polly's mum. It's not like that for me. And I don't know if I'm going to be able to do it all.'

'Oh, Jess, you're going to be great!' He chuckled.

‘But supposing I’m not?’ She took a deep breath.

Matthew smoothed her hair. ‘You are brilliant. You are clever and you can do anything that you put your mind to.’

‘But I’m not brilliant at everything. I can’t iron properly and you’re right that I’m a crappy cook. And I keep thinking about Danny. Mum and Dad did everything right, they were kind and hardworking and they loved us and yet they couldn’t keep him safe, could they? How do you keep them safe, Matt? I’m so worried about getting it wrong.’

Matthew sighed. His words when they came were slow and considered. ‘Danny died in an accident and it was no one’s fault. It’s just a terrible thing that happened, but that’s not going to happen to us. I know this is scary, but you are going to be an incredible mum and I will be right by your side, helping you figure it out. We can do this together, Jess, okay? Together.’

Jessica sniffed and nodded as she smeared the paste of tears and mascara onto her arm. ‘Okay.’

‘I’m sure from what I’ve been told about Danny he wouldn’t want your pregnancy spoilt worrying about things that are never going to happen. Would he?’

‘No he wouldn’t.’ Jessica pictured her brother’s face. ‘I’m sorry I ran out. I got a bit freaked.’

‘A little bit of freaking is allowed. But don’t run away in future; talk to me, give me a chance to fix things, okay?’

‘Okay.’ She nodded again.

‘That’s my girl.’ Matthew smiled.

She took another deep breath. ‘And we need to pick

names! It's bothering me. I want to be able to picture our baby and to do that I need to give it a name.'

'Okay. We can do that, Jess, but let's do it at the kitchen table. I need a snack, something to soak up all that red wine, and I have a couple of emails to send to Magnus. Don't forget, I need this job to keep young Phil in the style to which he will become accustomed.'

'Phil?' Jessica shook her head as they made their way along the hall.

'Yes, after Phil Parkes, the greatest player QPR have ever had. In my opinion.'

Jessica laughed again. 'That's not going to happen!'

'So what are we going to call our child?' Matthew asked his wife as he dipped his hunk of bread into the mix of extra-virgin olive oil and balsamic vinegar. 'How about Balsamica?' He closed his eyes in appreciation as he lowered the saturated bread into his mouth.

'For a boy or a girl?'

'Either. It's genius: we both love balsamic vinegar and we are not likely to encounter another!'

'This is our child we are talking about. Their whole future will be shaped by the name we saddle them with.' Jessica sighed and reached across the table for the loaf.

'Does it matter that much?' Matthew looked genuinely perplexed.

'Of course it does! Think back to when you were at school – who had the worst name?' She dunked her bread into the saucer, making sure she had a good mix of both ingredients, and thought about Stella Drew, who had spent her primary-school years unfairly dubbed Smella Poo.

Jessica silently chastised herself for wanting to laugh, even now.

'At school? No one that outlandish. I mean, it's not like we had Topaz in our class…' Matthew suddenly wagged his finger. 'But at uni there was a bloke in our department called Muriel Delahorn!' He laughed loudly. 'Poor bastard. He spent his entire life explaining that it was an old family name and should be pronounced Murrial, Murry for short.'

'Did you call him Murry?'

'No! Did we fuck! We called him Mavis, everyone did.'

'Why did you call him Mavis?'

'Because his name was Muriel and trying to hide it behind Murrial was worse, so Mavis it was!'

'Poor bloke.' She shook her head. 'But this is exactly my point: give a child a stupid or way-out name and they might suffer. I think we need to give them a name that means they can be a barrister or a dustman and carry off either.'

'Preferably the latter though, right?' Matthew was having a hard time at work.

Jessica ignored him. 'What about naming them after our parents?'

Matthew considered this. 'So for a girl, Margaret Coral—'

'Or Coral Margaret.' Jessica knew her mother would not want to play second fiddle to Granny Margaret, even if she was too polite to say.

'And for a boy… Roger Anthony!' Matthew guffawed. 'No, definitely not! Roger Anthony sounds like something Mavis Delahorn would get up to!'

'I like Joseph or Leo for a boy and I like Beth for a girl. Bethan.' She smiled.

Matthew smiled, realising she had given this a lot more thought than he had. 'Leo is good, strong! But let's talk about this later, when we've both had time to really think.'

Jessica nodded. But in her mind, she was already cradling a little girl called Beth.

14th October, 2013

I woke up crying and haven't stopped all day. I can't stop. I can't take a deep breath. I can't focus. Even now after two years in here. I get days like this, where I feel as if I am drowning in my sorrow. It's a horrible, horrible way to spend a day. One of the older women came up to me when we were outside; she hovered next to me as I breathed in my precious fresh air. It was obvious I'd been crying. She patted my shoulder and said, 'It's hard being away from your family, especially for a young'un like you. I still find it hard, even now. I miss them so much, I ache.' I stared at her, feeling a flicker of envy for this woman, clearly able to express her feelings and understand loss far better than me. I didn't want to chat to her, didn't want to open up. I didn't know how. Instead I sloped back to my room and picked up my sketchpad and pencils and I drew the first thing that came into my mind. It was a little striped sock. I studied it and lay my face in the pillow, to cry some more.

Ten

'Here we go, Mrs D!' Polly greeted Matthew's mother at the front door of Merton Avenue and shoved the baby bottle into her hand. 'It's easy once you get the hang of it and you need to get over the slightly rubbery aftertaste, but apart from that it's just like drinking a normal G&T!'

'Oh, goodness!' Margaret took the bottle but hesitated before placing the teat in her mouth. 'Is Coral coming?' she asked hopefully, wanting an ally.

'Yes, eventually.' Jessica smiled. 'She's coming straight from work.'

Music pulsed into the kitchen, which was filled with Jessica's friends. The French doors had been thrown open to accommodate the smokers and those who wanted to make the most of the warm June rays. Everyone had brought a pretty bag or parcel, wrapped in white, with ribbons tied into big bows. The gifts were stacked high on the dining table and sat invitingly like an Aladdin's cave of goodies, waiting to be revealed. Jessica couldn't believe that a tiny baby could need so much stuff, but apparently they did.

They had stuck to their decision of not wanting to know the sex of their unborn baby, due in a month's time, agreeing that the surprise was part of the fun. Matthew had hinted that he had seen something on their twenty-week scan, but Jessica ignored him, knowing it was almost impossible to accurately see anything through all those tears. She suspected that Matthew secretly wanted a boy, which was fine, as she secretly wanted a girl.

A large flipchart had been set up in the corner of the room and on it was a list of top names to vote on. Jessica watched her mother-in-law pull out her reading glasses from their natty little tartan case and run her eyes over the two lists, one in blue and one in pink. She saw how Margaret's hand flew to her throat. 'Kylie? Is that up for consideration?'

Jessica shrugged, feigning ignorance. The reality was they had beautiful names under consideration. She still favoured Bethan Rose and Leo Anthony Maxwell. She smiled, knowing that it would be one of these two that would become familiar to her mother-in-law, a name that would dance from her mouth as she regaled her book club and choir with all his or her latest achievements, which no other child had ever quite managed with the same degree of aptitude or brilliance.

Margaret pushed her specs further up her nose and walked over to the board. 'Adolph? Surely not, Jess! And what kind of a name is Kourtney?' She turned to her daughter-in-law, confusion and disgust clouding her face. 'That's not a real name, is it?'

'That's in homage to Polly's favourite Kardashian,' Jessica clarified.

'What's a Kardashian?' Margaret enquired. It was clear that whatever it was, she didn't want her first grandchild named after one.

'You know what, Margaret, don't worry too much about names. Matthew and I have it all under control. I am just letting Polly and the girls have a bit of fun. She's spent a week selling marquee services and is thinking of becoming a party planner; I think I'm her guinea pig!'

Margaret's shoulders visibly relaxed. Evidently the prospect of having to introduce Tupac or Miley to the wider family had not appealed.

The front doorbell rang. Jessica walked slowly down the hallway and greeted her mum, who stood there nervously, peering ahead into the kitchen, wondering what shenanigans Jessica's mates would be getting up to. She had never been to a baby shower before.

Jessica noted her freshly applied lipstick and her liberal application of perfume. 'Come through, Mum!' She placed her hand on her mum's back and pushed her along. Coral shrugged her arms from her coat and adjusted the locket that sat on her chest with pictures of her babies inside.

'Okay, everyone! It's time to play Measure the Cervix!' Polly held up a large watermelon with a hole cut into the front.

Jessica looked at her mum's face and was worried that she might actually faint. 'Would you like to come and see the crib, Mum? We can leave them to it. You too, Margaret.'

Margaret and Coral followed her out of the kitchen; neither needed the invitation repeating.

'Where's Matthew?' Margaret asked. She was, as ever, disappointed that her son wasn't on hand to fuss over.

'He's up the pub with Jake. I couldn't let him anywhere near this. I did take him to my antenatal class, though. I've only been to a couple – it didn't really feel like my thing,' she confessed, 'but at least I was better than him. God knows what he's going to be like at the birth. Every time the course leader said the word "vagina", which she did a lot, Matthew sniggered and giggled like a twelve-year-old. He's absolutely hopeless.'

Coral tutted as though her daughter had sworn.

'Think I'm rather with Matthew on that one.' Margaret rearranged her pearls and started up the hallway.

Jessica walked ahead, holding the banister and lumbering up the stairs, one step at a time. She had gained significant weight and was no longer nimble. She paused at the top and drew breath; her fatigue bloomed even after the smallest amount of exercise.

'All okay, darling?' Margaret looked concerned. Jessica liked the new warm tone with which her mother-in-law addressed her, as Matthew pointed out, she was now the goose that was carrying the golden egg.

'Oh yes, fine. I get so exhausted, even walking up the stairs. Ridiculous really!' She chuckled and rubbed her bump.

'No, not ridiculous, and all very normal. Everything will settle down, you'll see. But maybe not until it's been born and then you get a whole new level of exhaustion!'

'Oh, well, that's something to look forward to!' Jessica laughed. 'Mind you, the tiredness isn't the worst thing. I am so constipated! I've tried everything, but apparently that's quite normal too. And my horrible stretch marks, and the fact that I wake every half an hour trying to get comfy. All normal, apparently! So why does it all feel so very abnormal?' Jessica curled her lip.

'Welcome to motherhood!' Margaret laughed.

The nursery sat at the back of the house, with a lovely view beyond the sash window to the courtyard garden.

'Oh, Jess!' Coral gasped. 'This looks lovely. It's a good-sized room.'

Jessica smiled, pleased with the compliment.

'I mean, they don't need much space when they're little, do they? I slept in a drawer until I was a couple of months old, waiting for my sister to outgrow the cot.' Coral glanced at Margaret, seeking acknowledgement for the shared confidence.

Jessica looked around the room. She had taken a lot of time choosing the right shade of white: not too clinical or cold, but just the right tone to act as a canvas. A natural linen roman blind sat halfway up the window; its bottom edge was decorated with a fat band of grey-and-white gingham ribbon and an appliqued pale grey rabbit with one ear flopping over his eye.

'We've tried to keep it quite neutral and then when we know what we are getting, we can add colour in, like a pale pink cushion on the nursing chair or their initials on the wall in blue or whatever. I think we've got just about everything.' Jessica scanned the hand-painted off-white nursery furniture. The little wardrobe with its dinky hangers waiting for their contents, the changing station already packed to the gunnels with nappies, wet wipes, powder, sore bum cream, hand-sanitiser, nappy bags and a neatly folded pile of tiny white vests and linen squares.

'Look at these!' Jessica pulled open the top drawer of the chest and removed a pair of white socks. She laid them in her mother-in-law's flattened palm. 'I can't believe there are any feet in the world tiny enough for these socks. They make my heart melt!'

'I remember thinking the same when I was having you.' Coral smiled. 'Granny Maxwell knitted you a little matinee jacket and I held it up and thought she must have made a mistake; maybe she'd knitted a doll's version. I mean, let's be honest, she was going slightly loopy by that stage.' Coral shook her head at the memory. 'But then when you were born, it swamped you. You were so tiny and beautiful. It was a lovely time in my life, when you were a baby. The loveliest and the happiest.'

'Oh dear, sounds like it all went a bit downhill after that!' Jessica joked, aware that there was more than a grain of truth in that.

'Not downhill exactly. I've been very lucky, in some ways. But I do think about those years, with Danny little and you a baby. I remember tucking you both in every night and feeling like I was too lucky.' She drew breath as if to stem an outpouring of grief, a neat trick she had mastered.

'I think it is a special time. I know that when Matthew was tiny, that was the last time Anthony properly loved me.' Margaret toyed with the sock in her palm. Moments of emotional revelation like this were rare.

'Oh, he loves you, Margaret! Of course he does.' Jessica felt slightly awkward at the role reversal.

Margaret nodded. 'Oh I know, and I can't imagine things being different, not now. Too much water under the bridge and all that. But it was certainly different after Matthew was born. We were both utterly, utterly besotted with him. Still are. I think Anthony found it difficult to love more than one person, or maybe I just wasn't used to sharing him. I don't know.'

'God, and there was me hoping this baby would bind us even closer.' Jessica felt the sudden pooling of tears. They had been hovering much closer to the surface than usual in recent days, ready to roll at the smallest provocation.

'Oh, Jessica, don't cry! It will be wonderful. You and Matthew are a different kettle of fish. I can see you are best friends.' Margaret shook her head. 'Isn't that right, Coral?'

'Absolutely.' Coral thumbed her little girl's hand.

'Anthony and I were never as close as you two. In fact, Matthew is the one perfect thing we did right. Don't ever doubt what you are doing, Jess. You are going to make wonderful parents. I think we just loved Matt so very much and every decision we made, every plan, every thought was all about what was best for him. I would not change one single thing. I really wouldn't. But it did mean that as a couple we got a bit lost. We are parents first and foremost, but we used to be lovers first and foremost. I know some couples manage to retain all that, but not us.' Margaret straightened and replaced the sock in the drawer, next to its identical twin. 'Goodness me, I don't know how we got on to that!' She bristled. 'You have done so well in here, you know.' She ran her fingers over the hemmed fabric of the Roman blind. 'These are a good idea, aren't they? Very practical. Were they expensive?'

Jessica shrugged. She didn't know. Compared to what?

'I think I'll go and powder my nose.' Margaret left the

room. Jessica turned to her mum. 'Think we're all a bit emotional, Mum.'

Coral nodded. 'I think so. I don't tell you often enough, Jess, how very proud I am of you. Matthew is a wonderful catch, a professional man.' Jessica knew her grandparents had wanted more for her mother than to marry the salesman with the chirpy manner. 'You have this lovely home, a wonderful kitchen, a good car and he absolutely adores you.' At this Coral clapped.

Jessica didn't want her achievements to be measured by what her husband had acquired in terms of cars and a designer kitchen but knew that it was how her mum and dad gauged success. She was torn. 'I really love him, Mum.' This was the truth. 'We're a good team, always have been. He puts up with me and I make him laugh; it seems to work.'

Jessica thought of their evenings spent laughing over a bottle or two of wine, dancing around the kitchen or scrabbling for the best spot on the sofa and snuggling up to watch a crappy movie together under a soft blanket. 'I don't think things will change that much after the baby arrives. We are going to do it together and I'm determined not to become one of those couples who can't stay out past half past six and that walks into the pub like a human game of Buckaroo, weighed down with bags, bottles, toys and a bunch of nannies in tow, just in case.' She smiled at her mum. 'We plan on letting this baby become part of our lives, not having it take over our lives completely – if that makes sense.'

'Oh, it makes perfect sense, my love. And sounds wonderful, very sensible...'

'I feel a "but" coming on.' Jessica folded her arms and sat them on top of her rounded bump.

'But it's absolute rubbish.' Coral laughed. 'One look at that little face and you will do like the rest of us and fall in love. It's as if there is this balloon of love that fills you up so completely, there is no room for anything else. What that child wants and when they want it become the most important things in the world. You'll see.'

Jessica smiled at her mum. She couldn't wait for it all to happen. 'I've got something to show you.' She opened a drawer and removed a framed picture, holding it close to her chest. 'It's your grandchild.' She beamed.

'There you are!' Polly barged into the nursery, interrupting them. 'Phew, don't blame you, hiding up here. I've had about as much ribbing as I can stand: they are all going on about my new man, taking the piss. Excuse my French, Mrs M.'

Coral sniffed.

Jessica looked at her friend, who was clearly enjoying the ribbing. Polly and Paz were spending more and more time together and things were going great.

'So what do you think of our picture?' Jessica briefly flashed the image at her mate before handing it to her mum.

Polly squinted over Coral's shoulder. 'I can't really make anything out!'

Jessica found Polly's honesty irritating. 'What do you mean? Of course you can!' She pointed at the image. 'Look, that's clearly the face and the tum and you can even make out a little nose!' She purred.

Polly took the frame from Coral and, holding it up to her

nose, squinted hard. 'No. I can just see a blob thing. Oh, wait a minute... is that it?' She placed her finger on a dark shadow.

'No.' Jessica pulled the picture from her friend's grip. 'That is my bladder.'

'Oh! I was just going to say how much it looked like you!'

'Bugger off, Polly.' Jessica decided to ignore her friend. She beamed as she looked at the outline of her baby. She ran her fingers over the image and smiled at her mum, whose face was flushed with happiness. She couldn't wait for July the twenty-seventh.

'Anyway, enough! We are wasting precious time.' Polly clapped. 'I came to tell you we are just about to play "The Worst Godmother in the World". We all have to give a truthful reason why we can't possibly be considered for the post. I thought I stood a good chance with my drug arrest and everything.'

'Oh, Polly!' Coral squeaked and tutted, hoping Margaret hadn't heard.

'Never charged, Mrs M, never charged!' She wagged her finger. 'Anyway, it's a bit irrelevant. I think Gwen's going to win. Apparently she accidentally left her young cousin on a ferry bound for the Isle of Wight!'

'Oh, the poor child!' Margaret gasped, having heard the tail end of the conversation from the hallway.

'I know, right?' Polly nodded. 'They got him back though. Bit shaken, but unharmed.'

'Oh, I wasn't thinking he might be harmed, I just pity anyone that has to go to the Isle of Wight. Horrible place.'

Polly and Jessica fell against each other in giggles.

'Oh for goodness' sake, you two!' Coral reprimanded them and they laughed even harder, just as they had been doing since they were small.

Four hours later, the kitchen was still awash with cava, a baby-shower gift from Matt's parents, and pale pink and blue streamers. The floor was sticky underfoot and mountains of wrapping paper crowded the kitchen table and mingled with the remains of the cake. Jessica and Matthew decided to shut the door on the mess and deal with it tomorrow as they retreated to the sitting room.

'Did everyone have a good time?' he asked.

'I think so. It was very noisy – I bet Mrs Pleasant wishes she had accepted her invite and not had to listen through the wall!'

Jessica clambered onto the sofa. This was her favourite time of the day: early evening, when she could lie against her man and talk through things, knowing that her bed awaited her.

She was working on an idea that she wanted to submit to the agency. She stretched her legs out on the cushions and rubbed her feet together. 'You should have seen your mum's face today, it was priceless. She turned to Polly and said, "What is a Kardashian?" Oh God, I wish you'd been there!'

'I'm glad I wasn't, don't think I'd have coped with the Measure the Cervix game, although Jake would have loved it.'

'Oh, don't! Polly did suggest getting Paz in to read our

cards. I drew the line at that one. She's left loads of her stuff here – her black yoga bag full of sweaty kit, a box of books and a large plant. I've shoved it all under the stairs.'

'Christ, she's not moving in, is she?' Matthew bit his fingertips in mock terror.

'No! I think maybe she's storing things here to get a step closer to moving in with Paz.'

'Don't know who I feel more sorry for. She's stitching him up, planning his future, even though they've only just met. And God help her, the bloke's a nutter.'

'Matt, remember, we are going to give him the benefit of the doubt until we know him better.'

'I am.' He nodded. 'But he's still a nutter! I mean, *Toe-Paz...*' He shuddered.

'*We* should think about names.' Jessica grinned up at her man, knowing he found this too tricky to consider after a glass or two of wine.

'No need, I am still sold on Phil after Phil Parkes.'

'Ain't gonna happen.' Jessica shook her head. 'But I do like Leo and Noah or Joe, for boys.'

'I like Noah too, but it's a no-no.'

'Why?'

'Guy at work's just got a Noah, so that's out.' Matthew shrugged.

'Guy doesn't have the monopoly on Noahs!' she protested.

'True, but he and I have this unspoken competition thing going on. We're similar ages and abilities. He is definitely the biggest threat to my promotion and he plays golf, which I don't.'

'So?' Jessica was struggling to see what this had to do with picking their child's name.

'Magnus plays golf and Guy's always talking about bloody grand slams and bogies…'

'Urgh! Bogies!' Jessica knew it was childish, but laughed anyway.

'The point is, he makes it his thing because it excludes me and he got Noah first and he'd only rib me over it.'

Jessica bit her thumbnail. 'So that leaves Leo or Joe?'

'Joe Deane sounds a bit two syllabley – Leo Deane's better.'

Jessica laid her head on her husband's chest. 'Good. I like Leo best. He'll be strong, lion-like.'

'Absolutely.' Matthew liked the sound of that. 'And for a girl?'

She sighed. She'd given it a lot of thought but tried to make it sound casual, like they were choosing together. 'I rather like Bethan, Beth, Beth Deane. It's a great name. There was a girl in my class at primary school called Bethan and I wanted to be her, she was lovely.' She blinked against his shirt and waited for his response.

'Well, I'm glad you aren't her, I'm glad you are you!' He kissed her hair. 'How about Lilly? Lilly Deane is good.'

'Lilly Deane sounds a bit like a music-hall act: "And now, all the way from the streets of Bow, it's the famous Lilly Deane and her musical spoons!"' She laughed.

'Oh no, I don't want Lilly Deane to be a spoons player; I want her to be a supermodel!' Matthew declared.

'No you don't! You want her to be a botanist or an artist.'

'Do I?'

'Yes!' she shouted.

'So you like Lilly?' he pushed.

'I do, but only Lilly the botanist.' She smiled.

'I've always thought Lilly was a cool name, like Lily Cole or Lily Allen.'

'But I still prefer Beth,' Jessica asserted. 'I've always liked it. And I quite like Elsa.'

'Elsa, that's another lion name – have you been watching *Born Free*? If this is the route we're taking, what about Simba?'

Jessica laughed. 'No, Guy can have Simba for his next one.'

Matthew sighed. 'Shall we agree to disagree and see what we get?' he asked.

'Yep.' Jessica nodded. 'But it's good to have a top three at least.' *So that's settled. Leo for a boy and Bethan for a girl!*

'Absolutely.' Matthew took a large sip of his wine. 'Exciting, isn't it?'

Jessica nuzzled closer to her man, resting her head on his arm. 'It really is.'

20th January, 2014

I loved hearing my mum say that stuff at the baby shower about falling in love with me at birth. But then I remembered the time she took me shopping when I was about seven. We went into the only children's clothes shop on the High Street, run by a woman she knew from slimming club. I didn't really like the clothes – they were fussy and impractical, with too many buttons, itsy-bitsy ribbons and voluminous underskirts – but everyone wanted them because they were French. I pretended I did too, because I didn't want to be the odd one out. Anyway, my mum had no intention of buying anything: the clothes were way overpriced and out of our league. The woman was called Irene; she was short, had wild curly hair and wore scarlet lipstick. She greeted my mum loudly, as though they were great mates, and swooped forward and kissed her. As she did so, her sickly-sweet perfume tickled my nose. My mum was a little ruffled, to put it mildly; she didn't kiss anyone, not even us that often. Irene then glanced at me and said, 'Oooh, this little duckling might yet become a swan!' I felt tears gather as my cheeks burned and my heart beat loudly in my throat. I might have only been seven, but I knew she was calling me an ugly duckling.

Two things hurt me that day. Firstly, I hadn't realised I was a gosling. I hadn't given any thought as to my attractiveness or whether I was pretty. I was just happy being me. The realisation was hard. And secondly, I was floored by the fact that my mum didn't say anything in my defence. Nothing. Instead, she laughed nervously as if in agreement and clutched her handbag. It's funny how those little things come back to you so vividly. I can see now, of course, that she was just laughing politely to put her friend from slimming club at ease. But back then, aged seven, it stung so much. And then later at the baby shower, I remembered it again, and felt suddenly hollow. I vowed that when I had my baby, I would think it the most beautiful creature in the whole wide world. I would never let anyone call it an ugly duckling.

Eleven

It was July the twenty-fourth. Jessica sighed, blinked and turned slowly onto her side. It was now quite routine for her to wake in the early hours and have to rethink her sleeping position. Her eyes narrowed as she tried to focus on the clock. It was 4 a.m.

'Urgh.' She groaned, very loudly. Though not trying to wake her husband exactly, a small part of her was irked that he got to sleep like a baby while the real baby that was growing inside her was busy nudging her awake and squashing her bladder until she paid it the attention it demanded. It bothered her a little that Matthew got to be one half of this parenting duo and yet for the past nine months or so had carried on leading a normal life. He slept through the night and didn't look like he had swallowed a beach ball. How was that fair?

Waking at this ungodly hour had become a habit. Jessica would toss and turn until 6 a.m., when she could stand it no longer and, driven by boredom, would pop Matthew's sweatshirt over her pyjamas and go in search of tea and crap television. Then, as if Old Father Time was playing a trick on her, at 8 a.m., when the rest of the world was gearing up for the day ahead, she would be so drowsy she could sleep for hours.

She found some relief for her aching back and cramping legs by placing a small cushion between her thighs and moving onto her side. Reaching down to locate the cushion, which had previously sat on the spare bed in the guest room, she realised to her horror that she had wet herself.

'Oh God! What on earth?' Mortally embarrassed, she pulled her hand above the duvet and ran her thumb pad across the underside of her fingers. They were wet. Jessica reached over with difficulty and snapped the bedside lamp to life. Her heart rate slowed when she saw that it wasn't blood. She surreptitiously sniffed her hand; it smelt sweet and definitely wasn't pee. 'Okay. Okay.' She took a deep breath, realising that her waters had broken. This was quickly followed by the awareness that she had a new sensation in her stomach. It was a grumbly pain sitting in her lower abdomen, a bit like period pain, but tighter. She rubbed at the skin, taut across her swollen womb, and breathed out.

'Matt.' She gently rubbed his back. He made a small groaning noise, but remained on his side, deep in sleep. 'Matt!' She spoke a little louder and her rubbing turned into a small thump.

'What?' he croaked. This was never a good time for him.

'My waters have broken.'

'It's too early,' he mumbled and pulled the duvet up over his shoulder from where it had slipped.

'What do you mean it's too early?' Jessica sat up in the bed. She jabbed him in the back with her elbow. 'I'm having the bloody baby, Matthew!' She started laughing as the full realisation of what she was about to do flooded her body and brain.

Matthew pushed himself up into a sitting position and opened one eye fully. His hair was flat on one side, the other stuck up like a 1970s Gonk. 'What, really? What, now? How do you know?' He blinked furiously and rubbed his face.

Jessica nodded. 'I'm sitting in a pool of amniotic fluid.' She lifted the duvet and looked beneath it briefly. 'In fact, so are you.'

'Jesus Christ!'

Jessica laughed as her husband leapt from their marital bed as if he'd been stung.

He felt around on the floor for his pants. 'Aren't you supposed to be screaming and gripping the headboard or something?'

'I'm not really sure what I'm supposed to be doing. I've never had a baby before.' She smiled, patting the duvet flat around her.

'How do you feel?' He sat on the side of the bed and pushed his arms through the long sleeves of his QPR shirt.

'I feel okay, excited, nervous and happy!'

'Good, good. That's all very good.' Matthew exhaled through bloated cheeks. 'I'm feeling quite nervous too.'

'I can tell, Matt. You have your pants on back to front.'

Matthew looked down. 'Isn't it bad luck to reverse your clothes once you've put them on the wrong way round? I think it might be.' He put his jeans on over the top of his back-to-front pants.

Jessica studied her man. 'Are you sure you want to wear your football shirt? I don't want to sound like an old nag, but there will be photographs taken that we will want to keep, possibly forever and ever, and you will be immortalised in your QPR top.' She chewed the inside of her cheek.

'Exactly! That's why it's perfect. Plus I want Leo Anthony to see these beautiful blue and white hoops the moment he is born!' He pulled the fabric away from his chest and raised it to his mouth for a kiss.

Jessica rolled her eyes. 'Or your daughter...' she offered. *Bethan, my little Beth...*

'Yep. Or her. In fact, this is perfect – if it is a girl, she might marry a footballer who plays for QPR!' Matthew's face lit up at the idea.

Jessica lifted the duvet and shouted down into the depths, 'Stay where you are, baby. Your dad has lost the plot.' She resurfaced and looked at her husband. 'I don't really want that to be our daughter's highest aspiration.'

'Why not? They're loaded.' He grinned.

'Have you been talking to your mother?' she asked playfully. 'Ooh, ouch.' Jessica's expression changed as she sat forward and drew breath. The internal punch came out of nowhere. 'Shit, that hurt a bit.'

'You okay?' Matthew stroked the hair from her forehead. She nodded, feeling decidedly less perky than she had a minute ago. 'Are you going to be all right to sit in the car or shall I call an ambulance?' he asked, concerned.

'No, I'll be fine. We can just go slowly, right?' She didn't admit to the tiny tremor of fear that travelled up her spine. If this was how she was feeling at the beginning...

*

Jessica buckled herself into Edith, stretching the belt as far as it would go across her vast bump. She watched Matthew coming out of the house. Just as he was about to shut the front door, he dived back inside; he had clearly forgotten something. She closed her eyes briefly. Hurry up, Matt, please. She considered beeping the horn, but didn't want to incur the wrath of Mrs Not Very at this ridiculous hour. He reappeared, grinning and holding a bag up. 'Your bag!' he mouthed.

She smiled and nodded through the slightly foggy glass. The bag had been packed and sitting by the front door for the last fortnight. Twice she had checked its contents and on both occasions had removed items that had been surreptitiously inserted between her nursing bra and super-absorbent sanitary towels. The first was a vodka miniature with a label attached saying: 'DRINK ME!' and the second a picture of Zac Efron cut from a magazine and placed inside a rather cheap wooden frame, with the words 'I'm the baby's real dad!' scrawled across the front. Jessica giggled as she pictured Polly's handiwork.

Matthew raised his hand, about to grab the knocker and slam the front door, but then he nodded in her direction and dashed back inside again.

'For God's sake, Matt!' Jessica ran her fingers over her forehead and simultaneously rubbed the flat of her palm across her tummy; she was feeling uncomfortable and getting the occasional flare of pain. Her nerves were building and Matthew's unhurried excitement was threatening to make her shout.

Finally he skipped up the path and jumped into the car, throwing the bag on the back seat before fumbling with the ignition. 'Sorry. First I forgot your bag and then I had to go back for change for the car park. How we doing?'

'Okay. I'm good. Let's just get going.' Jessica bit her lip, trying not to cry. She knew none of this was Matthew's fault, and she managed a watery smile.

'That's my girl.' He winked and flicked the indicator as he pulled away from their house.

St Saviour's Hospital in Shepherd's Bush was approximately fifteen minutes away by car. Jessica knew this as they had driven there in a practice run in the early hours only last month. She looked at the clock: it was 4.30 a.m., which meant they would beat the rush-hour traffic.

Every traffic light was green and in no time at all Matthew was pulling Edith up on the yellow lines with the words 'DROP OFF' painted on the tarmac. Jessica smiled as she realised that the next time she'd be getting into the car it would be with her baby in tow. A wave of excitement swept through her.

Once inside the hospital, she felt her breathing regulate and her muscles relax slightly. Just being in a building where people were on hand for every eventuality made her feel more confident. Matthew abandoned her to the care of a silent porter who plopped her in a wheelchair while he went off to park the car. She hoped he wouldn't be too long. She wanted him by her side.

The nurse that met them at the entrance to the delivery suite was very calm, bored almost. She leant her elbow on the reception desk as she scanned Jessica's notes and tapped her chewed Bic pen against her teeth. Jessica would have liked a bit more urgency or at least attention; she noted the scruffy, faded scrubs and the way the woman's Crocs were heavily worn, sloping inwards. She decided this woman had the walk of an ambler – nothing was going to hurry her, not even the impending arrival of Leo or Bethan.

'We'll check you over and see what's happening,' bored nurse mumbled without looking up from the notes.

'I think what's happening is I am having a baby...' Jessica tried to make her comment humorous.

'Might be a false alarm; anything really.' She finally looked up.

'My waters have broken and I think I've started having contractions,' Jessica offered with a quiver of nerves. Supposing she had made a mistake? Was it her waters that had broken? Had she thoroughly checked? Could it have been pee? But she was in pain, of that she was certain.

'Okay, but things might still be a little way off.' The nurse smiled in a way that said she had seen it all before.

Jessica scanned the little room in which she found herself. The strip-lighting overhead was harsh and the suspended ceiling was stained with what looked like water damage from above. She was strangely glad of the sepia blobs and pondered them, trying to make countries out of the random shapes; one was almost Italy and another, if she squinted, a passable state of Texas. She sat on the bed with her back supported by four plump pillows that kept her upright. She was comfiest with her knees bent up towards her chest and her feet planted firmly on the plastic-coated mattress that crackled every time she moved or flexed her toes. The labour pains were occasional and each one was slightly more ferocious than the last. As the latest one subsided, she heard Matthew's laugh in the corridor. He pushed open the door, waving to the bored nurse and chuckling as he did so.

'Where on earth have you been?' Trust him to be making friends with the gloomy, Crocs-wearing woman. She hated the fact that she was alone in the brightly lit room while he was enjoying a jolly good laugh somewhere else.

'Oh God, you wouldn't believe it,' he puffed. 'Parking is a bloody nightmare even at this time of night. I don't know why anyone has a car in London, I really don't. They are more trouble than they're worth, even Edith! Think I might take Boris's advice and get a bike.' He sighed. 'That nurse seems nice.' He pointed to the corridor.

She ignored him.

'How are you doing, love?'

Jessica swallowed her irritation at the fact that only after discussing the traffic problems in W12 and how well he got on with his new nursey best friend, finally – finally! – he wanted to know how she was!

'I'm good,' Jessica muttered as tightness spread from the base of her stomach to the tops of her thighs. As a new contraction threatened, her legs began to shake. 'Oh shit!'

'What is it? Shall I get someone?' Matthew bent towards her, hovering an inch from her face, his fringe dangling close to her nose.

'No,' she breathed. 'Just move out of the way!'

'Right, sorry.' Matthew straightened and paced by the window. 'You are doing great,' he added for good measure.

'I haven't done anything yet!' she shouted.

'I know, but I was trying to motivate you. I read it in my book.'

This made her laugh despite the encroaching pain; she chuckled as she gripped her knees. 'Can you get the lavender oil out of my bag,' she managed, remembering her birth plan and that to combat anxiety she was going to inhale the sweet scent and let nature's essence work its magic.

'Yes of course.' Matthew scampered around the bed and retrieved the bag, glad to have something to do. He placed it on the bed. Unzipping the sides, he pulled out a jar of spirulina powder, a mesh bag full of misshapen crystals and a pair of neon-green Lycra leggings. Jessica instantly recognised them as her friend's belongings.

'What the...?' Matthew shook his head, confused.

'Oh no, Matt! Please, no! This is Polly's yoga bag. Not my maternity bag. What am I supposed to do with a sodding yoga mat and a block of rose quartz?' She grimaced.

Matthew looked from his pregnant wife to the items in his hands. He hastily shoved them back into the bag and zipped it up. 'One day we will laugh about this, Jess.' He smiled.

'One day maybe, but not today!' she shouted. Tears slithered across her temples as she threw her head back and almost instantly she started laughing.

'See, you're laughing already!' He was delighted.

'I know, but I really hurt and I'm a bit scared!' she wheezed.

'Then why are you laughing?' Matthew was unnerved by her giggles.

'I don't know!' Jessica wailed as she stared at the recessed spotlights in the suspended ceiling and thumped the mattress. 'Nerves, maybe. Do you remember when I shut my thumb in the car door but laughed because Mrs Not Very was watching and I didn't want to cry in front of her?'

'Yes.'

'Well, it's a bit like that.' She sighed.

'What, you think Mrs Not Very is watching?'

'No! Of course not!' She raised her voice and scrunched the top sheet in her fingers, in no mood for his humour. 'But it bloody hurts and I know people in the corridor can hear me, so I'm trying to stay happy and positive, even though I feel a bit shit.' Jessica took a deep breath and arched backwards; tears spilled from the corners of her eyes into her scalp.

'It's okay, baby.' Matthew smoothed her hair back over her forehead.

She lifted her head and smiled. 'I'm sorry.' She sniffed up her tears.

'Hey, don't be sorry. It must be scary. I wish I could magic it all over.'

Jessica saw his eyes crinkle with love and concern and it lifted her. 'Not too much longer and we will have our little baby.'

Matthew beamed at the realisation. 'I can't wait.' He gripped her hand.

'Me neither.'

The wave of pain subsided, a midwife came and went, things seemed to have slowed.

Jessica dozed. Matthew half straddled the mattress and with one foot on the floor, he held her close.

Opening her eyes, Jessica shifted her position and looked at her husband. He was drooling onto his QPR shirt. He snored loudly and woke himself up. 'Oh, hello, you.' He smiled. 'How are you? Any action?'

Jessica shook her head. 'I feel like a fraud. It was all happening so fast and now nothing. What will they do if nothing happens?'

'Well it's got to come out eventually.'

'Thanks for that, Einstein.' She shoved Matthew in the ribs and watched as he wobbled and slid from the mattress until both feet were firmly on the floor.

'Think I'll adjourn to the chair.' With his hands on the small of his back, he lumbered across to the blue vinyl chair by the side of the bed and plopped down into it.

'Do you want to play I Spy or Who Am I?' he offered cheerily.

'Neither. I want to play Let's Get this Bloody Baby Out and Go Home to our Comfy Warm Bed and our Nice New Nursery!' Jessica wriggled further down the mattress and smiled at the thought.

Matthew stood and bent in to kiss his wife on her forehead. 'It won't be much longer, Jess.'

Jessica raised her arms and leant forward to kiss her husband. At that very instant a powerful stabbing pain ripped through her lower abdomen. This was in a different league to any contraction she had previously experienced.

'Oh God... Matt!' Her eyes were squeezed shut as she held her breath and shrank back against the pillows, gripping the blanket inside her knotted palms.

'Shall I get someone?' Matthew hovered, placing his

hand over her bunched fingers and trying not to let the panic show in his voice. He had never seen her in pain like this and it scared him.

Jessica nodded as sweat poured from her forehead, her cheeks flushed, her face contorted. Matthew yanked the red cord that dangled loosely against the wall over her head.

'It's okay, Jess. It's all going to be okay. Hang in there, baby.' He looked towards the door. 'Where the fuck is everyone?' he shouted as he made his way over to it.

'Don't... don't leave me!' she managed through gulps of air that fuelled her pain.

'I have to leave you to go and get someone, but I am literally only going to poke my head outside and I'll be straight back. No one is responding to the cord!' He yanked at it twice more as he looked into her eyes. 'I'll only be a second. I promise.'

Matthew let go of her hand and ran from the room. As the warm gush of blood flowed over her inner thighs, Jessica sensed the bright lights swimming in front of her eyes. The room spun as if she was drunk. She looked above her head and tried to focus on the red cord that flickered in and out of focus. She wanted to pull it again, she wanted Matt to come back and she wanted someone medical to come and help her, but to reach for the cord or even call out felt impossible. She felt herself slipping as if drugged. Though she knew she had a job to do, a baby to deliver, she couldn't resist the black mass that pulled her in, sending her tense muscles soft and throwing a welcome veil of indifference over her panic.

14th March, 2014

Today we had a visit from the priest. He made his way along the corridor, popping into rooms with his usual fixed, happy smile and air of serenity. As one of the girls pointed out, it's all right for him, he only has to be here for an hour a week, no wonder he's bloody happy. I shy away from him, keep my distance, unable to look him in the eye. I don't want his words of kindness or understanding, as I deserve neither. His God knows what I have done. I do think about when I die and where I might go. When I was younger I used to wonder where Danny had gone. I would lie in my bed, trying to picture how something so solid could just disappear. Then I really did start looking at his bed and feeling sad and confused that he was not going to use it again. Half of me wished my mum and dad would throw all his stuff away so I wouldn't have to think about how he had disappeared and half of me wanted it preserved forever, so all I had to do was sit on his duvet and look at his books neatly lined up on the shelf, books that he had touched.

I went through a phase of picturing him sitting on a cloud with Grandad Maxwell and Flossy the rabbit; everyone we had ever lost all sitting together on their spongy white cushion, sharing memories and watching the world below as if we were tiny ants. I pictured them pulling crackers at Christmas. I realised one day that this was rubbish. There were no deceased relatives sitting on clouds: they would have dropped right through.

Graham Thornton was the cleverest boy in my school and he told me there was no heaven and that dead people were just like dead plants, but heavier. He told me that everything withered, died and returned to soil. I thought about this for years and it made a lot of sense: we were just like plants, but heavier and cleverer. But I still thought about the spark that Danny had, the things that made him unlike any other human, the stuff inside him – his soul, I suppose. Where did that go? I saw his soul as a mist, like smoke, that settled over those that had loved him. This would explain how Mum and Dad and all of us that had loved him still felt him close, because a little bit of him was settled on us.

Now I'm older and have time to think about this, and I do think about it a lot. I have almost come full circle. I remember asking my dad when I was little, 'What do you think, Dad? Do you think there is a heaven?' He sighed and said, 'Oh wow, now there's a question. Do I think there is a heaven?' I remember he looked skywards as though this might be where the answer lay. 'I think I don't know the answer to that, Jess,' he whispered, 'but if there is and there is a chance, just the smallest chance that we get to see those we've loved again, then I'm willing to keep an open mind.' I know those who have gone before don't sit in clouds, but I do think they might be in heaven. I hope that they are in heaven. Sometimes, sitting in my little room, I draw those I have loved, perching on the clouds. I always put Matthew in the middle. My baby, my beautiful baby, is an angel and I give her wings of elaborate feathers. I hope one day we all meet in heaven. I hope and pray with all my heart that this is true.

Twelve

Jessica was aware of the blink of the overhead strip-light and its irritating buzz, which drew her from sleep. She opened her eyes briefly and closed them again. She knew she had to concentrate, had to keep her lids open, but it was hard. The temptation to fall back into sleep was strong. She kept her eyes open long enough to realise that she was in a different room, a larger one. Her tongue was stuck to the dry roof of her mouth and every part of her hurt. Her bones ached and her muscles felt bruised. She was scared to move.

Staring at the ceiling, she noticed this one was pristine: no sign of Italy or the state of Texas. Her fingers flexed against the cool sheets. She felt confused and groggy. She plucked at the hospital gown that she was wearing, disliking its papery texture and wondering where her own nightie was. Slowly turning her head to the right, she was disappointed to see that she was alone; Matthew was nowhere to be seen.

The window blind was closed, but the silence of the hospital and subdued lighting told her it was night-time. How could that be? How much time had passed? It had been early morning when she arrived. *Baby*. The word leapt into her mind and the fog began to clear. Of course! She had been there to have a baby. What had happened? She placed her palm on her stomach, felt the wadding beneath her gown and she knew her baby was gone from her, but where was it now?

Using her arms to pull herself up slightly, Jessica managed to get into a sitting position, despite the sharp pain across her abdomen and the twinge in the back of her right hand as she flexed the cannula that was lodged there. She sat still for a few minutes before realising she was attached to a tube that snaked its way down the side of the mattress onto the floor. A catheter. She didn't know what had happened, but her instinct told her that it was something bad. Carefully sinking back down onto the mattress, Jessica lay very still and closed her eyes. Tears leaked from her as she tried to sift her jumbled thoughts. What had happened? Where was Matthew? And most importantly, had her baby survived? 'Matt…' she called weakly into the semi-darkness. 'Matt…' The darkness pulled at her senses as once again she slipped into a deep slumber.

It was some hours later that she heard Matthew's voice, which was quiet, soothing. 'Hey there.'

His words came from a space to the right of her head. She opened her eyes and looked first at the ceiling and then slowly turned to where her husband sat.

'Hey, my love. How are you feeling?' he whispered.

'Matt…'

'It's okay, Jess. I'm right here.'

'I don't…' Her voice was a warbled croak, issuing from a throat that was raw. Jessica lifted her arm, which felt peculiarly heavy as she ran her fingers over the base of her throat.

'It'll be sore, I expect, Jess. They put a tube down your throat to help you breathe. That'll pass in a day or so. Don't worry. Don't you worry about a thing. Everything is going to be just fine.'

I don't know what's happened. I'm in hospital. I hurt. I came here and I was laughing, I came to have a baby… baby… have I had my baby?

'Baby,' she rasped through parched lips, her eyes once again falling shut.

'Yes, Jess. Baby.' He sounded emotional, choked.

'Where?' she managed, wanting to ask so much more.

'Here she is. She's right here. We have a beautiful little girl and she is perfect!' Matthew stood up slowly and leant forward.

Jessica peered from beneath her heavy lids. In his arms was a wrapped white bundle, at the centre of which was a small squashed pink face. Jessica smiled, her eyes slowly blinking. *My baby! My beautiful, beautiful girl!*

'You did it, clever Jess. You did it! Say hello to your mummy.'

With tears in his eyes, Matthew tipped the blanket forward as Jessica lifted her fingers and clumsily stroked the side of her little girl's head. She felt warm to the touch. *Bethan, Beth… a little girl, my daughter.* The sedative once again pulled at her senses and she felt a deep sleep spread from her core and along her limbs until she had no choice but to succumb. She felt as if she was falling and did so with a sense of absolute peace, happy in the knowledge that her baby was safe. Her little girl, Bethan, resting safely in the arms of her dad.

The next time she opened her eyes, the fog of confusion had lifted a little. She felt a bit stronger than before, her arms felt less heavy and the raw scratch at the back of her throat had subsided to a dull ache.

'Ah hello, sleepyhead, how are you feeling?' The diminutive Indian nurse spoke as she entered the room and reached over Jessica's head to press a button on an upright machine behind her.

'Okay. Bit sore.' Her voice was still croaky. 'My husband was here...'

'Yes. He's popped home to freshen up and your little one is sleeping in the nursery. She is absolutely fine.'

Jessica smiled at the update. 'I feel horrible,' she confessed, her words slow and hoarse.

'You've had a Caesarean so you're bound to feel a bit tender, and the anaesthetic will make you feel groggy. You've had a rough old ride, poor love, but it all turned out okay in the end. They got to you in the nick of time and that's the main thing, right?' The nurse smiled, revealing fabulous even white teeth as she smoothed the blanket over Jessica's legs and reached for the thermometer in its little plastic holder. She popped a cover on it and inserted it into Jessica's ear, holding it until it beeped. Smiling, satisfied at the reading, she threw the little cone-like cover into the paper bag taped to the side of the bedside cabinet that served as a waste-paper bin and put the thermometer back in its holder.

'Your temperature is good, which means no infection, but we'll keep an eye on that. Do you need anything for pain right now?'

Jessica shook her head. 'I didn't know I was going to have a Caesarean.' She swallowed with difficulty. 'I had a birth plan.'

The nurse chuckled. 'Oh, birth plans are all well and good until something goes wrong and then they are chucked out the window and it's a case of doing whatever needs to be done to keep you and baby safe.'

So something went wrong. I don't remember. Why don't I remember? 'But she's okay now?' Jessica felt her heart hammer in her chest.

'Oh, she's safe and sound. Fed, watered, changed and as I said, sleeping right down the hall.'

Jessica nodded. It felt strange: she had a child that she hadn't properly met, a little girl who she hadn't seen born.

The nurse babbled as she filled Jessica's water jug. 'I fed her earlier and told her, "Lilly, your mum is going to be as pleased as punch when she sees you…"'

'Lilly?' Jessica shook her head slightly. Maybe the nurse had got the babies muddled. 'It's Bethan.' She was confused.

'Oh.' The nurse looked embarrassed. 'Well, I'll leave that for you and Dad to sort out. He seemed quite keen on Lilly, but you can always change it, of course.'

Lilly? That's not what we agreed.

'How long ago did I have her?' Jessica had lost all sense of time.

'Ah, well, let me see…' The nurse consulted the little fob

watch that hung upside down on her tunic. 'She is fifteen hours old.'

Fifteen hours... I was supposed to feed her. Jessica cupped her right breast, which felt as it always did. 'When can I feed her?'

'There's plenty of time for that. Her blood sugar was a bit low and she was hungry after her little adventure so she's had a few bottles of formula, but you can pick up right where you would be when you're ready. Okay?'

Jessica nodded. *Okay.* 'Can I go back to sleep now?' It was as if she had suddenly hit a new wall of tiredness.

'Of course! That's the best thing for you. Don't worry about Lilly, she's fine, and if she wakes up, I promise to bring her in. I'll just pull the door to and if you need anything at all, shout or pull the red cord over your head and we'll be straight in.'

'Thank you,' Jessica mumbled as she slid gingerly down the mattress, aware of the fresh wound across her abdomen. *Her name is Bethan. Beth.*

It was two hours later that Jessica was woken by the sound of the door opening.

'Good morning!' Matthew whispered as he wheeled in the plastic bassinet in which slept their daughter.

Jessica sat up as best she could and pushed her greasy locks behind her ears. 'Matt.' Her tears came quickly.

'Don't cry, darling. It's all going to be okay.' Matthew leant over the bed and cradled her awkwardly, not wanting to hurt her.

Jessica sniffed at her tears and closed her eyes, swallowing to try and alleviate the sting at the back of her nose.

'I'm sorry...'

'You don't have to say sorry. You've been amazing, Jess. I'm so proud of you.'

'I can't wait to hold her.'

'They are bringing her formula through in a second and then you can hold her and feed her, how about that?' he whispered.

Jessica nodded, staring at the fuzz of dark hair that poked from the top of the blanket in the bassinet. Relieved that she wasn't going to have to attempt breastfeeding, not just yet.

'She was going to be Bethan,' Jessica managed through her distress.

'Oh, I know, honey, but when I saw her, she was obviously a Lilly. She *is* Lilly! I didn't mean to go ahead and name her without you, it just kind of happened. I spoke to her and I said, "Hey there, Lilly!" And that was it. It stuck. The nurse then called her Lilly and then when I spoke to your parents, I said, "Lilly is here!" And that was that.' He gave a little laugh. 'Lilly is a beautiful name and I knew it was in your top three.' He sighed. 'Don't get upset, Jess; try not to think about anything. You've been through the mill. You both have.' He glanced at the little girl sound asleep beside them. 'But we have to put it all behind us and carry on. We are going to be an awesome little family and I am so grateful to have you both. I thought I might lose you.' Matthew exhaled as though limbering up and she noticed for the first time the dark, bruised hollows beneath his eyes. He caressed the back of her hand with his thumb, carefully avoiding the cannula.

'What happened to me?' Jessica sniffed her tears back down her throat.

Matthew shook his head and perched on the side of the bed. Jessica winced and tensed in anticipation of him coming too close to her tummy, which was very, very sore.

'After your contractions slowed, I thought things were going great. We were having a laugh in the delivery suite and then suddenly you were in terrible pain...' He closed his eyes at the memory.

'I remember that.'

'I didn't know what to do. I was shit scared, Jess. Totally shit scared. It was the worst moment of my life. I went to get help, I was only gone for seconds, literally, and when I came back into the room with the doctor, you were slumped, unconscious. It was awful. Things happened very quickly and the team here was marvellous. They shoved me out of the room – I asked to stay with you, but they wouldn't let me. They got you ready for theatre and wheeled you away. I just sat in the corridor and waited while they gave you a Caesarean. The longest hours of my life.'

Jessica nodded. That much she knew – as if the throb of the cut across her stomach wasn't proof enough.

'Your placenta ruptured, Lilly's heart rate dropped and she wasn't getting as much oxygen as she needed. And you were bleeding. Bleeding a lot...' He wiped his hand over his eyes and face as though trying to erase the image. 'It was all one God-awful panic. I don't want to go through that again, ever.'

'Oh God, Matt,' Jessica sobbed. The whole thing could not have been further from the dewy-eyed bonding experience she had envisaged. She felt confused. It was as if Matthew was talking about someone else, like waking up after a drunken night and having no knowledge of how she had arrived at a particular place or what she had done to get there. It was scary and disorientating. 'I don't like it, Matt.'

'I understand that, Jess. But it's all okay now and that's the main thing.' He used his authoritative tone. 'Your mum and dad have been worried sick. I spoke to them this morning and told them everything was good now.'

The sound of gentle mewling came from the crib. Matthew, as if programmed, hopped down off the bed and gathered their tiny daughter into his hands. 'Here she is and she is very keen to meet her mum!' Raising her gently and naturally as though he had been handling delicate newborns all his life, he supported her head and placed her in the crook of his wife's arm.

'She's tiny,' Jessica observed as she peeled back the blanket and studied her daughter in the pale pink onesie that Matthew's mother had bought. It swamped her. The sleeves were delicately rolled over her minute wrists and a surplus of material hung over her feet and pouched around her tummy. The first thing Jessica noticed was how light she felt against her arm, more like a little bag of bones than a real person. Then she took in the covering of thick, dark hair that stood up on her head as if it had been styled. Her tiny bunched fists darted about in front of her face, batting at some unseen object and her legs kicked and curled inside the terry-towelling suit. Her nose was a little flat and her eyes were tightly shut. Her fingernails were so tiny, and they were already a little too long.

'Isn't she beautiful?' Matthew stared at his daughter with an expression of pure joy.

Jessica nodded. She ran her finger over the rounded cheek of this little baby that was hers. She lifted her towards her face and inhaled the scent of her. She smelt wonderful.

A different nurse came into the room with a bottle of formula. 'Here we go, Mummy.' She beamed brightly at Jessica. The novelty of being able to call new mums by their title clearly hadn't worn off.

'Can *you* do it, Matt?' Jessica felt the swell of panic in her chest at the thought of having to feed her. She raised the child in her arms and watched as Matthew swooped and cradled his daughter to his chest. Her head rested neatly under the crook of his chin, where she fitted perfectly.

'Yes, of course. Don't you feel up to it?'

Jessica shook her head.

'That's understandable, Jess. Your body's had a shock. All in good time, my love.' He nestled back against the blue vinyl of the chair and fed his daughter, cooing and talking to her as he did so.

Jessica watched as the little girl's mouth sucked and gulped on the yellowy milk. She wished Bethan – no Lilly: she'd have to get used to that name – would go back to the nursery, leaving her and Matthew alone. All she wanted was to lie in her husband's arms and for him to tell her once again that everything was going to be fine.

Some time later, Jessica was woken by her mother-in-law's squeal. Margaret Deane came into the room ahead of her husband and smiled at her daughter-in-law as she dived towards the chair in which Matthew sat cradling their newborn. Her arms were outstretched, the navy cardigan balanced across her shoulders spreading like a little cape against her back and her fingers grasping the air as if she were up for a medal on the finishing line.

'Oh my goodness! Oh my, will you *look* at her! She is adorable.' This she addressed over her shoulder to her husband, who lumbered through the door with an enormous bunch of yellow roses obscuring his view and throwing him a little off balance.

'Quite hard to see anything at the moment, Margaret, I've got my hands full of bloody flowers!'.

Jessica watched as Matthew stood and gently handed Lilly to her grandma.

'Oh my! Oh look at you, my little darling!' Margaret's voice was thick with emotion as she hunched her shoulders and splayed her hands as though she were receiving a gift so fragile, the slightest movement or puff of wind might spirit it away. Jessica watched the tears course down Margaret's cheeks and noted the way she gazed lovingly at her husband, as though the act of holding her granddaughter had transported her back to that delivery room twenty-four years ago. The feel and smell of this newborn powerfully igniting the memory and the moment she became utterly, utterly besotted.

'Well, well! This is quite a moment.' Anthony Deane placed the huge bouquet of flowers on the side table and stood close to his wife. His hand rested on the small of her back and as he stared at Lilly Rose over his wife's shoulder, he turned and gently kissed her on the scalp; it was the most tender act Jessica had witnessed between them.

Anthony coughed and swallowed the emotion that threatened. Finally he turned to his daughter-in-law. 'Oh, Jess! Congratulations! Well done, my girl.'

'Hello, everyone!' Roger called from the doorway. He walked in beaming and clutching a pink teddy bear with a ribbon around its neck. Coral tripped in behind him, sporting a large badge that said: 'I'm a Granny!'

'Hello, darlin'!' Coral bent forward and kissed her daughter on the cheek. Jessica felt her tears pool. The relief at seeing her parents made her cry.

'Liking the badge, Coral!' Margaret smiled.

'That's good, Margaret, because I got you one too.' Roger pulled a second badge from his pocket and handed it to Anthony, who flipped it back and forth to make the pearlescent background change colour.

'Did I get one?' Anthony joked.

'No, mate, we've got these.'

Jessica watched as her dad pulled three tubed cigars from his shirt pocket and gave one to Anthony and one to Matthew. The men laughed, unified in their delight and excitement at the new arrival.

Margaret walked over and popped the tiny bundle into Coral's arms, who placed her lips against her granddaughter's head and closed her eyes. 'Hello, little one. Hello, Lilly. I'm your nan.'

Roger sat on the side of the bed and peered at the little girl's face. 'Oh, Jess, she's a proper stunner, just like her mum.' He leant over and kissed his daughter on the cheek. 'Had a rough old time, I hear.' He smiled as he stroked her hand.

Jessica nodded. 'A bit.'

'But all worth it, eh, Jess? And now your adventure really begins.'

She nodded. Again. Ignoring the quake in the pit of her stomach.

'My baby girl has a baby girl! How unbelievable is that?' He grinned.

'It is unbelievable,' she managed.

'Granny Maxwell would have eaten her up, that's for sure!' Roger smiled. 'She loved babies and she adored you. She's probably watching over you right now.' He patted her hand. 'And Danny. I bet he's pleased as punch for his little sister.' He swallowed.

Jessica nodded, meekly.

'Polly been in yet?' Coral asked casually, while repeatedly mouthing 'Hello' at Lilly Rose.

'No, not yet.'

'Do not leave her alone with this baby for a second. Before you could say jackrabbit, she'd have her ears pierced and a matching cherub tattoo on her little bottom.' She smiled knowingly at her daughter.

Matthew chuckled. 'Oh, don't! I'd kill her.' His voice caught in his throat. 'Anyone hurts so much as a single hair on Lilly's head and I'll kill them!'

Jessica was struck by the passion in his tone.

Roger laughed loudly. 'Now you know how it feels, Matthew. And believe me, that feeling only intensifies. Wait until she comes home from school and tells you Taylor was mean to her or, God forbid, she comes home with a rock on her finger and tells you she's in love with a bloody lawyer who supports QPR!'

'A lawyer who has given you Lilly,' Coral reminded him, nodding sagely.

Roger smiled. 'Ah, yes, and for that reason, Matthew, I will forgive you anything.' He winked at his son-in-law, whose cheeks flushed.

Emotions were running high and bouncing off the walls. Jessica watched those she loved engaged in the all-absorbing act of Lilly worship. She, however, felt more like an observer than a participant, a bit like the only sober person at a party, the only one who doesn't get the joke. She kept telling herself to smile. *Come on, smile!* This was supposed to be a happy day. She wanted everyone to leave so she could go back to sleep, but at the same time felt petrified of being left alone with her. Her. Her. Lilly, she meant Lilly. She didn't know who Lilly was. She had the overriding thought that she wasn't sure if she was hers – was she Lilly's mum? She hadn't seen her born, so how could she be sure? She knew it sounded ridiculous.

'Can you imagine not having her?' Margaret beamed, interrupting her thoughts. 'It's the weirdest thing, isn't it, Jessica? Even when they are absolutely brand new, like Lilly, you simply can't imagine not having them in your life. It's wonderful, isn't it? That instant love? Do you remember that, Coral?'

'I do indeed,' Coral murmured, unable to take her eyes from the baby in her arms.

Jessica stared at her mother, who looked star-struck, in love, besotted. Her words floated into her mind: '*One look at that little face and you will do like the rest of us and fall in love. It's as if there is this balloon of love that fills you up so completely, there is no room for anything else.'*

She couldn't stop the tears that spurted suddenly and without warning. She felt detached, disconnected from everyone and everything. She hurt, with every muscle aching in a different way, but it was more than physical discomfort that prompted her tears.

Coral noticed Jessica's stricken face against the pillow. She handed Lilly to Margaret. 'Poor love, you look so tired. It will all feel better after a good long sleep, I promise.' Coral's eyes crinkled in a smile and Jessica felt reassured by her mum's words. She didn't make promises lightly. Her dad nodded in agreement. Jessica wanted to believe that they knew best, but the trouble was she didn't just feel tired. She felt petrified. Panic clutched at her chest. What she wanted to say was, *'Take me home, Dad, please just pick me up and take me home. Carry me from the car and put me in my bed, set a glass of water on my bedside table and switch on my night light, tuck me in and leave the door ajar so you can hear me if I call... I don't know what's happened to me, Dad. I went to sleep and woke up and Lilly is here. I was expecting Bethan and I got Lilly. And Matthew has hardly looked at me because he can't tear his eyes from her and I look at her and feel... less than I think I should. All I want to do is go to sleep.'* But of course she didn't. Instead, she dried her tears on the tissue he offered and concentrated on keeping her smile in place.

7th April, 2014

You have to act sometimes, don't you? Hide your true thoughts or feelings. Make out one thing when you believe another. I do this in here all the time. I have to. I've a lot of time to think and I have met a lot of damaged people. I have learnt that you can't always tell good from bad, or right from wrong just by looking. And you can't always tell what someone believes from what they are saying. My doctor asked me to consider this and I do. I don't want to talk to anyone and I don't want to make friends. I get through this by being quiet and making myself invisible.

My therapist came into my room today and saw me sketching. I wasn't really thinking, just doodling, drawing swooping swirls that might have been clouds and shaded pools that looked a bit like puddles. Above one of the puddles I drew a face with spiky hair and tears pouring from the eyes and mouth that fell down into the puddle. I saw her eyes narrow, trying to decipher my random strokes. She had smiled, widely like I'd given a right answer. 'This is marvellous, Jess, really good that you express yourself, explore your thoughts through your art, is this something you are happy to do more of?' I nodded, mainly because I didn't want to disappoint her. She seemed so chuffed to see my random scrawl, funny really.

Thirteen

With her eyes closed and her pouchy tummy resting on her thighs as she hunched forward, Jessica sat on the closed loo seat in their bathroom and breathed very, very deeply. It was nearly two weeks since she had given birth and there was no sign of being able to zip up her skinny jeans, even if she had felt like changing out of her pyjama bottoms. Her scar had healed nicely into a pencil-thin red line that sat below her bikini line and the general soreness of her Caesarean had vanished. She could now stand upright without wincing. In truth, her body had bounced back well.

Opening her eyes, she stared at her reflection in the vast wall mirror and cringed at her appearance. Her hair needed a wash and she couldn't remember where her make-up bag was, much less when she had last delved into it. She ran her fingers through her fringe and bit her lips to give them a little colour. Not that it mattered how she looked, not really.

Lilly was crying. She had been crying for a minute and that was why Jessica was hiding in the toilet. She could hear Matthew pottering in the kitchen and knew that once he heard the baby monitor spring into life with its wailing siren, he would come running.

As if on cue, Jessica heard the heavy tread of her husband's footsteps as he bounded up the stairs, calling ahead, 'It's okay, Lilly, Daddy's coming. Don't cry, baby girl, I'm on my way!', followed by, 'Jess? Jess?' Whether intentional or not, she heard an accusatory tone in his call, and in her mind she fleshed out the subtext: *'Where are you? Why aren't you going to Lilly? She is crying and you are her mother and you should be running to her the moment she needs you...'*

'Sorry, Matt! I'm in the loo. A bit stuck. Have you got her?' she called through the closed door, smiling to add an authentic happiness to her voice.

'Oh right, no matter. Yep, I've got her!'

Jessica ground her teeth and listened to the sweet burble of banter that Matthew uttered every time he was with his little girl.

'Youarethemostgorgeousbabyinthewholewideworld! Yes you are! Yes you are!' Followed by the smack of his lips as he kissed Lilly's face. 'I could eat you up, Lilly! Yes I could! I could eat you in a sandwich!' And then more kissing.

Jessica felt her jaw tense and her fingers flex. Her jealousy flared from the smallest kindling and was immediately followed by a shot of guilt that fired through her veins and ricocheted around her stomach. *How can you be jealous? She is your baby, your little girl.*

'You okay in there, Mummy?' Matthew tapped gently on the bathroom door. She could hear Lilly hiccupping with relief and joy at being in her daddy's arms. 'We are going downstairs to make lunch and we'll see you down there!'

Jessica wasn't sure which she disliked most, his jovial tone or the way he called her Mummy and spoke on behalf of him and Lilly. She longed to have a conversation with just her husband. The way they used to.

Standing, Jessica stared at her reflection as she flushed the loo, reinforcing the charade. She ran her hand over her breasts, feeling nothing but relief that she had not been able to breastfeed her daughter. The midwife had clucked her tongue in sympathy and patted her arm as though offering an apology. 'Sometimes these things just happen,' she'd said. It didn't bother Jessica. With no milk production, there was no choice but to let Lilly continue on formula, the added advantage being that Matthew could take responsibility for the majority of her feeds, which he did very willingly, of course.

Come on, you can do this, Jess! Get your shit together and think positive. She tried to rally her reflection. *It's all going to be fine. It's all going to be just fine. So you're not like your own mum, with that instant love thing, that's okay. Everybody's different. For you, things might just take a little bit longer.* After taking one more deep breath, she crept down the stairs and made her way into the kitchen.

'We were just wondering whether you'd got stuck in that loo! Weren't we, Lilly? We were going to call the fire brigade.' Matthew addressed Lilly, who was lying in her Moses basket on its stand in the corner of the room, under the dresser.

'What's for lunch?' Jessica smiled, ignoring his comments.

'Oh, I thought the usual sixty-five mils of formula! Followed by a jolly good burp.' He waggled the bottle in her direction.

'I meant for us, idiot.' She sighed.

'Tell you what, you feed Lilly and I'll rustle up some cheese on toast. Sound good?'

Jessica nodded. 'Sounds great.' She hadn't had much of an appetite since having Lilly, but a quick bite of cheese on toast would be just the trick.

As Matthew handed her the bottle, Jessica felt the familiar squeeze on her intestines and an increase in heart rate as something close to panic spread from her core. The bottle sat awkwardly in her palm, slipping against her skin in a way that it didn't seem to for anyone else. Even her dad had looked like a pro as he jostled Lilly in one arm and with her feed in his other hand wandered around the kitchen, chatting to her idly as though he had been doing this forever. Jessica was only comfortable feeding her daughter in a certain position in a particular chair and preferably with no one around to watch. She crept over to the Moses basket and smiled down at her daughter, who kicked her legs up and grabbed at thin air, going cross-eyed with the effort of staring at nothing,

'Hello, Lilly. It's me, it's your mum.' She nodded.

'Of course she knows it's you! She loves you.' Matthew laughed as he reached for the block of Cheddar sitting alone in the depths of the fridge.

Jessica stared at him nervously. She knew he was trying his best, but even though his comment was meant to reassure her, it had the opposite effect, making her feel like she was saying the wrong thing. Why was this so hard? How could she begin to describe the embarrassment she felt at having to converse with a baby, her baby!

Reaching into the basket with one arm, she tried to scoop Lilly up with one hand under her little shoulders; realising she needed more leverage, she let her roll back down onto the soft mattress. Lilly, clearly unsettled by this lack of deftness, started to cry. Jessica saw Matthew's fingers twitch, desperate to take over, wanting to pick up his daughter with ease and juggle her mid air from one arm to the other as if to prove how easy it was.

Placing the bottle on the floor, Jessica tried for the second time. Using both hands this time, she lifted her little girl and placed her clumsily in the crook of her right arm. She then bent down awkwardly to pick up the bottle that sat by her feet. This wasn't so easy with the sting of her surgery flaring at any unusual movement. As she crouched, Matthew almost shouted, 'You have to support her head, Jess!' Unnerved and wide-eyed, she straightened and stared at the bottle, trying to figure the best way of picking it up without dipping too low or letting Lilly's head fall forward.

'C... can, can you bring her bottle through?' she almost whispered as she carefully made her way into the sitting room, walking as though trying to avoid broken glass, conscious of every step.

Matthew nodded silently and shoved the cheese back onto the counter top. Lunch could wait.

Jessica turned around and backed into the comfy chair upholstered in taupe linen that sat in the bay window of their Victorian home. With her left hand she pulled the cushion from behind her back and placed it in the gap below the arm of the chair; on this feather-filled pillow she rested Lilly's head. She exhaled, realising that she had been holding her breath.

'Here you go, love.' Matthew handed her the bottle, which she placed in Lilly's seeking mouth.

'She's a good little eater, isn't she?' he cooed. He placed his finger on the underside of the bottle. 'Just raise the end up a bit to make sure she doesn't swallow any air, then she'll settle better after.'

'Right.' Jessica nodded and lifted the bottle as if being instructed and wanting to take it all in.

Matthew sat at her feet and kissed her knee. 'It's all going to be okay, you know, Jess. Things will get easier when you are in more of a routine.'

She nodded, desperately hoping this was true.

'I think it's a good thing I'm going back to work tomorrow, it'll give you and Lilly a chance to get to know each other a bit better. And your mum's coming over for a couple of days, which will be fun.' He smiled. 'I know things haven't been that easy for you. I think it's because you had such a difficult birth and it was all a bit of a shock. Cathy the health visitor agreed.'

'I know,' she whispered.

'Do you want me to put Jake off?' Matthew asked.

'Hmmmmnn?'

'He's coming over for a cuppa this afternoon, would you like me to ask him not to?'

'Don't mind.' She shrugged. *Not Jake, please. Not today. I don't want to see anyone. Anyone.*

'He's desperate to see this little one.' Matthew stroked Lilly's little toes with his fingers. 'And I can't blame him, she is so beautiful!' There it was, the baby voice again... 'Must admit, I've missed the idiot. Be nice to catch up and I'm sure he won't stay long.'

Jessica nodded and kept her eyes on her baby. An hour later, Jake's booming voice shattered the fragile peace. 'Hey, amigos!' he shouted as he stepped inside the hallway.

Jessica felt the sleeping Lilly jump in her arms. She closed her eyes and tried to dig deep to find a smile and the warm welcome he would be expecting. She listened as he and Matthew chortled and bantered in the hallway, just like old times. She stared at the baby in her arms, hoping she wasn't going to wake up, not yet. Making mistakes with Lilly was bad enough, but doing so in front of an audience was worse.

'Well, well, well, Jessica Deane. Get you, you look like a mum!' Jake screeched as he came into the sitting room. 'Plonked there, looking knackered with your wee girl. How are you?' He bent to kiss Jessica, holding his jacket flat against his chest so as not to disturb Lilly.

'I'm good.' She smiled.

'You look like a natural,' he said. Her smile broadened. 'She's a bit small, I was expecting a larger model.' He raised his generous eyebrows and scrutinised the baby in her arms.

'She's a baby, Jake. They're meant to be small.' Matthew tutted.

'Suppose so.' Jake nodded. 'Does she look like anyone?' he asked.

'She looks like herself,' Jessica answered.

'Blimey, that's a relief. If she had a massive conk like her dad's, it would stand out a mile.'

'She happens to have the most exquisite nose ever created,' Matthew stated matter-of-factly.

'Oh, someone's got it bad!' Jake nudged his friend in the ribs.

'Mate, I am absolutely crazy about her. I knew I wanted to be a dad, but I had no idea how it would knock me for six. If anyone had told me I could feel like this about another human being, I wouldn't have believed them.'

Like you used to feel about me...

Matthew sighed. 'The moment I held her, it was like a punch to the gut. Like meeting Jess all over again, but more intense. She needs me, needs us. Having something so totally helpless rely on you is a huge responsibility but also the biggest privilege.'

There was a moment of silence while everyone considered Matthew's speech.

'Fucking hell, mate, you sound like Spiderman,' Jake said.

All three laughed and as Jessica dissolved into giggles, she felt a flicker of her old self reach up through the stifling veneer of motherhood and extend a waving hand through the crack.

'Polly been round with veggie bonkers hippy bloke yet?' Jake asked as he flopped down onto the sofa.

'Don't call him that. He's actually really nice.' Jessica felt the need to defend both her friend and Topaz, whose warmth and sincerity she had come to love.

'I didn't say he wasn't!'

'Calling him veggie bonkers hippy bloke is not a compliment, Jake!' Jessica felt the twitch of laughter on her face once again. It had taken the arrival of Jake in their home to remind her what normal felt like.

'Fair enough. Fair enough.' Jake nodded and raised his palm. 'I shall only refer to him by his real name of Topaz.'

And once again the three fell about laughing.

'Topaz? I mean, come on, Jess, what the fuck?' Jake roared.

Lilly slept on, oblivious. As Jessica laughed and chatted to their good friend with her baby girl in her arms, for the first time since giving birth she felt like a natural. *Maybe I can do this. I can.*

'Anyway, I don't want to be rude, but what does a man need to do to get a beer around here? If this is what parenthood means, you can shove it! I've been here for ten minutes and not so much as a cup of tea or a cold brewski. Your standards are slipping and I think it's all her fault!' Jake pointed at Lilly, who sighed and knitted her hands across her tummy as if on cue.

The doorbell rang. Matthew sprang up and Jessica heard her best friend's loud squawking. Her stomach flipped at the prospect of more guests.

She looked at Jake. 'Polly is really keen on this guy and you have to be nice and make him feel welcome.'

He threw his head back and laughed.

'I mean it!' she whispered. 'They are only popping in, so be nice.' She pointed her finger in his direction as if this somehow enhanced her threat.

'All right, Jess! Blimey, what's that tone for, are you practising your angry mummy voice?'

'I get plenty of practice with you around, Jake. I still haven't forgiven you for announcing to the whole wide world that I was pregnant!'

'Oh, thank God for that. I thought you were still mad at me for telling your parents about you and Matt shagging on your first date!' Jake raised his beer bottle in a self-congratulatory manner. 'I will of course be polite, but I bet he's a four-stone weakling with bad skin and a darting eye.' He shuddered. 'Vegetarians are always so worthy, desperate to tell you why meat is murder. I find I have very little in common with lentil munchers.'

Polly walked into the sitting room and curled her lip at Jake before smiling at her friend. 'Oh, Jess! Look at her! She is so beautiful, you clever girl. You look fantastic!' She graced her friend's cheek with a kiss. 'Can I hold her?' She rubbed her hands in anticipation as she sat down at Jessica's feet and took the sleeping Lilly in her arms.

'This is Topaz,' Matthew announced as they walked into the sitting room.

Jake looked from Polly's chisel-jawed beau to his mate. In their eyes, he ticked at least three boxes that usually invited derision: funny name, long hair and a collection of bangles and leather bracelets. Both recalled the time Scotty, their roommate at uni, had appeared after the summer break, sporting a leather thong around his neck and what looked suspiciously like highlights. He had been known ever since as Point Break.

'Congratulations, Jess. And you, Matt. You must be over the moon. Isn't it incredible?' He spoke as one who had plenty of experience of newborns.

'So, Topaz…' Jake paused as though expecting a ripple of laughter. 'That's an unusual name. Does it run in the family?' He shot Matthew a quick look before taking a sip of his beer. Ignoring Jessica's request for politeness, this line of questioning was entirely for his friend's benefit.

Topaz sat forward. 'Please, call me Paz. And actually no, it doesn't. I'm the first.'

'Really? You surprise me.' Jake feigned surprise.

Topaz joined his fingers and rested his elbows on his knees. 'I was actually christened Roland Raymond Jacques de Bouieller – it's the "Raymond Jacques de Bouieller" bit that gets passed on, so my elder brother is Simon Raymond Jacques de Bouieller. But my godfather took one look at my very blue eyes and called me Topaz. I was about two; we were at my parents' house in St Barts. It just kind of stuck.'

Polly smirked in Jake's direction. He hesitated, taken aback by the man's connections and apparent wealth. He stuttered briefly. 'So… so, Paz, you're a *yoga* teacher.' He smiled.

'Yes, yoga, meditation, spiritual health, that kind of thing.'

Jake looked at Matthew. 'And all that meditation gets you fit, does it?' He snickered.

Topaz stood and with two fingers gently lifted the hem of his white linen shirt to reveal a perfectly sculpted, tanned six-pack. 'Partly, but my mixed martial arts training and running help as well. I find that the combination and discipline of all three help maintain not only my fitness but my stamina too.' He let his shirt fall and ran his palms over his taut thighs.

Jake sucked in his slight paunch and turned to his friend. 'See the football at the weekend, Matt?'

Polly winked at Jessica. She loved watching Jake squirm. 'I don't think I'm ever going to let her go,' she gushed. Her eyes, which were fixed on Lilly, sparkled with tears. 'Holding her feels like the best medicine in the world.' She turned to Paz's tormentor. 'Have you held her, Jake?' she asked casually.

'No. I'm a bit too ham-fisted to be trusted with something so delicate. You know me, Mr Put-His-Foot-In-It Awkward Bastard.'

'Surely not?' Paz said and everyone bar Jake laughed loudly.

Matthew unbuttoned his shirt and threw it into the space behind the bedroom door where other items of dirty laundry lurked. 'It was nice to see everyone, wasn't it?'

'It was.' Jessica sipped from her water glass and settled back on the mattress.

'They loved Lilly.'

'They did.'

'Mind you, hard not to. Polly was surprisingly good with her, don't you think? Wonder if she's getting broody now that Paz is on the scene. Can't imagine Jake being a dad, though, can *you*?' Matthew stepped out of his jeans and hung them in his wardrobe.

Jessica shrugged. 'Don't know really.'

'I don't want to go back to work tomorrow. I've loved being home with my girls. I wish I could stay home forever and watch her all day. I don't want to miss anything.'

Jessica nodded, not trusting herself to comment for fear of the outpouring it might trigger.

Matthew dived onto the bed and wriggled over to where she lay. 'Come here, you,' he instructed as he pulled her towards him, pushing one arm beneath her until she was lying in his arms. He kissed her scalp and ran his palm over her shoulder and back as he kissed her neck.

Jessica tensed and placed her flattened palms on his chest, giving a small push. 'Don't! I can't... we can't do anything, Matt. The doctor said six weeks. So...'

Matthew pulled away and sat up. 'Christ, Jess, there's no need to look at me like that! I was only trying to make you relax. I was happy with a hug, I wasn't going to jump on you! I know what the doctor said. I was there, remember? And if you want to be specific, he said six weeks was a guideline, but if it felt comfortable before then—'

'It doesn't,' she interrupted, with more force than she'd intended.

'And don't I know it!' He gave a short derisory laugh.

'I'm sorry,' she mumbled. 'I just don't feel like...'

'No, I know. I know there's lots you don't feel like and that's fine.' His tone did not quite match his words. 'There's no rush. But don't ever push me away like that. We're on the same side, remember? And I love you.'

Matthew set the alarm, clicked off the lamp and turned onto his side. Jessica could see by the set of his muscles that he was far from sleep. She closed her eyes and waited for sleep. *I'm sorry, Matt. I'm sorry.*

17th May, 2014

The smiley nurse popped in today. Not a friend exactly, but a friendly face, which was nice. I see her occasionally when newbies arrive or she has to work in my wing.

'How are you doing, Jessica?' she asked, and not in the way the doctors or the guards do, but as if she really cared about my answer.

I put my sketchpad down and looked up at her. 'Bit better,' I said, which is the truth. I can't fully explain it, but since I have started drawing more, putting pencil to paper and sketching my thoughts and fears, it's as if I can exorcise the bad thoughts that have swirled around in there for too long. It certainly helps. And it helps my therapist see what I have difficulty in expressing.

Smiley nurse squinted at the pad. 'That's good.' She smiled and it felt good to know that in here there is someone that feels happy that I might be on the mend, even if she is just one person. 'What you drawing?' she asked, pointing to my sketch.

I lifted the page and let her stare at my pencil drawing of the Tramuntana mountaintops with the spiky trees and the terrace where the sun peeks over the iron railings.

'Wow, you're really good!'

I felt my heart swell at the compliment.

'Where is it?' she asked, folding her arms across her chest as though she had plenty of time to chat.

Again, I told her the truth. 'It's the place where I have been the happiest I have ever been. I think about it a lot.'

She smiled and said, ‘It’s good to have those places, isn’t it?’

I nodded. For me, it wasn’t only good, it was the one thing that kept me going, the thought that I might go there again and that happiness might be waiting for me.

Fourteen

At the sound of the front door closing, Jessica lay back against her pillow and took a deep breath. The day that Matthew had gone back to work, three weeks ago, had been a dark day. Jessica had spent the night before watching him iron his shirts and sort his notes, staring at him, imploring him to read her. She knew she should have been the one ironing his shirts – he had enough to think about with preparing to go back to work after a couple of weeks off – but she felt glued to the sofa. She feared giving voice to her ugly thoughts: 'Don't leave me, Matt, please stay here! I can't do it without you! I know I'm supposed to be getting the hang of it, but I'm not! I can't walk up and down the stairs with her as I'm scared I'll trip and fall. And how do I know when she has had enough bottle or when she needs a nap? How do you just know how to do these things and I don't?'

Now, as she heard him grab his keys from the console table and step outside into the big wide world, Jessica was overcome with desolation. It didn't matter how much she tried to reassure or remind herself out loud that all she had to do was stay at home, inside their beautiful house, and care for their healthy baby. It didn't even come close to easing the dark glue of despair that filled her completely. She was sensitive to the slightest hint of criticism. Just the thought that he and Cathy the health visitor had discussed her made Jessica feel so angry; her suggestion that the difficult birth had been a bit of a shock for her – well, no shit, Cathy! You think? Jessica's anger was quick to flare but even quicker to blacken into deep despair. She pictured her sadness like a thing inside her, creeping along her veins and settling into any void it could find. This dark mass was at present sitting below her throat and she knew that if not kept in check, it would rise up and drown her. This was her biggest fear.

She lay and let the cold blanket of dread wrap itself around her, wishing beyond hope that she could fast-forward the day until the sound of Matthew's key in the lock meant she could hand responsibility for Lilly over to him. There was nothing she could do to stop it. It mattered little whether it was sunny or raining, dark or light: every day felt like a challenge before it had even begun and it was exhausting.

Every offer of help from her parents or in-laws was accepted. Whenever she handed Lilly over, she felt ecstatic, but the high was quickly followed by a painful, guilt-ridden low. Jessica avoided the mother-and-baby groups, the gangs that gathered with their strollers, blocking the doors to coffee shops and swapping tips on parenting as they cooed over and compared each other's offspring. She wasn't like them. For her there was no healthy glow of motherhood, no bounce in her step as her post-pregnancy body shrank back into shape.

Jessica looked at the clock; it was 7 a.m. and already she felt utterly drained at the thought of what lay ahead. There was a knock of fear inside her chest at the prospect of spending hours alone with her baby. She closed her eyes and offered up a silent prayer. *Please, please let her sleep. Let her sleep and give me some peace. I can't do it. I can't do it all again today. I don't have the strength.* It was irrelevant that she had only just woken after a good nine hours, her night only briefly disrupted to settle Lilly, who had cried out and then gone straight back off.

Throwing her duvet in an arc from her body, she slid to the side of the bed and carefully pulled herself into a sitting position. Her feet reluctantly thumped against the floor; even getting out of bed required the utmost effort. She had a vague memory of herself running into the bedroom and leaping onto their bed, landing Matthew with a push as they both laughed and shed their clothes. It seemed like another person, one she could hardly relate to.

Jessica sat on the loo, reminding herself not to flush the handle – anything not to wake Lilly one moment before she had to. Creeping from the darkness of their en suite – she hadn't wanted to risk the click of the light switch – she leant forward on all fours on the mattress and prepared to lay her head in the nest of pillows that she had only just vacated, when the faltering bleat of her baby drifted across the hallway.

'No, no no! Please no.' Placing her hand over her mouth and closing her eyes, Jessica stayed still for a second or two, hoping that it was a mere blip and that Lilly would simply find her thumb and soothe herself back to sleep. There was a moment of silence. Jessica exhaled. She smiled. Even if this silence lasted mere minutes, she would make the most of it. It was in the very second that her head touched the pillow that Lilly started wailing in earnest.

Jessica pushed her face into the feathery depths and cried fat, hot tears that clogged her nose and throat. She forced herself up from the mattress. With leaden limbs she shuffled across the hallway and stood in the open doorway of the nursery. 'Shhhh…' she managed between gulps. 'Shhhh….'

Lilly's crying stopped, sputtered and recommenced. She wanted picking up, changing and feeding and no amount of reassurance from the doorway was going to alter that.

Jessica crept over to the cot and placed her palm on her daughter's chest. Lilly hiccupped and cried. 'Please, Lilly, go back to sleep. Shhhh…'

This suggestion seemed only to distress her baby more. Reluctantly, with tears streaming down her face, Jessica reached in and lifted her hiccupping child from her cot. With her baby perched on her straightened arm, she trod the stairs, carefully and deliberately, wary of tripping. How would she explain that to Matthew? She feared his wrath if she inadvertently did something wrong with Lilly. Not that he had ever shown his anger; in fact quite the opposite: he was patient, encouraging and supportive. But Jessica knew from experience what simmered beneath the surface when you loved someone as much as he did Lilly.

Jessica smiled as she entered the kitchen, wiping her tears on the back of her pyjama sleeve. Matthew had tidied, wiped down the surfaces and stacked the dishwasher. He had even placed her favourite mug by the kettle with a teabag resting in it, ready to make her first drink of the day. Lilly had quieted a little and now gnawed her thumb. Jessica clicked the kettle on to boil.

'I'm going to put you down while I make your bottle.' She still found it embarrassing and a little pointless talking to a baby that didn't and couldn't respond. She didn't know how Matthew and her parents did it, babbling away as Lilly stared past them into the middle distance.

Lilly screamed, as if she knew what was coming and being placed in her Moses basket was the last thing she wanted.

'Please don't cry, because that makes it doubly hard for me, don't you understand that?' Jessica walked over to the Moses basket and laid her little girl inside it. Lilly instantly started to shriek. 'I'm going to have to just ignore you because I need to concentrate!' Jessica pleaded, her words cutting no ice with her hungry, damp infant.

Matthew had placed the formula and its scoop next to the sterilising unit, in which nestled enough clean bottles for the day. In a sequence that was now familiar, Jessica washed her hands before shaking the excess sterilising fluid from the bottle teat. She put the required amount of formula into the scoop and levelled it off with a knife, just as she had been shown, before placing it in the bottle where she had put the cooling boiled water. She then fixed the teat and shook the bottle until all the powder had dissolved. Lilly screamed hard, going silent between sobs as though gathering strength to cry harder and louder. 'I'm going as fast as I can!' Jessica shouted towards the basket. She ran the cold tap and held the end of the bottle under the water to cool the mix.

'Just one more minute, Lilly!' she yelled and wiped away a few stray tears.

The doorbell rang.

'Oh shit!' Jessica plopped the bottle on the side and walked up the hallway.

Mrs Pleasant stood on the doorstep, her thin lips pressed together tightly and her cardigan buttoned up to the neck.

'Good morning.'

'Yes.' Jessica nodded. 'Good morning.' Willing her to get to the point quickly.

'What's wrong with your baby?' Mrs Pleasant got to the point very quickly.

'Nothing. I…' Jessica struggled to find the words.

'She is yelling fit to burst and I don't know if you are aware, but it's a sound that travels.' Her mean eyes shone like chips of amber.

'I'm sorry.' She felt her tears welling again.

'Well, sorry is all well and good, but I can't hear my programme. Does she need a doctor?'

'A doctor?' Jessica's heart hammered at the thought. Was that why Lilly was crying? Was she ill? 'I'm not sure. I don't think so, she just… she's just hungry.' She looked down at her grubby socks and felt terrible that her child was hungry.

'Well, can I suggest you feed her and do us all a favour?' Mrs Pleasant shook her head, her grey bowl-haircut barely moving as she made her way back up the garden path and closed the gate behind her.

Jessica looked from left to right up the street, trying to see who the 'all' in question might be. Did everyone think she was a bad mother?

Slamming the door, she rushed back into the kitchen. 'I'm here, Lilly. I was just getting the door. Please stop. Please don't cry! I've got your bottle, here it is!'

She grabbed the bottle and waved it in front of her daughter. This, unsurprisingly, did little to calm her. Jessica turned to place the bottle on the work surface while she reached for her daughter and in doing so she let the bottle slip from her hand. It hit the kitchen floor and immediately spread a white pool across the floor.

'Oh no, please no!' Jessica bent down, as if being closer to the fractured plastic could somehow miraculously fix the situation.

Lilly bawled. Her screaming had taken on a new, higher-pitched, urgent tone. The doorbell rang again. Jessica leapt up and headed towards the door. Her eyes were red from crying, but still she attempted a smile, ready to placate Mrs Pleasant. But it wasn't Mrs Pleasant who stood on the other side of the door. It was her Polly.

'Oh, Poll!' Jessica fell into her friend's arms.

'What is it, my honey? What on earth is the matter? I can hear Lilly.' Polly released her friend and pushed past, heading into the kitchen, where she scooped up the little girl and held her fast. 'It's okay. It's all okay, darling.' Polly kissed Lilly's little red face.

Jessica watched her friend and realised that yes, it was all okay now, because someone else was there who knew what to do.

Lilly's breath came in stuttering gasps. Jessica noticed little purple spots around her daughter's eyelids where she had cried so hard.

'Her bum's wet, I'll go change her. You make up her bottle, okay?' Polly's smile was fleeting.

'Do you think she's ill, do you think I should call Dr Boyd?'

Polly ran her hand over Lilly's brow. 'No. No, I think she's just a little hungry and soggy. Make her bottle, Jess, and we'll be down as soon as I've changed her,' Polly repeated as she trod the stairs. 'I've got loads of time – I'm between jobs at the mo, got the whole day off. I had been doing a little work experience as a florist, helping out, but it just wasn't for me.'

Jessica wandered over to the sink and reached for another bottle.

A few minutes later, as she watched across the kitchen table while Polly fed and burped her daughter before rocking her to sleep in her arms, Jessica felt guilty and grateful all at once.

'Thank you, Poll.' Her voice was barely a whisper.

'You don't have to thank me, Jess, that's what friends are for, right? Lilly is such a good little girl. She's the cleverest baby in the world!'

'Must take after her dad. I'm not much good at anything really.'

'Don't be daft!' Polly scoffed. 'You're good at lots. You are still on record for blowing the biggest Hubba Bubba bubble I have ever seen. What else...?' Polly tapped her mouth with her finger. 'Oh, you make the best fish pie, ever! And you can make me laugh like no one else. They're all good things.'

Jessica shrugged as she plucked at the belt of her dressing

gown, grateful her friend was there. She wondered who Lilly would call on for help when she became a mother; she doubted it would be her. 'How do you know what to do with her?' she asked.

'What do you mean?'

'When she's crying. I'm never really sure what she's crying for. Mrs Pleasant said I should call the doctor—'

'That's a great idea, Jess; let's start taking advice from Mrs Not-So! Maybe you could copy her hairstyle too. That'd make your mother happy!'

Jessica knew this was funny but couldn't quite remember how to laugh, not at that moment in time.

Polly sighed. 'You just have to run through a little checklist. It's usually just one of three things: bum – she needs changing; tum – she needs feeding; or mum – she wants a bit of company.'

Jessica nodded. Polly made it sound so easy. Maybe it was for her.

'Don't forget, I've had to look after my sister's three rug rats – she and Rich are always gallivanting off somewhere and so I'm well practised, but mainly I'm not knackered like you. When you're really tired it's hard to remember how to make a cup of coffee, let alone look after a baby. I get it.' She smiled.

'I am tired.'

Polly nodded. 'I'm a bit worried about you, Jess,' she whispered as she looked down at the sleeping Lilly.

'I'm fine.' The lie was swift and unconvincing.

'Do you want to tell me what's going on? You're just not yourself.' Her tone was cautious. 'And I need my bestie back. My life's not half as good without you making me laugh and making me food!'

Jessica shrugged, her words delivered slowly when she eventually spoke. 'I don't really know what's going on. I just know I've never cried so much in my whole life. I can't believe I have any more tears, but they just keep coming.'

'Is it anything to do with Matt? Is he treating you right? Because if he isn't, I'll proper duff him up.'

Jessica smiled at her friend's willingness to scrap on her behalf. 'No, Matt's great.'

'Good. I'll put my knuckle-duster away then. Is it Lilly? Do you not feel well? Are you lonely? Tell me, Jess.'

'I wish I could. I just know I feel sad, really sad.'

'Oh, Jess.' Polly placed Lilly over her shoulder and with her free hand held her friend's arm across the table. 'You are one of the strongest women I know. A real coper. Do you remember when Danny died, even though you were little, you just kind of knew that your mum and dad couldn't be there for you as much and you started getting your own packed lunch and making your bed? Do you remember? You held things together and you were only a child. You were amazing, you just got on with it, didn't you?'

Jessica nodded. She didn't know how to say it, but this was different. How could she explain that she was living under a big black cloud and the reason was she didn't know how to be a mum. The fact that even dippy old Polly was so happy to be in Lilly's company, so capable, only served to highlight her failings. Jessica knew she couldn't admit to just how bad it was. But she wasn't a coper. In fact she thought she might be mad.

Polly squeezed her arm and gave a little laugh. 'It's just a touch of baby blues, nothing to worry about. It'll pass in a flash; a couple of good nights' sleep and you'll feel brand new.'

'Did your sister have baby blues?' Jessica asked hopefully. Wanting to believe that she was cut from the same cloth as Polly's vivacious sister.

'Absolutely!' Polly patted her arm. 'I think everyone does. At least every woman I've ever known who's had a baby. Whether it's for that half an hour that you sit and sob and think what the hell have I done. Or whether it lasts longer and goes a bit deeper, one way or another, all women have it, I think. I know it can be really bad: my sister's friend was on the brink, they took her baby away from her, it was terrible. And even my gobby sis went to bed for a week or so and didn't put her fake tan on. But as I've said, you're such a strong bird, a coper. It will pass very quickly. You have a lot of support. You're right, Matt's a wonderful dad. And you've got me.' Polly gently rocked Lilly back and forth. 'Have you spoken to your mum about it?'

'Not really, but she did say she felt quite fed up when I was tiny. My dad had gone back to work, and apparently she sat on the sofa and cried and cried, thinking what on earth have I got myself into. When did your sister's baby blues go?' she asked, hoping there might be signs to indicate her ordeal was nearly over.

'I don't know exactly, but I know one day she just shoved her Uggs on, applied some lippy and seemed to get on with it, like she just knew what to do and what needed to be done. And you could tell that it had all started to come naturally.'

Jessica nodded. She couldn't wait for that day.

'Tell me how I can help you, Jess, and I'll do whatever I can, you know that.' Polly sipped her tea with her free hand.

Jessica considered how Polly could help her. She wanted to take her by the shoulders and ask her what she saw – was it still Jessica? Because it didn't feel like her, it didn't even look like her. That's how she felt, like she had disappeared. And if she had disappeared, where had she gone? And more importantly, when would she be coming back?

Instead, she dug deep to find a smile. 'Do you mind if I go and have a sleep?' she whispered.

'Of course, not. You go ahead.' Jessica felt her shoulders sag with relief. 'And then maybe after you've napped, you could have a nice bath? Lilly and I will be fine. We have a lot to catch up on. I need to tell her all about the incredible time I'm having with Paz and my plans to move him in and keep him as my sex slave.'

Jessica nodded. There was no humorous aside, no banter, no questioning; she just didn't have the strength. Not today. She pushed the chair away from the table and made her way up the stairs, unable to think about anything other than the dark space beneath the bedclothes into which she would crawl and disappear for a while.

Polly resettled Lilly over her shoulder and laid her cheek on her back. She sighed. 'I really miss your mum,' she whispered, before kissing Lilly's beautiful face.

4th August, 2014

I saw the psychiatrist today, along with three other women, none of whom I had spoken to before; they seemed to know each other and that made me feel a bit isolated, embarrassed. I don't like group therapy. In fact I hate it. It makes me feel exposed and nervous. I would be quite content to sit on my narrow bed alone, just thinking, but of course that's not allowed. We had to sit in a circle and talk about something we were good at. It could be anything. The girl opposite me told us she could juggle – she could juggle up to five things for a long time and had done it with apples, balls, socks, all kinds of things. Her boyfriend had taught her and it helped clear her head, apparently. This earned her a clap. The woman next to me broke the rules and said how she had messed up her life and was crap at most things. We had been told to stay away from anything negative and to try and focus on the positive. The psychiatrist changed tack and told us to try and think of the three words that best describe us. We had fifteen minutes to think about it. During this thinking time, I realised that I see my life in terms of before and after. The me before, I would describe as chatty, energetic and happy, and the me after, sad, regretful, lonely. So very lonely. It's like there are two of me. I picture the me before and it's like watching a film. I barely recognise the person who had so much to say, who was so hopeful for the future, who bounded into a room, laughing. I can't imagine being her, not for one day.

I was still considering this when negative woman was asked to list her three. She stood up, nervously pulling her jumper over her hands and said 'bonkers' and her friend laughed. The psychiatrist shushed her quiet and suggested to the woman she might want to look a bit deeper and expand on that. She then paused, giving the woman a chance to consider her next two descriptions. Eventually the woman nodded, sighed and said 'nutso and loopy'. Even the psychiatrist laughed as all five of us dissolved into giggles. It was a flicker of happiness in my unhappy world. It felt nice to be included. And it felt good to be laughing. I thought I might have forgotten how.

Fifteen

Uncharacteristically, Jessica had woken early. Slowly she'd washed her hair, applied a touch of make-up, poured bleach in the loos and wiped around the sink with a sponge until it gleamed. Each task had felt Herculean, requiring all her thought and concentration. Her movements were slow and laboured and her expression suggested they caused her pain. But it was important to get things right today.

When she opened the front door to her home, she did so with a straight back and a smile.

Cathy the health visitor was as chirpy and smiley as ever. 'Aww, she's gorgeous, Jessica. How's she sleeping?' She peered at Lilly lying on her beanbag, watching the world go by, her tummy gently rising and falling with each breath. At eight weeks, she had filled out; her features were more distinct and her movements smoother. She had also smiled twice, once for Matthew and once for her Granny Margaret. Both of whom were ecstatic, carrying the experience around like a precious gift.

Jessica pushed her newly washed locks behind her ears. 'She sleeps for about four or five hours, sometimes six, before waking up, but then she's not awake for long.

Sometimes she just needs a pat or help finding her thumb.' She gave a tentative smile.

'Well you can't grumble at that, can you?' Cathy beamed.

'No. You can't.'

'So, what I'm going to do today is weigh her and measure how long she is and her head circumference, things like that. I'll pop all the measurements in Lilly's red book to help us monitor her as she grows, okay?'

Jessica nodded. 'Smashing.'

'And I have a little questionnaire for you, Mum, just to see how *you* are doing. If you wouldn't mind filling it out for me.' Cathy opened her bag and removed her scales and notepad before casually passing the questionnaire to Jessica.

Jessica stared at the pad, wanting desperately to pass this test, wanting to get it right.

'Is there anything you want to ask me?' Cathy asked as she set up her weighing paraphernalia on the living room floor and reached for Lilly.

Mrs Pleasant's mean face and sharp comments flew into her mind. 'Lilly was crying the other morning and my neighbour asked if she should see a doctor.'

'Oh?' Cathy stopped what she was doing and gave Jessica her full attention.

'I mean, she was only crying because she hadn't had her bottle and her nappy needed changing. You know what it's like first thing when they wake up and there is a million things to do and it all needs doing at once!' Jessica chuckled and Cathy nodded. 'Well, I was just wondering, how would you know when to call a doctor, if she ever needed one?'

Cathy sat back on her haunches. 'It's tricky. There is no rule of thumb. But what I say to all new mums is, trust that little voice of instinct you have. If she has a high temperature or is in obvious pain, then yes, of course. But it's important to remember that you know your baby better than anyone and if you feel she needs to see a doctor, then call one. But a bit of a cry in the morning is quite normal. After all, it's her only way of telling you that she needs something, right?'

'Right.' Jessica tried out her brightest smile. 'Usually one of three things: bum, tum or mum!'

Cathy laughed. 'Exactly!' She smiled as she watched Jessica scan the questionnaire.

Jessica rested the clipboard on her legs and gripped the pen, feeling her fingers shake. The ten questions were easy enough, starting with 'I have been able to laugh and see the funny side of things', followed by a selection of boxes to tick, from 'As much as I always could' at the top to 'Not at all' at the bottom. Jessica was supposed to tick the most appropriate box for each statement.

She studied the questions and ran through what would be her honest answers. In response to 'I have been sad and miserable', she would have ticked 'Most of the time'. For 'I have looked forward with enjoyment to things', her response would have been 'Hardly at all'. Instead, Jessica went through each question meticulously lying to ensure her answers weren't going to cause any intervention from anyone and wouldn't embarrass Matthew in any way. She didn't want to be like Polly's sister's friend who had her baby taken from her; the very idea left her cold, it was unthinkable. She swung the pen between her knuckles and read: 'The thought of harming myself has occurred to me'; Jessica ticked the 'Not at all' box. She then slid the paper and pen across the floor for Cathy to read later.

Lilly gurgled after her great weigh-in and Cathy placed her back on her beanbag, where she sucked her thumb.

'She's doing great, Jessica. Gained two pounds since we last weighed her, which is spot on! A happy, healthy baby, that's what we like to see.'

Jessica picked Lilly up and gathered her to her chest, feeling a wave of unbridled relief. She was grateful that Lilly could not speak and tell Cathy how rubbish she really was.

'This is a lovely house, Jessica, refreshingly homely. How do you keep it so tidy *and* look after a baby? Mine are thirteen and fifteen and our place looks like a warzone!' Cathy laughed.

Jessica did her smile again. 'I just do. I don't like things to be a mess. What is it they say? Tidy house, tidy mind.' She let her eyes blink in time with her heartbeat.

'I should take photos and hold you up as an example. You've got a young baby and still manage to whizz the hoover over. Don't tell me you cook supper as well?'

'No, not every night.' Jessica thought of Matthew coming in from work and running the vacuum around before tackling the washing.

Immediately after Cathy left, Lilly started to wail. Jess took her upstairs and cooed desperately as she rocked her daughter back and forth on the spot. 'Please go to sleep. Shhhh... Come on, go to sleep, Lilly.'

Lilly wriggled inside her mother's grip.

'Stay still. Be a good girl and go to sleep please!' Jessica reclined her little girl's body until she lay flat against her arm. Lilly was now quiet.

'Shhhh...' Jessica whispered again, as though her baby still needed calming.

Lilly looked up at her mother and smiled, like it was some kind of game.

'Don't laugh. Close your eyes, baby.'

Lilly blinked and reached up to grasp her mother's hair.

'Stop it, Lilly! Go to sleep!' Jessica gently placed her fingers on her little girl's eyelids and tried to slide them shut.

Lilly instantly wailed again. She didn't like that at all.

'What on earth are you doing?'

Jessica turned abruptly towards Matthew's voice behind her. He leant, flush-faced, on the doorframe to their bedroom, in his suit, with his briefcase in his outstretched arms.

'I was just... I was trying to get her off to sleep.' She avoided eye contact.

'What?' He narrowed his eyes.

'I was getting her off to sleep. What are you doing home?' she whispered.

'Court was adjourned for the afternoon. I thought I'd come and surprise you.' His tone was stilted.

Lilly pulled herself upwards, lifting her head and looking towards her dad. Matthew placed his briefcase on the landing floor and reached for his daughter.

'I... I thought she might be tired.' Jessica swallowed.

Matthew patted his little girl's back as she lay against his shoulder. 'She doesn't look tired; in fact, she looks like she has just woken up. She's full of beans. Why would you think she's tired again, Jess?'

She shook her head. 'I don't know.' Jessica did know, but couldn't think how to confess to her husband that she needed the baby to sleep because *she* needed to sleep. Jessica didn't know how to be with her, didn't know what she was supposed to do. She only knew how to cope when Lilly was sleeping.

Matthew took Lilly downstairs, leaving Jessica alone. She stared out of the window and felt awkward, like a guest that didn't know or understand the rhythm of the house.

14th October, 2014

I think this is the first time I have been glad to have my diary to turn to. I'm sitting on my bed, huddled in the corner and I am shaking. I feel sick and afraid. I'm holding my acorn tightly in my palm. It brings me comfort, I can't explain why, today of all days, this present from my mum, from her hand to mine.

I walked to the dining hall for supper, as I have done countless times before. And as usual, I kept myself to myself. Tonight as I stood in line I realised I don't notice the smell any more. I placed my plastic tray, with its indents for food, on the rails, sliding it along, waiting for the feet in front to shuffle forward. I lifted it to receive a dollop of shepherd's pie and a large spoonful of diced mixed vegetables. I shook my head at the woman doling out pudding. I only eat because I have to. I always sit alone in the corner towards the back of the room, undisturbed – but not this evening. I was about to put a forkful of mash, peas and carrots into my mouth when I noticed one of the women I see in the exercise yard standing on the other side of the table, staring at me. She's a big woman with long blonde hair, which she scrapes so tightly into a ponytail that from the front she looks bald. She always has two dark rings of kohl around each eye, which make her eyes look tiny and sunken. She has plucked her eyebrows away.

I wondered if she was looking for a place to eat, which was unusual as she's one of the mouthy, popular women who everyone knows and fears, a bit of a queen bee in this rotten hive. I looked up and she sneered at me, 'Yeah, you!' She spoke as though we were mid conversation or she had called me and I hadn't heard, which is possible.

I opened my mouth to reply, but the words wouldn't come. I'm so used to being silent; it's harder to break the habit than you might think. I looked behind her to the sea of faces turned towards us, all eager to see what would happen next.

'How do you fucking sleep at night?' She took a step closer, her jaw twitched and her fingers flexed.

I felt my legs shake and my stomach churn. I was paralysed; the forkful of food shook and the peas fell.

'Don't you look at me!' she shouted.

I looked to my left and right, not really obeying her, but trying to see if there was a guard close by. There wasn't.

She shouted then. 'Sitting there like butter wouldn't melt, Miss Hoity-Toity, and all the time you are a fucking baby killer, isn't that right? You killed your little girl. What kind of animal are you?'

I couldn't speak. I couldn't swallow. I stared at her. She pulled her head back on her shoulders as though she was going to shout some more, but instead she coughed and a large splat of warm phlegm hit my face. It clung to the bottom of my fringe and my eyelashes and dripped from my nose, dropping slowly into my food. That's the second time I've been spat at in my life. It felt the same both times: confusing, shameful, soul-destroying.

'Problem here?' The guard arrived, finally.

I shook my head. No. No problem here. I waited until everyone had left before taking my tray to the rack. My legs were still shaking and I thought I might be sick. I saw the way the servers, inmates like me, looked at me, seeing me for the first time. I am no longer invisible. I am stripped bare, exposed and I want to die. I want to die.

Sixteen

Sunday was a bright autumnal day in Chiswick and the Deane household was preparing for guests. Matthew was happily pottering in the kitchen with the radio for company while Jessica ran Lilly's bath. She squeezed a liberal amount of bath foam under the stream from the tap and watched as it transformed into snowy peaks that sat on top of the water. Jessica removed Lilly's onesie and nappy and let her kick her bare legs out on the changing mat on the bathroom floor. Lilly squealed at her newfound nudey freedom and lifted her head as she giggled.

Jessica tested the water temperature and swirled her hand through the bubbles. She lifted her daughter from the mat, holding her under the arms as she dangled her over the bath. As usual, she let her kick the water, allowing her to get used to the temperature and the fact that she was going to have a bath. The oily foam must have made her hands slick. And like a well-oiled thing, in a split second, Lilly suddenly slipped from her mother's grasp and disappeared beneath the water and its foam topping.

Jessica hadn't heard Matt tread the stairs, had no idea that he was behind her. The first she knew of his presence was when he shouted over her shoulder, 'Jesus! Lilly! Jess! Grab her!'

While Jessica hesitated, peering at the water, Matthew barged her out of the way and shoved his arms into the bath. They emerged with Lilly, her hair plastered over her face. The little girl gasped, took a deep breath and howled. Matthew cradled his daughter to his chest and grabbed a towel, which he placed over her. Holding her close against his chest, he repeated, 'You are okay, my darling. It's all okay, Lilly. Daddy's got you.'

'Is she all right?' Jessica stood up, slowly whispering her question.

Matthew flashed her a look that made her intestines shrink. He ground his teeth and spoke through narrowed eyes. 'What the fuck, Jess? What the fuck?' A small fleck of spit left his mouth and landed on her cheek. She didn't remove it.

'What happened? You just froze!' he growled.

'I don't know. I don't know what happened.' She spoke to the floor, stung by his sharp snort of derision.

By the time their guests arrived, Matthew was calm and Lilly laughing, but Jessica carried the memory of the morning around with her like a bad smell that she couldn't shift.

It was the first time both sets of parents had met Polly's new man and despite the guffaws prior to his arrival about his name and profession, they all seemed to be getting along like a house on fire. Topaz had worked briefly as a builder on a project in Africa, renovating a school and helping to construct housing. Much to the annoyance of Jake, everyone sat and listened to his story, which was summed up by Anthony quite neatly: 'Doesn't matter where or how, bricks are bricks and a building's a building.'

Dinner was the usual lively affair, with Anthony verbally jousting with first Matthew and then Jake. 'You two boys make me sick, wouldn't know a hard day's graft if it kicked you up the arse!'

Roger followed this with a 'Hear! Hear!'

'I work hard, Dad! Very hard!' Matthew yelled.

'Rubbish. Sitting behind a desk isn't working hard, son. Working hard is being out in all weathers, carting bricks and mixing cement with fingers that are numb with cold. That's proper hard work!' Anthony emptied his glass.

'You sit behind a desk now,' Margaret reminded her husband.

'Only because I bloody have to. And I've earned the right to sit on my arse, I put the hard graft in!' Anthony banged the table.

Margaret tutted and rolled her eyes at Coral, who found the rambunctious nature of their relationship a little unsettling.

Polly complained about her annoying inability to lose weight, seemingly indifferent to the fact that she'd just polished off two healthy portions of coq au vin and a small bucket of ice cream.

'You shouldn't be so concerned about the outside, Polly. Beauty is a light that shines from within,' Topaz offered.

This insight caused Anthony, Roger, Matthew and Jake to guffaw loudly. Topaz joined in the laughter, almost as if he had been intentionally feeding their prejudices.

Matthew drank liberally from the bottle of chilled Chardonnay that never strayed too far from his reach. The wine and banter flowed well into the evening, apart from for Jessica, who hadn't resumed drinking. She was happy that everyone was having such a lovely time; it was the kind of evening she had dreamt about when they first bought the house in Merton Avenue. She, however, felt like a bystander. No longer confident in expressing her opinion or trying to be humorous. She looked at the mouths of her guests, wide open and unrestrained and felt strangely shy. Even she could see that this was ridiculous: these were the people that knew and loved her.

Coral smiled at her daughter across the table, noticing how she tried to participate and how hard she found it. Jessica smiled back. She watched as Margaret and her mum tidied away the dishes and rinsed the casserole pot, whispering and raising their eyebrows as they did so. Jessica instinctively knew they were talking about her.

Lilly was tucked up in the nursery, having fallen into an exhausted sleep after being much admired by all.

'Come on.' Margaret caught Jessica's eye and nodded towards the garden. She walked round and held her daughter-in-law's elbow, encouraging her to leave the kitchen table.

'Oh, was it something I said?' Anthony asked loudly as he noted his wife's departure.

'Oh, Anthony, if only it was *something* you said. I'm afraid the problem now is *everything* you say!'

Matthew, Jake, Topaz and Roger roared their approval. Polly sidled closer to her man, happy that he fitted in and was making an impression.

Jessica followed her mum and Margaret outside, each holding a warm mug of coffee to stave off the evening chill. They sat on the stone bench that during the day held a commanding view of their pretty courtyard garden.

'Gosh, I think we'll get numb bums sitting here. Wait a mo!' Margaret disappeared inside and returned with a thick plaid blanket, which they threw over their legs, and two oversized thermal fleeces that she had purloined from Matthew's walking kit.

'This is nice,' Coral said as she sipped her coffee. 'That was a lovely tea, Jess. I'm stuffed.'

For Margaret there were no preliminaries. As was her manner, she cut to the chase. 'Right then, Jessica, let's have it. Let's have it all.'

'What do you mean, "let's have it"?' Jessica laughed, finding her mother-in-law's directness both endearing and infuriating.

'You know very well what I mean. What's going on with you? And you are definitely not allowed to say "nothing". We know you better than that.'

Jessica sat in silence for some minutes, not knowing where, how or if to begin.

Coral tried to prompt her. 'We are all worried about you, Jessica. You are not yourself, love, and Matthew is beside himself...'

'Did he tell you that?' Jessica felt a flare of anger that her husband and parents had colluded in the great 'Let's Fix Jessica' project.

Margaret intervened, clearly not trusting Coral to strike the tone, making them sound like badly briefed accomplices.

'No, he hasn't said anything in great detail, but your mother and I aren't stupid. We all love you both so much. Is that the problem, darling? Is it something between you and Matthew? Because, you know, being a new mum isn't easy, there isn't always enough of you to go around. Isn't that right, Coral?'

Coral nodded, worried about saying the wrong thing.

Jessica laughed and shook her head as she gazed up at the stars. If only it were that simple, that brilliantly clichéd. Where to begin? How could she tell them that most of the time she felt as if she wasn't fully present. Her mind was elsewhere, with one ear permanently cocked, waiting for her daughter to wake up crying; and when she did, Jessica would cry too at the prospect of having to cope with her. Not that that was the only time she shed tears. Oh no; she could easily cry morning, noon and night, no longer consciously but as if her spirit leaked tears. Or how about the fact that she had so little energy, even the thought of standing up was sometimes more than she could bear.

Jessica looked at the two women who sat with concern etched across their foreheads. 'Not enough of me to go around? I like that phrase, but no, it's not that. I'm fine. Really. Just tired, very tired. Matthew is fine and Matthew and I are fine. He's wonderful and a really great dad.' She smiled at the truth. He was.

'So everything is *fine*?' Margaret asked with false bravado.

Jessica looked into her lap and nodded.

'So why don't I believe you, Jess?'

Jessica shrugged. The women sat in silence for a minute, each pondering how to continue.

'You have so much to feel happy about, darling.' Coral paused. 'I know life hasn't always been easy for you. Losing Danny was tough on you too, but you came out the other side. We are so proud of you for that. You are a very lucky girl: things have always landed in your lap and opportunities come to you. But being a mum means you have to take responsibility, smooth the path for Lilly. That's your job now.'

'Oh, well, thanks for that. I didn't realise I had to be punished for not having to scrub loos and live in poverty!' Jessica snapped.

'That's not what I meant at all. I am trying to say that I understand that looking after a little baby can be hard work, but she's an angel, Jess, an absolute angel. She sleeps so well, she's a great feeder and you have a lot of support.' Coral's tone was anguished.

'God, everyone keeps telling me how much support I have! Like I should be grateful. But everyone loves being involved with Lilly. It's not like I force any of you to come and help – you all hate to be away from her!'

Margaret took a gulp of coffee and considered her words. 'I hate to see you out of sorts. Anthony and I were thinking, why don't you and Polly go to the house in Majorca for a few days? You are right, we do love to look after Lilly and I know Coral would help out.'

Jessica's mum nodded, quickly.

'Maybe a little holiday might help you recharge your batteries and come back with a new head?'

Margaret's naive suggestion caused Jessica's temper to flare suddenly and in a manner entirely out of character. 'That's a great idea, Margaret – a week in fucking Majorca! Paella every night and a couple of jugs of sangria and I'll come back perky, the perfect mother! Jeez, why didn't I think of that?' she barked.

Margaret was shocked into silence: Jessica had never spoken to her like that before. She wasn't angry, however, but saddened and concerned.

Coral reached out and took her daughter's hand. 'Margaret is only being kind and trying to help you, Jessica Rose. There is no need to talk to anyone like that.'

Jessica slid down the bench and placed her head on her mum's shoulder. Coral allowed her to cry while the three sat in silence. No words were needed, just the odd pat on the shoulder or stroke on the back of the hand and a barely audible cluck or compassionate hum. 'Oh, Jessica, my little girl.'

Anthony wandered out onto the patio with a cafetière full of hot refill. He caught his wife's eye as, almost imperceptibly, she shook her head. He knew enough not to approach, retreating back into the shadows, happy to re-join his son and chums at the kitchen table.

Eventually, Jessica breathed deeply and felt her head clear. 'I'm sorry, Margaret,' she sniffed. 'I am really sorry, I shouldn't have spoken to you like that. I don't know what came over me, I...' She felt a mixture of huge remorse at having flared up at her mother-in-law, but also a strange kind of elation at having released some of the pent-up emotion that had been bubbling for some time.

'Darling, don't apologise. If you can't vent your spleen at those closest to you, then you are in big trouble.' Margaret smiled at her daughter-in-law; she meant it, every word.

Jessica tried to laugh. If only she knew just how big her trouble was.

Margaret continued. 'All I want to say to you, Jess, is that you know where we are if and when you need us. You're a big girl and more than capable of sorting out whatever it is that's eating at you; this I do know. I have masses of faith in you and your ability to be the best mum on the planet. Lilly is very lucky to have you.'

Coral chipped in. 'That's true, Jess. Please remember that you will always be my baby and if things get too much for you, I'm never more than a phone call away.'

'Thank you, Mum. Thank you both.'

'And remember, darling, you are never sent more than you can deal with.' Margaret nodded sagely.

Jessica smiled. 'I used to think that was true, but these days I am not so sure.'

Coral kissed the crown of her daughter's head as they stood and began to amble back inside the house.

'What's wrong with fucking Majorca anyway? I thought you loved it there? Matthew said it was the perfect honeymoon.'

'Margaret!' Jessica giggled; it was rare for her mother-in-law to use such language. The three laughed until the tears rolled down their cheeks.

Anthony nudged Roger and looked up from the table where he and Matthew were talking football. 'What's so funny, girls?' he called out.

None of the women could manage a response through their hysterics. Matthew smiled; it was so good to see his wife and mother laughing again. Roger winked at the boy and patted his arm. Matthew felt a heady combination of relief and optimism that it was all going to be okay.

Jessica lay in bed and thought about Margaret's words. She doubted very much that Lilly was lucky to have her, betting that Lilly wished she had a mum that didn't want to sleep day and night, didn't want a mum that would rather shut the world out and hide. What bothered Jessica most was the way everyone else seemed to mother naturally, by instinct, even Polly. And yet for her, nothing about it felt natural. She had assumed when she was pregnant that she would experience what everyone said she would: that she would take one look at her baby, her flesh and blood, and fall in love. Unless... A sudden thought made Jessica sit up as Matthew came into the bedroom.

'That's Lilly settled. She's had all her bottle and I reckon we are good for a few hours.' He sighed. 'That was a great evening, wasn't it? Really good to see everyone. And I must confess to rather liking Paz, he's up for a laugh and I like that. He and Polly are going to Romford next weekend. I said we might pop over there too, if you feel like it. Might be nice for Lilly to get some different air. Learn about her Essex roots...' He winked at his wife, who was distracted.

She spoke quickly, clearly agitated. 'Do you know, Matt, that sometimes babies get mixed up in the hospital? I read an article about it once, about this woman in Russia who took her baby home and fed it and looked after it and it wasn't until the child was about ten that the authorities contacted her to say there had been a mistake and she had been given the wrong baby and that another woman had been raising her child and they had to meet up and swap back.'

'God, that's really horrible! Why are you thinking about that?' Matthew asked as he sat on the side of the bed.

'I just am.' She shrugged.

'Well don't. It's silly to think about things like that, it'll only upset you. And it's very rare and probably only happens in Russia.' Matthew removed his socks and pulled his T-shirt over his head.

'We… we didn't see Lilly being born, did we? I mean, I was knocked out and you weren't in the room. I was thinking—'

Matthew stood and raised his palm. 'Stop right there.' He placed his hands on his hips. Jessica watched the heave of his chest and noticed the tense set of his jaw; she could tell he was angry. He put his T-shirt back on and made for the door. Stopping with his hand on the frame, he turned towards her. 'You need to snap out of this, Jess. You need to find a way to snap out of it. Okay?'

She nodded. 'I'm sorr—'

'Yes. Yes, so you've said. Often.' He hesitated. 'You know, Jess, I miss our sex life, of course I do. We were really good at that.'

Jessica felt the flush of awkwardness work its way up from the base of her chest to her neck. She hated it being mentioned and thought about the night near Halloween, the night they made Lilly, when she'd come home and stripped in the kitchen. His words from that night rang inside her head: *'How can I admit that I can't leave the house on time because my wife is too sexy. It doesn't make any sense!'* She opened her mouth to form a sentence, but realised the only words forming on her tongue were 'I'm sorry,' and she knew he didn't want to hear those. Instead she closed her mouth and stared at her husband, feeling the quake of her trembling thighs against the duvet.

'But that's not what I miss the most, surprisingly.' He shook his head. 'No. I miss the laughter. I miss my mate. You are not only my wife, you're my best friend. We used to laugh every day and I miss that more than I can say. You used to talk all the time and sometimes I'd think, "Shut up, Jess, just for a minute." But now...' He paused. 'I hate the silence. It saddens me how quiet you are.'

Jessica tried to think of something to say, but again she couldn't.

Matthew wasn't done. 'It's strange, isn't it? I see you every day and yet I actually feel quite lonely. I'm lonely.' He looked at her, his expression distraught, then made his way downstairs.

Jessica sank down under the duvet and lay very still.

'I'm sorry,' she whispered, closing her eyes and praying for sleep. She didn't understand how she could be so tired and yet sleep evaded her. She pictured Matthew's face and felt her heart crumple with fear. 'Please don't leave me, Matt. Please don't ever leave me!' she breathed into the night air.

The next morning, Jessica stared at Lilly and ran through a checklist. Her eyes were green, Lilly's were brown. Her hair was dark and Lilly's blonde. Her nose quite pointed, Lilly's flat.

This was the start of a very dark time. Jessica figured that if Lilly wasn't really hers, then that would explain why she couldn't do it, couldn't mother her properly. If she wasn't hers, then her lack of feelings, her guilt and disconnection, all made perfect sense. She was convinced that if Lilly was her baby, she would have found it easier and there would have been that instant love that she had eagerly anticipated. This idea was more palatable to her than the alternative. The truth. She googled 'DNA kits' and wondered if there was a way to do it without Matthew finding out.

2nd November, 2014

I have been cleverly hoarding pills. Any pills. I have a real cocktail. Painkillers, sleeping tablets, anything I can get my hands on, including one I found in the bathroom that's large and pink and looks ominous. One of the nurses must have dropped it without noticing. I thought about where to try and hide them, but everywhere is too obvious, like under my mattress or stuffed into a sock in my drawer. Instead, I decided not to hide them and so far this has worked. Rather than secrete them away, I lay them on a page inside my closed notebook, which is left casually on my bed or the chest of drawers for everyone to see. No one touches it; there are rules about people's personal things. Everyone can see it's just a harmless sketchpad, clearly visible, but what they don't know is that my pad is full of danger. Not only the pills that lie scattered across one of its pages, hidden by the sheet on top, dotted like the brightly coloured stepping stones of a path that leads to a much, much better place. But the ideas drawn in pencil on the pages, these are dangerous too. I try and capture images as they pop into my head. A bath full of water with broken glass littering the floor, a siren light swirling around a room, turning everything it touches blue and a crowd, surging forward, all with arms outstretched, grabbing for me, wanting a piece of me. And me with my eyes closed, craving peace with every cell of my being. A peaceful mind and a peaceful spirit. This is what I pray for.

Seventeen

Sunday lunch in Romford was a grand affair by Hillcrest Road standards. Her mum and dad had got out the best china, dusted off the spare chairs from the shed and laid the table with wine glasses and a bud vase full of flowers from the garden. Coral, she knew, would have ticked off the jobs from her list that lay by the cooker, making sure her timings were perfect. Potatoes in, check; plates warmed, check.

Jessica looked at her parents, Matthew and her friends. They all had their heads turned towards Lilly, who reigned supreme at the head of the table, sitting in her grandmother's lap. Polly had her hand clasped over the back of Topaz's as though he might disappear at any second. Did she and Matthew use to be like that? She didn't know who she could ask.

'She's such a good eater,' Coral confirmed as she wiped the milk trickle from Lilly's cheek.

'Gah!' Lilly suddenly shouted, waving her hands in the air.

'Gravy!' Roger called out. 'That sounded like gravy!' Roger held up the gravy boat.

'That definitely could have been gravy!' Coral agreed.

'Gravy! Clever girl. Gravy!' Matthew joined them, forming a chorusing trio. They did this as a rule, repeated every noise she made as though she were a deity dispensing wisdom.

'It wasn't gravy – she's only three months old, she can't speak, for goodness' sake! She laughs at her own farts.' Polly smiled.

'I do that too!' Matthew said. 'And she might only be three months, but maybe she's just super advanced, gifted!'

'Gifted, my arse!' Polly commented and reached for her plonk.

'Would that be your arse with the cherub on it, Pollywollydoodle?' Roger asked.

'Jessica! I can't believe you grassed!' Polly screamed, and banged the table. She turned to Coral. 'If you tell my parents, I am dead!' Polly stared at Coral and Roger, who had known her since she was small.

'Well, that depends on how well you do the dishes today.' Roger pushed the tray of buttery roasted spuds towards her.

'But that's blackmail!' Polly tutted.

'Yep.' Roger reached up and clinked glasses with Matthew.

Polly looked at her boyfriend, aghast.

'You can leave me out of it!' Topaz held up his palms.

Jessica found it odd that her family chatted and laughed despite her silence. They ate, giggled and stared at her daughter as though she were a television screen. Mimicking, echoing and praising her every noise and move. Jessica sat quietly, trying to nod and smile in all the right places, all the while trying to think of ways to escape.

Roger, finally beaten, pushed the bowl of uneaten pudding away from him and placed his splayed fingers across his little, rounded belly. He gave a slow yawn. Dinner had been a wonderful success. Succulent meat accompanied by vegetables roasted to perfection and a homemade fruit pie, the fruit for which Coral had picked, stewed and frozen for an occasion such as this. Lilly had been passed around like a prize and just the right amount of wine had flowed in all the right directions. There had been much hilarity as familiar family stories had been resurrected for the umpteenth time and told with a new twist, Roger and Coral alternately recounting their own parts. Everyone apart from Topaz knew how they ended; they knew that Polly ended up in a skip in the middle of Gidea Park and that Jessica had made out that she hadn't known her and had walked right by, leaving her best friend wedged between a discarded mattress and an old ironing board, with her legs in the air.

'I still haven't forgiven you!' Polly yelled. Jessica watched as Topaz now grasped her hand; things seemed to be going well for them.

Everyone present continued to coo over everything Lilly did and she responded by smiling on cue and giggling wide-eyed at her grandpa, much to his delight. Jessica thought how wonderful it was to be so loved and hoped that Lilly would remember this time in her life when she got older, remember the time when her every action was greeted with fascination, provoking a reaction of sheer delight. All she had to do was smile.

Jessica watched Matthew stride around the table, clearly as pleased as punch. She knew this was the kind of Sunday he had dreamt of: their lovely family, laughing and happy. He looked relaxed. It must make a pleasant change for him not to be walking on eggshells, watching and waiting to see how she was coping with the day. She knew Margaret would take the credit, positive that their presence the previous week had in some way contributed to the new-found peace that seemed to have settled over him, the boy that they adored. The truth was, Jessica had tried very hard in the last week to 'snap out of it'. She had got dressed, washed her hair and put on some perfume and when Matthew walked through the door, she made sure she was smiling and holding Lilly. It seemed to have done the trick. He kissed her more and didn't seem quite so anxious about leaving her alone. If only it was that easy to fool herself.

Jessica knew it was best for everyone if she kept up the pretence. But she was a bundle of nervous energy, fuelled by the adrenalin of the mentally exhausted. She felt like a reluctant circus act, spinning plates for the various members of the assembled audience and performing a different role for every individual. 'Ladies and gentlemen, let's have a drum roll please for Jessica, the Greatest Deceiver of Them All!' Matthew had winked at her when they arrived, a wink that said: *'I love you for having our baby. We are going to be okay. You are doing great!'* Polly had winked at her during the main course, a wink that said: *'You seem better, mate, and that is so good!'* Her dad had winked at her during pudding: *'That's my girl, holding it all together. I couldn't be any prouder of you.'* Jessica truly wanted to scream at them all, she wanted to hurl her parents' prized best china at the wall and watch it shatter, she wanted to clear the table with an outstretched arm and make a big noise and then when she had everyone's attention, she wanted to ask them, *'How? How exactly is it all going to be okay? You have no idea how I am feeling. None of you!'* But instead, she kept the words in her mouth; it was easier that way.

Lilly became a little unsettled, wriggling, whining and arching her back no matter how Coral held her or what method of distraction she employed. Her energetic outburst arrived just as the adults were feeling the torpor of full tummies, the haze of too much plonk and the lull after hectic conversation.

Jessica felt her mum studying her face; she knew that Coral would see beneath the smiling veneer and layers of concealer, noting that she looked absolutely shattered. It was hard to hide the two large, dark ovals under her eyes.

'Darlin', why don't you go and grab forty winks? Polly and I could take Lilly for a bit, read her a story, let her have a play?' Coral patted her granddaughter's back.

'Actually, I think I might go for a walk,' Jessica announced. 'I could do with a leg stretch and some fresh air.'

'Great idea!' Polly clapped her hands. 'I'll just grab my phone.'

'Actually, Poll, I think I'll go on my own, if you don't mind. I want a bit of time to myself, and besides, you shouldn't leave Paz. Dad'll get the photo albums out and you know you don't want that.' Jessica smiled at her dad, who, unused to drinking at midday, was now slumped back in his chair with a happy booze glow.

Lilly, clearly exhausted by her performance, started to

cry. Matthew lifted her from her grandma. 'I'm going to spirit away this grumpy baby and when she reappears she will be smiling and smelling far sweeter than she does now.' He kissed her cheek. 'Come on, you.' Lilly flopped onto her daddy's shoulder as he climbed the stairs to Jessica's old room, where the travel cot was set up. Jessica knew Matthew would probably collapse by her side and sleep too; the lure of the thick duvet on the freshly made bed would be too strong to resist. She couldn't blame him.

'I shan't be too long, just a quick stroll.' Jessica stood up from the table and threw her napkin onto her plate.

Coral shook her head. 'Sure you don't want company, love?'

'No. I'm fine. Really.'

'In that case, I shall make a start on the clearing up.' Margaret addressed this to her husband, whose eyes closed in a long blink. Clearly he was in no mood to help.

'I'll give you a hand, Mrs D. It's only fair, in exchange for your silence about my bottom.'

'Tell you what,' Topaz piped up, 'I'll do the dishes while you two natter. It's the least I can do after such a lovely lunch.'

'Oh, thank you, T— lovey.' Coral was still unable to call Polly's man Topaz. 'But you don't know where anything goes!'

'I'm sure I can figure it out.' Topaz flashed his winning smile and Coral felt her resolve melt.

Jessica kissed her mum on the cheek and watched her dad's head slump forward; he was slack-mouthed and already deep in sleep. 'See you in a bit.'

'Of course, darling. I'll pop the kettle on when you get back.'

Jessica smiled and nodded as her mum busied herself with the clearing of the table.

Pulling on her trainers and her old sweatshirt in the hallway, Jessica recalled the evening she had stopped by, less than a year ago, newly pregnant and full of joy at the prospect of what lay ahead. If only she could turn the clock back. If only. The thing that confused her most was how everyone else was so enamoured with Lilly and yet she was her mother and just couldn't feel the same level of connection. It left her feeling alienated from her family and lonely, so very lonely.

Topaz rinsed the dinner plates and then the cutlery under the hot tap and put them in the dishwasher.

Matthew came into the kitchen and placed the baby monitor on the work surface. 'She's zonked out, bless her. Rog asleep?'

'Yup!' Topaz nodded in the direction of the table. 'Polly and Margaret are in the sitting room. Think they'll be asleep too by now.'

'Lightweights.' Matthew laughed. 'You are going to give me a bad name if you keep offering to do the dishes.'

'You could always help, if you're worried about losing Brownie points?'

'Urgh, how can I refuse?' Matthew collected the pudding bowls and handed them to Topaz for a quick rinse.

With the dishwasher stacked and whirring away in the corner, the two men began tackling the heavy pots, pans and serving dishes. Topaz was quickly elbow-deep in the square stainless-steel sink, sporting the feather-trimmed pink rubber gloves that Coral had been given the previous Christmas. Rather than see them as a threat to his masculinity, Topaz wore them with pride, flashing the large fake diamond ring that was attached to one of the fingers. The two worked in amiable silence for some minutes, any awkwardness long gone.

'So how do you make a living, Paz? I mean, running the odd class for pregnant women, that can hardly cover your rent, can it? If that's not too personal.'

They both laughed, knowing it was far too personal.

'I get by.' Topaz smiled.

'You certainly do. Polly is smitten.'

'She's a great girl.' He nodded.

'Mad as a box of frogs!' Matthew added.

'I like a bit of mad.'

'Bloody good job, cos she's got it in bucket loads!' Matthew laughed.

Topaz laughed too. 'I'm not cut out to do an office job. I tried it for a couple of years, but putting a suit on every day, the commute, the stress... I felt strangled. I figured there had to be a better way to live and I found it.'

'So, what, you just woke up one day and felt the need to put on your MC Hammer pants?'

'No, not exactly.' Topaz smiled, refusing to rise to the jibe. 'I was working in my father's insurance practice. It felt like I was sinking a bit lower every day, day after day, until I no longer recognised myself. I lost my spark. Then one day I just stood up from the desk, pulled off my tie, resolved never to wear one again and got on a plane to India.'

'What did your dad say?'

'Nothing. He didn't talk to me for a year or so, which was horrible, but he carried on paying me as though I was still working for him, which answers your first question.'

'Ah, a trustafarian, you lucky bastard!' Matthew winked in envy.

'I had no plan, but I met some amazing people who took me on a spiritual journey. I discovered that my happiness doesn't lie in things and that being at peace, internal peace, is the most wonderful way to live. I travelled for a few years and the most valuable thing I learnt was to stay in the now and make the most of every second.'

'You see, that sounds like total and utter bollocks to me,' Matthew said.

Topaz stopped washing up and stood facing Matthew, willing him to look him in the eye. He placed his hands on his hips and stared at his doubter. 'The difference between you and me, Matt, is that I am willing to listen to other people's ideas, beliefs and experiences. I will then consider them and make up my own mind based on the facts presented to me. Whereas you seem to dismiss my ideas based on nothing more than the length of my hair! Who do you think would make the better lawyer?'

The two men stood facing each other, one resplendent in his pink rubber gloves and the other trying to muster some professional dignity. Matthew laughed first, a real deep belly-laugh that within seconds brought tears to his eyes. Topaz dissolved immediately after, and both men leant heavily on the work surfaces, trying to regain some composure. Matthew pulled the warmed tea towel from the oven door.

Topaz grinned. 'But you're on the biggest journey of all. Babies are an adventure in themselves, they eradicate the normal. Personally, I can't wait.'

Matthew nodded as he reached for the pan on the drainer. 'Yes, it's an adventure all right. My boss told me a while ago that all women turn into fruitcakes once they've had babies and I thought he was joking. But things have been...' He considered his words, not wanting to be disloyal, not wanting anything to get back to Polly and not wanting to confess that earlier in the day, whilst chatting to Lilly as he cleaned the kitchen, his hand had happened upon a square, shallow box at the back of the cupboard under the sink. He'd pulled it out and removed it from the anonymous plastic wrap in which it sat. There was a picture of a baby on the front of the box. The words had caused his heart to skip a beat: 'Maternity DNA Kit' he read out loud. 'This test will prove the biological relationship between mother and child. Results can be with you in three to five days!' Matthew had looked at his little girl, who lay on her stomach on a quilt, lifting her head and gurgling with happiness. He had thrown the box into the bin with more force than was necessary, before gripping the counter top and breathing deeply to control his anger.

He smiled at Topaz. 'Things have been really hard.'

Topaz kept his eyes on the suds. 'In what way?'

Matthew sighed. The wine had lubricated his tongue. 'Jess. She... she's...'

'I can see she's distant. Polly says it's as though she's lost her spark. I don't know her as well, obviously, but she does seem to be struggling a bit,' Topaz said, conscious that it might not be his place to comment.

'You see, that's the thing.' Matthew held Topaz's eye. 'Everyone talks about her struggle, but it's not like she's being sent down a mine every day or is living in a fucking refugee camp.' Matthew shook his head, regretting raising his voice. This was, after all, her parents' home. He looked over at Roger, who was snoring, oblivious.

'You sound angry.'

'I think I've every right to be angry.' He lowered his tone to a whisper. 'We don't shag any more, because she's too tired. Christ, to think we used to joke about not having sex any more, we just couldn't see that happening to us.' Matthew sighed. 'But that's not what gets me.' He paused. 'We don't laugh any more because she's too sad; we don't do anything any more, fuck all, and she's got this great life and this great baby.' Matthew set the pan down on the counter top. 'I sometimes...'

'You sometimes what?'

'I sometimes make out I'm working late and just sit at my desk because I can't face going home.' Matthew ran his fingers through his hair. 'I haven't told anyone that.'

'Is it really that bad?'

Matthew exhaled through bloated cheeks and rubbed his chin. 'I love her, Paz. I love her so much that I would die for her, you know.'

Topaz nodded. 'Not wanting to go home is really sad. Can you talk to her about it?'

Matthew shook his head. 'Not really. In fact not at all. She's very remote and sensitive and if I mention anything, she closes up even further and then we get the tears, or should I say more tears.' He ground his teeth.

'Do you think she might be depressed? I see it a lot through my classes.' Topaz let the idea hang.

Matthew gave a wry laugh. 'What does she have to be depressed about? Christ almighty, all she has to do is swan around our ridiculously expensive house, give her child the odd bottle and change her nappy. How hard can it be? I do it every second I'm not at work. It's not like she's juggling a career. She doesn't even have to go food shopping, I have it all delivered. I try and be the best husband I can, I do everything, including encourage her and support her and tell her that it doesn't matter even though it does matter. It matters a lot!'

'She probably knows all that, but after you've had a baby your hormones can go a bit crazy. If she is suffering from postnatal depression, it's not her fault, it's not her being lazy or off. She's poorly.'

'Who are you, Mr Giving Birth Expert as well?'

'No, I just like you both very much and sometimes it's easier to see what's going on from the outside looking in. And I bet you're both exhausted and that makes everything even harder to deal with.'

'I'm sorry I snapped. It's not your fault, and I appreciate your words and your concern, but she's my wife and I should be able to sort this out and the truth is it's killing me.' Matthew was mortified to feel tears gathering at the back of his throat.

'You could talk to your doctor, ask if he will come and see her?' Topaz removed his arms from the sink. This required his full attention.

Matthew shook his head. 'I don't want any bloody do-gooder coming round and making things worse. What would they do, give her pills?'

'Possibly.' Topaz shrugged. 'But if they helped…'

Matthew shook his head. 'I don't want her walking around like a zombie, it's bad enough now. The Jessica I married was strong and feisty, a real coper. I'm waiting for her to get back to that. I'm sure she will. I know she will. It's just going to take a little bit of time.'

Topaz nodded and put his arms back in the sink, unable to look at his new friend. 'You're probably right.'

Jessica walked out of her parents' house and skirted Hylands Park, able to breathe for the first time that day, out of sight of her family, who she was certain were always watching her, judging and waiting for her to mess up.

The park was full of families ambling across the springy grass, strolling hand in hand and working off overly large lunch portions. Dads chased toddlers and mums cradled babies in papooses slung across their chests. Jessica slowed her pace to watch the women, all seemingly managing with ease to perform the basic duty of looking after their children. *Lucky, lucky things.* She pictured running across the grass with Danny. Chasing after her big, fast brother, happy to run in his shadow while he led the way. Her mum and dad had strolled behind, hand in hand, happy. Happy because they didn't know what was around the corner, didn't know that this slice of bliss was temporary, that it would all be taken from them in the time it took for a brake to be applied and for a young boy to forget to look both ways. She thought back to dancing in her pants in the kitchen in Chiswick: maybe that had been their slice of bliss. She craved that feeling that the whole world was opening up and that as long as she and Matt were a team, they could conquer it. Her heart had nearly burst with joy to be in his arms. It felt like a long, long time ago.

Without warning, a powerful sob built in her chest and took her breath away. Raising her hand over her mouth, she cried into her cupped palm, looking to the left and right to check that none of her parents' friends or neighbours were around. 'Help me! Please someone help me,' she mumbled, walking quickly, without giving any thought to where she was heading, but knowing that she wanted to keep moving. She kept hearing Lilly's little voice saying 'Gah!' and squealing in delight. It reverberated round her head. She wished it would stop.

It started to rain. Two years ago, on that magical day in the soggy Sainsbury's car park when Matthew had proposed, when he had loved her so completely – her and her alone – he'd said, *'I want you to have my babies. And I can't imagine any other future than one with you.' But what about now, Matt? I bet you wish I would just disappear, leaving you and Lilly in peace. You are both better off without me. Everyone would be.*

She continued along Albert Road, eventually finding herself outside the train station on South Street. A tinny, nasal voice announced that the next train on platform three would not be stopping and that everyone should keep back behind the yellow lines – the place was deserted anyway. Feeling in her jeans pocket, Jessica pulled out her phone and her credit cards and travelcard that sat neatly in the little slots in its inside cover. Extracting her Oyster card, she hovered it over the barrier and made her way to the platform. She walked all the way along it to the point where a steep grassy bank sloped down to meet the track. She stared down at the litter that gathered there: a faded plastic bottle of Coke, an old copy of *Metro* and some cigarette stubs.

Standing very still, with her toes nudging the edge of the platform, she listened as the wind whistled about her, whipping her hair across her face and distorting the twangs and pings of the track so they almost echoed. The rain fell in large droplets, bouncing off the tracks and flattening her hair against her head. Jessica looked down the line and through the haze could see the lights of the oncoming train. They looked like eyes. Removing her hands from her pockets, she let them fall limply to her sides. She closed her eyes. Her pulse beat loudly in her ears and the rain cloaked everything in a misty haze. She took deep breaths and let the tears run down her face. She tipped her head back and welcomed the feeling of tranquillity that came over her.

'Jessica?'

Opening her eyes, she stared at the grey-haired man in the long dark coat who stood by her side in the rain. He reached out and gripped her arm and in that second the train hurtled past, pulling her towards the track. She teetered before stepping backwards with her heart pounding in her chest. It took a while for her to focus and recognise that it was Reverend Paul, from St Stephen's.

'Are you okay?' he asked, his voice soft, his forehead creased in concern.

She nodded.

'What in God's name are you doing, child?'

'Just... just stretching my legs, getting some fresh air.' She gave a false, bright smile. 'I... I need to go home.' She shrugged free from his grip and with legs that felt like jelly made her way out of the station and back towards her parents' house.

She let herself in via the back door and walked into the kitchen, where her parents, husband, Polly and Paz were seated around the table, drinking tea and chatting. The baby monitor lay in the middle of the table.

'Hey, Jess!' Roger smiled at his little girl.

Jessica unzipped her wet coat and slicked her hair back on her head.

'Look at you, you're soaking!' Coral pulled out a chair and placed her daughter in it, then fetched a towel that she rubbed over her wet hair. Jessica closed her eyes and enjoyed the sensation.

Coral tutted. 'I still wish you'd get these locks chopped, Jess. I'd love to treat you. A lovely bob would look so pretty on you. Your ends are rather tatty.'

Polly winked at her friend.

'I've been thinking...' Jessica whispered.

'Oh? What about, darling? Your haircut?'

Jessica shook her head as though she didn't have the foggiest idea what her mother was talking about. 'I think... I think Margaret might be right, a week in Majorca might do me good.' She swallowed. 'Is that okay, Matt?'

Matthew shot Topaz a glance. 'Yes, of course. Anything that helps get you back on form, Jess.'

'Will you come with me, Poll?' she asked.

'Oh God! You mean a whole week in your in-laws' lovely villa overlooking the sea with nothing to do but top up my tan and chat to my best friend? If I absolutely *have* to!'

Jess was silent, but the others laughed. And right on cue, Lilly started crying.

11th November, 2014

A nurse came and found me today as I sat in the recreation room, to tell me I had visitors. I wasn't expecting anyone and her words sent a stab of panic through my gut. I held my breath. I walked along the corridor towards the family room. The first thing I saw was Polly, shining, bright and beautiful. She was upright and had a smile in place; one I know she would have practised in the mirror before she arrived. Her blue jumper was vivid, unlike my clothes, which have suffered at the hands of the industrial laundry and the harsh chemicals they use to keep every sort of bug at bay. Her hair was shorter. She looked lovely – clean in a way that's hard to achieve in here – and happy to see me. I felt a small flash of envy. Our lives started out so similarly, how come they ended up so differently when we wanted the same things? Who chose this for me?

Paz was next to her. 'Hey, Jess.' He seemed very relaxed, as though we were meeting in a coffee shop or had bumped into each other in the street by accident. 'How you doing?'

How am I doing? I am broken. Completely broken. But to say so would have caused me pain, so instead I shrugged a little.

'We're worried about you, Jess.' He leant forward, with his elbows on his knees, his voice a conspiratorial whisper. 'We heard that there had been a hiccup. And you were doing so well.' He was right, I was doing so well, but the dip took me lower than I had been before. As low as I could go.

'Are you okay now?' he continued. 'Are you feeling a bit better after the incident?'

I couldn't look at him. Where to begin?

A hiccup? An incident? I tried to kill myself. It didn't work, obviously, and that upsets me more than anyone can know and now they watch me every second of every day.

'Is there anything you need?' He bent low, trying to make eye contact.

What did I need? I need the same thing I have always needed, to rewind to when my life was perfect. Paz smiled again at me, trying to make me listen. 'I want you to know that I am doing all I can to get you released. I am fighting for you in every way I can. We are not giving up and so you mustn't either. We are a team. You in here and us out there, we are a team and you are not alone. So even if there are moments when you feel alone, try and remember that you aren't. Try and remember that we are on your side and that we love you.'

'Talk to me, Jess,' he prompted.

But I couldn't talk to him, I can't talk to anyone. There is so much I want to say that it would take the rest of my life and so there is no point starting. No point in making small talk when my life is over. I have nothing. Nothing. Everything is destroyed. Everything. I remember my dad once said, 'Be patient on the dark days, because they pass.' That's a lie; sometimes they don't, sometimes they just get darker and darker until you can only feel your way, trying not to stumble.

I pictured Matthew, before life went wrong saying, 'Jess, my Jess. There is nothing you can do, nothing that would make me stop loving you.' But he didn't mean it. Nothing is forever, nothing.

'Don't cry.' Polly finally spoke.

Funny, I hadn't realised I was crying. I can't help it; it's my normal state in here. I am sad and homeless, like a snail without a shell. I have nowhere to hide and I am vulnerable and I would give anything, anything to make it stop.

'Would you like us to leave?'

I looked at Paz and managed a single nod. I didn't want them sitting there watching me. I don't want anyone to see me. I don't even look in a mirror. I don't want to see me.

Polly reached across the tabletop then and held my hands. I thought of all the times she had done this throughout our lives. We used to wear matching clothes and skip hand in hand when we were little and in my teens we'd hold hands if it thundered; she knew I hated the loud bangs.

'You are doing great,' she said, before trying to change the tone, whether trying to convince herself or me, I'm not sure. 'We had a shit journey here, you'd have laughed. We got stuck behind a bus that was behind a caravan that was behind a tandem bike – it was like a comedy sketch. I shouted out the window and beeped the horn, just to add to the drama.'

I looked at her trying to be funny, trying to be normal, but I knew her better than that. It struck me as very sad; that she didn't know how to 'be' with me after all we have shared. This slightly awkward imitation of Polly was what I was left with.

'I miss him.' I said it out loud. 'I miss him so much it hurts.'

I don't usually mention him, in fact I never do, wanting to spare people the trauma of having to respond, but it was automatic, the words just spurted out of me.

Polly drew breath and her smile slipped. Her eyes drooped and her shoulders sagged. 'I know. We do too. And you. We miss you too, so very much.'

She dropped her head until it lay on our joined hands and

she cried, deep, gulping sobs that made her whole body shake. Paz patted her back. And I was glad. Because finally her mask had gone and this was the real Polly, telling me something true. And I loved her for it.

Eighteen

The taxi engine ticked loudly, piercing the early morning hush on Merton Avenue. Jessica saw the twitch of a net curtain in Mrs Pleasant's bedroom. Let her look, there wasn't much to see. And anyway, she knew what was happening, after their conversation over the bins yesterday.

'So you're going away without your husband?' Mrs Not-So had asked, aghast.

'Yes.'

'Without the little girl?'

'Yes,' Jessica had sighed. Wanting to add, *'This is the twenty-first century; mothers don't need to be joined to their kids at the hip! And it's not like I'm leaving her in a cupboard, she's with her dad!'* Instead she'd nodded, sucking up the disapproval that came off their neighbour in waves. 'Join the club,' Jessica murmured as she retreated back inside.

Matthew now stood inside the open front door with Lilly on his hip. 'Kiss Mummy goodbye.' He leant forward so Jessica could easily reach.

As she kissed her little girl on the cheek, Lilly moaned and gripped Matthew's sleeve with both hands: being tilted unnerved her a little. 'Bye-bye, Lilly.' She smiled at her daughter.

Matthew reached forward and pulled his wife to him with his free arm. Jessica felt his words graze her scalp. 'Come back to me, Jessica.'

She gave a small laugh and hitched her bag over her shoulder. 'I will. I'm only going for a week. It'll fly by.'

Matthew moved away and held her by the top of her arm so that he could look directly into her face. His words were deliberate, earnest. 'No, Jessica. I mean, come back to me.'

She turned away from the glint of tears in his eyes and nodded as she made her way across the street to the waiting cab.

Later that day, the ancient Majorcan taxi juddered its way round the twists and turns of the narrowing coastal road, swerving around the bends as they meandered higher and higher. As the driver crunched through the whining gears, Polly mimed being sick into a bag. Jessica wanted to laugh but knew the cab driver was watching them in the rear-view mirror.

She strained to see the sea on the bends and every glimpse sent a bolt of joy through her. It didn't feel like running away exactly; more an attempt to preserve her fragile reserves of sanity, which were running dangerously low. Jessica loved it there: her happy, happy place, a place where she and Matthew had spent the best of times. Maybe at some unconscious level she figured that if she went to a place where she had known great happiness, some of it might creep back into her. Happiness by osmosis; it was worth a shot.

The fact that she had only been there before she'd become a mum also had an appeal; the place held no memories or images of Lilly. Jessica felt the familiar jolt of guilt shoot through her stomach. What kind of mother was she that she didn't long to be with her child constantly? She was a terrible mother, and an awful wife to Matthew. She bit her lip and looked out of the taxi window, hoping and praying that this holiday would be the tonic she needed. She decided to ignore the little voice in her head which told her it would take more than a holiday to fix what was broken inside her. Instead she made a vow that she would not think about Lilly at all and would simply focus on getting herself better. After all, she reasoned, in the long run that would help Matthew and Lilly most of all.

The temperature was noticeably warmer than at home; it felt like the summer and she welcomed it – no need for central heating or an extra jersey when you had the raw heat of the sun. Jessica could feel a bubble of excitement building in the base of her stomach as the taxi drove up to the villa, something she hadn't felt for quite a while. She breathed deeply and each breath of air in that foreign land seemed to clear her head.

The car stopped outside the wrought-iron gates of The Orangery, Matthew's parents' villa in Deià.

'Oh my God!' Polly screamed and ran across the gravel driveway. 'This place is amazing! Look at it!'

Jessica smiled as she fished behind the bush for the tin with the keys inside and pushed open the pale, solid-oak front door. Everything looked amazing. The gardener was evidently doing a great job. The grass had been neatly cut and the tubs were bursting with full-bloomed scarlet geraniums. The tightly packed stones of the semi circular driveway had been raked smooth, the random large rocks along the edges were freshly whitewashed and the dainty border of shrubs and flowers looked magnificent. It was beautiful. Alongside the villa ran the neat rows of orange trees, which Matthew had told her were beautiful whatever the time of year – whether laden with ripe oranges, peppered with delicate white blossom or simply a mass of shiny green leaves. Just inhaling their sweet, citrus scent made you feel better, he said, and he was right.

The Deanes had bought the house in the seventies when it was a mere ten years old, but its rough stone exterior and rustic grilled windows made you think it was much older. Anthony and Margaret had completely remodelled it in the nineties, ripping out the dated kitchen and bathrooms and introducing state-of-the art appliances and acres of white marble.

'Look at this place! God, I love it here!' Polly ran from room to room, jumping on the beds, running her fingertips over the counter tops and bouncing on sofas. 'Let's just move here and never, ever go home!'

Jessica smiled and walked over to the French doors, not wanting to admit how tempting that sounded. Turning the large key, she slid the wrought-iron bolts and pulled the doors wide. She walked out onto the vast circular terrace, which was dotted with a collection of wicker loungers, tables and chairs, each with a sumptuous caramel-coloured cushion and matching parasol. A small pool nestled in the shade of the corner nearest the house, in full view of the orange trees.

Jessica leant on the iron railings and drank in the view,

which from that height was unparalleled. Pockets of blue ocean twinkled in the distance, surrounded by the majestic Sierra Tramuntana, the beautiful craggy limestone mountain range that stretched the length of the north-west coast of the island. Oak and olive trees grew in clusters, decorating the rocky slopes in variegated greens. The arrow-like crowns of spiky pines poked up through the thinning cloud. Letting her eyes sweep left to right, she felt her muscles unknot. It was a world away from the view outside the window of Merton Avenue. She wondered what Matthew was doing at that very moment and tried to quell the knife of envy that sliced her gut when she thought of him and Lilly enjoying quality time without her. *This was your choice, Jess. No one made you leave.*

'Penny for them?' Polly's voice came from behind her.

'I was just thinking how beautiful this is,' Jessica lied.

'It really is. Bit scary though, it's so frigging high!' Polly inhaled the heady scent of pine and bougainvillea. 'It smells like air freshener!'

'I think you'll find that air freshener smells like this.' Jessica smiled at her mate.

'You are going to have to get lots of shots of me looking outdoorsy, Paz will love that.'

Jessica chuckled. She couldn't remember the last time Polly had cared so much what a man thought of her. She was glad she was happy. 'You really like him, don't you?'

'Well I should hope so, I'm going to marry him!' Polly screamed, then jumped up and down on the spot.

'Really?' Jessica did her best to sound enthused when all she could think was, *Enjoy this, it's the best bit.*

'Yes! He asked me yesterday and I said yes! Oh Jess, I am so, so happy! I love him, I really do. And we aren't going to wait, we're going to do it quickly while all the planets are aligned.'

Jessica stared at her friend and was silent.

'Well say something, Jess! I am getting married!'

'It's great, Polly,' she offered flatly.

'"Great"? Is that it?' Polly sighed.

Jessica could see she had taken the gloss off her friend's big announcement and it made her feel sad.

'So...' Polly suddenly clapped her hands. 'What shall we do first? Open a bottle to celebrate? Have a quick swim?' She pulled her sunglasses from her head and put them on.

'Actually, Poll, would you mind if I had a sleep? I just want to zonk out and recharge my batteries.'

'Oh! Sure.' Polly tried to hide her disappointment. 'You are quite right. This week is all about getting you back in tip-top shape.' Polly peeled off her T-shirt and unhooked her bra, before stepping out of her jeans and leaving the lot in a heap on the terracotta floor. 'You have a nap and I'll think about what we are going to have for supper! I'm going to lie here and tan my cherub for a bit.' She pointed at her bottom and jumped onto a sun-lounger.

Jessica wheeled her suitcase into a sparsely furnished bedroom, the smallest of the three, and parked it in the corner. This was the only room in which she and Matthew hadn't slept together and was precisely why she chose it. The one high window and whitewashed walls made her feel safe, protected, like no one could get to her and she could hide. Perfect. The multicoloured flat-woven rug cushioned her toes against the coolness of the tiled floor. Climbing between the starched white sheets on the single bed, she patted the white counterpane over her legs and laid her head on the bolster. She closed her eyes and instantly felt herself drifting off. She smiled, knowing she wouldn't be woken by Lilly. That felt like the biggest gift of all.

'Well strike a light, it's Sleeping Bloody Beauty!' Polly removed her sunglasses and sat up on her sun-lounger to get a proper look at her friend. 'Actually, better just make that Sleeping No Beauty – you look like shite.'

'How long have I slept for?' Jessica felt fuzzy, her tongue thick in her mouth.

'Three days.'

'What?' Jessica shook her head.

'Well, no, not three days, but it bloody well felt like it when I had no one to talk to.'

'Sorry, Poll. I couldn't help it.'

'Well it's now one in the afternoon and you went to sleep at three yesterday afternoon. That's got to be some sort of record. Usually we'd need to be mega hungover to achieve that kind of sleepage.'

Jessica yawned. 'God, I know what I need to do—'

'I know, I know, call your parents and check on Lilly. Go do it and then come out here for some sun!'

Jessica nodded. She had been about to say 'jump in the pool'. She had forgotten, just for a moment, all about Lilly. Her guilt washed over her in a familiar wave that left her feeling cold. *What's wrong with me? What is wrong with me?* she repeated as she went off to use the phone in the kitchen.

'Do I want to talk to her?' Jessica repeated her mum's question. *How can I speak to her? She can't talk!* 'Sure,' she replied, thinking this was what her mum wanted to hear.

'Go ahead!' Coral's voice could be heard in the background. 'You are on loudspeaker.'

Perfect. Jessica swallowed, hesitating. 'Hello there, Lilly. How are you? I hope you are having a nice time with Nanny and Grandad.' This was met by silence. Jessica felt her cheeks flush. Her words were stilted and she found the whole ordeal acutely embarrassing, but she knew she had to fill the void. 'I am at The Orangery. It's lovely here and Polly is with me.' She closed her eyes, her heart beat too quickly, her head swam a little and she cringed. Now her mum would know that she didn't know how to talk to Lilly.

'Ah, she's beaming here, Jess! She's very happy to hear your voice. Aren't you, darling?'

'Good. Have you spoken to Matt?'

'Yes! He's staying here too, commuting in. Don't think he could bear to be parted from this little one.'

I get it. Unlike me, who wants to be in another country, far, far away.

'Is the house okay? You and Polly settled? You must be careful, love, apparently there might be a storm coming in, your dad saw it on the internet.'

'Yes. I—'

'Oh, love, sorry, got to go!' Lilly's cry filled the room like a siren. 'She's a bit grumpy; you've caught her just before her nap! Speak soon, Jess. Bye!'

The phone went dead. Jessica held the receiver between her palms. 'Bye, Mum.'

Jessica went back outside and sank down onto a sun-lounger, still in her pyjamas.

'Take your clothes off!' Polly shouted. 'It's not like I haven't see it all before.' She threw a magazine at her friend, who caught it and placed it on the ground.

'I'm okay.' Jessica drew her knees up and placed her arms around them. She didn't know how to explain how she felt about her post-pregnancy body. It wasn't that she looked dramatically different; in fact the changes were subtle. Her body was softer, more rounded. Her newly filled-out breasts, hips and tummy carried stretch marks that gave her skin a crêpey texture; silvery-purple jagged lines that seemed to peek from beneath her skin. She hated them. Her nipples were larger and darker than before and the linea nigra, the dark stripe that started below her bikini line and worked its way up over her belly button, showed little sign of fading. She felt marked by the changes and didn't want to expose them, not even to Polly, who had seen her body countless times.

Polly lit a cigarette. She always smoked on holiday. 'Paz says that the female form in any shape or size is to be worshipped as it's been created to give life, the greatest achievement of all.'

'Well that's easy for Paz to say, he won't have to go through it!'

'He's genuine, Jess. He is the kindest person I've ever met.'

'That's nice.' Jessica smiled, but still refused to remove her pyjamas. 'Do you mind if I go back to bed, Poll?'

'Seriously?' Her friend sat up and stared. 'You want to

go back to bed? You've only just got up. It's like holidaying with Rip Van Winkle!'

'I think if I can sleep some more then maybe we could go out for supper this evening.' Jessica looked out towards the mountains. She hated having to negotiate with her friend and realised she might have been better off coming there alone, free to sleep and sit in her pyjamas without comment or judgement.

'Whatevs!' Polly turned onto her front and closed her eyes.

True to her word, Jessica drew on all her mental reserves and got out of bed, showered, and even managed to drag a brush through her long hair. She dug deep, trying to find enthusiasm for the evening ahead.

The fish restaurant was on the water, at the foot of the mountain, a stone's throw from the shingle beach. The taxi driver that had dropped them there was a friend of the Deanes and more than happy to converse, wanting to know all about Lilly and when she would be making her debut trip to the island. Jessica had been polite but evasive.

Their table had a wonderful view of the sea and the jagged rocks either side.

'Do you know, Jess, I have never known you be so quiet. You've hardly said a word since we arrived. And poor old taxi-man had to practically interrogate you to get an answer.' Polly gulped at her sangria.

'I'm sorry.' She paused. 'Matt says all I do is apologise. Maybe he's right.'

Polly sighed. 'I want you to know that if I met you now, I would definitely not choose you to be my best friend. In fact you wouldn't even make the top three. You're a bit boring.'

Jessica smiled into her lap. 'Well, luckily for me, you chose me before I got boring and now you are stuck with me, so that's that.'

'Are you going to have a drink?' Polly poured her second glass of sangria and knocked it back like it was squash.

'Maybe a glass of wine.' Jessica nodded. This would be her first drink in a year; she had got out of the habit.

'Atta girl!' Polly clapped as though her friend had given the correct answer. 'I miss getting pissed with my girl; it was a big part of our lives. Do you remember the first time we got drunk? In your mum and dad's back garden, swigging from a bottle of Blackthorn. I remember your dad coming out to see what we were laughing at and you'd just been sick in his conifer.'

Jessica smiled at the memory and toyed with the napkin on the table. 'I didn't want to drink when I was pregnant and I just haven't taken it up again.'

'Yet!' Polly laughed. 'You haven't taken it up again yet, but tonight could be the night!'

'Just one then.' She smiled.

'In celebration of my marriage!' Polly squealed. She banged her feet under the table, beyond excited.

'Yes. It's great news, Poll.'

Polly sighed, concerned and upset by her friend's muted reaction. 'Is Matt treating you right?' The question came out of the blue.

'What?'

'You heard. Is Matt being mean or hurting you in any

way?' Polly's jaw was set.

'No!' Jessica laughed her answer. 'You asked me this before and the answer is still no, he's great. More than great.'

'Good, because even though you are too boring to be my best friend, if he is maltreating you, I'll go berserk. Really.' Polly drained her glass.

Jessica closed her eyes and accepted the glass of wine that Polly poured her. She sipped it, enjoying the chilled sparkle of Codorníu as it slipped down her throat.

'I just need to know how you are feeling and what's going on. I am so worried about you.'

'I know I'm boring now, Poll, but I've changed, things are different.' She concentrated on the little bubbles that rose to the top of her glass.

'You haven't changed, Jess. You've only had a baby. Millions of people do it and it doesn't change them, not really.'

'Well, it's changed me.' She nodded and glugged her wine, reaching for the bottle. 'I am permanently exhausted.'

'Have you told your doctor or health visitor?'

She shrugged. 'Not really.'

'Maybe you're anaemic?'

'Yes, that'll be it. Thank you, Nurse Polly.' Jessica smirked as she finished her second glass and sat back, waiting for the booze to lower its veil for her to hide behind. She refilled her glass and ordered a second bottle.

'Wow! So much for your one glass!' Polly laughed.

Jessica raised her palms in submission and looked at the menu.

By the end of the evening, the girls were drunk and happy,

giggling and picking at their spicy paella as they chatted.

'I can't tell you how happy I am to have found Paz!' Polly raised her glass. 'Here's to me, who is actually going to become Mrs Veggie Bonkers Hippy Bloke!'

'I'll drink to that!' Jessica slurred. 'And you need to give me credit for coming to that horrible smelly class with you. And I only did it because of Conor Barrington and his cheese-and-onion breath and octopus hands!'

The two girls roared and banged the table. An older couple on the table next to them looked over to see what the sudden noise was.

'A promise is a promise!' Polly giggled. 'And you promised to help me find my man and you did.' She closed her eyes and was tempted to keep them closed as her head lolled onto her chest.

'I promise to always be there for you, Polly. You are my girl. After Matt, you are my number one!' Jessica raised her glass in salute.

'No, no. Lilly is your number one! You are a mummy now, with your own little girl. So, so cute.'

And just like that, the veil was lifted and Jessica was reminded of the sadness and fear she dragged around inside her like a rock. 'Sometimes, Polly, you're such a dickhead. Why do you have to spoil things? I'm going for a walk,' Jessica shouted as she wove her way across the restaurant terrace and down onto the shingle beach.

'Okay, Mrs Moody!' Polly mumbled, lifting her glass to her absent companion. Her mouth and mind were having difficulty coordinating. The other diners were not oblivious to the drama, the pair having drawn so much attention throughout the evening. Their whispers echoed around the tables.

Jessica welcomed the solitude as she stood on the pebbles, staring out into the blackness. The water was a dark pool of tar. The waves crashed and foamed in their relentless battle against the pull of the moon. The pretty beach that tomorrow would see lovers laughing as they ran into the water and families unpacking picnics, tonight felt like a place of foreboding. Jessica longed for the morning and the return of the light.

The red glow from a moored yacht swayed on the horizon, a tiny speck that could be swallowed up in one gulp by the vast, endless ocean. The chill breeze made her shiver; it took her breath away, causing her chin to dip involuntarily towards her chest as she tried to muster some warmth. She remembered lying back in the ocean, safe in Matthew's arms, partially submerged and feeling as if she was flying. *'Fly high, golden girl. I've got you.'* That's what he'd said.

The wind was loud in her ears as fine strands of her hair meshed with her long eyelashes. A squall suddenly skittered across the calm, expectant sea. The incoming clouds were beautiful, a rich palette of mauves as the storm brewed behind them. Where they split in the distance, flesh-pink sky was revealed; it would be warm tomorrow. The tempest was almost upon her, yet still no rain had fallen. A plastic chair crashed along the patio. It was coming.

Jessica glanced over her shoulder at the curtains that billowed from the upstairs windows of the fish restaurant; no longer simply sheets of fabric, they now assumed sinister shapes and forms. Darkness closed in quite suddenly, as though a heavenly shopkeeper had decided it was time to draw a blind on the day.

Jessica wasn't particularly angry with Polly. She was angry with herself, angry and disappointed. How had her life gone from being so perfect to such a bloody mess? 'What is wrong with me?' She shouted into the darkness, knowing there would be no response. *Please, someone help me! Show me what to do, please!*

Her thoughts were interrupted.

'Jess!' Polly shouted through the wind as she tottered up the beach, pulling her pashmina around her shoulders. 'I'm sorry I upset you.' When she finally reached her friend, she was slightly out of breath; she hung on to Jessica's arm, with her head hung low, eager to make amends. 'I never thought I would say this, but I just don't know what to say to you any more. It's not like you, Jess.' Polly's legs swayed beneath her, the alcohol seemed to have gone straight to her knees. 'Paz and Matt said they thought you might be depressed and I told them that you didn't do depression, that you weren't that kind of girl—'

Jessica turned to face her friend, shrugging her arm free of Polly's grip. 'Not that kind of girl? What kind of girl am I then, Polly? You don't know! You don't know anything about me!' she shouted.

'I do. I do know you! You're my best friend and you always will be.' Polly's bottom lip trembled.

'No!' Jessica shook her head. 'No you don't. You don't know me any more! I'm not funny old Jess who you knock for on the way to school, or good old Jess that lets you come into her house and nick her food! Game for a laugh Jess, the first to get pissed, the last to leave. Let me tell you about me, would you like that?' she yelled.

Polly's tears fell in silent response.

'Listen to this, Polly.' Jessica turned to face her; her words were loud and slow, delivered with consideration. 'I hate being a mother. I hate it! I can't do it and I can't understand it. I am so crap at it; I can't even hold her bloody head properly. I wish I'd known how I was going to feel because I honestly would have tried harder not to get pregnant. I hate every second of my life now, and I want my old life back!'

Polly sobbed. 'Jess... Jess, no...' She reached for her friend's arm, but Jessica backed away.

'Yes, Polly, yes! I don't love Lilly. I don't love her. I don't even *like* her!' She was now screaming. 'I hate her fucking name and I hate her room in my house. I hate seeing her things in my kitchen and I don't want to spend any time with her, none at all! And I hate myself for saying such a terrible thing, even for thinking it, but it's the truth.'

'You don't mean it, Jess! You've had too much to drink...'

'Oh, I mean it! I mean every word of it! The sound of her waking is like torture to me. I wish we'd never had her.' Jessica balled her hands into fists. 'I don't know who she is or why she is in my life! Who the fuck is she? I wish I could wind back the clock to when it was just Matt and me in our lovely house. When I was happy! I was so happy!' Jessica thumped her thighs as her tears broke the surface. 'I can't do it. I can't. And I can't tell Matt because he loves her and that kills me too. I don't want him to love her, I want him to just love me.' Jessica collapsed onto the beach as the rain came. She cared little that the stones bit into her knees or that the fat raindrops plastered her hair to her face. 'And I don't know what to do...'

Polly sank down beside her friend and wrapped her arms around her. 'It's okay, Jess. It will all be okay.' She held her shivering form tight in the rain.

'How? How, Polly? I feel like giving up. I am so, so sad and I can't go on like this. I just can't. Everyone is telling me how lucky I am and how much support I have, but it makes no difference, none at all. I'm going mad.'

'Shhhh....' Polly soothed. 'You are not going mad. We'll find a way, Jess. We will find a way to make it all better. I promise.'

The two lay side by side on the pebbles and let the storm wash over them. Polly held her friend tight as she sobbed into the rain. They cried and talked until morning broke and the sun crept over the horizon and the sea became calm again.

Birds circled overhead, eager to scoop up any spoils that the storm had brought to the surface. The two friends sat on the beach with their elbows resting on their raised knees, each replaying and analysing the previous night's events. Jessica's revelations sat between them like an unwanted third person that demanded their attention.

'Do you fancy a coffee?' Polly asked quietly. 'I'll nip up to the bistro and grab us a couple, if you like?'

Jessica nodded.

'Will you be okay? I shan't be a sec.'

Jessica nodded again.

Polly jumped up and wiped the sandy residue from her bottom. She returned a quarter of an hour later with welcome china mugs of hot, dark coffee and resumed her place next to her best friend on the beach. They sat in silence for a while longer, until eventually Polly felt able to phrase the words that were tumbling around inside her head.

'How are you feeling now?' she whispered.

Jessica looked up through swollen eyes and smiled briefly. 'A bit better and a bit worse.' She sipped her coffee, comforted by the warmth as it slipped down her throat, which was raw from crying. 'Better because I've told someone and worse because I'm so ashamed that you know how I feel.'

Polly sighed and nodded. 'I think you were very brave to tell me how you are feeling. It can't have been easy for you.'

'I was drunk.'

'Drunk or not, now you've had the courage to say it, we can start to put you right.'

'You make me sound like a broken thing, like a doll whose arm's come off or something.'

'I... I think you are a broken thing, Jess.' Polly's voice was small.

Jessica stared at her friend. 'I don't know why this is happening to me. I don't understand how my mum and my nan and everyone else can just cope, get on with being a mum, but I can't and I... I don't want to.'

'Don't get mad with me,' Polly said, 'but I just called Paz and spoke to him.'

'Did you tell him?' Jessica's chest heaved at the thought of him knowing her horrible secret.

Polly shook her head. 'Not the detail, no. But the outline,

the basics, and he agrees with me: you are poorly, Jess. This isn't something that a week in Majorca or a good night's sleep can cure. You need to go your doctor and be as honest as you can.'

'What will Matt think?' Jessica wondered aloud.

'Knowing Matt, he will just be happy to know what is going on and that you are getting it sorted. He meant every word of his wedding vows, Jess: in sickness and in health. He loves you, he really does.'

Jessica glanced at Polly. 'He is always going on about how strong I am and how capable and clever, but I'm not. I'm a mess and I don't want him to leave me.' She buried her head in her arms and cried again.

'He's not going to leave you, Jess. He loves you. He really does.' Polly ran her hand over her friend's hair.

Jessica straightened up and nodded through her tears. 'Okay.' She held the mug between her palms. 'Can I ask you something, Poll?'

'Of course you can, babe. Anything.'

'Do you think I can get better?'

Polly reached out and gripped Jessica's hand inside her own. 'I think that you can do anything, my lovely mate, anything you set your mind to, and you won't be doing it alone. We will be with you, every step of the way. I'm taking you home. We are going home today and we are going to get this sorted out. I don't know how it works, but we will do it together, one step at a time. Okay?'

'Okay,' she mumbled.

Jessica watched as the sun shifted higher in the sky, throwing its warm rays across the ocean and falling on her skin. She lifted her head and smiled. She felt warm, as if a chill had shifted from the pit of her gut. Warm and hopeful.

10th January 2015

You Are Not Alone: Post Natal Depression and its Aftermath. These are the words I am digesting. Whenever Paz visits, he always brings me a new book to read. I haven't read any of them so far – I don't want to listen to some doctor who has no idea what I have been through talking about hormones and telling me how my brain is messed up. But this book's cover awoke something inside me, and yesterday, I opened it in the middle and started reading. Then I went back to the beginning and I have just finished reading the whole thing. And I feel, god, how do I feel? Shocked, sad and strangely relieved. Paz is right, people need to know more about this, people need to talk about it because I think that maybe if I had known more about it, known what was happening to me and just how many women it affects, then I wouldn't have felt so alone, so frightened and so isolated. I have been wondering, had I known how common it was, would this information have helped me in any way and I think it would. I think I would have found it easier, knowing I was in a club of many thousands, rather than a club of one. The scariest thing has always been how it crept up on me, throwing its dark cloak over my head so I couldn't see what was happening. 'You know it's an illness?' the psychiatrist asked me this over and over again, practically every week since I arrived here, but I just never really believed her. I suppose I couldn't believe that an illness could make you behave in such a terrible way. I didn't want to let go of the guilt. Today I told her about the book and how I was beginning to see it.

Nineteen

Jessica sprinted around the kitchen table at the sound of the front gate creaking. 'Daddy's home! Ah! Daddy's home! Quick, quick, come on, let's hide.' She grabbed Lilly, who squealed with delight, and ran up the stairs before jumping onto their bed. She tugged the sheet over their heads and wrapped her daughter in her arms, inhaling the scent of her as she pulled her towards her chest, cuddling her like a soft cushion. Lilly giggled and kicked her feet.

'Where are my best girls?' Matthew called, shutting the front door behind him and placing his briefcase on the floor.

Jessica heard him throw his keys on the console table and pad around the kitchen. Next came the click of his wedding ring on the banister and the sound of his tread on the stairs.

'Well… they are not in the bathroom!' he shouted.

Lilly yelled out an excited response.

'Oh, dearie me, I think I need to bash the lumps out of this very bumpy mattress. Like this!' Matthew gently thumped the space to the left of his wife, who chortled gleefully, as did their daughter.

'Oh no, Lilly, he is getting us!' Jessica lifted her legs to form an arc and avoid Matthew's prods.

He growled and poked his head under the sheet. 'There you are!' He wriggled under the cover and lay down next to his girls in their makeshift hideaway. 'How was your day?'

'Our day was good! Lilly went for a walk around the furniture with only a little bit of help from me. And she has acquired a taste for broccoli, which I told her was little trees and that she was a giant tearing them up and gobbling them whole! And, drum roll please, she said sock!'

'Sock! How marvellous!' Matthew lifted his daughter and kissed her feet. 'At least we know we can turn her out into the big wide world and her toes will always be warm.' He smiled.

'Hey, we're not turning her out quite yet; she's only nine months old. I think another twenty-nine years and two months and I might just consider it.'

Matthew kicked off the sheet and sat up as Lilly climbed up her mum to reach the lamp on the bedside table.

'Oh no you don't, little wriggler!' Jessica pulled her back and, standing, popped Lilly on her hip. 'Right, come on, Lilly Rose, we have a table to set and wine to chill because when you are asleep, I am going to ravage your dad, yes I am! I shall ravage him stupid!'

Lilly laughed.

Matthew undid his shirt and slipped off his tie. 'You're going to have to start moderating your speech with her soon. She'll be repeating everything you say!' He laughed.

'Love, she just managed sock. I think ravaged might be a few months away yet.'

'Ock!' Lilly shouted, before clapping her hands together.

'That's close enough!' Matthew grinned.

'And I cooked dinner. A big fat chicken is, as we speak, roasting in the oven, and there's mash and veg, all ready to be slathered in gravy.'

'Gah!' Matthew laughed.

'Yes, lashings of gah!'

Jessica turned and looked at her lovely man. The combination of antidepressants, counselling and Topaz's mindful relaxation techniques were working. Just a few months ago, when she and Polly had cried on the pebble beach, Jessica could not have imagined feeling like this. But ever since the doctor had said the words 'You have postnatal depression,' it was as if a great weight had been lifted from her shoulders. Jessica didn't feel sad, or ashamed; she felt relieved. So, so relieved. Someone clever, medical and experienced was giving a name to the thing that was destroying her and not only did that thing have a name, it was an illness. She was ill. Not mad; ill.

She and Matthew had held hands, tears streaming down their faces, as the doctor explained to them how the disease worked. He had described how it was most likely brought on by changes in hormone levels, and that it affected between ten and fifteen women in every hundred who'd recently given birth. Polly had been right: it was quite common. Unlike with the health visitor's questionnaire, this time Jessica had been honest about her negative thoughts, her guilt at being a bad mother and even that she had at times considered hurting herself and her baby. Matthew had been aghast, but he had gripped her hand even tighter, for which she was entirely grateful. The doctor had then prescribed a daily dose of mirtazapine to help combat the depression. He also emphasised that she needed to eat regularly and recommended that she exercise and have sessions with a relaxation therapist; she chose Paz.

Despite wishing for it, Jessica did not feel magically better overnight, but she clung to the diagnosis like an anchor. She was poorly and, just like having a headache or the flu or something more sinister, she had to take drugs to enable her to feel better. And so take them she did. Slowly but surely, she began to feel a little better every day, until finally one morning it was as if she had woken up from a very bad dream. Her senses were sharper and her thoughts positive, but best of all, she started to love every second she got to spend with her little girl. It was as if Jessica and Lilly were on catch-up. Lilly would snuggle into her mother's lap as Jessica read to her and they would go for long walks and feed the ducks. The best thing about it all was that she felt like a regular mum. That day, she spent a whole hour bathing Lilly, marvelling at her little pink toes, her chubby bottom and her infectious giggle. She was perfect. Preparing her breakfast was no longer a chore; it was a joy to watch her daughter each morning, listening to her burble away.

Life, however, was not perfect. She still fell into bed each night knackered, like any other new mum, and there were still moments when she felt a longing for her old life, missing the way she and Matthew had once been able to focus solely on each other. And the sex... well, their pre-Lilly exploits were still more of a memory. The difference now was that she was able to snatch moments of joy with her daughter and if she thought about the future, she no longer felt quite so afraid. The black cloud under which she had been living hadn't disappeared entirely, but it had turned to grey and was full of very large holes through which Jessica could poke her head and take a breath.

Matthew was standing on the landing, smiling. He loved the new Jess, who was very like the old Jess, but perhaps just a bit less bonkers and a bit more responsible. The vision of her going to feed the ducks with Lilly filled him with unimaginable joy. He could barely believe that only three months ago he had been scared of leaving the two of them alone together.

'So, a good day?' he asked as his wife made her way out onto the landing.

'Yes, Matt.' She smiled. 'A very good day.'

2nd March, 2015

Something very strange and wonderful happened to me today. I walked to my art therapy session and halfway down the corridor I started humming. I stopped in my tracks and was so stunned I had to lean on the wall. 'Are you okay?' one of the cleaners asked me. I nodded. I was more than okay, I was beaming. I had been singing a song in my head, and humming as I walked! This might not sound like much, but let me tell you this is a really big deal. I cannot remember the last time I had sung. Can't remember the last time there was space in my head that allowed lyrics and music to fill my mind. It was lovely. The song was one that Matt and I danced to in the kitchen, it made me feel happy, remembering the old me. I arrived at my class feeling positive, me positive! Amazing. I was told to sketch the first thing I thought of and I drew a ravine. Lilly, Matthew and my parents were on one side and I was on the other, they were waving for me to join them, but there was no bridge, no rope, nothing. I was stuck. 'Look!' My therapist pointed at the image, 'You want to cross that ravine, but you are unable, circumstance is preventing you. Circumstance, not something you have done. This isn't your fault, you have no control. No matter how badly you want to, you don't have the means to get across.' I looked at her and I got it. Sometimes no matter how badly you want to do one thing, you just can't, no matter how much you wish it. Circumstances beyond your control won't allow it. I thought about the terrible thing that I did and I used to think that if someone offered me the chance to rewind time, would I stop and do something differently, change the outcome? And the answer had always been no, I don't think I would or could and that frightened me. But with my new head and clearer thoughts I was able to say, Yes! Of course and if I could have that day back and do things differently, then I would. I would in a heartbeat.

This has been a very good day.

Twenty

Matthew woke to Jessica kissing his cheek.

'Good morning,' she whispered.

'Well, good morning to you. This makes a pleasant change from the alarm.' Matthew reached out and pulled his wife towards him. His touch was hesitant at first; as a couple they were still a little out of practice. They kissed in a way they hadn't for a long, long time. This was no obligatory peck hello or goodbye, but a slow, full-mouthed kiss full of love and passion, a kiss that cemented their desire for each other. Jessica shed her nightdress as Matthew pulled her on top of him. There she lay, smiling, skin to skin with the man she loved.

'Matthew, my Matthew...' She ran her fingers over his face and chest. 'Polly's wedding day!'

'Yep. I remember every second of ours.' He kissed her throat.

'Me too. It was perfect. I love you so very much, you know that, don't you?'

'I do.' Matthew held her close and whispered into her hair. 'I feel like you've come back to me, Jess, and that's brilliant.'

She nuzzled the space under his chin and kissed his face repeatedly. The young couple held each other tightly, wrapped in the promise of what lay ahead.

Jessica looked over Polly's shoulder into the large mirror of the dressing table in the bridal suite of Orsett Hall, where she was to be married.

'You look incredible.' Jessica smiled. 'Really hot.'

'Are you allowed to look hot on your wedding day? I thought I was demure!' Polly laughed.

Jessica surveyed her friend's ample bosom, which was squashed into an ivory basque. 'Yeah, I'm not sure demure is the word, but fabulous, definitely!'

'I'm so proud of you, Jess.' Polly beamed at her reflection.

'Don't be daft; it's you who's getting married! How do you feel?'

'Nervous. Happy. A little sloshed.' Polly lifted her glass.

'Perfect.'

'It is perfect.' Polly sighed. 'Do you remember when we were little and we used to play brides?'

'Yes! We used to walk up and down the front path with pillowcases on our heads instead of veils and holding a bunch of weeds!'

'I always thought I'd marry you!' Polly laughed. 'That was until I discovered blokes and snogging.'

'Which reminds me, Poll. We need to have a conversation.' Jessica pursed her lips. 'Your husband might want to do *S-E-X*.'

'Way ahead of you on that one!' Polly opened her dressing gown to show off her ivory silk stockings and suspenders to match her basque.

'Wow!' Jessica grinned. 'You are amazing!'

'Thanks. You're amazing. I meant what I said, I am proud of you, Jess. Proud of your journey. You are one of the strongest women I know.' Polly sipped her cold champagne.

'God, you sound like that hippy Paz!' Jessica laughed.

'I don't think you are allowed to talk about my future husband like that.'

'You know I love him, Poll. We both do. Paz has helped save me, him and my little yellow pills.' She patted her glittery clutch bag, in which sat her drugs, just in case. 'And do you know the best thing about you getting married, Poll?'

'What?'

'It means the end of our bet. I agreed to help you land the man of your dreams and now that you have, I am officially off the hook. The Conor Barrington card can never be used again.'

'Well, not unless this all goes tits up and he leaves me for someone who actually knows what "Love, Light, Universe" means.'

'You have told him you're not really vegetarian, haven't you?' Jessica raised an eyebrow. 'I don't want you sneaking bacon sandwiches at three in the morning in the airing cupboard.'

'He knows all about me, Jess, and he still loves me. That's quite something, isn't it?' Polly smiled. 'And if we have a tenth of what you and Matt have got going on, we'll be just fine.'

'You were right what you said in Majorca about Matt: he did mean every word of his vows. He is my rock.'

'And you're his.'

'Blimey, then we might both be in trouble, we all know I'm not that anchored.' She gave a small laugh.

'You are doing great. You know you are.'

'Things are good.' Jessica nodded. 'It's still not all plain sailing. I get so tired and with a baby it's hard to fit in time for each other sometimes. But everything is on the up and it *feels* better.'

'Even the *S-E-X*?' Polly asked.

'Yes.' She smiled, remembering that very morning. 'Even that. And I plan to take full advantage of spending the night in this fab hotel: no chores, a glass of plonk and no alarm clock! Apart from Lilly.'

Jessica bent forward and kissed her mate on the cheek.

'Talking of Lilly, do you think my little bridesmaid is going to wear her shoes or is she still refusing?' Polly asked as she straightened up and shook off any tears that threatened; this was no time to be crying, not while she was putting the finishing touches to her make-up.

'In fairness to Lilly, she does walk better in bare feet. She's only one but already has the gait of a drunk!'

'So she does take after her mother.' Polly winked in the mirror.

'Yes, she does.' *That's me. I'm Lilly's mum. That's my job and it's the best job in the whole wide world!*

Roger and Coral made a fair attempt at the Twist and Jessica danced with Paz, who held Lilly high above the crowd. Polly boogied with Paz's father, who seemed to be enjoying every minute.

Jake pulled out the vacated chair next to Matthew and plonked himself down; he reached for the bottle of champagne in the middle of the table and filled his glass. 'Christ, this must be costing a pretty penny.' He looked around the ornate reception room.

Matthew nodded and sipped his beer. 'Lovely though.'

'Oh yes, lovely.' Jake pulled his collar. 'And if that slender red-haired dolly to your right plays her cards right, this evening could get a whole lot lovelier.'

Matthew turned to look at a bored bridesmaid who was repeatedly stabbing a fork into a piece of wedding cake. 'Lucky girl.' He nodded at his friend.

'I notice Polly didn't actually marry Topaz, but rather Roland Raymond Jacques de Bouieller blah di blah di blah!'

'Yep, but the vicar did refer to him as Paz throughout, which I thought was nice, personal.'

'I guess.' Jake sniffed.

Matthew turned to his friend. 'You've got to give him a break, mate. He's in. He is one of the circle now, a friend, a good friend, and Polly's husband, no less! And you can't laugh at his name or his ponytail every time you see him for the rest of our lives, okay?'

Jake shrugged. 'I suppose so. And you are right, it's time I embraced him.'

'Good.' Matthew sounded happy; he'd experienced enough discord to last him a lifetime.

Jake drained his glass, adjusted his tie and ran his fingers through his hair in preparation for wooing the bored bridesmaid. 'Still think he's a tosser though,' he whispered, just loud enough for Matthew to hear.

Jessica grabbed her dad's hand and danced with him in the corner of the crowded dance floor. She leant in and shouted into his ear, 'Polly and I were talking earlier about how we used to play brides!'

Roger nodded, pulling Jessica to the side of the mêlée where he could be heard without having to yell. 'That feels like five minutes ago.' He shook his head. 'I remember the day you both snipped the heads off all my roses, to make bride perfume. I went spare! All bloody year cultivating those beauties for you two to lop them off and mush them up in a bucket with one of my screwdrivers!'

'They weren't entirely wasted, we did smell lovely.' Jessica laughed.

'Ah, Jess, happy, happy days. And poor old Danny always had to be the vicar, didn't he? I can see him now, standing by the front door with a black T-shirt on and a serious expression.'

Jessica looked into her dad's eyes. 'He was a good brother; he used to play whatever I asked him to. We liked each other very much, that's always made me really happy. You hear stories of some kids who war constantly, don't you, but we were never like that, we were mates.'

'You were.' Roger inhaled. 'You did have your moments, though. It wasn't all playing and friendly. I remember you both rowing in the back of the car: he'd hit you and you'd punched him back. Blimey. I wished you'd both shut up. Cor, Jess, the times I've wished I could go back and listen to you both. Listen to him...'

'I don't remember that.' She shook her head.

Roger sighed. 'That's the thing about people who've passed on, Jess. It changes the way they're remembered. If I think about my old mum, I only think about the good bits, her laughing and Christmas Day with us all around the table. I never think about her taking to her bed, her hypochondria or the fact that she wasn't that keen on Coral when I first took her home. Death gives you an altered perspective, it lets those left behind pick out the best bits and disregard the bad.'

'That's a good thing, Dad, isn't it?'

Roger squeezed his daughter's hand. 'I suppose it is, my love.'

Topaz interrupted them. 'I think this little bridesmaid is a bit fed up with my dancing!' He handed Lilly to her mum, who took her into her arms. 'I'm off to rescue my wife!' He laughed as he danced through the crowd.

'I love you, Dad,' Jessica said over her shoulder as she headed towards Matthew.

'And for that I am thankful. Every day, my girl.' Roger smiled, watching his little girl and her little girl make their way from the dance floor over to the table.

'Well, if it isn't the most gorgeous girl in the room – and her daughter's quite pretty too.' Matthew smiled at his wife, who sat on his lap and plonked Lilly on hers, the layers of tulle on her tutu frock bunched up beneath her.

'Why, thank you.' She kissed him on the mouth, feeling the longing leap in her stomach. 'Lilly's on her last legs, Matt. I think I might take her up to the room.'

'I'll come with you.' Matthew downed his pint.

'No, no, you stay. I don't want to shorten your evening. Lilly and I will be fine. She'll be out for the count in five minutes.' Lilly laid her head on her mum's chest and closed her eyes, her thumb firmly in place.

'That's what I'm hoping.' Matthew wriggled his eyebrows at his wife.

'Oh purlease, you two, get a bloody room!' Jake bellowed, winking at his new companion.

'We've got one actually!' Matthew shouted as he followed his wife out of the grand reception hall. 'Have I told you that you look absolutely stunning tonight?' he whispered in his wife's ear as they made their way up the wide staircase.

'You have, but you can tell me again.'

'How much did that dress cost, was it expensive?' He looked serious.

'Why?' Jessica hovered on the stair, shifting Lilly and resting on the banister.

'Because I intend to shred it, rather quickly, to get at you, and I just wondered how much it was going to cost me...'

Jessica giggled and did her best to race up the stairs.

Lilly lay on her back and snored loudly from the travel cot on the floor, which sent them both into paroxysms of laughter.

'She sounds like an old man!' Jessica observed.

'Is that right? And exactly how many old men have you slept with to know that?' Matthew kissed his wife's bare shoulder.

'Far too many to recall!' Jessica flung herself back on to the mound of plump pillows and stroked her husband's head, which rested on her stomach. 'I can't believe Polly actually got married!' she squealed. 'I think they'll be really happy.'

Matthew yawned. 'Me too. All we need now is for Jake to get sorted and that's everyone settled.'

'Yeah, well, don't hold your breath on that one. He can be so rude.' She tutted.

'Actually, he had his eye on a certain grumpy bridesmaid.'

Jessica sat up in the bed. 'Which bridesmaid? Red hair, tall, aloof?'

'That's the one. Why?'

Jessica climbed on top of her husband and kissed his face as she laughed. 'Oh, no reason. But we cannot miss breakfast tomorrow morning.'

'I'd better get me some sleep then,' he whispered as he ran his palm over her back.

'You just have one more chore to perform. Lie back and sing "Jerusalem", and with any luck we should be done by the second verse.'

12th April, 2015

One of the girls had a visitor today who told her they had seen my story on the news, we don't get the news in here. Paz was on the campaign trail standing on a step, flanked by my mum and dad as he spoke about postnatal depression and what to look out for. How do I feel about this? Part of me is proud of the stand he is taking and that he is doing all he can to get me out of here and part of me wants him to keep quiet and not to have my picture beamed into people's televisions while they eat their tea. I want them to forget about me, forget about what I did. I don't want to be known as 'that girl'. It's difficult.

Twenty-One

Jessica had received a text from Polly, who on her extended honeymoon in India had taken time out to inform her that she had been forced to go to the loo behind a bush – her second al fresco wee ever! Jessica smiled as she recalled the first occasion and Mrs Pleasant's horrified disapproval. However, Polly's text wasn't the only notable event of the day. The other one sat on the counter top, propped against the bread bin. Jessica glanced at it and bit her nails, using the pain as a distraction.

Matthew walked into the kitchen to find Jessica sitting at the kitchen table. She looked as if she had been crying. His heart lurched inside his chest. It had been a while since he had come home to this.

'Jess?' He placed his briefcase on the floor and threw his keys on the console table before crouching down by her side. 'Hey, baby. What's wrong? Are you having a bad day?'

She bent forward until her arms were lying flat on the table.

'Where's Lilly?' he asked.

'My mum's got her,' she managed through her sniffles. 'She's staying there tonight.'

'Jess, sit up, come on. What's going on? You are scaring me.'

Eventually she lifted her head. Her mascara sat in two black smudges around her eyes.

'What's up?'

She tried to get her breath.

Matthew was impatient, concerned. 'Do you need me to call your counsellor or Dr Boyd?'

'No, I don't.' She shook her head.

'Have you had your tablets today?' he whispered.

'Yes, I've had my tablets. Of course I have.' She didn't like him asking.

'Why don't we go for a walk, get some fresh air and get your breathing in check?' He knew this sometimes helped.

'I don't want to go for a walk!' she wailed.

'Okay, okay. We don't have to, I just want to help you.' He raised his palms.

She gave a reluctant nod.

'I'm here to make things better, remember? You just tell me what you need.'

'I don't need anything.' She sniffed.

'Come on, Jess. Help me out. What's wrong?'

'I'm pregnant,' she whispered.

'What?'

'I'm. Preg-nant,' she enunciated.

'Oh, honey! Oh, Jess! Are you sure?'

'Yes, I'm sure.' She pointed to the pregnancy test on the counter top.

Matthew pulled her up and into his arms. 'Then why have you been crying? This is fantastic news, a baby brother or sister for Lilly. It'll complete our little family. It'll be wonderful! We will make it wonderful.'

She leant against his solid chest as he stroked her hair. 'Supposing… supposing I can't cope again. I don't want to feel like that again, Matt. I don't. I can't go backwards. I'm so scared. I still have off-days and I need to focus and now this…' She hiccupped.

'Hey, listen to me. It will be far easier this time because we know what to expect. We can talk to Dr Boyd and make sure we plan and put things in place that make it better for you. We know what to look out for this time, right? And Lilly's birth was a horrible shock, an emergency, but this won't be like that. It will be much, much better. Everything will be different, okay?' He tilted her chin with his finger and kissed her.

'Okay,' she whispered. 'Don't leave me, Matt.'

'I'm never going to leave you, that's a daft thing to say.' He kissed her head.

'I love you.'

'I love you too.' He held her fast and closed his eyes, offering a silent prayer that his words of reassurance would prove to be true.

And things were fine, for a while.

Jessica's initial misgivings about increasing her dose of anti-depressants during her pregnancy had disappeared after a consultation with her GP. She had to agree, it was far, far better for her, Lilly and their unborn child that she remain on an even keel. Lilly knew she was getting a baby brother or sister and was given a big-girl's bed in the larger spare room, which became her bedroom. The cot got a good scrub, ready for the new arrival.

And then, without warning, Jessica had woken one morning and simply didn't want to get out of bed. It was as if some unseen force had come along in the night and switched off her happy.

Lilly called out, rousing her from her sleep. 'Matt? Matthew?' she called, but he had already left for work. It was as though she had caught a bug: she felt hungover, fuzzy-headed and sad, just like she had before. Within minutes of waking, the tears that she had kept at bay had begun leaking from her puffy eyes.

She had hoped it was a one-off, a blip. But the cloud of despair had now hovered over her for weeks, as dark and forbidding as it was before. Try as she might, she couldn't find a chink big enough through which to come up for air. She waited with bated breath for Lilly to call out again. A hammering headache beat out its rhythm inside her skull and opening her eyes caused her physical pain. When Lilly finally did yell out, Jessica felt the all too familiar sinking feeling in the pit of her stomach. 'Oh no, please no,' she whispered as she crept across the landing.

Lilly was now steady on her feet and happy to trot up and down the stairs when holding her mummy's hand. They trod the stairs in silence. Lilly's bare feet slipped a little on the wide treads. Her crumpled nightie hung off her and her nappy needed changing.

When they reached the kitchen, Jessica gave Lilly her breakfast in silence: a little bowl of baby porridge with three slices of banana that she squished between her chubby fingers and ate like a lollipop. Lilly then started to cry. It sounded to Jessica like breaking glass; it grated on her senses and put her on edge. Without giving it too much consideration, she reached into the cupboard and pulled out the bottle of strawberry-flavoured liquid paracetamol. She no longer needed to read the instructions and used the plastic syringe to squeeze the required dose into Lilly's mouth. The little girl swallowed it between sobs; some of it dribbled down her chin in a sticky slick that Jessica pushed back in with the tip of her finger. She then refilled the syringe and Lilly duly swallowed the second dose. After the third, Jessica stopped.

Lilly reached out a sticky hand and placed it on Jessica's stomach. 'Baba!' She was most disappointed not to get a reply.

Jessica nodded, answering flatly, 'Yes, another baba.' Inside, her heart twisted. How would she cope with another baby? She was sure that Matt had noticed she was using the strawberry medicine to keep Lilly quiet. She had taken to buying it secretly and stashing it under their bed, unable to explain the amount she got through. It had become a habit.

Almost every evening now, Matthew would run his finger around Lilly's gums, looking for new teeth, convinced this was the reason for her fretfulness and night-time waking. Jessica lived in fear of Matt discovering that she was once again not coping. She laughed falsely as she prepared supper and tried not to notice the growing mountain of laundry, the way the kitchen floor was so sticky underfoot it gripped her heel with every step, or the growing piles of paper and detritus that littered the work surfaces and crowded the table.

At eighteen weeks, Jessica's rounded baby bump was starting to show. Coral called daily, trying to offer support by way of chirpy conversation, careful never to mention the word depression or ask how her daughter was feeling, a little fearful of the response. Jessica tried to sound grateful for the calls and upbeat messages of support, but in reality it was simply another intrusion, another pressure for her to deal with.

Lifting her little girl as best she could, Jessica carried her back up the stairs and laid her in their double bed, with pillows around the outside so she wouldn't fall out. This became the pattern for the next week. She and Lilly would spend most of the day sleeping or lying in the darkened bedroom, getting up just before Matthew came home. Lilly, weepy and disorientated, would then cry incessantly.

Walking to the window, Jessica glanced down in time to see Mrs Pleasant looking up at the bedroom window. 'Fuck off!' she mouthed, before drawing the curtains tightly and shutting the bedroom door, making the room as quiet and dark as she possibly could.

Jessica then climbed into bed beside her daughter and placed her head on the pillow. She screwed her eyes shut and she made a wish, just like she used to when she was little. 'Please, please don't let me have this baby. I don't want it. I can't do it and I wish... I wish it would disappear.' This she whispered into the ether as Lilly began to snore. It wasn't long before both of them had fallen asleep.

25th May, 2015

An unforgettable day. During quiet time, while the others were playing a board game and some were watching television, I opted to sit and look out of the window. I stared at the small patch of grass in the middle of the courtyard. I have a trick, keeping my eyes low so I only see the grass and not the high barbed-wire fence or the carefully positioned cameras and security lights that surround us. I make out I am in the park. I jumped as someone suddenly screeched in the hallway, a horrible sound, shrill and animal-like. I felt a wave of pity for them and a flicker of fear, followed by a burst of happiness, because I never used to notice the grunts, shouts and screams. I was part of the noise, part of the fabric, but I figured that if I now notice them, feel separate from them then maybe I don't belong here any more and that thought makes me happier than I can say.

The nurse disturbed my thoughts: I had a visitor. Paz came on his own, Polly was working, but that's not important. What is important is what he brought with him, a letter. A letter! He pushed the envelope across the table, slowly and carefully as though it was fragile. It had been opened, read and checked. Two whole sentences had been blocked out with a black marker pen. This didn't really bother me. I was too busy digesting what was legible. I ignored Paz pretty much. I read it four times over and over and have read it again and again all afternoon. I have run my fingers over the paper that he has touched and have inhaled it, trying to detect his scent. I know it by heart. It says this,

Jess, even writing your name makes my heart jump. But I want you to know that I feel calmer. (And then there is the thick black strip that I can't see beneath and I have tried, even holding it up to the light and squinting with it close to my eye, then it says) I have been through a range of emotions, phases if you like, hatred, rage, guilt, regret and am now as I mentioned, a little calmer. I still don't fully understand how our situation spiralled into hell and how it happened so quickly. I blame myself for not seeing the signs, not intervening sooner. (And then there is another black strip. Then it continues) I am able now with the buffer of four years between now and then to think of some of the good aspects of our life and that helps. Life is a strange and difficult journey and I could never in a million years have imagined how mine would unfold, I am sure it is the same for you. The purpose of this letter is to tell you that I don't wish you any harm, not any more. I forgive you. By forgiving you it will make that journey easier and less painful for us all. Matthew.

My tears came readily and I am crying again now. He forgives me! It is more than I could ever have wished for. I am also crying at the sight of his name. Matthew – followed by a full stop. A single dot. I could never have imagined a time when he would put pen to paper and not draw big X's after his name, not when writing to me. I can picture the countless notes he has scribbled to me and each and every one ends with his name and a little line linking the top of the w to a large kiss. I wonder if he hesitated, if habit urged him to put an X or whether the Jess he wrote to is so far from the girl he married, the girl he loved that it didn't occur to him. Matt, my Matt. Your forgiveness is like a beacon of hope at the end of a very dark tunnel and I am so so grateful. We did spiral into hell; this letter is proof of how far we fell.

Twenty-Two

Matthew sat on the sofa with Jessica's head in his lap. It was the middle of the evening, just before bedtime and bar the odd groan from a radiator, the house was quiet. He stroked her hair away from her forehead.

'This pregnancy feels very different from when you were carrying Lilly, doesn't it.'

She closed her eyes. 'Does it?'

Matthew sighed and chose his words. 'Yes, I think so. It's nice and calm, much better in some ways. First time round we were really over-excited, weren't we? This feels better, like we are more in control. Don't get me wrong, I loved it when you were having Lilly – not the drama and panic at the end, but the first bit was lovely, while we waited, not knowing what we were going to get.'

'We don't know what we're getting now,' she murmured.

Matthew reached down and held her hand. 'No, and that's the best bit, isn't it? Getting to meet our little one for the first time! I can't imagine Lilly being a big sister, can you?'

Jessica didn't answer.

'And I think our names are good: Leo for a boy and Sophia for a girl. Are you sure you don't want to go with Bethan?'

Jessica shook her head.

'D'you remember when you were in labour with Lilly and I couldn't park the car and then I brought Polly's yoga bag instead of your maternity bag! God, that moment when I pulled out a bag of bloody crystals! I knew you wanted to go mad at me. I felt like such an idiot! But it didn't matter in the end, did it?'

'Nothing matters, nothing. Not really, not in the great scheme of things,' Jessica whispered into the still sitting room, her words sending a shiver of fear along her husband's spine.

Much later that night, Jessica fumbled for the door handle in the pitch dark, needing the loo but not wanting to rouse herself fully. With her PJs around her ankles, she slumped on the loo, her eyes still closed. This was a neat trick she had perfected, remaining half asleep so she could slip back between the covers as if nature had never called.

The pain in her stomach came quite without warning. Jessica bent double and tried to focus as the shock pulled a guttural yell from her throat that woke her husband.

'Jess?'

She heard him get out of bed, heard the creak of the mattress and the snap of the lamp as she sat flopped over, trying to catch her breath. Matthew came into the bathroom and pulled on the light. He looked stricken. She stared down at her bunched-up pyjama bottoms and saw that they were drenched in a pool of bright red. She was bleeding, heavily.

'Oh God! Stay there! Don't move.' Matthew ran back into the bedroom to grab his phone. Who he was planning to call she wasn't sure. She looked down, fixated by the vast scarlet stain that had now transferred to her thighs, hands and calves. It felt as if time was suspended.

This was what she had wished for and yet Jessica felt none of the relief she had expected, only pain, fear and self-loathing. But it was too late to rewind. Her wish was coming true. This was her fault.

In the hospital, Matthew answered all the preliminary questions while Jessica got cleaned up. Then she lay flat on a paper-sheeted couch with her hospital-issue gown pulled up to reveal her stomach. Matthew sat by her side, occasionally laying a tentative hand on her shoulder, nervously letting her know he was right there, while trying to remain unflustered. She heard him exhale loudly several times.

'Okay, Jess, where are we?' The sonographer was chatty, composed and efficient as she came into the cramped room, shutting the door firmly behind her. Her friendly, business-like demeanour brought calmness to the situation. 'You were due to have your twenty-week scan next week, is that right?'

Jessica nodded.

'Try to relax, my love,' she coaxed, her gaze never lifting from the monitor in front of her.

Jessica stared at the screen. Almost immediately the grainy grey and white image was apparent. Just like her earlier scan, but bigger and more obvious. Her baby. Matthew now gripped her arm; she wasn't sure who was supporting whom.

Jessica watched the sonographer place the tip of her tongue against her bottom lip in concentration as her eyes narrowed, focusing on a fixed point on the screen, performing the task slowly, in silence. Eventually, she removed the wand from Jessica's stomach and sat up straight.

'Bear with me a second, Jessica. I'm just going to go and fetch one of my colleagues. I'd like their opinion on something. Shan't be a second.' Her smile was fleeting and forced as she hopped off her stool and left the room.

'How you doing?' Matthew spoke to the side of her head.

Jessica shrugged. How was she doing? She didn't know. She felt remote, third-party, as though watching herself from above, hovering somewhere near the strip-light with the dead flies trapped inside it.

'Morning, morning.' The balding doctor was brusque. He didn't waste time on pleasantries and went straight over to the screen to gaze through his glasses at a spot marked with a cross.

'Yup.' He nodded at the woman before standing upright and pulling his glasses from his face. He briefly tapped one arm of his glasses against his teeth before he spoke. When his words came, his eyes were half closed as if in prayer.

'We have had a good look at what's going on following your bleed, Mrs Deane.' He took a deep breath. 'And I'm afraid that it isn't good news.' He paused, smiling benignly at Matthew. 'My colleague and I are in agreement that there is no heartbeat on the screen.'

There was a moment's silence.

'Could... could it be that you just can't see it? Should we try again?' Matthew asked.

'I'm afraid not.' The doctor smiled again. 'We have been very thorough and I would say that, looking at the measurements, this has been the case for a week or two. I am very sorry.'

All four stood in silence, letting the information sink in.

'What happens now?' Matthew hardly dared ask.

'We'll give you a minute or two and then come back in and explain your options.' He nodded at them both and made his way from the room, with his colleague creeping diffidently behind him.

Matthew stood and looked down at his wife as she lay impassively on the couch. She pulled her gown down, covering the redundant bump.

'I want it gone in the quickest possible way, Matt. I don't want to be like this any longer than I have to.' She looked at him for the first time, aghast to see his face contorted with tears.

'It'll be okay, it'll all be okay.' He took her hand inside his and kissed her knuckles.

Jessica ran her palm over the plastic-coated mattress and felt her mind slip in a fog of confusion. She was given a pre-med and had a cannula fitted in her hand, just as she had when Lilly was born, but this was for a procedure of a different kind. A procedure – those words said it all; a procedure and not a birth. The 'evacuation of retained products of conception' was a horrible, unemotional term, but presumably that was the point. Jessica for one was grateful.

Matthew kissed her cheek as she was wheeled into the operating theatre. 'I'll be right here, waiting, my love,' he said.

She nodded and closed her eyes, submitting to the dark that enveloped her.

Arriving home without the baby, Jessica felt strangely detached from her body. She was vaguely aware of how her stomach cramped as if it was in labour, but it was like it was happening to someone else. She felt drained and her brain was all jumbled up, trying to distinguish between labour and loss. She couldn't understand why the hospital had insisted she rode to the car in a wheelchair, since the moment they arrived home she'd be climbing stairs and hopping on and off the loo, but when she tried to point this out her tongue couldn't form the words.

Margaret and Anthony had spent the day at Merton Avenue, looking after Lilly, who was beyond excited to see her mummy and daddy back home. Matthew made his way up the path with his arm around his wife's waist. She made slow progress, holding the gate and wincing a little at every movement, her womb throbbing with each step.

Mrs Not-Very was on the pavement. She'd watched in silence as Jessica hesitantly folded her limbs from the car. 'So that's you back then,' she said. 'I wish you all luck.' It was as close to kindness that the woman had ever come and it made Matthew tear up.

Indoors, Lilly waddled past her mum and up the stairs, with Granny Margaret in hot pursuit.

'I'll make you a cup of tea, Jess, in one second.' Margaret kissed her daughter-in-law as she passed her in the hallway. 'I've spoken to Coral, she sent all her love of course and says she'll be over just as soon as you feel up to it.'

Jessica nodded her appreciation at their concern.

'Come and sit down, Jess.' Anthony's tone was soft.

'Actually, Dad, I think she wants a sleep and a bit of a lie down.' Matthew looked across at his wife.

'Yes, of course. Of course,' Anthony breathed, unsure of the right thing to do or say.

'Come on, Jess, let's get you tucked up.' Matthew placed his hand on the small of his wife's back and guided her up the stairs.

The clean bed linen was peeled back. Jessica lowered herself gently onto the mattress and Matthew removed her slippers and lifted her legs, pulling the cover over her. He bent and kissed her forehead, fatherly, concerned. 'You go to sleep, my love, and I'll come and check on you in a bit. I'll feed Lilly and get her settled.'

'Matt?'

'Yes?'

'I made this happen. It's all my fault. But I did it for us, for us and Lilly,' she murmured.

'No. No, Jess. Of course it's not your fault! It just happens, there's not always a reason. You mustn't think that. Don't worry about a thing.' He gently kissed his wife again, her eyes already closed.

She just wanted to blot out the world, wanted to disappear. She lay in the dark and listened to Margaret, Anthony and Matthew fussing over Lilly. She heard the click of the kettle, the chink of china mugs being placed on the table and the scrape of cutlery. She heard the phone ring, the tap run, the loo flush and the echoes of their hushed words. She felt like she was floating, like she was on the outside looking in. She heard the occasional sob, sensed the sad, regretful atmosphere, the whispered grief. But she felt nothing but guilt and relief. Like she had been given a reprieve. And that was the truth. Her wish had come true.

5th June, 2015

Sometimes, I think about what my life would be like if my wish hadn't come true. I think about a life where I am a different kind of person and time has moved on. I picture myself at a kitchen window, with Lilly playing in the garden outside; she is quite grown-up, inquisitive, but still sweet and beautiful. Oh so beautiful. And my other child, my boy, who lived, because I hadn't wished it otherwise, is sitting by my feet playing with his cars while I prepare vegetables for supper, in readiness for Matthew who is on his way home from work. In this vision that makes me smile, the sun is shining, life is good and I am even wearing a pinny.

Twenty-Three

The days following the miscarriage were a rollercoaster. There were times when Jessica felt full of energy and brimming with joy at being with Lilly; she whizzed around the house like a whirling dervish, vacuuming behind sofas, cleaning windows and scrubbing the oven, belting out tunes while she did so. Lilly clearly loved these days: the house had the atmosphere of a party and the buzz was infectious. And then there were other days, when even the thought of having to make up a bottle or prepare a slice of toast and honey left Jessica crying and weary with fatigue. Today was one of those days. Today she felt so pulled by the demands of her little girl, it felt like her head might explode. Lilly refused to nap and when she wasn't eating wanted Jessica to play with her. Jessica raced around the house, trying to cope. The clock ticked and she felt like there wasn't a moment that wasn't allocated. It was relentless. She felt a squirm of guilt as she put Lilly in front of a movie so she could doze by her side on the sofa. Usually, when the credits rolled, she would wake with such guilt that she would smother her daughter in kisses of apology, before the next wave of tiredness hit and she was once again reaching for the remote control to replay a Disney classic. But this time the phone rang, jolting her out of her sleep and making Lilly cry loudly. Desperately scrabbling for the strawberry paracetamol with one hand and the phone with the other, Jessica answered the phone on the tenth ring.

'I'd nearly given up!' It was Lavinia, Jessica's favourite children's editor, who worked with the agency that had commissioned her before. 'I heard you had a baby! Congratulations! But that's not why I'm ringing. I want you to get involved in this fantastic new project. Another nature-type book, but this time it's talking ladybirds and bugs who take tea and tend gardens. It's just delightful and you'd be absolutely perfect!'

Jessica gritted her teeth and forced a smile into her voice. 'How lovely to hear from you! But I'm afraid I'm rather tied up right now.' She looked around at the chaos of the kitchen in which she stood and burst out laughing. The thought of being able to work to a deadline or concentrate long enough to produce anything was indeed laughable. 'To be honest, Lavinia, I think I'll be tied up for a very long time. I'm a mum now and as you may have heard, it's kind of a full-time job!' She laughed again, more drily this time. It wasn't as if her work was valued; it was, as Matthew had implied, a glorified hobby.

Lavinia seemed vaguely insulted by Jessica's comment. 'Fine, well, when you get bored of being a yummy mummy you just let me know.'

She hung up the phone, and Jessica stood still for a moment, trying not to howl at the thought of being anything like a yummy mummy. On days like this, with greasy hair and still in her pyjamas, Jessica felt transparent, invisible, light as air, not of this world. As she went back into the sitting room to replace the phone, she caught sight of her reflection in the window and gasped, astonished to see that she was a solid living thing.

Lilly was now very quiet, withdrawn and for this Jessica was grateful. They were getting through another day.

Later that week, Jessica woke and listened to the noises of morning, dogs barking, cars hooting and the boiler whirring into life. Matthew stood alone in the kitchen, waiting for the kettle to boil. He needed that first cup of tea of the day to remove some of the grit from his throat and provide a small amount of fuel to see him through the first few hours. The days tumbled into one another, there was no time to stop and think. Magnus had called him out over his performance and late delivery a couple of times, he knew he was going to have to come clean soon and confess to the nightmare in which he existed. For a nightmare it was.

'You off now?' Jessica appeared at the kitchen door, her face imploring him to stay for just one more minute.

'Yes, off to see a client, so I'm driving in. My dad would like him – he builds houses, lots of them. I shan't be late. Will you be okay?'

Jessica nodded as though trying to convince them both.

Gripping Edith's steering wheel, Matthew cracked open the window an eighth of an inch, hoping the slight breeze might stir the air and help him focus. It didn't. The constant stream of cars travelling in the opposite direction on the dual carriageway blurred under his gaze as they swept past him. He ran his fingers over the glossy brochure that lay on the passenger seat, his client's latest project. Glancing at the image unleashed a whole new level of sadness. The picture on the front was of a sparkly car in a driveway and a woman waving from the open front door, grinning as she half turned with a toddler on her hip, both eager to get back inside her brand new, shiny home. The wording promised a life of peace and tranquillity and that was what he craved, more than anything: peace. His fingers hovered over the neat front lawn, where there was a swing and an abandoned football; it made his heart constrict and stopped the breath in his throat.

He took a large lungful of air. 'Oh, Jess! Jess. I can't go on like this. I can't.' Hot tears ran down his nose and streaked his face. He hadn't cried like this with any regularity since he was a boy and yet this was the second time in as many weeks. He had almost forgotten how to give in to the tears. It felt like drowning and once he started, he couldn't stop. The embarrassment of crying so hard in a semi-public place made it even worse.

He pushed at his eyes, trying to stem the flow, but it was useless. 'I can't do this. I can't do it any more. I've had enough. What the fuck is wrong with her!' He slammed the steering wheel with the heel of his hand. 'It's such a bloody mess and so tiring. I am tired.' He spoke aloud as he travelled alone; his crying found a new rhythm as he took two short intakes of breath for every release.

Jessica didn't know which kind of day it was going to be until she opened her eyes or tried to stand, but today was a good day. She and Lilly had just got back from the park; they had fed the ducks and chased each other around a tree. A good day indeed.

Her GP, Dr Boyd, was kind and supportive, adjusting her dosage of antidepressants and encouraging her to contact him as and when she needed to. She did so less and less. There were only so many times that she could repeat how she was feeling, detailing the misery of her routine, only to be told, in a tone usually reserved for the elderly or infirm, to hang in there and that she would turn a corner, eventually. The loop of depression in which she lived sapped her of energy and the will to live. These were the darkest of days.

It was after three days of observing Jessica operate on a fairly even keel, watching her smile and converse as though all was well, that Matthew came home with a surprise. He beamed at her from the foot of the stairs as she came down with an armful of laundry and Lilly.

'Really?' she asked.

'Really. A whole weekend, just you and me. A big bed, room service, large TV and no alarm clock – how does that sound?' He smiled, knowing he needed this as much as she did.

Jessica grinned at her man. 'That sounds like absolute heaven.'

'Good. Because it's all arranged. Your parents are coming here to look after Lilly and you and I are off to Cliveden for a bit of spoiling.'

'Oh, Matt! No way. Can we afford it?'

'No, we can't. But my mum and dad are treating us.'

'Bless them. It'll be wonderful, just me and my man. I can't wait.' She slipped her arm around his waist and held him tight. 'I really can't wait.'

'Good. Me too. Now go pack because we leave in the morning! And don't worry about laundry and clothes: apart from breakfast, when you will be in public, you won't be needing much.' He winked at her.

Jessica kissed her husband on the cheek as she passed him in the hallway. She had a good, good feeling about this weekend.

Coral gathered Lilly into her arms to wave her mum and dad off from the front doorstep. She caught her son-in-law's arm. 'Look after her, lovely.'

'I will.' He smiled.

'It will all be okay, Matthew. She just needs a bit of down time and some TLC.' Coral smiled, confident that this weekend would be the break they both needed.

Matthew nodded and gathered their overnight bags from the hall floor.

Lilly waved in earnest and then cried before waving some more.

'Don't worry about a thing, we'll all be fine! See you on Sunday!' Roger shouted as they threw their luggage in the boot and jumped in Edith.

Jessica watched her family getting smaller and smaller in the wing mirror. She sank down in the seat and popped the radio on. Adele's 'Someone Like You' was playing.

'Do you remember dancing to this in the kitchen?' she asked as she watched the houses of Merton Avenue and then the shops, restaurants and bars of Chiswick High Road glide by. Both of them turned their thoughts to that enchanted evening, which felt like a lifetime ago. Jessica looked across at her handsome husband. She reached over the console and rested her hand on his thigh. 'We can get back to that, Matt. We can. I know it.' She squeezed his leg beneath his jeans. 'I love you. And that's all that matters, isn't it? I love you.'

'I know.' Matthew looked at his wife. 'I love you too.'

Less than an hour later, Matthew flicked the indicator and turned Edith into the gravel driveway of Cliveden House.

'Oh, wow!' Jessica sat forward in her seat and peered at the grand house in front of them. 'This is stunning!'

Matthew patted Edith's dashboard. 'Don't feel inferior, Edith. You might not be the flashiest motor ever to grace this driveway, but what you lack in grandness, you make up for in reliability.'

Jessica giggled. 'You sound as nuts as me!'

'Blimey, Jess, that's saying something.' And they both laughed, a good belly laugh, just like they used to.

Their room was sumptuous: fancy and decadent, with a large four-poster bed and beautiful antique half-moon tables on which sat ornate lamps that gave the room just the right amount of cosy. The large sash windows, whose plush drapes were tied back, gave the best view of the incredible manicured grounds. The en-suite bathroom had a large roll-top bath and a vintage brass radiator.

'I rather like it here,' Jessica murmured from the depths of the bed as she finished off a healthy portion of lobster ravioli, washed down with champagne. She had questioned whether the alcohol was a good idea, given that she was taking medication, but she and Matthew agreed that for one night it would be fine; this was, after all, a treat. After her second glass, she had to agree, it was a splendid idea!

The two lay in the middle of the disarranged bed and looked at the large moon through the window. The night was silent, the air warm and the atmosphere perfect.

Jessica laid her head on the flat space between her husband's shoulder and chest, feeling the soft rhythmic pulse against her cheek. She blinked. 'I'm giving you a butterfly kiss,' she whispered, beating her lashes against his pale flesh. She felt Matthew's arms envelop her in a hug. Their conversation was slow, unhurried.

'I didn't know what a butterfly kiss was when I met you. Do you remember?'

She smiled. 'There were lots of things you didn't know.'

'That's true.' He grazed the top of her head with a kiss.

'You didn't know the car-name rule. I remember asking what your little Fiat was called and you looked at me as though I was crackers. His number plate was R zero fifty-five – you'd been driving around in "Ross" and you didn't even know it.' She felt his chuckle grow in his chest.

'And I didn't know the rule concerning red sauce and brown sauce.'

'But it's so easy to remember.' She rolled her eyes. 'It's always red unless it's a dish that starts with P, like pie or pasty, then it's brown. Other than that, it's red. Easy.'

'What about paella?'

'Neither sauce required, clever clogs, although we didn't

eat much paella when I was growing up. We had a fair few fish fingers though.'

They laughed and lay against each other, relaxed, with the flames of happiness flickering from long-forgotten embers. Jessica felt contentment swirl inside her like a swallowed cure. She felt better, so much better. This was her medicine, this was what she needed: to lie in the arms of her husband, enjoying the quiet of being alone together. When she spoke, her voice was small, conscious of spoiling the moment and wary of being heard.

'I love it here,' she whispered.

'Me too,' Matthew mumbled drowsily.

'Do... do you ever wish it could be like this all the time?'

'Hmmm?' Matthew was close to sleep and needed it repeating.

Jessica drew breath. 'Do you ever wish we could turn back the clock to when there was just the two of us?' She let the idea hang in the air before continuing. 'Back to when we could do what we wanted, sleep when we wanted. Just the two of us?' She heard him sigh, but he didn't say anything. Jessica took this as her cue to continue. 'I sometimes think of the night we made Lilly. She should have been called Pimm's. Do you remember, we were so drunk on it when we made her, I was convinced she'd come out with slices of cucumber and a strawberry on her head.' Jessica laughed.

Matthew laughed too. 'We'd best not tell her that! Far better she think that we planned her and yearned for her rather than she was the result of a few drinks too many!'

Jessica raised her head and propped it on his shoulder. 'I wish... I wish I'd not drunk so much that night. I wish we'd waited a few years, stuck to our five-year plan and had more moments like this.'

Matthew shifted, easing her head from his body until he sat up.

She ran her fingers over his strong, bare back and continued. 'If I hadn't been so sloshed, I wouldn't have been so unlucky and then if we hadn't had Lilly, there wouldn't have been the next baby.'

Jessica's words tailed off; she was only half aware that she was actually voicing the thoughts that she dwelt on with regularity in private. It was as if she was lulled into her chatterbox state by a rare moment of euphoria, helped by the champagne. 'I think about it a lot. I imagine what we'd be doing if it was just us. We wouldn't know what it was like to be truly knackered or to have every second of every day hijacked by a baby. We'd be free… And I think about the miscarriage and I feel guilty because you were so upset, but I was just relieved, that's the truth!'

Matthew brought his knees up beneath the sheets until his elbows rested on them and with his head in his hands he began to cry. Jessica at first thought he was laughing, until she heard the unmistakable sound of sobbing.

'Matt! Oh no, Matt! Don't cry. Please don't cry! Why are you crying?' She sat back against the pillows and wondered what to do.

All Matthew could mutter was, 'Oh God. Oh my God!' His tears were a mix of grief and rage. His breathing was erratic. He couldn't talk.

Jessica listened to him and watched, wide-eyed from the other side of the bed.

His words when they did come were delivered with a newly hardened edge to his voice. 'No! No, Jess. I never, ever think that. I love my girl, I love my family and I could never, ever think of Lilly in terms of being *unlucky*.' This word he almost spat. 'There was nothing unlucky about being given our beautiful little girl.' He swiped at his tears with the back of his hands and threw back the sheet as he stumbled from the bed.

Jessica shrank back against the padded headboard. 'I didn't mean it like that,' she whispered.

'No? How did you mean it, Jess? How the fuck did you mean it? I don't know what's got into you. I don't know what's happened. I try to understand. I do. I have been more than patient, but sometimes I don't know what the fuck is going on! I can't keep pace with your moods. Every time I put the key in the door, I never know what I'm going to find. Your highs and lows have a massive effect on Lilly and me. It's like holding a mirror up to your mood: the rest of us take our cues from you and it's shit, really shit!' Matthew stood by the side of the bed, staring at her like she was a stranger.

'I know it's shit. I… I just get so tired,' she said. 'So tired that I can't stay awake, can't think. And when I do think, I feel so sad that it saps every ounce of strength that I have ever possessed and I miss me. I miss the me I used to be. The me that bounced and laughed and looked forward to things.'

'Christ, *you* miss her? Try being me! I fucking miss her – if I ever knew her, that is.' He placed his hands on his hips and stared at his wife, his tone, clipped. 'I'm not so sure sometimes.'

'I'm still here, Matt.' Jessica patted her chest. 'I'm sorry I'm not the woman you need me to be. I need you to help me, Matthew, and I need you to wait for me, please!' She was almost begging. 'It will be okay when I'm not so tired. It will.' She nodded, trying to convince them both.

'*You're* tired?' He snorted his anger. 'I'm busting my balls commuting in and out of town every day, an hour there and back just so you can have the fucking house of your dreams and *you're* tired? I do everything in the house because if I don't it all goes to pig shit, which you seem happy to wallow in, but I'm not.'

'It's not just tired, it's... it's like I'm in this dark place—'

'Dark place? I tell you what, I'll swap you. I'll take wandering around in my pyjamas and playing with Lilly all day. I'll fucking take it any day of the week. Christ, it's not as if you're cooking dinner or cleaning the place regularly! What the fuck is it that you do all day that is making you so tired?'

Jessica slunk further down the bed. Crawling into a ball, she pulled the sheet up under her nose.

'Paz said I had to give you time and space. Said that it wasn't your fault and that you were fragile.'

Jessica closed her eyes, hating the level of detail with which he and Topaz had discussed her. It made her feel less of a person and if she was less of a person then what was she? She knew that everyone was talking about her – her parents, Polly, everyone. It left her feeling as if she had no one to talk to, no one to keep her secrets. She was on her own. Completely on her own.

Matthew continued. 'How much time and space do you need, for God's sake? Because I tell you what, Jess, I'm at my fucking wits' end and I'm finding it very hard to reconcile you with the girl I married.'

'I don't know where she is, Matthew. But I want her to come back. I do. But I feel as if I am drowning. I am drowning,' she whispered, mouth hidden by the sheet as she stared at him.

'And even now, you can't say anything, not one word. Not one fucking word. You're just lying there in silence.' Matthew grabbed his pants, jeans and shirt from the floor. 'Lilly is the most amazing thing we have ever done. Our greatest achievement. She comes first, always. Before us and before you. Got it?'

'I'm sorry,' she managed.

'Oh God! Please! Not "sorry" again! I don't want to hear sorry. It feels a little thin.' He reached for the door handle before turning back to look at his wife, who lay in the middle of the grand bed. 'To be honest, Jess, sometimes you make it really hard to keep loving you.'

Jessica heard the door close and looked up at the space that he had vacated. Her tears fell hot and fast. The thought, the very idea of Matthew not loving her, was absolutely the worst thing that she could imagine. Jessica just wished that things could go back to the way they were when she and Matt were happy. She would do anything, anything to recapture those days.

18th July, 2015

This morning I got the sweetest news you can imagine. I met with my doctor and he told me that I will be released in six weeks. Six weeks! I can't quite believe it. I can't! I will be free of these walls and I will no longer have to force down food that sits like ashes in my mouth. I can't wait to stare at the clouds, walk barefoot and breathe clean lungfuls of fresh air. I shall take in the view and feel the breeze on my face. My heart is singing. I have smiled for the first time in as long as I can remember and I have songs in my head. It's wonderful. Music has been gone from me for such a long time. I have missed it. I have missed lots of things.

My doctor tells me I have to write everything down, everything that I can remember from the day itself. So that's what I'll do. Not for anyone else to read, just for me. He says it will help greatly as I work towards my release day. It's going to be hard, because much of it I have blocked out of my mind since. I have had to, to survive. But mainly it's hard because it's like writing about a person I don't know, a person I don't recognise. It's as if she was this dark shadow of me lurking inside and now she has gone I can only look back at that time with deep, deep sadness and regret. It is hard for me to accept what I did, whether in an altered state of mind or not, I know I will pay for it, for the rest of my life.

Twenty-Four

Polly paced the kitchen floor.

'So how was the weekend? Did you guys catch up, get good sleep?'

'Something like that. The place was beautiful and the food was great.' Matthew avoided eye contact.

Polly picked up a new black and white framed photo of Lilly. 'She is so beautiful! Look at her little nose, Paz! I've loved seeing her today. She has really grown.'

'Think someone's getting broody.' Matthew winked at his friend.

'Hey, she's pushing on an open door. I think when the time is right it'll happen for us and it will be such a gift.'

'I want one just like this! She's so good and so gorgeous!' Polly squeaked.

'And she's a great little sleeper. It certainly makes things easier.' Matthew hesitated, smiled a little and filled the kettle.

Polly knew that nothing was easy, not for Jessica. 'How's she doing?' she asked, her voice quieter.

Matthew pinched the bridge of his nose and sighed. 'Not... err... Not great.'

'Is she still taking her medication?' Topaz asked.

'She says she is.' Matthew gave the honest answer; he wasn't sure what was going on. Jessica had hardly spoken to him in the past week, most of which she had spent in bed with the curtains closed.

'And what about counselling, is that still happening?' Paz prompted.

Matthew shook his head. 'She doesn't want to see anyone. Which makes things hard. I'm worried about her. I know it's a dip she's going through – losing the baby has hit her hard – but she won't talk about it and of course it sent her hormones haywire again.' He sighed. 'We need to give her time, I know that, but I can't watch her like a hawk every minute, that'll send us both crazy. Even crazier.' He smirked.

'Is she interested in Lilly?'

'No. Not really.' Matthew busied himself with the gathering of mugs and the making of coffee. 'Not at all, in fact. I do everything for her and Jess is happy to let me. Her mum and dad pop over when they can, but it's not a good situation, not good at all.'

'Well, Lilly certainly looks happy,' Polly interjected.

'Yep. It's funny. She's being an angel, almost like she knows she has to be.'

'Can I go up and see her?' Polly asked.

'Yes, of course.' Matthew nodded. 'She might be sleeping.'

Topaz smiled at his wife as she left the room. 'I'm worried about you, Matt.'

Matthew scanned the cluttered work surface and turned to his friend. 'Shall we go and sit down?'

The two men picked up their cups of coffee and made their way into the sitting room. The dishes could wait.

'So, come on, how are you doing?'

'Truthfully?' Matthew paused. 'I don't know how much more I can take.' This was the first time he had shared this with anyone other than his wife. He exhaled. 'The weekend was a complete disaster. I'm hoping that when she's fully rested—'

'How much sleep do you think she needs?'

'I know what you're saying, Paz. But it's difficult. I lost it a bit when we were away and she's kind of closed me out since then. I didn't mean to and I regret it, but we rowed and I said some things… I don't want to push her, I want to support her and I think there is a fine line.'

'I agree with you, Matt, but leaving her to stew under the duvet is not going to help her. Not going to help anyone. It's not addressing anything. The problem won't just go away.'

'What do you suggest?'

'You won't like what I suggest.' Topaz looked serious.

'Try me.'

Polly knocked on the bedroom door as she pushed it open. The window needed opening. The room smelt of stale air and a body in need of a shower. Jessica lay very still on her side of the bed. Polly crept in and sat on the flattened side of the duvet.

'Hey, bud. I just came up to let you know that you are back to being Mrs Boring, in case you were wondering, and yet again, if I could choose a more exciting and engaging best friend, I definitely would.' Polly lay on her back with her head on Matthew's pillow and crossed her legs at the ankle.

Jessica felt the springs fold under Polly's weight. She could hear her friend's breathing. She wanted Polly to go away. She was in no mood for her humour or her company.

'I know you are awake,' Polly said. 'I can tell because you are being extra quiet and not moving. Don't forget how often I've bunked in with you over the years. So, because you are my best friend whether I like it or not, I'm going to ignore your silence and chat anyway. Like I used to when we shared a tent at Guide camp and you wanted to sleep and I wanted to chat.' Polly cleared her throat. 'So I think Matthew is a bit worried about you, doll. We all are, because we love you. We love you very much.'

Jessica blinked rapidly and pushed her face further into the pillow.

'Paz and Matt are downstairs putting the world to rights. Lilly is zonked out. She's been so funny today.'

Jessica screwed her eyes shut. The last thing she needed was an update on what everyone was doing. As ever, she hated the fact that they were all talking about her. All talking about her and not to her. Having to listen to Polly, who sounded happy, caused bile to rise in her throat, which threatened to choke her. It took all of her strength not to shout at her friend that she should enjoy this bit, make the most of every second before a child came along to spoil it.

'I'm sorry about the baby, Jess. I really, really am. You were doing so well, this is just a bump in the road. And you will bounce back out the other side, I know you will.' Polly sighed. 'And the good news is, I've found you a cleaner! A great girl called Paula; she lives near here. She could come in for a couple of mornings and run the hoover over or help with the ironing, whatever. I shall leave her card on the fridge in case you want to call her, okay? Okay.'

Polly sat in silence for a minute more. 'I bought you a present. I'll pop it on your bedside cabinet and you can look at it later if you feel up to it.' She stood up and placed her gift by the lamp and a half-empty glass of water. 'I'll leave you now, Jess, let you sleep. But when you're ready to talk, just shout and I'll be here like a shot. I love you. Don't ever forget that.' She patted her friend's still form and walked towards the door.

Jessica opened her eyes and lifted her head; on her cabinet was a beautiful red leather notebook.

'One more thing,' Polly said before closing the door behind her. 'You can't stay up here forever. You need to make a plan. A plan that gets you out of this room and allows you to start living your life. I'll help you if you like, we all will. But it needs to happen and it needs to happen soon. We miss you.'

Polly made her way back downstairs, where Matthew and Topaz were mid conversation.

'That's not going to happen, Paz! No way am I sending her away.' Matthew's tone was sharp.

'Well, if you change your mind, I have the details.'

Matthew wrinkled his nose and swallowed. He gave a small nod in acknowledgement.

'She's sleeping,' Polly lied, preferring this to the fact that her best friend had just ignored her. 'Maybe another week in Majorca is in order?'

‘Christ, Poll, that can’t be the bloody solution. We’d be bankrupted by childcare and flights within three months!’

‘I know it’s not practical. I’m just trying to think of how to fix things.’

‘We all are.’ Topaz looked at Matthew and smiled.

The doorbell rang, once, twice and a third time.

‘Who the hell...?’ Matthew jumped up and sprinted to the front door, relieved that Lilly hadn’t stirred.

‘Maaate!’ Jake shouted as he leant on the doorframe, his eyes glazed, hair mussed and shirt buttons undone to reveal his pale, hairless chest. He swayed a little as he held up the thin plastic strip off which hung four cans of Stella Artois. ‘Sunday night is brewski night!’ He staggered forward as if to enter the house, but Matthew raised his arm to block him.

‘Not now, Jake. It’s not a good time.’ Matthew looked at his unshaven friend and felt a flicker of anger.

‘Come on, Deano! Bit of Eurosport, couple of cold tins – where’s my wingman? Hey? Where’s my boy gone?’ The alcoholic fumes wafted off him.

Lilly started crying. Matthew sighed. ‘I’ve got to go, Jake.’ He gestured towards the sitting room.

‘That’s not your job, mate. That’s women’s work! Let Jess sort her out. No point having a dog and barking yourself, isn’t that what they say?’

Topaz appeared in the hallway. ‘Hey, Jake.’ He nodded in the direction of the stairs. ‘Sorry, Matt, Lilly’s crying, do you want us to go up? Or...’

‘It’s okay, I’ll go.’ Matthew looked flustered.

Jake stared down the hallway. ‘Hey, veggie bonkers

hippy bloke! I see how it is. What we all doing in there, chanting around a joss stick?' He raised his arms and tried to wave his hands, dropping his beers in the process. One dented can started spraying golden foam all over the path. Lilly's cries increased in volume, quickly followed by her calling from the top of the stairs.

'Not tonight, Jake.' Matthew turned and headed up the stairs to quiet Lilly.

'You playing mummy, are you, Toe-Paz? Helping with the baby? Are you living in the "now"?' He used his fingers to draw speech marks in the air and chuckled.

Topaz stepped forward and in the blink of an eye had bunched Jake's shirt under his throat. The muscles in his broad forearm corded and his jaw was set. It caught Jake by surprise. He tried to draw breath as his face turned pink.

Topaz's voice was quiet, calm. 'I have tried to like you, Jake. I have tried really hard. I make it my policy to try and like everyone. But you're an arsehole. If you ever talk to me again, even one word, I will hurt you. Properly hurt you. Do you understand?'

'C... c... an't breathe!'

Topaz released his grip and watched as Jake fell against the wall, gasping and reaching for something solid.

'I'll let you off with those two, but no more. Got it?'

Jake nodded.

'Good.' Very calmly, Topaz closed the front door.

'Was that Jakey?' Polly asked as her husband came back into the room.

'Yes.' Topaz smiled.

'Aww, how is he?' she asked.

'He's grand, Polly. Really grand.'

Jessica could hear Jake's voice coming from downstairs and then Polly and Paz chatting and Matt coming upstairs to see Lilly. She closed her eyes in an attempt to shut out what she had heard earlier, but it echoed in her head. 'You won't like what I suggest,' Topaz had said. And Matt, her Matt, who once said he would love her forever had said, 'Try me.' Jessica knew that they had all had enough of her. They were trying to get rid of her. She felt a rush of bitter, bitter disappointment followed by utter, utter hopelessness. Polly was right about needing a plan but she would need it sooner than she thought.

25th July, 2015

What I *do* remember is that I knew October the fourteenth was the day. I hadn't planned it as such, but if I'm being honest, I knew it was coming and that thought sustained me. Like an appointment marked on the calendar with a big red cross, a beacon, it shone at me in the early hours while I scrabbled with half-closed lids to locate the tap, kettle, bottle and milk for mixing. And even if the date wasn't something to look forward to exactly, it still had a calming effect, knowing that afterwards I would be able to breathe properly for the first time in… I don't know how long.

I was obsessed with sleep because I was tired. Not just tired, not the run-of-the-mill sleepiness that you feel at the end of the day when you stretch, yawn and long for your bed, hoping the alarm isn't set too early. No, this was a bone-deep fatigue that meant I could hardly think straight. Words and thoughts tumbled inside my head, knotting together in random formations that slowed me down as I tried to decipher them. I stared at people I knew, willing their names to come to me before I embarrassed us both. Tears leaked from my eyes, but I wasn't actually crying – there were no fractured breaths, no sobs, none of that. It was as if my soul was weeping. As if my sadness and my exhaustion were indivisible. I didn't recognise myself, which was scary in itself. My eyes looked sunken, skull-like, the sockets wide and the half-moon crescents the colour of purple bruises against my pale, jutting cheekbones.

In the supermarket that morning, I chatted idly to a girl, or rather she chatted to me. 'I'm knackered, *so* tired...' she said as she scanned my pasta and a four-pack of loo roll. I laughed out loud, snorted a derisory, sneering chuckle. I wanted to put my face an inch from hers and speak through gritted teeth, saying, 'You don't know tired! You have no idea of what real tiredness is! You think staying out late and working a full day makes you tired? Just wait, just you wait...' But of course I didn't because it wasn't her fault. She didn't know. No one knows until they are in it and then it is too late.

I walked back from the shops, initially with a bit of a spring in my step. It was nice to be out in the fresh air. And then I thought about going back inside the house and it made me feel quite desolate. If there had been a way to avoid walking through the front door, I would have taken it. I cried as I rounded the corner. There were times when it was a relief to cry out loud because often I thought I was crying and actually I was just staring ahead in silence, crying on the inside. That was the worst feeling in the world. My hair was irritating me – greasy and grubby, it hung lankly against my skin and I thought how much easier it would be if I didn't have any hair at all.

Twenty-Five

Jessica pulled the band from her hair and felt her greasy locks cling to her face. It irritated her beyond belief. Putting the key in the lock, she dumped the shopping on the kitchen table and looked in on Lilly, who was in front of the TV, exactly where she had left her. 'I'm back now.' She sniffed up her tears and smiled briefly at the little girl.

Jessica trod the stairs and stood at the sink in the bathroom. With her legs splayed, she threw her head forward until her thick, chocolate-coloured curls hung over her head in a curtain that nearly reached the bathroom floor. Gathering her locks into a ponytail in her left hand, she righted herself and smiled. She looked a bit like a genie with a big fat rope of hair sitting on top of her head. With the scissors poised in her right hand, Jessica started to cut. The sound the blades made as they sliced into her hair was very pleasing; hypnotic. When she had chopped all around the ponytail and it came away in her hand, she shook her head and stared in the mirror. It was surprisingly even. She threw the discarded mass of hair onto the floor and cut the right side until it sat over her ear. This made the whole thing ridiculously lopsided and so, turning her head to the right, she cut the left side to match. Next she trimmed the long licks of hair that hung from her crown and then a little more from the back. When she had finished, her hair was short in places and shorn in others.

Jessica placed her hand on her reflection in the mirror and stared. She didn't recognise the face that stared back and that suited her just fine. Gripping the scissors, she drew back her fist and jabbed their point at the glass. The top of the mirror fell away in long shards that clattered to the floor. The image of her face was now bisected by the fractured glass still hanging on the wall. 'Seven years bad luck…' she whispered.

Jessica picked up the phone in the bedroom. 'Mum…' She spoke quickly, gabbling, making little sense. 'Just wanted you to know that I have done it, finally! It was annoying me, much better this way. I know you'll be happy. One less thing to worry about.'

'Done what?' Coral was a little flustered by her daughter's directness and couldn't think what she was referring to.

'My hair!' Jessica laughed, loudly, as though her mum wasn't keeping up. 'I've cut it all off.'

'Have you? Who did that for you, love? Is it a bob?'

'*I* did. *I* cut it. And it's not just short, it's gone. All gone. It's for the best. It's all for the best, part of the plan.' With that she replaced the receiver, straightened the bedspread and reached under the bed for a bottle of strawberry paracetamol liquid. Then she made her way downstairs.

Jessica poured half a pint of milk into the saucepan, watched it start to bubble, then removed it from the heat to cool. She collected a bottle and teat from the cupboard and gave it a rinse before filling it three quarters full with the warm milk. Next she took the strawberry liquid from its box and tipped over half of it into the milk. She shook the bottle gently.

I padded up the stairs one at a time and walked into our bedroom. Lilly had relocated onto the rug beneath our window and was stirring a plastic spoon into an empty bowl. The clatter ricocheted like gunfire inside my head.

'It's a conspiracy, you know, Lilly,' I told her. 'It's as if all the women that have given birth are swimming in a pool of quicksand and they beckon you in from the depths, waving and smiling and saying, "Come in, the water's lovely!" And so you jump, and almost immediately you start to sink and it's only when you are close to them that you can see their looks of panic, but by then it's too late, solid ground beneath your feet is something you will never feel again. Never. And it's a burden. It really is.'

Lilly just laughed, like she did at everything. Her fat, nappy-covered bottom meant she crouched awkwardly, with her feet planted firmly on the floor. Her blue eyes were bright, her dimpled cheeks raised in a smile that showed all her teeth, like she was excited. She was always like that, exuberantly happy. That's because she didn't understand. She had no idea of what lay ahead, was ignorant of the price she would have to pay for my shortcomings; she didn't know about the quicksand, how it would suck her in until she had no choice but to let it rise above her head or how, strangely, she, like me, would be glad of the dark escape that I was offering.

'I makin' cake now!' Lilly shouted. Always shouting.

When she saw her baby bottle in my hand, she shrieked, 'We play bubbas!' Whenever a new idea presented itself, her voice always got even louder.

She abandoned the bowl and spoon and kept one foot on the ground while she hopped on the other. She was clapping in time like a lame dancer as she turned in a circle. Her laugh was too high-pitched and again very loud. I watched her chubby hands smack together with fingers splayed, palm-to-palm, and it was as though it was happening in slow motion.

It's hard to explain, but I felt like the more energy she expended, the less I had. It had always been that way. Like we were a machine and I was the fuel that kept her going. But I was running out and she just wanted to go faster, faster.

I placed my hand across her little round tum and lifted her up onto our unmade bed. She settled herself back on the deep pillow, wiggling her bottom, trying to get comfortable as she pulled down her pretty white smocked top over her little jeans, which had a cluster of pink and green flowers sewn onto the hem of one leg. Her socks were stripy – pink and white – and when she lay flat, her little feet fell naturally inward. She flattened the front of her blouse, which had become bunched up inside her pale pink cotton cardigan, arranging and smoothing her clothes as if she was a grown-up and not a little girl who was not yet two.

'I all tangly, Mummy!' She smiled and hunched her shoulders briefly as though everything she said was a revelation.

I nodded in response. She didn't expect anything else from me.

Lilly was giggling, kicking her heels against the floral Indian cotton bedspread that was a wedding present. I heard my dad's voice saying, 'I don't think I can go any further without mentioning quite how beautiful my daughter looks today,' and I heard the roll of laughter and clapping that followed. It was such a lovely, lovely day. Perfect, in fact.

I lifted the bottle and Lilly lay ramrod straight apart from her arms, which stuck up, fingers flexing, grasping. A bit greedy, I thought.

'Mweh, mweh!' She did her best impression of a crying baby and my head automatically jerked towards the door. *Is that Lilly awake?* My heart rate increased at the prospect of dealing with that tiny baby and I felt the familiar band of angst tighten across my forehead. *No, no, it's okay. It's just Lilly pretending, playing bubbas, she's here on the bed and she's a little older now.*

'I a baby now.' She opened and closed her mouth like a little goldfish, trying to remember what being a baby was like.

That made me smile briefly – like her, I often tried to imagine not being me. I used to try and imagine what it would feel like not to be alive. I tried to imagine what it was like before I was born and what it would be like after I'd gone. It brought me fleeting moments of peace.

I handed the bottle to Lilly and she rammed it into her mouth. I watched as her very red lips worked quickly, gorging on the milk that I had flavoured with strawberry syrup. She was drinking very quickly and I could tell she couldn't taste the over-generous slug of sedative. Which was a good thing.

I ran my fingers through her pale golden hair with its bounce of curl on the end of each strand. It felt like silk.

She removed the bottle suddenly and it exited her mouth

with a loud sucking noise. Like everything else, that made her laugh. 'Loveoo, Mummy.' A glug of sticky milk slipped down her cheek and soaked into the pillowcase. Something else to wash. The blots, scuffs and dents on every surface in the house were so numerous I hardly noticed them any more. She blinked and immediately placed the bottle back in her mouth. Her eyes never left mine.

I stroked her cheek and watched as she finished it, saying 'Shhhh...' as though it was bedtime. I glanced at the clock on the bedside table; it was half past four in the afternoon. The dappled sunshine through the trees cast a moving image across the wall. The branches dipped and rose in the breeze, giving the impression of sea diamonds on the wall behind her head. It was all so quiet, so peaceful, until the phone rang and shattered the silence.

Jessica reluctantly picked up the phone.

'Jess?'

'Hello, Matthew. I've decided, I'm going to start work now. It's been far too long since I've worked on anything and now is the right time for me. I'm going to call Lavinia tomorrow and say I'm finally ready to tackle my next project. I feel quite excited about it.'

'Oh, well, that's good.' He noted her energetic tone and wondered if maybe Coral had got the wrong end of the stick; she had sounded panicked when she called, but things seemed fine. 'Your mum said you had cut your hair?'

'What?'

'Your hair, Jess. What have you done to your hair?'

'Oh, I cut it off.' She ran her free hand over her scalp. It was a little uneven, admittedly; some of it was just bristles, and where the scissors had slipped, there were one or two little cuts. But at least she didn't have to think about it.

'I don't...' Matthew started.

'You don't what?'

'I don't know why you did that.'

Jessica walked back and forth, her overly long pyjama bottoms dragging across the floor, gathering dust bunnies in their wake. 'I made our baby disappear, Matt. It was my fault. I wished it.' Jessica held the receiver close.

'You wished it?'

'Yes. I didn't want it and I made it happen.' She blinked.

'No you didn't, love.' Matthew swallowed the tears that massed at the back of his nose and throat. He covered his eyes and lowered his voice. He was as usual sitting within earshot of Guy.

'If you make a bad world, Matthew, then bad things are going to happen. My mum and dad made a bad world and they lost Danny, he got taken from them. And I have made a bad world,' she whispered.

'You didn't make a bad world, Jess. Any world you are in is infinitely more beautiful because you are in it.' His breath caught in his mouth.

'I'm sorry I didn't open the door,' she said, urgently.

'What? You don't have to answer the door, I have a key.'

'I should have let you in sooner, but I kept you out there in the rain.' She chewed her lip, which was quite raw. 'That was bad of me.'

'When, Jess?'

'When you asked me to marry you. In the car park. With your soggy bread and your jumper full of rain. I didn't like it because you hugged Jenny and she put her leg up on you. I remember it. I've always thought she was the type of girl you should be with.'

'Oh yes.' Matthew sniffed. 'Yes, you did, you kept me out in the rain!' He laughed through his tears.

'You are not really married to me any more, Matthew, you know that, don't you?' Her voice was quiet but steady.

'Yes I am, Jess. I am married to you now and I always will be. In sickness and in health, for richer or poorer, that's what we agreed, remember?' He raised his volume, no longer caring if Guy or anyone else heard.

She shook her head. 'I don't think it counts. Not now. I went and bought loo roll and pasta. We'd run out. The girl in the shop bothered me. I can't explain why.'

'It's good you went out. Did you manage okay with Lilly and the pushchair?'

'No, I left her here. I went on my own. It was quite nice just to have five minutes.'

'You... you left her?' he stuttered.

'Yes.' She smiled. 'She was fine. I was only gone for a little while.'

'Where is Lilly now?' he asked softly.

'Hmmm?' she hummed, needing the question repeating, unable to remember what he had asked.

'Where is Lilly?' he asked more firmly.

'She's here.' She looked at their little girl, who was sleeping. Sleeping very soundly.

'Jess, hang in there. I will be home very soon.' Matthew replaced the receiver and dialled for a taxi as he grabbed his case and jacket.

Jessica walked into their bathroom, popped the plug in and began to run a bath.

I hung up the phone and looked again at the hypnotic display of the alarm clock. Ten minutes had passed, maybe more, since I had given Lilly the strawberry syrup. I watched her tummy rise and fall as her blinks got slower and longer and her mouth fell open, slack and dribbling.

I laid my head next to hers on the pillow and I whispered, 'You are perfect, Lilly Rose. Far too perfect for this horrible world, where things change so fast that you feel like you might fall off. I'm so sorry. I'm so sorry you got me and not a different mum, a mum that knows how to do it. But I just don't. No matter how much I want to, I can't. And this is not a world I want you to live in. A world where you can't keep the people you love safe. You will suffer because of me – I will be punished, I know it, and you deserve better. So much better. Go to sleep, knowing that you are loved.'

I realised I was crying as I kissed her forehead and walked into our en-suite bathroom. I ran my thumb over the jagged edge of the large mirror, hardly noticing that it sliced deep, causing a crimson line to appear almost instantly. I swiped my thumb along my jawbone, touching the tip of my tongue against it, taking in the iron flavour.

I ran my hand under the tap, making sure the water wasn't too hot. I sat on the loo and stared at the running water, mesmerised. I held my hand under the stream and watched as my trickling blood left a strawberry trail suspended in the water. Pink. Lilly loved anything pink.

Once, not long after we met, I came home to find Matthew had run me a bath. There were candles flickering around the room and he brought me a cup of tea on a little tray. I thought it was the nicest bath I had ever had. It probably was.

The bath was nearly full, but I left the taps running. I liked the sound of the thundering spray. Constant noise helped dull the chatter in my head.

I went into the bedroom and over to the bed. Gently, I picked Lilly up. Her head lolled backwards against my arm. 'Out for the count, my darling.' I kissed her nose. Her arms dangled. One of her socks had fallen off, onto the bed; I grabbed it and stuffed it into my pyjama pocket.

Walking into the bathroom, I felt the water soaking my socks. I moved my toes against the wet floor and it felt quite nice, warm. I thought that I should probably turn the taps off, but I liked the thin wall of water that cascaded like shimmering glass over the rim. I watched it for a second or two and then stepped forward. Lilly was getting heavy.

I rested her against my stomach and kissed her scalp one last time. 'You'll never get sucked in, Lilly. I won't let that happen to you.'

I walked closer to the tub and she seemed to roll out of my arms. It made a big splash.

I was so tired. I closed my eyes and enjoyed the sound of the running water and the warmth around my feet.

I took a step and slipped slightly on the wet floor. The water was over my feet by then. My socks were heavy. That made me laugh a little. Heavy socks? What a ridiculous thing.

Before I left the bathroom I looked back, just once. Lilly's hair was fanned out like fine strands of pale gossamer in the water.

It was the most beautiful thing I had ever seen.

And just like that, I had done it, the very worst thing a woman could do.

Twenty-Six

I sat on the sofa, breathing deeply. My head felt quite clear. I don't know how long I sat for, but I felt very calm. For the first time in a long time, I felt peaceful and that was good.

I took a deep breath and ran my fingers over the little pink and white striped sock in my hand. The sock was dotted with blood, quite a lot of blood actually. I knew that I'd cut myself, but I couldn't really remember where or how.

The key clicked in the door. I sat upright and smiled, trying to look my best. I wondered if it was too late to go and find my perfume and spray some scent behind my ears. It probably was. I knew I needed to make more effort but decided that he would just have to take me as he found me. *Oh, Matthew!* I was so glad he was home. I missed him dreadfully during the day. I loved him so much. I wanted him to sit by my side and hold my hand and just enjoy the fact that I was feeling calm. The poor love, things hadn't been easy for him. I knew he wanted the house to be tidier and for me to be a bit more together.

'What the fuck?' he shouted, very loudly.

I could tell he wasn't happy. My stomach shrank and I shuddered. I so wanted him to be happy and I definitely didn't want him to be angry with me, especially not then, when I was feeling so peaceful.

He ran into the sitting room and he looked... crazy. Scared and crazy.

'What...? What the...?' he shouted, gasping for breath. He held his arms away from his body, as though he didn't know where to go or what to say next.

Finally he managed, 'Where's Lilly?'

'Where is Lilly?' he asked again, louder the second time. And then, pointing at Lilly's sock, 'Is that blood?'

I laughed and lifted the sock towards him. 'Don't worry, Matt. It's *my* blood. I cut my thumb on the mirror.' I smiled and nodded. 'I'm so glad you're home. Come and sit with me.' I patted the space on the sofa next to me. I could see his chest was heaving and his mouth was open.

He ran his hand through his hair and raced out of the room.

Then I heard it.

Matthew was screaming. I had never heard him scream before. I'd heard him shout, when he was angry or laughing. Yes, I'd heard him being very loud on more than one occasion, but this was something different. It sounded as if... as if he was dying, and I didn't like it one bit.

I blinked very quickly and put my hands over my ears. I wasn't very good with loud noises or bangs. I felt scared because he not only sounded sad but angry too and I didn't want him to be angry with me, that was the last thing I wanted. I just wanted him to come and sit by my side and hold me in his arms. His words from when we'd stood locked together in the rain were loud and clear in my head: 'Jess, my Jess. There is nothing you can do, nothing that would make me stop loving you.'

Even though my hands were over my ears and I was trying to hum to block out the noise, I could hear him shouting, 'Fuck! No!

Oh my God! Help me! Help! NO! Someone please help me! Please!'

He thundered down the stairs and out of the hallway into the street. And then I heard lots of pairs of feet hammering back up the stairs, all making lots of noise, banging around overhead. I wondered who he had invited in and why they were upstairs. We usually brought guests into the kitchen to have a cup of tea. There were lots of shouts and crying and a couple of different screams. And then more crying. It wasn't just Matt crying, other people were *howling* too. One sounded like a woman.

A little while later a man came into the sitting room. He poked his head around the door and scanned the walls and the floor before walking towards me. He was wearing a green jump-suit and very thin blue rubber gloves and he was carrying a little plastic box.

'Hello,' he said.

I looked at him, wondering if we had met before.

'My name is Chris.'

'Hello, Chris.' I smiled at him. He was about fifty, with short grey hair and he looked slim and fit, like a cyclist. 'Do you own a bike?' I asked.

He ignored my question and I wondered if he'd heard me. I was deciding whether or not to repeat it, when he said, 'I have come to help you.'

His voice was calm and I thought it was a very nice thing to say. But I wasn't sure how he could help me or what he meant by that exactly.

'Are you hurt, Jessica?' he asked.

I thought I must know him because he knew my name. I held up my thumb and flexed it. This caused the blood to pump again, breaking through the congealed crust. 'I've already told Matt it's just a little cut. Nothing to make a fuss about.'

He looked over my shoulder.

I turned around and noticed for the first time that part of the ceiling had fallen away, quite a large part, in fact.

'Oh no! Oh my God!' I gasped. I couldn't think how this had happened, but it had made a terrible mess. I could see up into the dark space: there were the soggy edges of a board hanging down and, behind that, wooden strips that reminded me of lolly sticks, the kind Danny and I used to make things out of when we were little. There were chunks of dark material and dust, lots of dust. Now that I could see it, I could smell it too. It smelt old.

Wide chunks of plaster had fallen onto the sitting room floor and lay like white mountains with powdered snow scattered around. I became aware of a different sound. I looked back towards the ceiling and noticed there was a steady stream of water running down and pooling onto the floor, which was so sodden, it had changed colour. I noticed too for the first time that water was running through the light socket above me and dripping from the modern green glass chandelier we had bought from Heal's.

'Oh goodness!' I said. 'I didn't notice that! It's going to take quite a lot of clearing up, isn't it? We have a lady that Polly has recommended. I can't remember her name. Shall I fetch her card?' I pointed towards the kitchen. 'It's in there somewhere.' I laughed, embarrassed by the mess on the counter tops.

'No, that's okay. We'll get all that taken care of.' Chris's voice was quite soothing.

'That's very kind of you.' I thought it was lovely that Chris wanted to help sort things out and I was in fact quite relieved by his intervention. I liked the idea of someone else taking control for a while and getting everything straight.

'Let's get you checked out, Jessica. Come with me, my love.'

I stood up.

'Checked out for what?' I asked.

'Just to see how you are doing.' He smiled.

'Actually, Chris, I've been feeling very, very tired.' It felt good to tell him this.

He nodded as he placed his arm under my elbow and helped me towards the door.

I noticed I was still wearing my wet socks. 'Heavy socks!' I pointed at my feet and laughed.

Chris didn't laugh but held my arm tightly.

We walked outside together, his hand on my back keeping me steady. I noticed a small gathering of people on the other side of the street, crowding the pavement and standing near the ambulance. I didn't recognise many of the faces, neighbours possibly or just passers-by. But then I spotted Mrs Pleasant: her tiny eyes were shining, her mouth was open, revealing little, yellow teeth. I turned to smile at her and, quite unexpectedly, she spat at me. I was really shocked: how was I supposed to react? I decided to ignore her. I always knew she was horrid, but that proved it. I couldn't wait to hear what Matthew would have to say about it. I thought he might give her a new nickname, like Mrs Cobra or Mrs Gobalot. I laughed as I thought about that. *Mrs Gobalot...*

A policeman was standing in front of them with his back to me. He opened his arms wide, shooing the crowd backwards. There were flashing blue lights in the street, maybe four or five. From the corner of my eye I saw a stretcher being carried out of the house. On it lay something tiny and motionless. It pricked my conscience, but I wasn't able to say why and I dismissed it from my thoughts immediately.

Chris helped me into the back of the ambulance. A policewoman climbed in too. She was not smiling; her lips were thin and pressed together. I didn't like her nearly as much as I did Chris, who laid me down on a stretcher and placed a soft red blanket over me that came up to my chin. He clicked a seatbelt across my body. I liked the feeling of being tucked in, cosy.

Looking back towards the house, I asked, 'Can you get Matthew for me?'

'Not right now, Jessica,' he said.

'I need to speak to him.' I smiled, still polite, even though I was feeling a little anxious. I wanted my husband. I needed to tell him that I was going with Chris but that I would see him later. I had also remembered the name of the lady that could help tidy up the mess; her name was Paula and I knew where I had put her card, on the front of the fridge under our 'I heart NY' magnet.

'Matthew is busy right now. Would you like me to give him a message?' he asked, his eyes darting towards the police lady.

I sighed. That would be the next best thing, if he couldn't come to me at that very moment.

'Can you tell him...' I paused. What was it I wanted to say to the man I loved, my husband, my Matthew?

'Can you tell him, everything is going to be okay.' And I nodded and closed my eyes, happy that it would be.

Twenty-Seven

1st September, 2015

I was released today. I've got the newspaper; they always use that same photograph. Flashbulbs were popping all around me. I was caught unawares and I'm looking slightly dazed into the lens as they lead me away from the court. It doesn't look anything like me. My eyes are wide, full of fear and grief. I hate that picture. Here's a clipping:

> Today will see the release of Jessica Deane, who notoriously tried to kill her baby daughter Lilly, aged fourteen months, in what became known as 'The Baby in the Bath' case. She has been detained in the secure psychiatric unit of Mountside Prison for four years. Her crime, like her release, polarised opinion. Women's campaigners have insisted from the outset that Deane needed medical help and understanding, not imprisonment. But there are others that believe she should have been tried for attempted murder and sentenced accordingly.
>
> Justice Andrea Silver in her summing up at the trial made these comments:
>
> 'This is a case that has touched the nation. You are a woman who stands before me with her life entirely devastated. Your disturbance of mind at the time, due to severe postnatal depression, coupled with your guilty plea, enables me to take a course that will offer rehabilitation and medical

treatment. I see no benefit to society in awarding a custodial sentence. Your unwillingness to seek help sooner, afraid of the stigma of being labelled depressed and the inability of the organisations involved in your care to identify the level of threat, is something that we as a society need to look at.'

Her husband, Matthew Deane, now lives in the USA with their daughter Lilly who is five years of age. Experts say that she was too young to fully understand the circumstances of her early life, and apparently she is now thriving in her new home. Matthew Deane has refused to comment specifically on his wife's release.

Deane has shown remorse for the crime and is known to have made two suicide attempts whilst in the care of Mountside Hospital NHS Trust.

Her friend and spokesman Roland de Bouieller, who has campaigned tirelessly for greater understanding of postnatal depression, gave this statement:

'We are delighted that today will see Jessica Deane released. No system can punish her as much as she has punished herself; she has lost her husband, her beloved daughter and her liberty. Depression is a terrible, terrible illness that needs to be much better understood. For all those screaming for her sentence to be increased and for her to be incarcerated, I would ask that you walk a mile in her shoes.'

We have been told that Ms Deane will be moved to an undisclosed address.

'All set?' Polly held both her hands.

Jessica nodded. 'Yup. Thank you. Thank you both.' She hugged her tightly, getting as close as she could across her friend's bump.

'Careful, mate, I am a coveted vessel.' Polly winked at her best mate.

Topaz stepped forward and enveloped them both with his arms. 'I'm so happy today. You've worked hard, Jess, and here you are, new beginnings!'

Jessica nodded, *yes, new beginnings…*

'I want you to think about what we discussed. A retreat for women recovering from postnatal depression, with yoga, fresh air, good food. Margaret and Anthony were really keen and your mum and dad thought it was a great idea. And we'd love to be involved, wouldn't we, Poll?'

Polly nodded. 'You bet. We go where you go, you can't shake me off!'

Jessica smiled; she didn't want to shake her off, ever.

'I could teach relaxation and you could run art classes. It could really do some good and would be a nice place for you to continue your journey.'

Jessica pulled away from her friends. 'We'll see.' It was the best she could offer, wanting to take one day at a time.

'Let us know when you're settled and we'll be there on the first available flight, promise?' Polly fought back the tears that threatened.

'Promise.' Jessica blew a kiss.

Five hours later, Jessica paid the cab driver and smiled her thanks. She retrieved her hand luggage from the boot of the rusting car and breathed in the warm evening air. Her eyes roved over the garden, remembering her honeymoon, when she and Matthew had wandered around the villa naked, eaten biscuits in bed and sat on the terrace drinking cold beer. She had never felt so carefree, so happy. She walked slowly down the path to the front door; bent down on all fours and with her arm outstretched scrabbled around in the dirt under the shrub. To her relief, her fingers soon touched cool, hard metal. She had found the ancient tin. Picking it up, she shook it, the sound of the key making a pleasing rattle. Margaret had reassured her; confident it would be where they left it.

Jessica let herself into the The Orangery and made her way to the master bedroom, where she removed her clothes and climbed between the stiff, white sheets of the double bed that she and her husband had once shared. She pulled the bolster pillow into her arms and held it close. She set her alarm clock before slipping into a peaceful slumber.

The high-pitched beep woke her some four hours later. She climbed slowly from the mattress and put her dressing gown on before tidying the bed, pulling the top sheet taut and smoothing the creases from the pillows. After drinking a solitary glass of red wine, she made her way outside on to the terrace. It was midnight.

Jessica lit a candle and held it up at arm's length as she looked out over the majestic Tramuntana Mountains, their jagged profiles grey against the dark sky. She let the warm wind flow over her. For her this was the most special time of day, as the sea sparkled in the moonlight and the land was covered with a blanket of hush. Aubergine-coloured clouds rolled on the horizon. Jessica faced them head on, no longer afraid, remembering a time when her survival was dependent on punching very large holes in them, through which she could poke her head and take a breath. Not any more.

She looked at the sun-lounger on which Polly had reclined in the nude. *'I'm going to lie here and tan my cherub for a bit!'* Jessica smiled, picturing her, dear, dear

Polly, her lifelong friend and now about to become a mum herself. She and Paz had shown such love and support; Jessica knew she would never be able to repay them. She considered their idea for a retreat. This would certainly be the perfect spot.

Jessica inhaled the heady floral and citrus scent that wafted on the breeze. She placed the candle on the table behind her and pulled the beautiful red leather notebook from her pocket. Opening it at random, she ran her fingers over the thick creamy pages of her journal. Alongside the words, beautiful illustrations were dotted throughout, a study of her and Matthew's hands, entwined. Lilly's rosebud mouth, breaking into a smile. Her mum, dad and Danny, sitting on a Devon riverbank, all wishing their holiday would never end. A diary full of thoughts and recollections never meant for anyone's eyes but hers. She raised it to her mouth and kissed the cover of this little book that had become a friend, a friend that had helped her through her darkest of days. Days that were now behind her. Gripping a few sheets between her fingers, she ripped the pages from the spine and tore them into smaller squares before flinging the confetti over the rails to drift hundreds of feet below, scattering on the wind as they sailed away from her. She stood watching and laughed into the night wind.

Jessica tightened her dressing gown around her waist and stood pressed against the railings. There she balanced, with her fingers gripping the barrier and the candle flickering in the darkness behind her. Her gift of an acorn nestled safely inside her palm. She spoke into the darkness. 'Oh Lilly.' Her words when they came were delivered slowly and calmly.

'Your grandad once told me that death changes the way people are remembered, lets those left behind pick out the best bits and disregard the bad. I think in one sense he's right. But I want you to know that I cling to the remote possibility that we might reconnect and that I might, one day, get the chance to tell you just how much I miss you…' Jessica closed her eyes and took a deep breath. 'I don't know why I got sick, Lilly, and I don't know how I could ever make it up to you,' she sighed, 'but I do know that I'm your mum and I love you. I love you. Don't ever doubt it, I love you!'

The candle flame faltered and went out.

Epilogue

Lilly was crouching in the garden, gathering stray petals from the vividly coloured lilac shrub. She would use them to make perfume that she would wear at her wedding later, when she married her teddy bear. Several dolls and her fat penguin were attending as guests. Her teddy was already dressed in his bow tie in readiness for the occasion.

Matthew smiled as his little girl chattered to herself. The New England sun warmed her skin on another bright, beautiful spring day. He watched her through the open kitchen window while he trimmed broccoli spears and prepared cauliflower for lunch.

Suddenly Lilly stood and with a tilt to her chin, looked up towards the sky and shouted, 'Daddy?' Her little voice was clear and golden.

Matthew beamed, knowing he would never tire of hearing that word. It made his heart sing. He placed the knife on the counter. 'Coming!' He made his way to the garden from the square hallway of their grand American Colonial home, glancing at the photograph of Lilly with her Grandad Roger and Nana Coral when they had come to visit. Their faces shone with joy, happy to be hand in hand with Lilly once again as she gathered acorns from the wood and gave one to her nan, a present. It had been lovely to see them; strange, but lovely. Familiar. He hoped they were well.

'What are you doing there, Lilly Rose?' he asked as he bent down to match her height.

'I'm making perfume for my wedding!' she sang rather haughtily, flicking her long curtain of hair over her shoulder. Matthew laughed; she always added a sense of the theatrical.

'You can be a guest after you have been the vicar.'

'Right. Got it.' He nodded as if learning his part.

'Daddy?'

'Yes?'

'When you got married, did my mummy have a pretty white dress?'

Matthew thought about his beautiful bride, his golden girl. 'Yes. Yes she did.'

'Did she look like a princess?' Her eyes widened.

Matthew nodded and held his little girl's hand. He pictured Jessica standing to take a bow, remembering how the tiny crystals sewn into the delicate cream lace of her fitted bodice sparkled in the candlelight, her awkward bow before she took her place next to him, gripping his hand on the tabletop. 'Yes. She looked exactly like a princess. She looked beautiful.'

'Daddy?' She did this, said his name while she thought of what next to say. He loved it.

'Yup?'

'I sometimes think I'd like to see my mummy. Not the

photos but my in-real-life Mummy. I'd like her to do my plaits.' She paused, placing her finger in her mouth and blinking rapidly, worried she had given too many of her inner thoughts away. Even aged five, she knew this was a sensitive area.

'Well, we should consider that. We can talk about it some more and have a good old think about what's best.' He squeezed her hand, anxious as ever of shattering the peace they had found and yet torn, riddled with guilt that Lilly was without a mother and Jessica denied her little girl.

Lilly twisted her foot into the grass. 'Do you think she's better now, or is she still poorly?'

'I think she's a lot, lot better.' He acknowledged this.

'Madison's mummy was poorly and she was in the hospital for a long, long time.'

Matthew nodded. The school fundraiser still fresh in his mind for Madison's mum.

'But…' Lilly paused and drew breath. 'But Madison and her sister got to see her even when she was really sick. They made her a card and when it was Madison's birthday they took her cake into the hospital and her mum sang to her and they opened all her presents right there on the bed!' she added wide-eyed. 'And… and I would like to tell Mummy about my sleepover and show her my ballet stertificate.' Quite suddenly, her eyes filled with tears and she threw herself into her dad's arms.

'It's okay, Lilly Rose. It's okay, darling. Your mummy loves you so very much. I've always told you that.'

'I love her too, Daddy, but I want to speak to her. I need to ask her something.'

Matthew sighed as they made their way inside. 'Come on, let's dry those tears and get you cleaned up, you've got a wedding to get ready for, remember?'

Lilly wiped her nose and tried out a smile. Her dad was right, brides were supposed to be happy on their wedding day.

The phone rang on the breakfast bar. Paz grabbed it. 'Hello? Hey, mate! Oh God! So good to hear your voice!'

He gesticulated wildly to Polly who stood by his side.

'No, we're just here for a visit – what a place. Yes. Yes of course. Hang on.' He covered the mouthpiece with his cupped palm. 'Go and get Jess, quickly!' He spoke with urgency.

Jessica came in from the terrace, her shoulder-length hair hung in a glossy curtain. Her nose was peppered with freckles. 'Who is it?' she asked quietly, still slightly nervous of contact with the outside world, they had already had to field several calls from quote-hungry journalists.

Paz held the phone at arm's length and struggled to find the words. 'It's...' He swallowed and pushed the phone into her hands before leaving her alone.

'Hello?' Jessica whispered as she cradled the phone.

There was a pause on the end of the line. 'Errmm... Mummy?' Lilly used the word with familiarity, warmth. 'I'm doing a project about when I was a baby...' Lilly spoke as if it had been weeks not years since she had last had contact with her mother.

Jessica pulled the mouthpiece towards her face as the strength left her legs and she sank down onto the cool, tiled floor. Lilly's voice was sweet and older, with a lisp. No longer a baby, she was a little person! It was beautiful, the most beautiful sound she had ever heard.

'... and I wanted to ask you something.'

Jessica nodded through her haze of tears, leaning back against the breakfast bar, struggling for composure, trying to catch her breath. 'Okay.' It was the first word she had spoken to her daughter in nearly four years and not what she had envisioned. In her dreams she gushed *I have missed you more than I can say. And I'm sorry. I'm sorry.* She concentrated on breathing and tried to keep her sobs at bay.

'My teacher Mrs Liddiment said we had to ask our mummy what was the first thing you thought when you saw me for the very first time. That's it,' Lilly added, calm and assertive.

Jessica exhaled, struggling to stay calm, the whole encounter felt surreal. 'Now, let me see.' She swallowed, gathering her thoughts. Her hands shook. 'The first time I saw you...' Jess closed her eyes, picturing the moment. 'Well, Daddy had you in his arms; you were wrapped up like a bundle in a white blanket. Your little face was squashed.' Jessica smiled at the memory. 'And I remember thinking,' she struggled to form the words as tears clogged her nose and throat, 'that's my baby! My beautiful, beautiful girl!'

Matthew leant on the banister as he listened to his daughter, watching as she smiled and twirled on the spot with happiness, chatting to her mum. His thoughts flew to a rain-soaked car-park some years ago – what was it he had said? *I can't stand the idea of not spending every night with you or not seeing your face on the pillow next to mine when I wake up. I want you to have my babies. And I can't imagine any other future than one with you. I love you.* He twisted the gold band that sat on the third finger of his left hand. And he smiled.

Amanda Prowse

Perfect Daughter

'A powerful page turner'

CLOSER

Prologue

When the last of the guests had left and Jacks had wrapped the leftover sausage rolls in clingfilm, the newlyweds kicked off their shoes and lay on their donated double bed, looking up at the ceiling.

'That all went well, didn't it?'

It had been a small, low-key wedding at the Register Office on the Boulevard. The registrar had mumbled and Pete's mum had cried. And then everyone had piled back to their new home in Sunnyside Road, bought with the help of both sets of parents. Pete scooted round putting coasters under cans of beer, Jacks passed around plates of sandwiches and cakes, and her best friend Gina teased her for acting like a grown-up married woman. Jacks had looked around the small, square kitchen of their little Weston-super-Mare terrace, trying to stop her mind flying to the vast kitchen in the seafront villa where she had not so long ago lain on a daybed and succumbed to the charms of a boy who had told her about the big wide world beyond her doorstep and had made her believe that one day, she might see it.

Then she had spied her dad, Don, with his arm around

Pete's shoulder, and felt a strange sort of contentment. She sidled up between them.

'I was just saying to young Pete here, the best advice I can give you is never go to bed on a cross word. And if you can smile through the bad times, just imagine how much you will laugh in the good.'

'And the best advice I can give is don't take advice from him!' Jacks' mum jerked her thumb in her husband's direction. She spoke a little louder than she would normally – but normally she wouldn't have polished off three glasses of Asti and four Martini-and-lemonades.

'Thank you, Don.' Pete had beamed at his new wife. 'I'll look after her, I promise,' he'd said, as if she wasn't present.

Pete stroked Jacks' shoulder and brought her back to the present. 'Feels weird having all these rooms to wander around in and only us to live in them. Three bedrooms, the bathroom and two rooms downstairs – I'm still used to being in my little bedroom at my mum's!'

'I know, me too. It'll be great, Pete, all this space.'

She scratched the itching skin, stretched taut across her stomach. 'There'll be one more occupant before we know it!'

'Yep. Can't wait. Shall we decorate the littlest room, make it cosy?'

'What with? Don't think we've got any spare cash for decorating right now.' She hated having to point out the practicalities and quash his enthusiasm.

'I know, and I don't mean anything flash, but we can manage a lick of paint. And Gina's arty, couldn't we get her to draw something on the walls?'

'Blimey, I've seen her artwork. No thanks! Poor baby would be waking up to the Take That logo every morning.'

They both laughed. Pete reached for her hand. 'I've got a wife.'

'Yes, you have.' She smiled.

'Do you feel like a wife?' he asked.

'I suppose I do. What are wives supposed to feel like?'

She felt him shrug. 'Don't know. I guess like they are part of a pair, and no longer having to face the world on their own.'

'Oh, Pete, you old softie! That's lovely, and yes, in that case I do feel like a wife.' She leant across and kissed him.

'I wonder how long we'll live here.' Jacks let her words float out into the darkness.

'I reckon a couple of years, just till we are on our feet. We should get this place shipshape, replace the windows, get the garden nice, put a new kitchen in and then move up.'

She smiled into the darkness, loving the idea of a new kitchen and a lovely garden. 'Poor house, we've only been in it for three weeks and already we are planning on moving!'

'It's good to plan, Jacks, set our path and find a way. That's how you get on in life, isn't it. You work hard and you fight for better.'

'I like that, Pete. Work hard and fight for better – it sounds like a plan.' She squeezed his hand. 'I wouldn't want much more than this, mind. Maybe an en-suite bathroom and room in the kitchen for one of them big fridges.'

'I'd love a garage. I could have a workbench and a place to store all my tools and I could make things.'

She could tell he was smiling. 'What would you make?'

'Dunno. Things from wood and I could do repairs, fix things. I'd love to be out there tinkering.'

Jacks chuckled. 'You sound like my dad!

'I'll take that as a compliment.'

'I tell you what I would love, a conservatory, with wicker furniture in it. I'd sit in it and read a magazine and have a coffee, somewhere to put my feet up.'

'That sounds like a plan.'

She nestled up to him and laid her head on his chest.

'Funny how things work out, isn't it, Mrs Davies?'

Jacks smiled at the unfamiliar title. 'It sure is.'

One

She supposed it was a talent of sorts, her ability to wake a couple of minutes before her alarm roused her every single morning. It didn't seem like a big deal – who worried about a measly two minutes here or there? But when she multiplied them over a year, it amounted to an extra seven hundred and thirty minutes of sleep that she was missing out on. And when you were as tired as she was, those extra twelve hours over the course of a year would have been most welcome. She wished she could take them all at once, literally just lie in bed, in silence and drift off without fear of disturbance. Bliss.

She lay back and stared at the ceiling with its fringed blue paisley lampshade housing a single dull bulb hanging from the centre. They had meant to change the shade for something yellow to match the wallpaper, that had been the plan, they might even have had a look at a few in British Home Stores, she couldn't remember, but fifteen years later it still hadn't happened. Like everything else in the house that was defunct, mismatched or ageing, they had got used to it, lived with it, until it was just how things were. This even applied to the cardboard boxes full of clothes and bits and bobs that had been packaged up and stacked in the front hallway. They were intended for the loft. What had he said? 'Pop 'em there, love, and I'll shove them up in the loft next time I bring the ladder in.' But three years later, they had taken root in the hallway, become furniture. She hoovered around them and stacked clean laundry on the top, and the kids threw their school bags on to them rather than take them upstairs. In fact she wasn't even sure what was in a couple of them.

Opening her eyes wide, she tried to force herself into a greater state of wakefulness. Her nightie was twisted in an uncomfortable ring around her midriff; she lifted her bottom and in her crab-like pose pulled the fabric until it lay flat beneath her. She had got into the habit of wearing both a nightie and pyjama bottoms, whether for warmth, comfort or an added obstacle for Pete to navigate should the mood take him, she wasn't sure. Although she had to admit the mood hadn't taken him for quite some time and, if she was being honest, that was something of a relief.

She glanced across at her husband, who slept without a pillow, his head tipped back, mouth open, his dark stubble poking like little sticks through skin that could do with a good dollop of moisturiser. Chance would be a fine thing – he considered owning hair gel a statement of questionable sexuality. Unaware of her scrutiny, he raised his arm and scratched his nose. Then he turned and breathed open mouthed in her direction. She looked away; anything his body emitted at that time of the morning was less than fragrant. He was still a young man, still good-looking when he was spruced up, but there was something about him in the early-morning light, with the sweat of a warm night clinging to his skin and his breath laced with spices, that made her shrink from him.

She smiled at the irony as she flexed her toes inside his old sports socks that she slept in. Hardly sexy. He still on occasion had the ability to elicit a longing deep inside her, especially when he smelt good and was confident, reminding her of the self-assured banter of their youth. She remembered when they left school, eighteen years ago. She had been a beauty then, with her long, slim legs, blonde hair and a tan that seemed to last year round. Her nose was freckled and her long eyelashes framed her green eyes without the need for mascara. Whenever she stumbled across photographs from that era, it always shocked her how lovely she had been and how unaware of it she was. She recalled her many insecurities and how she had worried about the slight cleft to her chin, her gangly limbs.

They had married soon after they had started dating and in those days slept skin to skin, her face pressed into his chest, arms and legs entwined. Any time separated was considered a waste. They would wake in the early hours to make love before falling asleep again. Not that she had needed much sleep, not then. Neither sleep nor food sustained her, all she needed was him, him and her new baby. The sight of him, the thought of him, the feel of him against her, he was everything.

Jacks crept from their bed and looked back at him as he screwed his eyes shut, wrinkled his nose and farted. She rolled her eyes. 'Those were the days,' she whispered as she collected her towel from the back of the old dining chair in the corner of the room and headed for the shower.

'Mum?'

'What?' Jacks answered without lifting her head from the newspaper. It was 7.15. She had shoved on some clothes, run a brush through her hair, turned on the lights, flicked on the heating, placed the breakfast cereal on the table and made a hot drink. She now sat at the kitchen table. This was her one small window of opportunity at the beginning of every day when she was able to read the local news. A brief moment before the world came rushing up to meet her and she had to run to keep up, like a lady she'd once seen balancing on a glittery ball in the circus. Her smile had been fixed, but under her elaborate false eyelashes Jacks had seen the terror in her eyes. One wrong step and she would fall off. Jacks knew exactly how she felt.

'Mum?' The shout was louder this time.

She closed her eyes. 'For God's sake, Martha, you know I hate this shouting up and down the stairs.' She tapped her palm on the kitchen table, liking the sound of her wedding band on the wooden surface. 'How many times have I told you, if you want to ask me something, come down here!' She shook her head and returned to the article in the *Weston Mercury*, interested in how to get a smear-free shine on your conservatory windows with nothing more than warm water and a squirt of vinegar.

Her daughter's footsteps thundered down the uncarpeted stairs. Jacks drew breath: how many times *had* she told her? Too many to count, but Martha, aged seventeen, who had lived in this house since she was born, still hadn't mastered conversing face to face, preferring to holler from room to room. Neither, it would seem, had she learnt how to walk down the stairs without shaking the rafters.

'Have I got a shirt for school?' She practically bounced on the spot, her tone was urgent. It amazed Jacks that despite the fact that they left the house at 7.45 every morning and had done so for the last six years, time always seemed to sneak up on Martha like it was a shock or a deviation from the norm, each and every morning.

Jacks looked at her daughter in her tight black school skirt, thick woolly tights and pyjama top, reeking of perfume and trying to tease her roots with her fingers as she loitered in the doorway. She decided not to comment on the dark ring of black kohl that masked her daughter's pretty blue eyes and made her heart-shaped face look top-heavy. There were only so many times she could have that conversation. Besides, when she was a lawyer, rushing up the court steps in a crisp white shirt with her briefcase full of important notes, she would surely rethink her knotty hair and over-the-top eye make-up. She would want to emulate her colleagues. Jacks smiled at the thought. Her brilliant girl, soon to take her A levels, which would put her on the path to a university education and then a dazzling career. Jacks would never forget Mrs Fentiman, the woman who had come into Martha's school and given a talk, extolling the virtues of doing law and painting a picture so vivid, Jacks could taste the champagne with which they toasted their wins and could smell the leather-topped desk at which she sat and enjoyed a perfect view of St Paul's Cathedral. Her suit was elegantly tailored and she wore Chanel earrings.

Jacks wanted that life for Martha, all of it. She wanted Martha to go into schools and inspire girls to strive for better, she wanted her to drink flutes of champagne in chambers instead of pints of cider-and-black under the pier.

'So have I got a shirt?' Martha prompted.

Jacks nodded. 'In the airing cupboard.'

'The airing cupboard on the landing I just came from?' Martha pointed to the ceiling.

'That's the one.' Jacks traced the words of the newspaper article with her finger, ignoring her daughter's sarcasm.

'If you don't mind me asking, what is it you're reading?' Martha was chewing gum, which Jacks found inexplicable before breakfast. It must make everything taste of mint and what if she accidentally swallowed it? That didn't bear thinking about.

'It's an article about conservatory windows and how to clean them.' She looked at her daughter as her tortoiseshell-framed glasses slipped down her nose.

'But we haven't even got a conservatory!' Martha rolled her eyes.

Jacks removed her specs and looked at the back wall of the kitchen that ran the width of their house. 'Yet. I don't have a conservatory yet.'

Martha rolled her eyes again. 'Instead of a conservatory, can't you just build an extra bedroom in the loft so I don't have to share with Jonty? I hate sharing with him. It's not fair!'

'Really, Martha? Funny how you've not mentioned it.' She gave a wry smile as her daughter thumped back up the stairs. Jacks felt a familiar flicker of guilt. Martha was right;

she shouldn't have to share with her little brother. Jonty had been moved into his big sister's room with a set of open bookshelves dividing the space when Jacks' mum had come to live with them. It was Martha's favourite topic of conversation. Jacks had hoped the complaints about just how hard done by she was might have waned. They hadn't.

For the first time that day she considered the seven thousand, four hundred and eighty-two pounds that sat in their savings account and had done so for a little over a year. It was the sum that remained from the sale of her parents' house, a couple of streets away in Addicott Road, once they had paid for the hoist to be installed in the bathroom. A hoist her mum never used because it scared her and anyway, as it turned out, it was so much easier to pop her in the shower, less palaver. The hoist, however, hadn't cost as much as the stair lift that had been fitted. A stair lift on which Jacks bashed her shins in the dark of night and about which she had to continually reprimand Jonty, who liked using it as a ride and to ferry his Transformers up and down.

'I'll be late tonight. City are playing at home, Tuesday-night friendly, so don't worry about tea, I'll get a pie at Ashton Gate.' This her husband Pete yelled excitedly from the landing. She shook her head; no wonder Martha thought shouting was okay.

'Righto.' She sighed, reaching for her mug and draining the contents. The best cup of tea in the whole day was undoubtedly this first one.

'Mu-um?' Jonty hollered from behind the bedroom door.

'I give up.' Jacks closed the paper and placed her empty

mug and toast plate in the sink. 'Yes, love?'

'I need to take in some things to make a model of a famous building!'

'What?' Jacks spun round and marched from the kitchen into their narrow hallway, avoiding the sports bag that blocked her path and the stack of boxes, hoping she had misheard.

'Mrs Palmer says we need to take in things from our household rubbish and recycling that we can use to build a model of a famous building.' He was precise, probably reading from whatever scrap of paper he had discovered bearing this information.

'When do you need it by?' *Not today, please not today...*

'Today!' he answered.

'God, Jonty! And you are telling me *now*?' Jacks snapped. Placing her hands on her slender hips, she tried to think of a solution: what had they thrown away recently that might resemble a building?

'Thought we weren't supposed to shout up the stairs?' Martha poked her head around the bathroom door, her hand gripping the straightening irons that were plugged in on the landing.

'Don't be sarky to your mum,' Pete interjected as he thundered down the stairs in his baggy sweatpants, thick socks, long-sleeved T-shirt and body warmer, the uniform of a man who worked outside.

'I would have told you before, but I forgot!' Jonty explained.

'We out of milk?' Pete called.

Jacks turned her head towards the kitchen. 'No, it's on

the side, near the kettle!' Then she trod the first stair. 'Forgetting is no good, Jonty. I've told you to let me have any notes or pieces of paper as soon as you bring them out of school. That way we can make sure we have a bit of notice for things like this.'

'Yeah, we don't want a repeat of the Harvest Festival embarrassment!' Martha laughed.

'Thank you for that, Martha! Just get yourself ready.' Jacks felt her cheeks flame as she remembered sending him off for the grand Harvest Festival service with an offering of a tin of pinto beans and a Cadbury's Creme Egg. It was all she could lay her hands on at the last minute as they had walked out of the front door. Apparently Mrs Palmer had sniffed at the items and asked what pinto beans were. To which Jonty had replied, 'They're for making pinto.' Jacks had grabbed them in error from the supermarket shelf and was secretly quite glad not to have them lurking in the cupboard, taunting her with their fancy label, confirming her lack of culinary knowhow.

'Sorry, Mum,' Jonty offered.

'That's okay.' She smiled, the sound of his eight-year-old baby voice and his contrition twisting her heart. He was a good boy, her baby. 'Can you both come down and have your breakfast as soon as you're ready, I don't want to be late today!'

'*I* gave you a piece of paper a week ago, about that art trip to Paris and you still haven't said if I can go or not!' Martha said.

'Your dad and I are still discussing it.' Jacks nodded. She placed her hand on her forehead, simultaneously trying to think about what Jonty could take in and how to explain to Martha that there just weren't the funds for a trip to Paris. The savings-account money was for a rainy day or any expenses her mum might have. Her own conservatory was a pipe dream and so, sadly, was her daughter's desire to go to Paris. Paris indeed! It made her chuckle. In her day they'd had a trip to Oldbury Power Station, with a packed lunch thrown in.

'What are we still discussing?' Pete asked from the kitchen.

'Martha's trip to Paris!' Jacks replied.

'So I *can* go?' Martha said.

Jacks shook her head. 'No, we are still discussing it!'

'I don't know why anyone would want to go to Paris!' Pete joined in from the kitchen table. 'Dirty, 'orrible place where you'll get mugged and you need a mortgage just to buy a cup of tea!'

'Dad, you think I'm going to get mugged everywhere! You said I'd get mugged if I went to Worle on my own on the bus, and I didn't!'

'You was just lucky, girl. And just cos you survived Worle, doesn't mean you'll have the same luck in Paris.'

'And anyway, how do you know what Paris is like, you've never even been!' Martha pointed out.

'No interest in it, love, that's why.'

'God, Dad, you think going up to Bristol is a big day out!'

''Tis when the mighty City are playing.' Pete clapped his hands together, making a big noise.

'Can I come with you tonight, Dad, to see the mighty City?' Jonty asked.

'No, mate. No midweek games till you can stand a round at The Robins, them's the rules.'

'I think you make up the rules as you go along.' Martha jumped to her little brother's defence. 'It's not up to Dad if I go to France or not, is it, Mum? You know what he's like!'

'I *can* hear you, Miss Martha!' Pete yelled.

'What building am I making, Mum?' Jonty asked.

'Errmm...' Jacks was trying to think of something when the bell rang out, loud and clear above the chatter and accusations flying back and forth up and down the stairs.

'Nan's ringing!' Jonty and Martha shouted in unison.

I know. I heard it.

When Jacks' mum, Ida Morgan, had first come to live with them eighteen months ago, she had seemed disorientated, uncomfortable and confused, so Jacks had given her a small hand bell, to be rung whenever she needed tending to. Turned out she needed tending to quite a lot.

When Ida's dementia had first become apparent, several years ago now, it was ignored. Jacks' dad, Don, had trivialised it and they had all just gone along with it, joining in the banter of distraction. What did it matter if Ida forgot where she lived and served frozen oven chips without cooking them first? Called everybody by the wrong name, put eggs in the tumble dryer and the car keys in a jar of coffee? Jacks' dad had made light of it as he tried to keep things ticking along, not wanting to frighten his wife or distress their only daughter. But after he died, Ida declined rapidly; or maybe it was that Jacks' dad had shielded her from the extent of her mum's condition. Either way, it was a shock.

To begin with, Jacks would go round to Addicott Road and sit with her mum during the day and Pete would pop in on her every night, checking up on her and locking the doors and windows for bedtime. One night he found her in the garden, wearing nothing but her nightie as she placed food on the small patch of lawn. He watched as she piled up uncooked potatoes, scattered cereal from boxes and threw down an old chicken carcass and some cheese on to the grass.

'What are you doing, Ida?' he had asked gently.

She looked at him without recognition. 'I'm putting food out for the rabbits,' she replied. 'They don't feed themselves, you know!'

'You really shouldn't do that, Ida. It will attract rats,' he said softly, racking his brain, trying to recall if they had ever had a pet rabbit.

'Don't be stupid!' she snapped. 'This isn't food for the rats, it's for the rabbits!'

He had guided her inside the house, where she made a cup of tea as though nothing had happened.

Not long after that, Jacks and Pete decided she should move in with them, to Sunnyside Road. Eighteen months on and her mum was now frail. She was quiet mostly, with the odd burst of lucidity, preferring to be in bed than on the sofa and favouring things that were familiar and routine. Sometimes she recognised her family and at other times not. For Ida it was a dark, difficult and lonely way to live. And, awful though it was to admit, for Jacks, Pete and the kids it was as if a ghoulish spectre lurked in the rooms Ida occupied, visible and scary; given the choice, they avoided sitting in its shadow. They loved her of course, but the kids could find little to recognise in the old lady who yelled and whistled; she was quite unlike the nan who used to make the best apple pie in the world and who would sneak them sweets before bedtime when their mum wasn't looking.